Henry Morley, Robert Herrick

Hesperides

Works Both Human and Divine

Henry Morley, Robert Herrick

Hesperides
Works Both Human and Divine

ISBN/EAN: 9783337366612

Printed in Europe, USA, Canada, Australia, Japan

Cover: Foto ©Andreas Hilbeck / pixelio.de

More available books at **www.hansebooks.com**

HESPERIDES

OR

Works both Human and Divine

OF

ROBERT HERRICK

WITH AN INTRODUCTION BY HENRY MORLEY

LONDON

GEORGE ROUTLEDGE AND SONS

BROADWAY, LUDGATE HILL

NEW YORK: 9 LAFAYETTE PLACE

1885

MORLEY'S UNIVERSAL LIBRARY.

VOLUMES ALREADY PUBLISHED.

SHERIDAN'S PLAYS.

PLAYS FROM MOLIÈRE.   By English Dramatists.

MARLOWE'S FAUSTUS & GOETHE'S FAUST.

CHRONICLE OF THE CID.

RABELAIS' GARGANTUA and the HEROIC DEEDS OF PANTAGRUEL.

THE PRINCE. By Machiavelli.

BACON'S ESSAYS.

DEFOE'S JOURNAL OF THE PLAGUE YEAR.

LOCKE ON CIVIL GOVERNMENT & FILMER'S " PATRIARCHA."

SCOTT'S DEMONOLOGY and WITCHCRAFT.

DRYDEN'S VIRGIL.

BUTLER'S ANALOGY OF RELIGION.

HERRICK'S HESPERIDES.

COLERIDGE'S TABLE-TALK.

BOCCACCIO'S DECAMERON.

STERNE'S TRISTRAM SHANDY.

CHAPMAN'S HOMER'S ILIAD.

MEDIÆVAL TALES.

VOLTAIRE'S CANDIDE & JOHNSON'S RASSELAS.

INTRODUCTION.

ROBERT HERRICK — whose name was written also Hearicke, Heyricke, Eyrick, and Erick—belonged to a Leicestershire family, out of which came in after years the Abigail Erick, who was mother to Jonathan Swift. The poet's father, Nicholas Herrick, was a goldsmith in Cheapside, who in 1582 married a Julian Stone and had seven children, of whom Robert, the youngest, was baptized on the 24th of August, 1591.

In November, 1592, Nicholas Herrick, being sick in body, made his will, and within a day afterwards fell or threw himself from a window of his house in Cheapside and was killed. Dr. Fletcher, Bishop of Bristol, father of John Fletcher the poet, claimed, as High Almoner, the goods left by the dead man. He claimed them as goods and chattels of a suicide, but accepted upon arbitration an award of £220. In the following year a posthumous child was born to Mrs. Herrick. He was named William, after the uncle who acted as guardian to the children. The father's possessions realized for the family about £5,000

Robert Herrick had been named after the eldest of his uncles, an ironmonger, who was three times Mayor of Leicester, lived to keep his golden wedding-day, and died when his nephew and godson was twenty-seven years old. The poet had rich relatives, and many of them. His grandmother, when he was twenty years old, died at the age of ninety-seven, and it is said on her tomb that "she did see, before her departure, of her children and her children's children, to the number of 142." Herrick had on his mother's side an Aunt Anne, married to Sir Stephen Soame, who was Lord Mayor of London in 1598. This brings the name of Soame into his poems.

After an education of which nothing is known but that it laid foundations for a keen enjoyment of the Latin lyric poets, Robert Herrick was apprenticed, at the age of sixteen, to his uncle William, who obtained knighthood, and, like the poet's father, was a goldsmith. He lived in Wood Street, Cheapside, and had a manor—Beau Manor Park—in Leicestershire. Before he was out of his time as apprentice, Robert Herrick had given up the pursuit of trade and was studying as a Fellow Commoner at St. John's College, Cambridge. But it was from Trinity Hall that he graduated as B.A. in the year of Shakespeare's death, and as M.A. in 1620, when his age was twenty-nine. Herrick was one of Nature's poets, and had by that time written many a line that gave him place among the younger men of genius who gathered about Ben Jonson, and thought it fame if any one of them was called by him "son" and so sealed of the tribe of Ben. Herrick, who was no poetaster, could not fail of the just reverence that caused him afterwards to set up little shrines to Jonson in his verse. He became known among the lyric poets of the town, and songs of his were set by the composers then in fashion.

It was not until nine years after the completion of his course at Cambridge that Robert Herrick—in 1629, the year of his mother's death—took orders and was presented by Charles I. to the living of Dean Prior, in what he calls " dull Devonshire." Though he was happiest as comrade of the poets of the town, and loved no scenery so well as that of Cheapside and the Strand ; though he abuses the rocky stream of Dean Burn that breaks down from the moor through a wild little valley and feeds watercresses by the long and empty road between his parsonage and the few houses of Dean Prior ; the love of flowers runs through all his verse. The watercresses of Dean Burn are not forgotten among the simple havings of his grange ; and if he shows no interest in rural scenery, he was full of sympathy with all that was human in his little world among the hills. Dean Prior is on the borders of Dartmoor, and within easy reach of some of the best scenery in Devonshire. For eighteen years Herrick lived in his Vicarage, and then reverse of fortune seemed to him almost a blessing, when he came to be among the deprived clergy; for when he gave place in 1647 to John Syms he returned to London, the blest place of his nativity.

Herrick's source of income was cut off, but he belonged to a numerous and monied family. He had, as a poet and good Royalist, many patrons among whom the cause of his reverse entitled him to ready welcome, and he could dine well when he pleased at tables not his own. His first business when he came to London was to print, in 1647–8, the collection of poems he brought with him from Devonshire, and named, as being from the West, " Hesperides : Works Human and Divine." He was at that time about fifty-seven years old.

The book strengthened friendships, but failed to win general attention in the troubled times of the last years of Charles I., or to touch the spirit that prevailed under the Commonwealth. Herrick published after this no other book, though he was for thirteen years, in London and elsewhere, withdrawn from his duties as a clergyman. It was not until August, 1662, that John Syms was in his turn ejected, and Robert Herrick, at the age of seventy-one, returned to his Vicarage. There he resumed his duties and spent the last twelve years of his life. He was buried there, on the 24th of October, 1674, aged eighty-three. Milton, whose age then was about sixty-six, died on the 8th of the next month.

But Herrick lives with us for ever in his book. It was shaped during the eighteen years of his life in the Vicarage at

Dean Prior, before his deprivation in 1647; brought then to
London, and printed with the date of 1647 on the section contain-
ing " Noble Numbers," and the date of 1648 on the " Hesperides."
There was no reprint of it until that of 1823, which followed
a book of Selections in 1810. but Herrick knew well that
his book was for all time. In the quiet of his parsonage, the
music of his life found utterance in every mood. His whole
mind expressed itself, animal and spiritual. In the texture of his
book he evidently meant to show the warp and woof of life.
He aimed at effects of contrast that belong to the true nature
of man, in whom, as in the world at large, " the strawberry grows
underneath the nettle," and side by side with promptings of the
flesh, spring up the aspirations of the spirit. Even the dainty
fairy pieces written under influence of the same fashion that
caused Shakespeare to describe Queen Mab and Drayton to
write his Nymphidia, even such pieces of his, written in earlier
days, Herrick sprinkled about his volume in fragments. He
would not make his nosegay with the flowers of each sort bunched
together in so many lumps. There is truth in the close contact
of a playful sense of ugliness with the most delicate perception
of all forms of beauty. Herrick's " epigrams" on running eyes
and rotten teeth, and the like, are such exaggerations as may
often have tumbled out spontaneously, in the course of playful
talk, and if they pleased him well enough, were duly entered in
his book. In a healthy mind, this whimsical sense of deformity
may be but the other side of a fine sense of beauty.

A lyric poet must need sing of love, and Herrick was a bachelor
who tells his tombmaker to write over him—

> " Chaste I lived, without a wife,
> ' That's the story of my life."

and who made it the last word in his Hesperides that, " Jocund
his muse was, but his life was chaste." But he could shape an
ideal Julia, and play about her with many a dainty song ; could
shape what music he pleased about Perilla, Sappho, Dianeme :
while, in other moods, the doles to the poor at his parsonage
door ; his spaniel Tracy ; his servant Prudence Baldwin in her
fidelity, her sickness, her death ; the relatives and friends whom
he loved, and to whom one after another he gives a place in his
white Register, that they may live with him immortal upon earth ;
his loyalty to his king, not unmixed with a sense of limit to a
king's authority ; his lament over the tumults of the Civil War ;
his loyalty to God ; his sense of grey hairs, age, and the quiet
looking of his soul toward the passage from this life into the
next ; in these and a hundred other moods, the whole mind
speaks. The careful opening and close, the successive refer-
ences to the early or late place in his book which he gives
to a friend, are among many clear indications of the poet's
order in disorder, of his design to use poems as foils and
settings to one another [illegible]

blended notes that make the full music of life, by expressing
the whole nature of man. He passes, as we daily pass, from
grave to gay, from lively to severe. When he is treading
what is now forbidden ground, he may offend grossly against
modern convention, but he never is immoral. He and his time
held with Catullus, that—

> "—castum esse decet poetam
> Ipsum : versiculos nihil necesse est :
> Qui tum denique habent salem ac leporem,
> Si sunt molliculi, ac parum pudici,
> Et quod pruriat incitare possunt."

Or as he himself put it—

> "Numbers ne'er tickle, or but lightly please,
> Unless they have some wanton carriages."

Accordingly he played sometimes upon what is now forbidden
ground, in lines that glanced only upon the animal side of life.
They are left out of this volume, but how much is lost by the
omission ? Here is Herrick's book just as he published it, with
only the rust of age rubbed off, in accidents of spelling and bad
punctuation that have nothing whatever to do with the expression
of a poet's mind, except as dust upon a mirror that may make its
images less clear ; and as to those lines which for us are " parum
pudici " and would interfere with the free reading of Herrick in
our English homes, how much is lost by their omission ?
Precisely 728 lines, or only as much as would fill another eighteen
pages in the present volume. Those eighteen pages being away,
the rest is as strong as all was formerly. There are only two
places (on page 61 and page 109) where I have changed a line or
word, and the two changes were very trivial. I have long felt
how few were the omissions that would suffice to secure for
Robert Herrick, his due place among the familiar English poets.
As a lyric poet, he is, in range of thought and fulness of natural
music, second only to Robert Burns. Those who wish to
read Herrick in the old spellings and without any omissions,
will have all they can desire in the edition of him published
in 1876 in three volumes by Dr. Grosart, whose "memorial
introduction" contained some valuable results of search for facts
touching the poet's life. Those who wish for a volume of choice
extracts, made by a critic with fine taste, and grouped according
to their matter, will find that in a little book that has been
included in Macmillan's Golden Series—"Chrysomela: a Selection
from the Lyrical Poems of Robert Herrick, arranged with notes,
by Francis Turner Palgrave." Here the desire is that Herrick
himself, brought home to all, should speak in his own clear
way in the tongue we speak ourselves, and that, with only the
few omissions become necessary by the change of times, he
should speak through his whole book just as he uttered it.

H. M.

May, 1884.

HESPERIDES.

To the Most Illustrious and Most Hopeful Prince Charles, Prince of Wales.

WELL may my book come forth like public day,
When such a light as You are leads the way,
Who are my works' creator, and alone
The flame of it, and the expansion.
And look how all those heavenly lamps acquire
Light from the sun, that inexhausted fire ;
So all my morn and evening stars from You
Have their existence, and their influence too.
Full is my book of glories ; but all these
By You become immortal substances.

The Argument of his Book.

I SING of brooks, of blossoms, birds, and bowers,
Of April, May, of June, and July flowers ;
I sing of May-poles, hock-carts, wassails, wakes,
Of bridegrooms, brides, and of their bridal cakes.
I write of youth, of love, and have access
By these, to sing of cleanly wantonness ;
I sing of dews, of rains, and, piece by piece,
Of balm, of oil, of spice, and ambergris ;
I sing of times trans-shifting ; and I write
How roses first came red, and lilies white ;
I write of groves, of twilights, and I sing
The court of Mab, and of the fairy King.
I write of Hell ; I sing, and ever shall,
Of Heaven, and hope to have it after all.

To his Muse.

WHITHER, mad maiden, wilt thou roam ?
Far safer 'twere to stay at home ;
Where thou may'st sit, and piping please
The poor and private cottages.

Since cots and hamlets best agree
With this thy meaner minstrelsy.
There with the reed thou may'st express
The shepherd's fleecy happiness,
And with thy Eclogues intermix
Some smooth and harmless Bucolics.
There, on a hillock, thou mayst sing
Unto a handsome shepherdling,
Or to a girl that keeps the neat,
With breath more sweet than violet.
There, there, perhaps, such lines as these
May take the simple villages ;
But for the court, the country wit
Is despicable unto it.
Stay then at home, and do not go,
Or fly abroad to seek for woe ;
Contempts in courts and cities dwell ;
No critic haunts the poor man's cell,
Where thou may'st hear thine own lines read,
By no one tongue there censured.
That man's unwise will search for ill,
And may prevent it sitting still.

To his Book.

WHILE thou didst keep thy candour undefiled
Dearly I loved thee, as my first-born child ;
But when I saw thee wantonly to roam
From house to house, and never stay at home,
I brake my bonds of love and bade thee go,
Regardless whether well thou sped'st or no.
On with thy fortunes then, whate'er they be ;
If good I'll smile, if bad I'll sigh for thee.

Another.

To read my book, the virgin shy
May blush while Brutus standeth by ;
But when he's gone, read through what's writ,
And never stain a cheek for it.

To the Sour Reader.

IF thou dislik'st the piece thou light'st on first,
Think that, of all that I have writ, the worst ;
But if thou read'st my book unto the end,
And still dost this and that verse reprehend :
O perverse man ! If all disgustful be,
The extreme scab take thee and thine, for me

To his Book.

COME thou not near those men, who are like bread
O'er-leavened, or like cheese o'er-renetted.

When he would have his Verses read.

IN sober mornings do not thou rehearse
The holy incantation of a verse ;
But when that men have both well drunk and fed,
Let my enchantments then be sung or read.
When laurel spirts in the fire, and when the hearth
Smiles to itself and gilds the roof with mirth ;
When up the thyrse is raised, and when the sound
Of sacred orgies flies around, around ;
When the rose reigns, and locks with ointment shine,
Let rigid Cato read these lines of mine.

Upon Julia's Recovery.

DROOP, droop no more, or hang the head,
Ye roses almost withered ;
Now strength and newer purple get,
Each here declining violet.
O primroses ! let this day be
A resurrection unto ye ;
And to all flowers allied in blood,
Or sworn to that sweet sisterhood.
 For health on Julia's cheek hath shed
Claret and cream commingled ;
And those, her lips, do now appear
As beams of coral, but more clear.

To Silvia to Wed.

LET us, though late, at last, my Silvia, wed,
And loving lie in one devoted bed.
Thy watch may stand, my minutes fly post haste ;
No sound calls back the year that once is past.
Then, sweetest Silvia, let's no longer stay ;
True love we know precipitates delay.
Away with doubts, all scruples hence remove,
No man, at one time, can be wise and love.

The Parliament of Roses to Julia.

I DREAMT the Roses one time went
To meet and sit in parliament ;

The place for these, and for the rest
Of flowers, was thy spotless breast
Over the which a state was drawn
Of tiffany, or cobweb lawn ;
Then in that Parley all those powers
Voted the Rose, the queen of flowers :
But so as that herself should be
The maid of honour unto thee.

No Bashfulness in Begging.

To get thine ends, lay bashfulness aside ;
Who fears to ask, doth teach to be denied.

The Frozen Heart.

I FREEZE, I freeze, and nothing dwells
In me but snow and icicles ;
For pity's sake, give your advice
To melt this snow, and thaw this ice.
I'll drink down flames, but if so be
Nothing but love can supple me,
I'll rather keep this frost and snow,
Than to be thawed or heated so.

To Perilla.

AH, my Perilla ! dost thou grieve to see
Me, day by day, to steal away from thee ?
Age calls me hence, and my grey hairs bid come
And haste away to mine eternal home ;
'Twill not be long, Perilla, after this,
That I must give thee the supremest kiss :
Dead when I am, first cast in salt, and bring
Part of the cream from that religious spring,
With which, Perilla, wash my hands and feet ;
That done, then wind me in that very sheet
Which wrapped thy smooth limbs when thou didst implore
The gods' protection but the night before ;
Follow me weeping to my turf, and there
Let fall a primrose, and with it a tear .
Then lastly, let some weekly strewings be
Devoted to the memory of me ;
Then shall my ghost not walk about, but keep
Still in the cool and silent shades of sleep.

A Song to the Maskers.

COME down, and dance ye in the toil
    Of pleasures, to a heat ?
But if to moisture, let the oil
    Of roses be your sweat,

Not only to yourselves assume
  These sweets, but let them fly
From this to that, and so perfume
  E'en all the standers by ;

As goddess Isis, when she went
  Or glided through the street,
Made all that touched her, with her scent,
  And whom she touched, turn sweet.

To Perenna.

WHEN I thy parts run o'er, I can't espy
In any one the least indecency,
But every line and limb diffused thence
A fair and unfamiliar excellence ;
So that the more I look the more I prove
There's still more cause why I the more should love.

Treason.

THE seeds of treason choke up as they spring :
He acts the crime that gives it cherishing.

Two Things Odious.

TWO, of a thousand things, are disallowed :
A lying rich man, and a poor man proud.

The Wounded Heart.

COME, bring your sampler, and with art
  Draw in 't a wounded heart,
  And dropping here and there ;
Not that I think that any dart
  Can make yours bleed a tear,
  Or pierce it anywhere ;
Yet do it to this end, that I
              May by
          This secret see,
        Though you can make
That heart to bleed, yours ne'er will ache
          For me.

No Loathsomeness in Love.

WHAT I fancy I approve,
No dislike there is in love.
Be my mistress short or tall,
And distorted therewithal ;

Be she likewise one of those
That an acre hath of nose ;
Be her forehead and her eyes
Full of incongruities ;
Be her cheeks so shallow too
As to show her tongue wag through ;
Be her lips ill hung or set,
And her grinders black as jet ;
Has she thin hair, hath she none,
She's to me a paragon.

To Anthea.

IF, dear Anthea, my hard fate it be
To live some few sad hours after thee,
Thy sacred corpse with odours I will burn,
And with my laurel crown thy golden urn.
Then, holding up there such religious things
As were, time past, thy holy filletings,
Near to thy reverend pitcher I will fall
Down dead for grief, and end my woes withal ;
So three in one small plat of ground shall lie,
Anthea, Herrick, and his poetry.

The Weeping Cherry.

I SAW a cherry weep, and why ?
  Why wept it ?   But for shame ;
Because my Julia's lip was by,
  And did out-red the same.
But, pretty fondling, let not fall
  A tear at all for that
Which rubies, corals, scarlets, all,
  For tincture, wonder at.

Soft Music.

THE mellow touch of music most doth wound
The soul, when it doth rather sigh than sound.

The Difference betwixt Kings and Subjects.

'TWIXT kings and subjects there's this mighty odds :
Subjects are taught by men ; kings by the gods.

His Answer to a Question.

SOME would know
Why I so
Long still do tarry,
And ask why,

Here that I
Live, and not marry?
Thus I those
Do oppose:
What man would be here
Slave to thrall,
If at all
He could live free here?

Expenses Exhaust.

LIVE with a thrifty not a needy fate;
Small shots paid often waste a vast estate.

Love, what it is.

LOVE is a circle, that doth restless move
In the same sweet eternity of love.

Presence and Absence.

WHEN what is loved is present, love doth spring;
But being absent, love lies languishing.

No Spouse, but a Sister.

A BACHELOR I will
Live, as I have lived still,
And never take a wife
To crucify my life;
But this I'll tell ye too,
What now I mean to do;
A sister in the stead
Of wife about I'll lead,
Which I will keep embraced,
And kiss but yet be chaste.

The Pomander Bracelet.

TO me my Julia lately sent
A bracelet, richly redolent;
The beads I kissed, but most loved her
That did perfume the pomander.

The Carcanet.

INSTEAD of Orient pearls of jet,
I sent my love a carcanet;
About her spotless neck she knit
The lace, to honour me or it.

Then think how wrapped was I to see
My jet to enthral such ivory.

His Sailing from Julia.

When that day comes, whose evening says I'm gone
Unto that watery desolation,
Devoutly to thy closet gods then pray,
That my winged ship may meet no Remora.
Those deities which circum walk the seas,
And look upon our dreadful passages,
Will from all dangers re-deliver me
For one drink-offering poured out by thee.
Mercy and Truth live with thee! and forbear,
In my short absence, to unsluice a tear ;
But yet, for love's sake. let thy lips do this,
Give my dead picture one engendering kiss ;
Work that to life, and let me ever dwell
In thy remembrance, Julia.   So farewell.

How the Wallflower came first, and Why so Called.

WHY this flower is now called so,
List, sweet maids, and you shall know.
Understand, this firstling was
Once a brisk and bonny lass,
Kept as close as Danae was ;
Who a sprightly springall loved,
And to have it fully proved,
Up she got upon a wall,
Tempting down to slide withal ;
But the silken twist untied,
So she fell ; and bruised, she died.
Love, in pity of the deed,
And her loving luckless speed,
Turned her to this plant, we call
Now the Flower of the Wall.

Why Flowers Change Colour.

THESE fresh beauties, we can prove,
Once were virgins, sick of love.
Turned to flowers, still in some
Colours go and colours come.

To his Mistress objecting to Him neither Toying nor Talking.

YOU say I love not, 'cause I do not play
Still with your curls and kiss the time away.

You blame me, too, because I can't devise
Some sport, to please those babies in your eyes ;
By Love's religion, I must here confess it,
The most I love when I the least express it.
Small griefs find tongues ; full casks are ever found
To give, if any, yet but little sound.
Deep waters noiseless are ; and this we know,
That chiding streams betray small depths below.
So when Love speechless is she doth express
A depth in love, and that depth bottomless.
Now since my love is tongueless, know me such,
Who speak but little, 'cause I love so much.

Upon the Loss of his Mistresses. 39

I HAVE lost, and lately, these
Many dainty mistresses :
Stately Julia, prime of all ;
Sappho next, a principal ;
Smooth Anthea, for a skin
White and heaven-like crystalline ;
Sweet Electra, and the choice
Myrrha, for the lute and voice.
Next, Corinna, for her wit,
And the graceful use of it ;
With Perilla : all are gone,
Only Herrick's left alone,
For to number sorrow by
Their departures hence, and die.

The Dream.

METHOUGHT, last night, Love in an anger came
And brought a rod, so whipped me with the same :
Myrtle the twigs were, merely to imply,
Love strikes, but 'tis with gentle cruelty.
Patient I was : Love pitiful grew then,
And stroked the stripes, and I was whole again.
Thus like a bee, love gentle still doth bring
Honey to salve where he before did sting.

To Love.

I'M free from thee, and thou no more shalt hear
My puling pipe to beat against thine ear ;
Farewell my shackles, though of pearl they be,
Such precious thraldom ne'er shall fetter me.
He loves his bonds who, when the first are broke,
Submits his neck unto a second yoke.

Love's Play at Push-pin.

LOVE and myself, believe me, on a day,
At childish push-pin, for our sport, did play ;
I put, he pushed, and heedless of my skin,
Love pricked my finger with a golden pin ;
Since which, it festers so, that I can prove
'Twas but a trick to poison me with love :
Little the wound was, greater was the smart ;
The finger bled, but burnt was all my heart.

The Rosary.

ONE asked me where the roses grew ?
 I bade him not go seek ;
But forthwith bade my Julia show
 A bud in either cheek.

√ The Parcæ ; or, Three Dainty Destinies.
The Armilet.

THREE lovely sisters working were,
 As they were closely set,
Of soft and dainty maiden-hair,
 A curious Armilet.
I, smiling, asked them what they did,
 Fair destinies all three ?
Who told me they had drawn a thread
 Of life, and 'twas for me.
They showed me then how fine 'twas spun :
 And I replied thereto,
I care not now how soon 'tis done,
 Or cut, if cut by you.

Sorrows Succeed.

WHEN one is past, another care we have,
Thus woe succeeds a woe, as wave a wave.

To Robin Redbreast.

LAID out for dead, let thy last kindness be
With leaves and moss-work for to cover me ;
And while the wood-nymphs my cold corpse inter,
Sing thou my dirge, sweet warbling chorister.
For epitaph, in foliage, next write this :
Here, here the tomb of Robin Herrick is !

Discontents in Devon.

MORE discontents I never had,
 Since I was born, than here ;
Where I have been, and still am sad,
 In this dull Devonshire.
Yet, justly too, I must confess,
 I ne'er invented such
Ennobled numbers for the press,
 Than where I loathed so much.

To his Paternal Country.

O EARTH ! earth ! earth ! hear thou my voice, and be
Loving and gentle for to cover me ;
Banished from thee I live, ne'er to return,
Unless thou giv'st my small remains an urn.

Cherry Ripe.

 CHERRY ripe, ripe, ripe, I cry,
 Full and fair ones, come and buy ;
 If so be you ask me where
 They do grow? I answer, there,
 Where my Julia's lips do smile
 There's the land or cherry isle,
 Whose plantations fully show
 All the year where cherries grow.

To his Mistresses.

PUT on your silks, and piece by piece,
Give them the scent of ambergris ;
And for your breaths, too, let them smell
Ambrosia like, or nectarel ;
While other gums their sweets perspire,
By your own jewels set on fire.

To Anthea.

Now is the time when all the lights wax dim,
And thou, Anthea, must withdraw from him
Who was thy servant. Dearest, bury me
Under that holy-oak or gospel-tree ;
Where, though thou see'st not, thou may'st think upon
Me, when thou yearly goest procession ;
Or, for mine honour, lay me in that tomb
In which thy sacred relics shall have room :
For my embalming, sweetest, there will be
No spices wanting when I'm laid by thee.

The Vision to Electra.

I DREAMED we both were in a bed
Of roses, almost smothered ;
The warmth and sweetness had me there
Made lovingly familiar,
But that I heard thy sweet breath say,
Faults done by night will blush by day
I kissed thee, panting, and I call
Night to the record, that was all.
But, ah ! if empty dreams so please,
Love, give me more such nights as these.

Dreams.

HERE we are all by day ; by night we are hurled
By dreams, each one into a several world.

Ambition.

IN man, ambition is the commonest thing ;
Each one by nature loves to be a king.

His Request to Julia.

JULIA, if I chance to die
Ere I print my poetry,
I most humbly thee desire
To commit it to the fire ;
Better 'twere my book were dead,
Than to live not perfected.

Money Gets the Mastery.

FIGHT thou with shafts of silver, and o'ercome,
When no force else can get the masterdom.

The Scar-fire.

WATER, water, I desire,
Here's a house of flesh on fire ;
Ope the fountains and the springs,
And come all to bucketings.
What ye cannot quench pull down,
Spoil a house to save a town.
Better 'tis that one should fall
Than by one to hazard all.

Upon Silvia.

WHEN some shall say, Fair once my Silvia was,
Thou wilt complain, False now's thy looking-glass;
Which renders that quite tarnished which was green,
And priceless now what peerless once had been.
Upon thy form more wrinkles yet will fall,
And coming down, shall make no noise at all.

Cheerfulness in Charity; or, the Sweet Sacrifice.

'TIS not a thousand bullocks' thighs
Can please those heavenly deities,
If the vower don't express
In his offering, cheerfulness.

Once Poor, still Penurious.

GOES the world now, it will with thee go hard;
The fattest hogs we grease the more with lard.
To him that has there shall be added more;
Who is penurious, he shall still be poor.

Sweetness in Sacrifice.

'TIS not greatness they require,
To be offered up by fire;
But 'tis sweetness that doth please
Those eternal essences.

Steam in Sacrifice.

IF meat the gods give, I the steam,
High towering, will devote to them,
Whose easy natures like it well
If we the roast have, they the smell.

Upon Julia's Voice.

So smooth, so sweet, so silvery is thy voice.
As, could they hear, the damned would make no noise,
But listen to thee, walking in thy chamber,
Melting melodious words to lutes of amber.

Again.

WHEN I thy singing next shall hear,
I'll wish I might turn all to ear,

To drink in notes and numbers such
As blessed souls can't hear too much ;
Then melted down, there let me lie
Entranced, and lost confusedly,
And by thy music stricken mute,
Die and be turned into a lute.

All Things Decay and Die.

ALL things decay with time : the forest sees
The growth and downfall of her aged trees;
That timber tall, which threescore lustres stood
The proud dictator of the state-like wood,
I mean the sovereign of all plants—the oak,
Droops, dies, and falls without the cleaver's stroke.

The Succession of the Four Sweet Months.

FIRST, April, she with mellow showers
Opens the way for early flowers ;
Then after her comes smiling May,
In a more rich and sweet array ;
Next enters June, and brings us more
Gems that those two that went before ;
Then, lastly, July comes, and she
More wealth brings in than all those three.

No Shipwreck of Virtue.—To a Friend.

THOU sailest with others in this Argus here,
Nor wreck or bulging thou hast cause to fear ;
But trust to this, my noble passenger,
Who swims with Virtue, he shall still be sure,
Ulysses-like, all tempests to endure,
And 'midst a thousand gulfs to be secure.

Upon his Sister-in-law, Mistress Elizabeth Herrick.

FIRST, for effusions due unto the dead,
My solemn vows have here accomplished ;
Next, how I love thee, that my grief must tell,
Wherein thou liv'st for ever.   Dear, farewell !

Of Love.—A Sonnet.

How love came in I do not know,
Whether by the eye, or ear, or no ;
Or whether with the soul it came,
At first infused with the same ;

Whether in part 'tis here or there.
Or, like the soul, whole everywhere,
This troubles me : but I as well
As any other, this can tell ;
Then when from hence she does depart,
The outlet then is from the heart.

The Rock of Rubies, and the Quarry of Pearls.

SOME asked me where the Rubies grew
    And nothing I did say ;
But with my finger pointed to
    The lips of Julia.
Some asked how Pearls did grow, and where
    Then spoke I to my girl,
To part her lips and show me there
    The quarelets of Pearl.

Conformity.

CONFORMITY was ever known
A foe to dissolution ;
Nor can we that a ruin call,
Whose crack gives crushing unto all.

To the King, upon his Coming with his Army into the West.

WELCOME, most welcome to our vows and us,
Most great and universal genius !
The drooping West, which hitherto has stood
As one, in long-lamented widowhood,
Looks like a bride now, or a bed of flowers,
Newly refreshed both by the sun and showers.
War, which before was horrid, now appears
Lovely in you, brave Prince of Cavaliers !
A deal of courage in each bosom springs
By your access, O you the best of Kings !
Ride on with all white omens, so that where
Your standard's up, we fix a conquest there.

Upon Roses.

UNDER a lawn, than skies more clear,
Some ruffled Roses nestling were,
And snugging there, they seemed to lie
As in a flowery nunnery :
They blushed and looked more fresh than flowers
Quickened of late by pearly showers ;

And all, because they were possessed
But of the heat of Julia's breast,
Which, as a warm and moistened spring,
Gave them their ever flourishing.

To the King and Queen, upon their Unhappy Distances.

WOE, woe to them, who by a ball of strife,
Do, and have parted here a man and wife ;
Charles, the best husband, while Maria strives
To be, and is, the very best of wives ;
Like streams you are divorced, but 't will come when
These eyes of mine shall see you mix again.
Thus speaks the oak here, C. and M. shall meet,
Treading on amber with their silver feet ;
Nor will 't be long ere this accomplished be ;
The words found true, C. M. remember me.

Dangers wait on Kings.

As oft as night is banished by the morn,
So oft we'll think we see a King new born.

The Cheat of Cupid ; or, the Ungentle Guest.

ONE silent night of late,
    When every creature rested,
Came one unto my gate,
    And knocking, me molested.

" Who's that," said I, " beats there,
    And troubles thus the sleepy ?
" Cast off," said he, " all fear,
    And let not locks thus keep ye.

" For I a boy am, who
    By moonless nights have swerved ;
And all with showers wet through,
    And e'en with cold half starved."

I pitiful arose,
    And soon a taper lighted ;
And did myself disclose
    Unto the lad benighted.

I saw he had a bow,
    And wings too, which did shiver ;
And looking down below,
    I spied he had a quiver.

I to my chimney's shine
  Brought him, as Love professes,
And chafed his hands with mine,
  And dried his dropping tresses.

But when he felt him warmed,
  " Let's try this bow of ours
And string, if they be harmed,"
  Said he, " with these late showers."

Forthwith his bow he bent,
  And wedded string and arrow,
And struck me that it went
  Quite through my heart and marrow.

Then laughing loud, he flew
  Away, and thus said flying,
" Adieu, mine host, adieu,
  I'll leave thy heart a-dying."

To the Reverend Shade of his Religious Father.

THAT for seven lustres I did never come
To do the rites to thy religious tomb ;
That neither hair was cut, or true tears shed
By me o'er thee, as justments to the dead ;
Forgive, forgive me ; since I did not know
Whether thy bones had here their rest or no.
But now 'tis known, behold, behold, I bring
Unto thy ghost the effused offering :
And look, what smallage, nightshade, cypress, yew,
Unto the shades have been, or now are due,
Here I devote ; and something more than so,
I come to pay a debt of birth I owe.
Thou gavest me life, but mortal ; for that one
Favour I'll make full satisfaction ;
For my life mortal, rise from out thy hearse,
And take a life immortal from my verse.

Delight in Disorder.

A SWEET disorder in the dress
Kindles in clothes a wantonness ;
A lawn about the shoulders thrown
Into a fine distraction ;
An erring lace, which here and there
Enthrals a crimson stomacher ;
A cuff neglectful, and thereby
Ribbons to flow confusedly ;
A winning wave, deserving note,
In the tempestuous petticoat ;

A careless shoe-string, in whose tie
I see a wild civility ;
Do more bewitch me, than when art
Is too precise in every part.

To his Muse.

WERE I to give thee baptism, I would choose
To christen thee the Bride, the Bashful Muse,
Or Muse of Roses ; since that name does fit
Best with those virgin verses thou hast writ ;
Which are so clean, so chaste, as none may fear
Cato the Censor, should he scan each here.

Upon Love.

LOVE scorched my finger, but did spare
　The burning of my heart ;
To signify in love my share
　Should be a little part.
Little I love, but if that he
　Would but that heat recall,
That joint to ashes should be burnt,
　Ere I would love at all.

Dean-Bourn, a rude River in Devon, by which sometimes he lived.

DEAN-BOURN, farewell ; I never look to see
Dean or thy warty incivility ;
Thy rocky bottom, that doth tear thy streams
And makes them frantic, even to all extremes,
To my content I never should behold,
Were thy streams silver, or thy rocks all gold.
Rocky thou art ; and rocky we discover
Thy men, and rocky are thy ways all over.
O men, O manners ; now, and ever known
To be a rocky generation !
A people currish, churlish as the seas.
And rude almost as rudest savages.
With whom I did, and may resojourn when
Rocks turn to rivers, rivers turn to men.

Kissing Usury.

BIANCHA, let
Me pay the debt
I owe thee for a kiss
Thou lend'st to me,
And I to thee
Will render ten for this.

If thou wilt say,
Ten will not pay
For that so rich a one ;
I'll clear the sum,
If it will come
Unto a million.
He must of right,
To the utmost mite
Make payment for his pleasure,—
By this I guess,—
Of happiness,
Who has a little measure.

To Julia.

How rich and pleasing thou, my Julia, art,
In each thy dainty and peculiar part !
First, for thy Queenship, on thy head is set
Of flowers a sweet commingled coronet ;
About thy neck a carcanet is bound,
Made of the ruby, pearl, and diamond ;
A golden ring, that shines upon thy thumb ;
About thy wrist the rich Dardanium ;
Between thy breasts, than down of swans more white,
There plays the sapphire with the chrysolite.
No part besides must of thyself be known,
But by the topaz, opal, chalcedon.

To Laurels.

A FUNERAL stone
Or verse, I covet none;
But only crave
Of you that I may have
A sacred laurel springing from my grave,
Which being seen
Blest with perpetual green,
May grow to be
Not so much called a tree
As the eternal monument of me.

His Cavalier.

GIVE me that man that dares bestride
The active sea-horse, and with pride,
Through that huge field of waters ride :
Who, with his looks, too, can appease
The ruffling winds and raging seas,
In midst of all their outrages,

This, this a virtuous man can do,
Sail against rocks, and split them too;
Ay, and a world of pikes pass through.

Zeal required in Love.

I'LL do my best to win whene'er I woo;
That man loves not who is not zealous too.

The Bag of the Bee.

ABOUT the sweet bag of a bee,
 Two Cupids fell at odds;
And whose the pretty prize should be,
 They vowed to ask the gods.
Which Venus hearing, thither came,
 And for their boldness stripped them,
And taking thence from each his flame,
 With rods of myrtle whipped them.
Which done, to still their wanton cries,
 When quiet grown she'd seen them,
She kissed, and wiped their dove-like eyes,
 And gave the bag between them.

Love Killed by Lack.

LET me be warm, let me be fully fed,
Luxurious love by wealth is nourished.
Let me be lean, and cold, and once grown poor,
I shall dislike what once I loved before.

To his Mistress.

CHOOSE me your Valentine;
 Next let us marry:
Love to the death will pine,
 If we long tarry.
Promise and keep your vows,
 Or vow ye never;
Love's doctrine disallows
 Troth-breakers ever.
You have broke promise twice,
 Dear, to undo me;
If you prove faithless thrice,
 None then will woo ye.

To the Generous Reader.

SEE and not see, and if thou chance to espy
Some aberrations in my poetry;

Wink at small faults, the greater, ne'ertheless,
Hide, and with them their father's nakedness.
Let's do our best our watch and ward to keep ;
Homer himself, in a long work, may sleep.

To Critics.

I'LL write, because I'll give
You critics means to live ;
For should I not supply
The cause, the effect would die.

Duty to Tyrants.

GOOD princes must be prayed for ; for the bad
They must be borne with, and in reverence had.
Do they first pill thee, next pluck off thy skin ?
Good children kiss the rods that punish sin ;
Touch not the tyrant, let the gods alone
To strike him dead that but usurps a throne.

Being once Blind, his Request to Biancha.

WHEN age or chance has made me blind,
So that the path I cannot find ;
And when my falls and stumblings are
More than the stones i' th' street by far ;
Go then afore, and I shall well
Follow thy perfumes by the smell ;
Or be my guide, and I shall be
Led by some light that flows from thee.
Thus held, or led by thee, I shall
In ways confused, nor slip nor fall.

Upon Blanch.

BLANCH swears her husband's lovely, when a scald,
Has bleared his eyes ; besides, his head is bald.
Next, his wild ears, like leathern wings full spread,
Flutter to fly and bear away his head.

No Want where there's Little.

To bread and water none is poor ;
And having these, what need of more ?
Though much from out the cess be spent,
Nature with little is content.

Barley-Break ; or, Last in Hell.

WE two are last in hell ; what may we fear
To be tormented or kept prisoners here ?

Alas ! if kissing be of plagues the worst,
We'll wish in hell we had been last and first.

The Definition of Beauty.

BEAUTY no other thing is than a beam
Flashed out between the middle and extreme.

To Dianeme.

DEAR, though to part it be a hell,
Yet, Dianeme, now farewell ;
Thy frown last night did bid me go,
But whither only grief does know.
I do beseech thee, ere we part
(If merciful as fair thou art,
Or else desirest that maids should tell
Thy pity by love's chronicle),
O, Dianeme, rather kill
Me, than to make me languish still !
'Tis cruelty in thee to the height,
Thus, thus to wound, not kill outright ;
Yet there's a way found, if thou please,
By sudden death, to give me ease ;
And thus devised, do thou but this,
Bequeath to me one parting kiss :
So superabundant joy shall be
The executioner of me.

A Country Life : To his Brother, Mr. Tho. Herrick.

THRICE, and above, blest, my soul's half, art thou,
  In thy both last and better vow.
Couldst leave the city, for exchange, to see
  The country's sweet simplicity,
And it to know and practise, with intent
  To grow the sooner innocent
By studying to know virtue, and to aim
  More at her nature than her name.
The last is but the least, the first doth tell
  Ways less to live than to live well ;
And both are known to thee, who now canst live,
  Led by thy conscience, to give
Justice to soon-pleased nature, and to show
  Wisdom and she together go,
And keep one centre ; this with that conspires
  To teach man to confine desires,
And know that riches have their proper stint
  In the contented mind, not mint ;

And canst instruct that those who have the itch
    Of craving more are never rich.
These things thou know'st to the height, and dost prevent
    That plague, because thou art content
With that Heaven gave thee with a wary hand
    (More blessed in thy brass than land)
To keep cheap Nature even and upright
    To cool not cocker appetite.
Thus thou canst tersely live to satisfy
    The belly chiefly, not the eye ;
Keeping the barking stomach wisely quiet,
    Less with a neat than needful diet.
But that which most makes sweet thy country life,
    Is the fruition of a wife,
Whom, stars consenting with thy fate, thou hast
    Got not so beautiful as chaste ;
By whose warm side thou dost securely sleep,
    While love the sentinel doth keep,
With those deeds done by day which ne'er affright
    Thy silken slumbers in the night.
Nor has the darkness power to usher in
    Fear to those sheets that know no sin.
The damasked meadows and the pebbly streams
    Sweeten and make soft your dreams ;
The purling springs, groves, birds, and well-weaved bowers,
    With fields enamelled with flowers,
Present their shapes, while fantasy discloses
    Millions of lilies mixed with roses.
Then dream ye hear the lamb by many a bleat
    Wooed to come suck the milky teat,
While Faunus in the vision comes to keep
    From ravening wolves the fleecy sheep.
With thousand such enchanting dreams that meet
    To make sleep not so sound as sweet ;
Nor can these figures so thy rest endear,
    As not to rise when chanticleer
Warns the last watch, but with the dawn dost rise
    To work, but first to sacrifice ;
Making thy peace with Heaven for some late fault,
    With holy-meal and spirting salt ;
Which done, thy painful thumb this sentence tells us
    " Jove for our labour all things sells us."
Nor are thy daily and devout affairs,
    Attended with those desperate cares,
The industrious merchant has, who for to find
    Gold, runneth to the Western Inde,
And back again ; tortured with fears, doth fly,
    Untaught, to suffer poverty.
But thou at home, blest with securest ease,
    Sitt'st, and believ'st that there be seas

And watery dangers, while thy whiter hap
    But sees these things within thy map ;
And viewing them with a more safe survey
    Mak'st easy fear unto thee say,
"A heart thrice walled with oak and brass that man
    Had, first durst plough the ocean."
But thou at home, without or tide or gale,
    Canst in thy map securely sail,
Seeing those painted countries, and so guess
    By those fine shades their substances ;
And from thy compass taking small advice,
    Buy'st travel at the lowest price.
Nor are thine ears so deaf but thou canst hear,
    Far more with wonder than with fear,
Fame tell of states, of countries, courts, and kings,
    And believe there be such things
When, of these truths thy happier knowledge lies
    More in thine ears than in thine eyes.
And when thou hearest by too true report,
    Vice rules the most or all at court,
Thy pious wishes are, though thou not there,
    Virtue had, and moved her sphere.
But thou liv'st fearless ; and thy face ne'er shows
    Fortune when she comes or goes,
But, with thy equal thoughts prepared, dost stand
    To take her by the either hand ;
Nor car'st which comes the first, the foul or fair.
    A wise man every way lies square ;
And like a surly oak with storms perplexed,
    Grows still the stronger, strongly vexed.
Be so, bold spirit ; stand centre-like unmoved ;
    And be not only thought but proved
To be what I report thee, and inure
    Thyself if want comes to endure.
And so thou dost ; for thy desires are
    Confined to live with private Lar,
Nor curious whether appetite be fed,
    Or with the first or second bread.
Who keep'st no proud mouth for delicious cates ;
    Hunger makes coarse meats delicates.
Canst, and unurged, forsake that larded fare,
    Which art, not nature makes so rare ;
To taste boiled nettles, coleworts, beets, and eat
    These and sour herbs as dainty meat,
While soft opinion makes thy genius say,
    "Content makes all ambrosia."
Nor is it that thou keepest this stricter 'size
    So much for want as exercise ;
To numb the sense of dearth, which, should sin haste it,
    Thou might'st but only see 't, not taste it ;

Yet can thy humble roof maintain a quire
    Of singing crickets by thy fire ;
And the brisk mouse may feast herself with crumbs,
    Till that the green-eyed kitling comes ;
Then to her cabin, blest she can escape
    The sudden danger of a rape.
And thus thy little well-kept stock doth prove,
    Wealth cannot make a life, but love.
Nor art thou so close-handed, but canst spend
    (Counsel concurring with the end)
As well as spare ; still conning o'er this theme,
    To shun the first and last extreme ;
Ordaining that thy small stock find no breach,
    Or to exceed thy tether's reach.
But to live round, and close, and wisely true
    To thine own self, and known to few.
Thus let thy rural sanctuary be
    Elisium to thy wife and thee ;
There to disport yourselves with golden measure :
    For seldom use commends the pleasure.
Live, and live blest, thrice happy pair ; let breath,
    But lost to one, be the other's death.
And as there is one love, one faith, one troth,
    Be so one death, one grave to both.
Till when, in such assurance, live, ye may
    Nor fear nor wish your dying day.

Divination by a Daffodil.

WHEN a Daffodil I see
Hanging down his head t'wards me,
Guess I may what I must be :
First, I shall decline my head ;
Secondly, I shall be dead ;
Lastly, safely buried.

To the Painter, to Draw him a Picture.

COME, skilful Lupo, now, and take
Thy bice, thy umber, pink, and lake ;
And let it be thy pencil's strife
To paint a Bridgeman to the life.
Draw him as like too as you can,
An old, poor, lying flattering man ;
His cheeks bepimpled, red and blue,
His nose and lips of mulberry hue.
Then for an easy fancy, place
A burling iron for his face ;
Next, make his cheeks with breath to swell,
And for to speak, if possible ;

But do not so, for fear, lest he
Should by his breathing poison thee.

Upon Cuffe.—Epigram.

CUFFE comes to church much, but he keeps his bed
Those Sundays only whenas briefs are read ;
This makes Cuffe dull, and troubles him the most,
Because he cannot sleep in the church free-cost.

Upon Fone, a Schoolmaster.—Epigram.

FONE says, those mighty whiskers he does wear
Are twigs of birch and willow growing there ;
If so, we'll think, too, when he does condemn
Boys to the lash, that he does whip with them.

A Lyric to Mirth.

WHILE the milder fates consent,
Let's enjoy our merriment ;
Drink, and dance, and pipe, and play,
Kiss our dollies night and day ;
Crowned with clusters of the vine,
Let us sit and quaff our wine ;
Call on Bacchus, chant his praise,
Shake the thyrse and bite the bays ;
Rouse Anacreon from the dead,
And return him drunk to bed ;
Sing o'er Horace ; for ere long
Death will come and mar the song ;
Then shall Wilson and Gotiere
Never sing or play more here.

To the Earl of Westmorland.

WHEN my date's done, and my grey age must die,
Nurse up, great lord, this my posterity :
Weak though it be, long may it grow and stand,
Shored up by you, brave Earl of Westmorland.

Against Love.

WHENE'ER my heart love's warmth but entertains,
O frost ! O snow ! O hail ! forbid the banes.
One drop now deads a spark, but if the same
Once gets a force, floods cannot quench the flame.
Rather than love, let me be ever lost,
Or let me 'gender with eternal frost.

Upon Julia's Ribbon.

As shows the air when with a rainbow graced,
So smiles that ribbon 'bout my Julia's waist ;
Or like—— Nay, 'tis that zonulet of love,
Wherein all pleasures of the world are wove.

The Frozen Zone ; or, Julia Disdainful.

WHITHER ? Say, whither shall I fly,
To slack these flames wherein I fry ?
To the treasures shall I go,
Of the rain, frost, hail, and snow ?
Shall I search the underground,
Where all damps and mists are found ?
Shall I seek, for speedy ease,
All the floods and frozen seas ?
Or descend into the deep,
Where eternal cold does keep ?
These may cool ; but there's a zone
Colder yet than any one ;
That's my Julia's breast, where dwells
Such destructive icicles,
As that the congelation will
Me sooner starve than those can kill.

An Epitaph upon a Sober Matron.

WITH blameless carriage I lived here,
To the almost seven-and-fortieth year.
Stout sons I had, and those twice three,
One only daughter lent to me :
The which was made a happy bride,
But thrice three moons before she died.
My modest wedlock, that was known
Contented with the bed of one.

To the Patron of Poets, M. End. Porter.

LET there be patrons ; patrons like to thee,
Brave Porter ! Poets ne'er will wanting be.
Fabius, and Cotta, Lentulus, all live
In thee, thou man of men ! who here dost give
Not only subject-matter for our wit,
But likewise oil of maintenance to it.
For which before thy threshold we'll lay down
Our thyrse for sceptre, and our bays for crown.
For, to say truth, all garlands are thy due ;
The laurel, myrtle, oak, and ivy too.

The Sadness of Things for Sappho's Sickness.

LILIES will languish, violets look ill,
Sickly the primrose, pale the daffodil ;
That gallant tulip will hang down his head,
Like to a virgin newly ravished.
Pansies will weep, and marigolds will wither,
And keep a fast and funeral together ;
If Sappho droop, daisies will open never,
But bid Good-night and close their lids for ever.

Leander's Obsequies.

WHEN as Leander young was drowned
No heart by love received a wound ;
But on a rock himself sat by,
There weeping superabundantly.
Sighs numberless he cast about,
And all his tapers thus put out ;
His head upon his hand he laid,
And sobbing deeply, thus he said:
"Ah, cruel sea !" and, looking on't,
Wept as he'd drown the Hellespont.
And sure his tongue had more expressed,
But that his tears forbad the rest.

Hope Heartens.

NONE goes to warfare, but with this intent :
The gains must dead the fear of detriment.

Four Things make us Happy Here.

HEALTH is the first good lent to men ;
A gentle disposition then :
Next, to be rich by no byways ;
Lastly with friends to enjoy our days.

His Parting from Mrs. Dorothy Keneday.

WHEN I did go from thee, I felt that smart
Which bodies do when souls from them depart ;
Thou didst not mind it, though thou then might'st see
Me turned to tears, yet didst not weep for me.
'Tis true I kissed thee, but I could not hear
Thee spend a sigh, to accompany my tear.
Methought 'twas strange, that thou so hard shouldst prove,
Whose heart, whose hand, whose every part spake love.
Prithee (lest maids should censure thee) but say
Thou shedd'st one tear whenas I went away ;
And that will please me somewhat ; though I know,
And love will swear 't, my dearest did not so.

The Tear sent to Her from Staines.

GLIDE, gentle streams, and bear
Along with you my tear
    To that coy girl,
    Who smiles yet slays
    Me with delays,
And strings my tears as pearl.

See, see, she's yonder set,
Making a carcanet
    Of maiden-flowers!
    There, there present
    This orient
And pendant pearl of ours.

Then say I've sent one more
Gem to enrich her store;
    And that is all
    Which I can send,
    Or vainly spend,
For tears no more will fall.

Nor will I seek supply
Of them, the spring's once dry;
    But I'll devise,
    Among the rest,
    A way that's best,
How I may save mine eyes.

Yet say, should she condemn
Me to surrender them;
    Then say, my part
    Must be to weep
    Out them, to keep
A poor, yet loving heart.

Say, too, she would have this;
She shall: Then my hope is,
    That when I'm poor,
    And nothing have
    To send or save,
I'm sure she'll ask no more.

Upon one Lily, who married with a Maid called Rose.

WHAT times of sweetness this fair day fore-shows,
Whenas the Lily marries with the Rose!
What next is looked for, but we all should see
To spring from these a sweet posterity?

An Epitaph upon a Child.

VIRGINS promised when I died,
That they would each primrose-tide
Duly morn and evening come
And with flowers dress my tomb.
Having promised, pay your debts,
Maids, and here strew violets.

The Hour-Glass.

THAT hour-glass which there you see,
With water filled, sirs, credit me,
The humour was, as I have read,
But lovers' tears incrystalled ;
Which, as they drop by drop do pass
From the upper to the under-glass,
Do in a trickling manner tell
(By many a watery syllable)
That lovers' tears in lifetime shed,
Do restless run when they are dead.

His Farewell to Sack.

FAREWELL, thou thing time past so known, so dear
To me, as blood to life and spirit.   Near,
Nay, thou more near than kindred, friend, man, wife,
Male to the female, soul to body.   Life
To quick action, or the warm soft side
Of the resigning, yet resisting bride.
These, and a thousand sweets, could never be
So near or dear as thou was once to me.
O, thou the drink of Gods and Angels ! wine
That scatterest spirit and lust ; whose purest shine,
More radiant than the summer's sunbeams shows,
Each way illustrious, brave ; and like to those
Comets we see by night, whose shagged portents
Foretell the coming of some dire events ;
Or some full flame, which with a pride aspires,
Throwing about his wild and active fires.
'Tis thou, 'bove nectar, O divinest soul !
Eternal in thyself, that canst control
That which subverts whole Nature, grief and care,
Vexation of the mind, and damned despair.
'Tis thou alone, who, with thy mystic fan,
Work'st more than wisdom, art, or Nature can,
To rouse the sacred madness, and awake
The frost-bound blood and spirits, and to make

Them frantic with thy raptures, flashing through
The soul like lightning, and as active too ;
'Tis not Apollo can, or those thrice three
Castalian sisters sing, if wanting thee.
Horace, Anacreon, both had lost their fame,
Hadst thou not filled them with thy fire and flame,
Phœbean splendour ! and thou, Thespian spring,
Of which sweet swans must drink before they sing
Their true-paced numbers and their holy lays,
Which makes them worthy cedar and the bays.
But why ? why longer do I gaze upon
Thee with the eye of admiration ?
Since I must leave thee, and enforced must say,
To all thy witching beauties, Go, away !
But if thy whimp'ring looks do ask me why ?
Then know that Nature bids thee go, not I.
'Tis her erroneous self has made a brain
Incapable of such a sovereign,
As is thy powerful self.   Prithee, not smile,
Or smile more inly, lest thy looks beguile
My vows denounced in zeal, which thus much show thee
That I have sworn but by thy looks to know thee.
Let others drink thee freely, and desire
Thee and their lips espoused, while I admire
And love thee, but not taste thee.   Let my muse
Fail of thy former helps, and only use
Her inadulterate strength ; what's done by me
Hereafter shall smell of the lamp, not thee.

Upon Glasco.—Epigram.

GLASCO had none, but now some teeth has got,
Which though they fur, will neither ache nor rot.
Six teeth he has, whereof twice two are known
Made of a haft, that was a mutton-bone ;
Which not for use, but merely for the sight,
He wears all day, and draws those teeth at night.

Upon Mrs. Eliz. Wheeler, under the name of Amarillis.

SWEET Amarillis, by a spring's
Soft and soul-melting murmurings,
Slept ; and thus sleeping, thither flew
A robin redbreast ; who at view,
Not seeing her at all to stir,
Brought leaves and moss to cover her ;
But while he, perking, there did pry
About the arch of either eye,

The lid began to let out day,
At which poor Robin flew away;
And seeing her not dead, but all disleaved,
He chirped for joy to see himself deceived.

The Custard.

FOR second course last night, a custard came
To the board so hot, as none could touch the same;
Furze, three or four times with his cheeks did blow
Upon the custard, and thus cooled so,
It seemed by this time to admit the touch;
But none could eat it, 'cause it stunk so much.

To Myrrha, Hard-hearted.

FOLD now thine arms, and hang the head
Like to a lily withered:
Next, look thou like a sickly moon,   .
Or like Jocasta in a swoon.
Then weep, and sigh, and softly go,
Like to a widow drowned in woe;
Or like a virgin full of ruth,
For the lost sweetheart of her youth:
And all because, fair maid, thou art
Insensible of all my smart,
And of those evil days that be
Now posting on to punish thee.
The gods are easy, and condemn
All such as are not soft like them.

The Eye.

MAKE me a heaven, and make me there
Many a less and greater sphere:
Make me the straight and oblique lines,
The motions, lations, and the signs;
Make me a chariot and a sun,
And let them through a zodiac run;
Next, place me zones and tropics there,
With all the seasons of the year.
Make me a sunset and a night,
And then present the morning's light,
Clothed in her camlets of delight.
To these make clouds to pour down rain;
With weather foul, then fair again;
And when, wise artist, that thou hast,
With all that can be, this heaven graced:
Ah! what is then this curious sky,
But only my Corinna's eye!

Upon the Much Lamented Mr. J. Warr.

WHAT wisdom, learning, wit, or worth,
Youth or sweet nature could bring forth,
Rests here with him, who was the same,
The volume of himself, and name.
If, reader, then thou wilt draw near,
And do an honour to thy tear,
Weep then for him, for whom laments
Not one, but many monuments.

Upon Gryll.

GRYLL eats but ne'er says grace.   To speak the troth,
Gryll either keeps his breath to cool his broth,
Or else because Gryll's roast does burn his spit,
Gryll will not therefore say a grace for it.

The Suspicion upon His overmuch Familiarity
with a Gentlewoman.

AND must we part, because some say,
Loud is our love and loose our play,
Aud more than well becomes the day?
Alas, for pity! and for us,
Most innocent and injured thus.
Had we kept close, or played within,
Suspicion now had been the sin,
And shame had followed long ere this,
To have played what now unpunished is.
But we, as fearless of the sun,
As faultless, will not wish undone
What now is done; since, where no sin
Unbolts the door, no shame comes in.
Then, comely and most fragrant maid,
Be you more wary than afraid
Of these reports; because you see
The fairest most suspected be.
The common forms have no one eye
Or ear of burning jealousy
To follow them: but chiefly where
Love makes the cheek and chin a sphere
To dance and play in; trust me, there
Suspicion questions every hair.
Come, you are fair, and should be seen
While you are in your sprightful green,
And what though you had been embraced
By me, were you for that unchaste?
No, no, no more than is yond moon,
Which, shining in her perfect noon,

In all that great and glorious light
Continues cold as is the night.
Then, beauteous maid, you may retire ;
And as for me, my chaste desire
Shall move towards you, although I **see**
Your face no more ; so live you free
From Fame's black lips, as you from me.

Single Life most Secure.

SUSPICION, discontent. and strife,
Come in for dowry with a wife.

The Curse.—A Song.

Go, perjured man, and if thou e'er return
To see the small remainders in mine urn,
When thou shalt laugh at my religious dust,
And ask, Where's now the colour, form, and trust
Of woman's beauty? and with hand more rude
Rifle the flowers which the virgins strewed ;
Know, I have prayed to Fury that some wind
May blow my ashes up, and strike thee blind.

The Wounded Cupid.—Song.

CUPID, as he lay among
Roses, by a bee was stung ;
Whereupon in anger flying
To his mother, said, thus crying :
" Help! O help! your boy's a-dying."
" And why, my pretty lad?" said she.
Then blubbering, replied he,
" A winged snake has bitten me,
Which country people call a bee."
At which she smiled, then with her hairs
And kisses, drying up his tears,
" Alas!" said she, " my wag, if this
Such a pernicious torment is,
Come, tell me then how great's the smart
Of those thou woundest with thy dart!"

To Dews.—A Song.

I BURN, I burn, and beg of you
To quench or cool me with your dew ;
I fry in fire, and so consume,
Although the pile be all perfume.
Alas! the heat and death's the same
Whether by choice or common flame.

To be in oil of roses drowned,
Or water, where's the comfort found ?
Both bring one death; and I die here,
Unless you cool me with a tear.
Alas! I call; but ah! I see
Ye cool and comfort all but me.

Some Comfort in Calamity.

To conquered men, some comfort 'tis to fall
By the hand of him who is the general.

The Vision.

SITTING alone, as one forsook,
Close by a silver-shedding brook,
With hands held up to love, I wept,
And after sorrows spent, I slept.
Then in a vision I did see
A glorious form appear to me.
A virgin's face she had; her dress
Was like a sprightly Spartaness.
A silver bow, with green silk strung,
Down from her comely shoulders hung ;
And as she stood, the wanton air'
Dandled the ringlets of her hair.
Her legs were such Diana shows,
When tucked up she a-hunting goes ;
With buskins shortened to descry
The happy dawning of her thigh :
Which, when I saw, I made access
To kiss that tempting nakedness ;
But she forbade me, with a wand
Of myrtle she had in her hand :
And chiding me, said, " Hence, remove.
Herrick, thou art too coarse to love."

Love Me Little, Love Me Long.

YOU say, to me-wards your affection's strong ;
Pray love me little, so you love me long.
Slowly goes far ; the mean is best : desire
Grown violent does either die or tire.

Upon a Virgin Kissing a Rose.

'TWAS but a single rose,
  Till you on it did breathe
But since, methinks, it shows
  Not so much rose as wreath.

Upon a Wife that Died Mad with Jealousy.

In this little vault she lies
Here with all her jealousies ;
Quiet yet, but if ye make
Any noise they both will wake,
And such spirits raise, 'twill then
Trouble death to lay again.

Upon the Bishop of Lincoln's Imprisonment.

Never was day so over-sick with showers
But that it had some intermitting hours.
Never was night so tedious but it knew
The last watch out, and saw the dawning too.
Never was dungeon so obscurely deep,
Wherein or light or day did never peep.
Never did moon so ebb or seas so wane, ·
But they left hope-seed to fill up again.
So you, my lord, though you have now your stay,
Your night, your prison, and your ebb ; you may
Spring up afresh when all these mists are spent,
And star-like, once more gild our firmament.
Let but that mighty Cæsar speak, and then
All bolts, all bars, all gates shall cleave, as when
That earthquake shook the house, and gave the stout
Apostles way, unshackled, to go out.
This, as I wish for, so I hope to see ;
Though you, my lord, have been unkind to me :
To wound my heart, and never to apply,
When you had power, the meanest remedy.
Well, though my grief by you was galled the more,
Yet I bring balm and oil to heal your sore.

Dissuasions from Idleness.

Cynthius pluck ye by the ear,
That ye may good doctrine hear.
Play not with the maiden-hair,
For each ringlet there's a snare.
Cheek and eye, and lip and chin,
These are traps to take fools in ;
Arms and hands, and all parts else,
Are but toils and manacles,
Set on purpose to enthral
Men, but slothfuls most of all.
Live employed, and so live free
From these fetters, like to me,
Who have found, and still can prove
The lazy man the most doth love,

Upon Strut.

STRUT, once a foreman of a shop, we knew ;
But turned a ladies' usher now, 'tis true.
Tell me, has Strut got e'er a title more ?
No, he's but foreman as he was before.

An Epithalamium to Sir Thomas Southwell and his Lady.

Now, now's the time, so oft by truth
Promised should come to crown your youth.
   Then, fair ones, do not wrong
   Your joys by staying long ;
   Or let love's fire go out,
   By lingering thus in doubt ;
   But learn, that time once lost,
   Is ne'er redeemed by cost.
Then away ; come, Hymen, guide
To the bed the bashful bride.

These precious, pearly, purling tears,
But spring from ceremonious fears.
   And 'tis but native shame,
   That hides the loving flame,
   And may a while control
   The soft and amorous soul ;
   But yet love's fire will waste
   Such bashfulness at last.
Then away ; come, Hymen, guide
To the bed the bashful bride.

On, on devoutly, make no stay,
While Domiduca leads the way ;
   And Genius, who attends
   The bed for lucky ends ;
   With Juno goes the Hours,
   And Graces strewing flowers.
   And the boys with sweet tunes sing,
   Hymen ! O Hymen ! bring
Home the turtles, Hymen, guide
To the bed the bashful bride.

Behold, how Hymen's taper-light,
Shows you how much is spent of night.
   See, see the bridegroom's torch
   Half wasted in the porch ;
   And now those tapers five
   That show the womb shall thrive.

   Their silvery flames advance,
   To tell all prosperous chance
Still shall crown the happy life
Of the goodman and the wife.

Move forward then your rosy feet,
And make, whate'er they touch, turn sweet.
   May all like flowery meads
   Smell where your soft foot treads;
   And everything assume
   To it the like perfume;
   As Zephirus, when he 'spires
   Through woodbine and sweetbriars.
Then away; come, Hymen, guide
To the bed the bashful bride,

And now the yellow veil at last,
Over her fragrant cheek is cast.
   Now seems she to express
   A bashful willingness;
   Showing a heart consenting
   As with a will repenting;
   Then gently lead her on
   With wise suspicion;
For that, matrons say, a measure
Of that passion sweetens pleasure.

You, you that be of her nearest kin,
Now o'er the threshold force her in.
   But to avert the worst,
   Let her her fillets first
   Knit to the posts; this point
   Remembering, to anoint
   The sides, for 'tis a charm
   Strong against future harm;
And the evil deeds, the which
There was hidden by the witch.

No fatal owl the bedstead keeps,
With direful notes to fright your sleeps;
   No furies here about,
   To put the tapers out,
   Watch, or did make the bed;
   'Tis omen full of dread:
   But all fair signs appear
   Within the chamber here.
Juno here, far off doth stand,
Cooling sleep with charming wand.

On your minutes, hours, days, months, years,
Drop the fat blessing of the spheres.

That good which Heaven can give
To make you bravely live,
Fall, like a spangling dew,
By day and night on you.
May fortune's lily hand
Open at your command,
With all lucky birds to side
With the bridegroom and the bride.

Let bounteous fate your spindles full
Fill, and wind up with whitest wool.
Let them not cut the thread
Of life until ye bid.
May death yet come at last,
And not with desperate haste;
But when ye both can say,
Come, let us now away.
Be ye to the barn then borne,
Two, like two ripe shocks of corn

Tears are Tongues.

WHEN Julia chid, I stood as mute the while
As is the fish or tongueless crocodile;
Air coined to words, my Julia could not hear,
But she could see each eye to stamp a tear:
By which mine angry mistress might descry,
Tears are the noble language of the eye;
And when true love of words is destitute,
The eyes by tears speak, while the tongue is mute.

His Wish.

IT is sufficient if we pray
To Jove, who gives and takes away:
Let him the land and living find;
Let me alone to fit the mind.

His Protestation to Perilla.

NOONDAY and midnight shall at once be seen;
Trees at one time shall be both sere and green;
Fire and water shall together lie
In one self-sweet conspiring sympathy;
Summer and winter shall at one time show
Ripe ears of corn and up to the ears in snow;
Seas shall be sandless, fields devoid of grass;
Shapeless the world, as when all chaos was,
Before, my dear Perilla, I will be
False to my vow, or fall away from thee.

To Julia.

PERMIT me, Julia, now to go away,
Or by thy love decree me here to stay.
If thou wilt say that I shall live with thee,
Here shall my endless tabernacle be ;
If not, as banished I will live alone
There, where no language ever yet was known.

On Himself.

LOVE-SICK I am, and must endure
A desperate grief that finds no cure.
Ah me ! I try, and trying, prove,
No herbs have power to cure love.
Only one sovereign salve I know,
And that is death, the end of woe.

Virtue is Sensible of Suffering.

THOUGH a wise man all pressures can sustain,
His virtue still is sensible of pain ;
Large shoulders though he has, and well can bear,
He feels when packs do pinch him and the where.

The Cruel Maid.

AND, cruel maid, because I see
You scornful of my love and me ;
I'll trouble you no more, but go
My way, where you shall never know
What is become of me ; there I
Will find me out a path to die,
Or learn some way how to forget
You and your name for ever ; yet
Ere I go hence, know this from me,
What will in time your fortune be ;
This to your coyness I will tell,
And having spoke it once, farewell.
The lily will not long endure,
Nor the snow continue pure ;
The rose, the violet, one day
See, both these lady-flowers decay ;
And you must fade as well as they.
And it may chance that love may turn,
And, like to mine, make your heart burn
And weep to see it ; yet this thing do,
That my last vow commends to you :

When you shall see that I am dead,
For pity let a tear be shed,
And, with your mantle o'er me cast,
Give my cold lips a kiss at last ;
If twice you kiss, you need not fear,
That I shall stir or live more here
Next, hollow out a tomb to cover
Me ; me, the most despised lover ;
And write thereon, " This, reader, know,
" Love killed this man." No more, but so.

To Dianeme.

SWEET, be not proud of those two eyes,
Which, star-like, sparkle in their skies ;
Nor be you proud that you can see
All hearts your captives, yours yet free ;
Be you not proud of that rich hair,
Which wantons with the love-sick air ;
When as that ruby which you wear,
Sunk from the tip of your soft ear,
Will last to be a precious stone,
When all your world of beauty's gone.

To the King, to Cure the Evil.

To find that tree of life, whose fruits did feed,
And leaves did heal, all sick of human seed ;
To find Bethesda, and an angel there,
Stirring the waters, I am come ; and here
At last I find, after my much to do,
The tree, Bethesda, and the angel too ;
And all in your blest hand, which has the powers
Of all those suppling healing herbs and flowers.
To that soft charm, that spell, that magic bough,
That high enchantment I betake me now,
And to that hand, the branch of Heaven's fair tree,
I kneel for help ; O lay that hand on me,
Adored Cæsar ! and my faith is such,
I shall be healed, if that my King but touch.
The evil is not yours ; my sorrow sings,
Mine is the evil, but the cure the King's.

His Misery in a Mistress.

WATER, water I espy ;
Come and cool ye, all who fry
In your loves, but none as I.

Though a thousand showers be
Still a-falling, yet I see
Not one drop to light on me.

Happy you, who can have seas
For to quench ye, or some ease
From your kinder mistresses.

I have one, and she alone,
Of a thousand thousand known,
Dead to all compassion.

Such an one as will repeat
Both the cause and make the heat
More by provocation great.

Gentle friends, though I despair
Of my cure, do you beware
Of those girls which cruel are.

Upon Jollie's Wife.

FIRST, Jollie's wife is lame ; then next, loose-hipped,
Squint-eyed, hook-nosed ; and lastly, kidney-lipped.

To a Gentlewoman, objecting to Him his Grey Hairs.

AM I despised, because you say,
And I dare swear, that I am grey ?
Know, lady, you have but your day,
And time will come when you shall wear
Such frost and snow upon your hair ;
And when, though long it comes to pass,
You question with your looking-glass,
And in that sincere crystal seek
But find no rose-bud in your cheek,
Nor any bed to give the show
Where such a rare carnation grew.
Ah ! then too late, close in your chamber keeping,
   It will be told
   That you are old,
By those true tears you are weeping.

To Cedars.

IF 'mongst my many poems, I can see
One only worthy to be washed by thee,
I live for ever, let the rest all lie
In dens of darkness, or condemned to die.

Upon Cupid.

LOVE like a gipsy, lately came,
 And did me much importune
To see my hand, that by the same
 He might foretell my fortune.

He saw my palm ; and then, said he,
   " I tell thee, by this score here,
That thou, within few months, shalt be
   The youthful Prince D'Amour here."

I smiled, and bade him once more prove,
   And by some cross-line show it,
That I could ne'er be Prince of Love,
   Though here the princely poet.

How Primroses came Green.

VIRGINS, time past, known were these,
Troubled with green sicknesses,
Turned to flowers ; still the hue,
Sickly girls, they bear of you.

To Jos. Lord Bishop of Exeter.

WHOM should I fear to write to, if I can
Stand before you, my learned Diocesan,
And never show blood-guiltiness or fear,
To see my lines excathedrated here.
Since none so good are, but you may condemn,
Or here so bad, but you may pardon them.
If then, my lord, to sanctify my muse
One only poem out of all you'll choose,
And mark it for a rapture nobly writ,
'Tis good confirmed, for you have bishoped it.

Upon a Black Twist, rounding the Arm of the Countess of Carlisle.

I SAW about her spotless wrist.
Of blackest silk, a curious twist,
Which, circumvolving gently there.
Enthralled her arm as prisoner.
Dark was the gaol, but as if light
Had met to engender with the night ;
Or so, as darkness made a stay
To show at once both night and day.
I fancy more ; but if there be
Such freedom in captivity,
I beg of love that ever I
May in like chains of darkness lie.

On Himself.

I FEAR no earthly powers,
But care for crowns of flowers,

And love to have my beard
With wine and oil besmeared.
This day I'll drown all sorrow :
Who knows to live to-morrow ?

Upon Pagget.

PAGGET, a school-boy, got a sword, and then
He vowed destruction both to birch and men ;
Who would not think this younker fierce to fight ?
Yet coming home but somewhat late last night,
Untruss his master bade him, and that word
Made him take up his shirt, lay down his sword

A Ring Presented to Julia.

JULIA, I bring
To thee this ring,
Made for thy finger fit ;
To show by this,
That our love is,
Or should be. like to it.

Close though it be,
The joint is free ;
So when love's yoke is on,
It must not gall,
Or fret at all
With hard oppression.

But it must play
Still either way,
And be, too, such a yoke,
As not too wide,
To over-slide,
Or be so strait to choke.

So we, who bear
This beam, must rear
Ourselves to such a height,
As that the stay
Of either may
Create the burden light.

And as this round
Is nowhere found
To flaw, or else to sever;
So let our love
As endless prove.
And pure as gold for ever.

To the Detractor.

WHERE others love and praise my verses, still
Thy long black thumb-nail marks them out for ill.
A felon take it, or some whit-flaw come
For to unslate or to untile that thumb !
But cry thee mercy ; exercise thy nails
To scratch or claw, so that thy tongue not rails ;
Some numbers prurient are, and some of these
Are wanton with their itch; scratch, and 'twill please.

Upon the Same.

I ASKED thee oft what poets thou hast read,
And lik'st the best ? Still thou repliest, " The dead."
I shall, ere long, with green turfs covered be ;
Then sure thou'lt like, or thou wilt envy me.

To Music.

BEGIN to charm, and as thou strok'st mine ears
With thy enchantment, melt me into tears ;
Then let thy active hand scud o'er thy lyre,
And make my spirits frantic with the fire ;
That done, sink down into a silvery strain,
And make me smooth as balm and oil again.

Distrust.

To safe-guard man from wrongs, there nothing must
Be truer to him than a wise distrust ;
And to thyself be best this sentence known.
Hear all men speak, but credit few or none.

Corinna's going a-Maying.

GET up, get up for shame, the blooming morn
Upon her wings presents the god unshorn.
    See how Aurora throws her fair
     Fresh-quilted colours through the air ;
    Get up, sweet slug-a-bed, and see
    The dew bespangling herb and tree.
Each flower has wept, and bowed toward the east,
Above an hour since, yet you not dressed,
    Nay ! not so much as out of bed ;
    When all the birds have matins said,
    And sung their thankful hymns ; 'tis sin,
    Nay, profanation to keep in,
Whenas a thousand virgins on this day
Spring, sooner then the lark to fetch in May.

Rise, and put on your foliage, and be seen
To come forth, like the spring-time, fresh and green,
    And sweet as Flora. Take no care
    For jewels for your gown or hair ;
    Fear not, the leaves will strew
    Gems in abundance upon you ;
Besides, the childhood of the day has kept
Against you come, some orient pearls unwept.
    Come, and receive them while the light
    Hangs on the dew-locks of the night,
    And Titan on the eastern hill
    Retires himself, or else stands still
Till you come forth. Wash, dress, be brief in praying ;
Few beads are best, when once we go a-Maying.

Come, my Corinna, come ; and coming mark
How each field turns a street, each street a park
    Made green, and trimmed with trees ; see how
    Devotion gives each house a bough
    Or branch ; each porch, each door, ere this,
    An ark, a tabernacle is,
Made up of white thorn neatly interwove,
As if here were those cooler shades of love.
    Can such delights be in the street
    And open fields, and we not see't ?
    Come, we'll abroad, and let's obey
    The proclamation made for May :
And sin no more, as we have done, by staying ;
But, my Corinna, come, let's go a-Maying.

There's not a budding boy or girl, this day,
But is got up and gone to bring in May.
    A deal of youth, ere this, is come
    Back, and with white-thorn laden home.
    Some have despatched their cakes and cream
    Before that we have left to dream :
And some have wept, and wooed and plighted troth,
And chose their priest, ere we can cast off sloth ;
    Many a green gown has been given,
    Many a kiss, both odd and even,
    Many a glance, too, has been sent
    From out the eye, love's firmament ;
Many a jest told of the key's betraying
This night, and locks picked, yet we are not a-Maying.

Come, let us go, while we are in our prime,
And take the harmless folly of the time.
    We shall grow old apace and die
    Before we know our liberty.
    Our life is short, and our days run
    As fast away as does the sun,

And as a vapour, or a drop of rain
Once lost, can ne'er be found again;
    So when or you or I are made
    A fable, song, or fleeting shade,
    All love, all liking, all delight
    Lies drowned with us in endless night.
Then while time serves, and we are but decaying,
Come, my Corinna, come, let's go a-Maying.

On Julia's Breath.

BREATHE, Julia, breathe, and I'll protest,
    Nay more, I'll deeply swear,
That all the spices of the East
    Are circumfused there.

Upon a Child.—An Epitaph.

BUT born, and like a short delight,
I glided by my parents' sight.
That done, the harder fates denied
My longer stay, and so I died.
If pitying my sad parents' tears,
You'll spill a tear or two with theirs,
And with some flowers my grave bestrew
Love and they'll thank you for 't.   Adieu.

A Dialogue betwixt Horace and Lydia, translated Anno 1627, and set by Mr. R. Ramsay.

Hor. WHILE, Lydia, I was loved of thee,
Nor any was preferred 'fore me
To hug thy whitest neck; than I,
The Persian King lived not more happy.

Lyd. While thou no other didst affect,
Nor Chloe was of more respect;
Then Lydia, far-famed Lydia,
I flourished more than Roman Ilia.

Hor. Now Thracian Chloe governs me,
Skilful i' th' harp and melody;
For whose affection, Lydia, I,
So fate spares her, am well content to die.

Lyd. My heart now set on fire is
By Ornithes' son, young Calais;
For whose commutual flames here I,
To save his life, twice am content to die.

Hor. Say our first loves we should revoke,
And severed, join in brazen yoke;
Admit I Chloe put away,
And love again love cast-off Lydia?

Lyd. Though mine be brighter than the star;
Thou lighter than the cork by far,
Rough as the Adriatic sea, yet I
Will live with thee, or else for thee will die.

The Captived Bee; or, The Little Filcher.

As Julia once a-slumbering lay,
It chanced a bee did fly that way,
After a dew, or dew-like shower,
To tipple freely in a flower;
For some rich flower he took the lip
Of Julia, and began to sip;
But when he felt he sucked from thence
Honey, and in the quintessence,
He drank so much he scarce could stir,
So Julia took the pilferer.
And thus surprised, as filchers use,
He thus began himself to excuse:
" Sweet Lady-flower, I never brought
Hither the least one thieving thought;
But taking those rare lips of yours
For some fresh, fragrant, luscious flowers,
I thought I might there take a taste,
Where so much sirup ran at waste.
Besides, know this, I never sting
The flower that gives me nourishing;
But with a kiss, or thanks, do pay
For honey that I bear away."
This said, he laid his little scrip
Of honey 'fore her ladyship,
And told her, as some tears did fall,
That that he took, and that was all.
At which she smiled, and bade him go
And take his bag; but thus much know,
When next he came a pilfering so,
He should from her full lips derive
Honey enough to fill his hive.

Upon Prig.

PRIG now drinks water, who before drank beer;
What's now the cause? We know the cause is clear;
Look in Prig's purse, the cheveril there tells you
Prig money wants, either to buy or brew.

An Ode to Master Endymion Porter, upon his Brother's Death.

NOT all thy flushing suns are set,
Herrick, as yet ;
Nor doth this far-drawn hemisphere
Frown, and look sullen everywhere.
Days may conclude in nights, and suns may rest,
As dead, within the west ;
Yet the next morn regild the fragrant east.

Alas for me ! that I have lost
E'en all almost :
Sunk is my sight ; set is my sun ;
And all the loom of life undone ;
The staff, the elm, the prop, the sheltering wall,
Whereon my vine did crawl,
Now, now blown down ; needs must the old stock fall.

Yet, Porter, while thou keep'st alive,
In death I thrive,
And like a Phœnix re-aspire
From out my nard and funeral fire ;
And as I prune my feathered youth, so I
Do mar'l how I could die,
When I had thee, my chief preserver, by.

I'm up, I'm up, and bless that hand
Which makes me stand
Now as I do ; and but for thee,
I must confess, I could not be.
The debt is paid ; for he who doth resign,
Thanks to the generous vine,
Invites fresh grapes to fill his press with wine.

To his Dying Brother, Master William Herrick.

LIFE of my life, take not so soon thy flight,
But stay the time till we have bade good night.
Thou hast both wind and tide with thee ; thy way
As soon despatched is by the night as day :
Let us not then so rudely henceforth go
Till we have wept, kissed, sighed, shook hands, or so.
There's pain in parting, and a kind of hell
When once true lovers take their last farewell.
What ? shall we two our endless leaves take here
Without a sad look, or a solemn tear ?
He knows not love that hath not this truth proved,
Love is most loth to leave the thing beloved.

Pay we our vows and go, yet when we part,
Then, even then, I will bequeath my heart
Into thy loving hands ; for I'll keep none
To warm my breast, when thou my pulse art gone.
No, here I'll last, and walk, a harmless shade,
About this urn, wherein thy dust is laid,
To guard it so as nothing here shall be
Heavy, to hurt those sacred seeds of thee.

The Olive Branch.

SADLY I walked within the field,
To see what comfort it would yield,
And as I went my private way,
An olive branch before me lay ;
And seeing it I made a stay.
And took it up, and viewed it ; then
Kissing the omen, said "Amen:
Be, be it so, and let this be
A divination unto me ;
That in short time my woes shall cease,
And love shall crown my end with peace."

Upon Much-more.—Epigram.

MUCH-MORE provides and hoards up like an ant,
Yet Much-more still complains he is in want.
Let Much-more justly pay his tithes, then try
How both his meal and oil will multiply.

To Cherry Blossoms.

YE may simper, blush, and smile,
And perfume the air a while ;
But, sweet things, ye must be gone ;
Fruit, ye know, is coming on :
Then, ah ! then where is your grace,
When as cherries come in place ?

How Lilies came White.

WHITE though ye be, yet, lilies, know,
From the first ye were not so ;
     But I'll tell ye
     What befell ye.
Cupid and his mother lay
In a cloud ; while both did play,
He with his pretty finger pressed
The ruby niplet of her breast ;

Out of the which the cream of light,
    Like to a dew,
    Fell down on you,
And made ye white.

To Pansies.

AH, cruel love! must I endure
Thy many scorns, and find no cure?
Say, are thy medicines made to be
Helps to all others but to me?
I'll leave thee, and to Pansies come;
Comforts you'll afford me some:
You can ease my heart, and do
What love could ne'er be brought unto.

On Gilly-flowers Begotten.

WHAT was it that fell but now
    From that warm kiss of ours?
Look, look, by love I vow
    They were two gilly-flowers.
Let's kiss, and kiss again;
    For if so be our closes
Make gilly-flowers, then
    I'm sure they'll fashion roses.

The Lily in a Crystal.

YOU have beheld a smiling rose
    When virgin's hands have drawn
    O'er it a cobweb-lawn;
And here, you see, this lily shows,
    Tombed in a crystal stone,
More fair in this transparent case
    Than when it grew alone,
    And had but single grace.

You see how cream but naked is,
    Nor dances in the eye
    Without a strawberry;
Or some fine tincture, like to this,
    Which draws the sight thereto,
More by that wantoning with it
    Than when the paler hue
    No mixture did admit.

You see how amber through the streams
    More gently strokes the sight
    With some concealed delight
Than when he darts his radiant beams

Into the boundless air;
Where either too much light his worth
    Doth all at once impair,
    Or set it little forth.

Put purple grapes or cherries in-
    To glass, and they will send
    More beauty to commend
Them, from that clean and subtile skin,
    Than if they naked stood,
And had no other pride at all,
    But their own flesh and blood,
    And tinctures natural.

Thus lily, rose, grape, cherry, cream,
    And strawberry do stir
    More love, when they transfer
A weak, a soft, a broken beam,
    Than if they should discover
At full their proper excellence,
    Without some scene cast over,
    To juggle with the sense.

Thus let this crystalled lily be
    A rule, how far to teach
    Your nakedness must reach
And that no further than we see
    Those glaring colours laid
By art's wise hand, but to this end
    They should obey a shade,
    Lest they too far extend.

So though you're white as swan or snow
    And have the power to move
    A world of men to love;
Yet, when your lawns and silks shall flow,
    And that white cloud divide
Into a doubtful twilight, then,
    Then will your hidden pride
    Raise greater fires in men.

To his Book.

LIKE to a bride, come forth, my book, at last,
With all thy richest jewels overcast;
Say, if there be 'mongst many gems here one
Deserveless of the name of Paragon;
Blush not at all for that, since we have set
Some pearls on queens that have been counterfeit.

Upon some Women.

THOU who wilt not love, do this ;
Learn of me what woman is.
Something made of thread and thrum ;
A mere botch of all and some ;
Pieces, patches, ropes of hair ;
Inlaid garbage everywhere.
Outside silk, and outside lawn.
Scenes to cheat us, neatly drawn ;
False in height, and false in size.
False in breast, teeth, hair, and eyes ;
False in head, and false enough ;
Only true in shreds and stuff.

Supreme Fortune Falls Soonest.

WHILE leanest beasts in pastures feed,
The fattest ox the first must bleed.

The Welcome to Sack.

So soft streams meet, so springs with gladder smiles
Meet after long divorcement by the isles,
When love, the child of likeness, urgeth on
Their crystal natures to an union ;
So meet stolen kisses, when the moony nights
Call forth fierce lovers to their wished delights ;
So kings and queens meet, when desire convinces
All thoughts but such as aim at getting princes,
As I meet thee.   Soul of my life and fame !
Eternal lamp of love ! whose radiant flame
Outglares the heavens' Osiris ; and thy gleams
Outshine the splendour of his midday beams ;
Welcome, O welcome, my illustrious spouse ;
Welcome as are the ends unto my vows.
Ay, far more welcome than the happy soil
The sea-scourged merchant, after all his toil,
Salutes with tears of joy ; when fires betray
The smoky chimneys of his Ithaca.
Where hast thou been so long from my embraces,
Poor pitied exile ? Tell me, did thy graces
Fly discontented hence, and for a time
Did rather choose to bless another clime ?
Or went'st thou to this end, the more to move me
By thy short absence to desire and love thee ?
Why frowns my sweet ? Why won't my saint confer
Favours on me, her fierce idolater ?

Why are those looks, those looks the which have been
Time past so fragrant, sickly now drawn in
Like a dull twilight? Tell me, and the fault
I'll expiate with sulphur, hair, and salt:
And with the crystal humour of the spring,
Purge hence the guilt, and kill this quarrelling.
Wilt thou not smile, or tell me what's amiss?
Have I been cold to hug thee, too remiss,
Too temperate in embracing? Tell me, has desire
To thee-ward died in the embers, and no fire
Left in this raked-up ash-heap, as a mark
To testify the glowing of a spark?
True, I confess I left thee, and appeal
'Twas done by me, more to confirm my zeal,
And double my affection on thee; as do those
Whose love grows more inflamed by being foes.
But to forsake thee ever, could there be
A thought of such like possibility,   .
When thou thyself dar'st say, thy isles shall lack
Grapes, before Herrick leaves canary sack.
Thou mak'st me airy, active to be borne,
Like Iphyclus, upon the tops of corn.
Thou mak'st me nimble, as the winged hours,
To dance and caper on the heads of flowers,
And ride the sunbeams. Can there be a thing
Under the heavenly Isis, that can bring
More love unto my life, or can present
My genius with a fuller blandishment?
Illustrious Idol! could the Egyptians seek
Help from the garlic, onion, and the leek,
And pay no vows to thee, who wast their best
God, and far more transcendent than the rest?
Had Cassius, that weak water-drinker, known
Thee in thy vine, or had but tasted one
Small chalice of thy frantic liquor, he
As the wise Cato, had approved of thee.
Come, come and kiss me; love and life commends
Thee and thy beauties; kiss, we will be friends
Too strong for fate to break us. Look upon
Me with that full pride of complexion,
As queens meet queens; or come thou unto me,
As Cleopatra came to Antony,
When her high carriage did at once present
To the Triumvir love and wonderment.
Swell up my nerves with spirit; let my blood
Run through my veins like to a hasty flood;
Fill each part full of fire, active to do
What thy commanding soul shall put it to;
And till I turn apostate to thy love,
Which here I vow to serve, do not remove

Thy fires from me ; but Apollo's curse
Blast these-like actions, or a thing that's worse;
When these circumstants shall but live to see
The time that I prevaricate from thee,
Call me the Son of Beer, and then confine
Me to the tap, the toast, the turf ; let wine
Ne'er shine upon me, may my numbers all
Run to a sudden death and funeral.
And last, when thee, dear spouse, I disavow,
Ne'er may prophetic Daphne crown my brow.

Impossibilities to his Friend.

My faithful friend, if you can see
The fruit to grow up, or the tree ;
If you can see the colour come
Into the blushing pear or plum ;
If you can see the water grow
To cakes of ice, or flakes of snow ;
If you can see that drop of rain
Lost in the wild sea, once again ;
If you can see how dreams do creep
Into the brain by easy sleep :
Then there is hope that you may see
Her love me once, who now hates me.

Upon Gubbs.—Epigram.

Gubbs calls his children kitlings ; and would bound,
Some say, for joy, to see those kitlings drowned.

To Live Merrily, and to Trust to Good Verses.

Now is the time for mirth
   Nor check or tongue be dumb ;
For the flow'ry earth,
   The golden pomp is come.

The golden pomp is come ;
   For now each tree does wear,
Made of her pap and gum,
   Rich beads of amber here.

Now reigns the Rose, and now
   The Arabian dew besmears
My uncontrolled brow,
   And my retorted hairs.

Homer, this health to thee,
   In sack of such a kind,

That it would make thee see,
 Though thou wert ne'er so blind.

Next, Virgil I'll call forth,
 To pledge this second health
In wine whose each cup's worth
 An Indian commonwealth:

A goblet next I'll drink
 To Ovid; and suppose
Made he the pledge, he'd think
 The world had all one nose.

Then this immensive cup
 Of aromatic wine,
Catullus, I quaff up
 To that terse muse of thine.

Wild I am now with heat,·
 O Bacchus! cool thy rays;
Or frantic I shall eat
 Thy thyrse, and bite the bays.

Round, round, the roof does run;
 And being ravished thus,
Come, I will drink a tun
 To my Propertius.

Now, to Tibullus next,
 This flood I drink to thee;
But stay, I see a text,
 That this presents to me.

Behold! Tibullus lies
 Here burnt, whose small return
Of ashes scarce suffice
 To fill a little urn.

Trust to good verses then;
 They only will aspire,
When pyramids, as men,
 Are lost i' th' funeral fire,

And when all bodies meet
 In Lethe, to be drowned;
Then only numbers sweet,
 With endless life are crowned.

Fair Days; or, Dawns Deceitful.

FAIR was the dawn; and but e'en now the skies
Showed like to cream, inspired with strawberries:

But on a sudden all was changed and gone
That smiled in that first sweet complexion ;
Then thunder-claps and lightning did conspire
To tear the world, or set it all on fire.
What ! trust to things below, whenas we see
As men, the heavens have their hypocrisy.

Lips Tongueless.

FOR my part, I never care
For those lips that tongue-tied are.
Tell-tales I would have them be
Of my mistress and of me ;
Let them prattle, how that I
Sometimes freeze and sometimes fry ;
Let them tell how she doth move
Fore or backward in her love ;
Let them speak by gentle tones,
One and the other's passions :
How we watch, and seldom sleep,
How by willows we do weep,
How by stealth we meet and then
Kiss and sigh, so part again.
This the lips we will permit
For to tell, not publish it.

To the Fever, not to trouble Julia.

TH'AST dared too far ; but Fury, now forbear
To give the least disturbance to her hair ;
But less presume to lay a plait upon
Her skin's most smooth and clear expansion.
'Tis like a lawny firmament, as yet
Quite dispossessed of either fray or fret.
Come thou not near that film so finely spread,
Where no one piece is yet unlevelled.
This, if thou dost, woe to thee, Fury, woe !
I'll send such frost, such hails, such sleet, such snow,
Such flesh-quakes, palsies, and such fears, as shall
Dead thee to th' most, if not destroy thee all ;
And thou a thousand thousand times shalt be
More shaked thyself, than she is scorched by thee.

To Violets.

WELCOME, maids of honour,
You do bring
In the spring ;
And wait upon her.

She has virgins many,
    Fresh and fair ;
      Yet you are
More sweet than any.

Y'are the maiden posies,
    And so graced,
      To be placed,
'Fore damask roses.

Yet though thus respected.
    By-and-by
      Ye do lie,
Poor girls, neglected.

Upon Bunce.—Epigram.

MONEY thou owest me : prithee fix a day
For payment promised, though thou never pay :
Let it be doomsday ; nay, take longer scope ;
Pay when thou'rt honest, let me have some hope.

To Carnations.—A Song.

STAY while ye will, or go,
    And leave no scent behind ye :
Yet trust me, I shall know
    The place where I may find ye.

Within my Lucia's cheek
    (Whose livery ye wear),
Play ye at hide or seek,
    I'm sure to find ye there.

To the Virgins, to make much of Time.

GATHER ye rosebuds while ye may,
    Old time is still a-flying ;
And this same flower that smiles to-day,
    To-morrow will be dying.

The glorious lamp of heaven, the sun,
    The higher he's a-getting,
The sooner will his race be run,
    And nearer he's to setting.

That age is best which is the first,
    When youth and blood are warmer ;
But being spent the worse and worst
    Times still succeed the former.

Then be not coy, but use your time,
  And while ye may, go marry ;
For having lost but once your prime,
  You may for ever tarry.

Safety to Look to One's Self.

FOR my neighbour, I'll not know
Whether high he builds or no ;
Only this I'll look upon,
Firm be my foundation.
Sound or unsound let it be,
'Tis the lot ordained for me.
He who to the ground does fall,
Has not whence to sink at all.

To his Friend on the Untuneable Times.

PLAY I could once ; but, gentle friend, you see
My harp hung up here on the willow tree.
Sing I could once ; and bravely, too, inspire,
With luscious numbers my melodious lyre.
Draw I could once, although not stocks or stones
Amphion-like, men made of flesh and bones,
Whither I would ; but, ah ! I know not how
I feel in me this transmutation now.
Grief, my dear friend, has first my harp unstrung,
Withered my hand, and palsy-struck my tongue.

His Poetry his Pillar.

ONLY a little more
    I have to write,
    Then I'll give o'er,
And bid the world Good-night.

'Tis but a flying minute
    That I must stay,
    Or linger in it ;
And then I must away.

O Time, that cuts down all,
    And scarce leav'st here
    Memorial
Of any men that were !

How many lie forgot
    In vaults beneath,
    And piecemeal rot
Without a fame in death !

Behold this living stone
    I rear for me,
    Ne'er to be thrown
Down, envious Time, by thee.

Pillars let some set up,
If so they please,
Here is my hope,
And my pyramides.

Safety on the Shore.

WHAT though the sea be calm?   Trust to the shore :
Ships have been drowned, where late they danced before.

A Pastoral
Upon the Birth of Prince Charles, presented to the King, and set by Mr. Nic. Laniere.

The Speakers—*Mirtillo, Amintas,* and *Amarillis.*

Amin. GOOD day, Mirtillo.   *Mirt,* And to you no less ;
And all fair signs lead on our shepherdess.
   Amar. With all white luck to you.   *Mirt.* But say, what news
Stirs in our sheep-walk?   *Amin.* None, save that my ewes,
My wethers, lambs, and wanton kids are well,
Smooth, fair, and fat, none better I can tell :
Or that this day Menalcas keeps a feast
For his sheep-shearers.   *Mirt.* True, these are the least.
But, dear Amintas, and sweet Amarillis,
Rest but awhile here by this bank of lilies ;
And lend a gentle ear to one report
The country has.   *Amin.* From whence?   *Amar.* From whence?   *Mirt.* The Court.
Three days before the shutting in of May
(With whitest wool be ever crowned that day !)
To all our joy, a sweet-faced child was born,
More tender than the childhood of the morn.
   Chor. Pan pipe to him, and bleats of lambs and sheep
Let lullaby the pretty prince asleep.
   Mirt. And that his birth should be more singular,
At noon of day was seen a silver star,
Bright as the wise men's torch which guided them
To God's sweet babe, when born at Bethlehem,
While golden angels, some have told to me,
Sung out his birth with heav'nly minstrelsy.
   Amin. O rare ! But is't a trespass, if we three
Should wend along his baby-ship to see ?
   Mirt. Not so, not so.   *Chor.* But if it chance to prove
At most a fault, 'tis but a fault of love.
   Amar. But, dear Mirtillo, I have heard it told,
Those learned men brought incense, myrrh, and gold,
From countries far, with store of spices sweet,
And laid them down for offerings at his feet.

Mirt. 'Tis true, indeed; and each of us will bring
Unto our smiling and our blooming King,
A neat, though not so great an offering.
   Amar. A garland for my gift shall be,
Of flowers ne'er sucked by the thieving bee;
And all most sweet, yet all less sweet than he.
   Amin. And I will bear along with you
Leaves dropping down the honeyed dew,
With oaten pipes, as sweet as new.
   Mirt. And I a sheep-hook will bestow
To have his little king-ship know,
As he is prince, he's shepherd too.
   Chor. Come, let's away, and quickly let's be dressed,
And quickly give, the swiftest grace is best.
And when before him we have laid our treasures,
We'll bless the babe, then back to country pleasures.

To the Lark.

GOOD speed, for I this day
Betimes my matins say;
   Because I do
   Begin to woo.
   Sweet singing lark,
   Be thou the clerk,
   And know thy when
   To say, Amen.
   And if I prove
   Best in my love,
   Then thou shalt be
   High-priest to me,
   At my return,
   To incense burn;
   And so to solemnize
   Love's and my sacrifice.

The Bubble.—A Song.

To my revenge, and to her desperate fears,
Fly, thou made bubble of my sighs and tears.
In the wild air, when thou hast rolled about,
And, like a blasting planet, found her out;
Stoop, mount, pass by to take her eye, then glare
Like to a dreadful comet in the air:
Next, when thou dost perceive her fixed sight,
For thy revenge to be most opposite,
Then like a globe, or ball of wild-fire, fly,
And break thyself in shivers on her eye.

A Meditation for his Mistress.

You are a Tulip seen to-day,
But, dearest, of so short a stay,
That where you grew, scarce man can say.

You are a lovely July-flower,
Yet one rude wind, or ruffling shower,
Will force you hence, and in an hour.

You are a sparkling Rose i' th' bud,
Yet lost, ere that chaste flesh and blood
Can show where you or grew or stood.

You are a full-spread, fair-set Vine,
And can with tendrils love entwine,
Yet dried, ere you distil your wine.

You are like Balm, inclosed well
In amber, or some crystal shell,
Yet lost ere you transfuse your smell.

You are a dainty Violet,
Yet withered, ere you can be set
Within the virgin's coronet.

You are the queen all flowers among,
But die you must, fair maid, ere long,
As he, the maker of this song.

The Bleeding Hand; or, the Sprig of Eglantine Given to a Maid.

From this bleeding hand of mine,
Take this sprig of Eglantine.
Which, though sweet unto your smell,
Yet the fretful briar will tell,
He who plucks the sweets, shall prove
Many thorns to be in love.

Lyric for Legacies.

Gold I've none, for use or show,
Neither silver to bestow
At my death; but thus much know,
That each lyric here shall be
Of my love a legacy,
Left to all posterity.
Gentle friends, then do but please
To accept such coins as these,
As my last remembrances.

A Dirge upon the Death of the Right Valiant Lord Bernard Stuart.

HENCE, hence, profane; soft silence let us have,
While we this Trental sing about thy grave.

Had wolves or tigers seen but thee,
They would have showed civility;
And in compassion of thy years
Washed those thy purple wounds with tears.
But since thou art slain, and in thy fall
The drooping kingdom suffers all,—

Chor. This we will do; we'll daily come
And offer tears upon thy tomb;
And if that they will not suffice,
Thou shalt have souls for sacrifice.

Sleep in thy peace, while we with spice perfume thee,
And cedar wash thee, that no times consume thee.

Live, live thou dost, and shalt, for why?
Souls do not with their bodies die;
Ignoble offsprings, they may fall
Into the flames of funeral,
Whenas the chosen seed shall spring
Fresh, and for ever flourishing.

Chor. And times to come shall, weeping, read thy
glory,
Less in these marble stones than in thy story.

To Perenna, a Mistress.

DEAR Perenna, prithee come,
And with smallage dress my tomb:
Add a cypress sprig thereto
With a tear, and so adieu.

Great Boast, Small Roast.

OF flanks and chines of beef doth Gorrel boast
He has at home; but who tastes boiled or roast?
Look in his brine-tub, and you shall find there
Two stiff-blue pig's-feet, and a sow's cleft ear.

Upon a Blear-eyed Woman.

WITHERED with years, and bed-rid, Mumma lies
Dry-roasted all, but raw yet in her eyes.

The Fair Temple; or, Oberon's Chapel.   Dedicated To Mr. John Merrifield, Counsellor-at-Law.

RARE temples thou hast seen, I know,
And rich for in and outward show;
Survey this chapel, built alone
Without or lime, or wood or stone,
Then say, if one thou hast seen more fine
Than this, the fairies' once, now thine.

The Temple.

A WAY enchased with glass and beads
There is, that to the chapel leads,
Whose structure, for his holy rest,
Is here the Halcyon's curious nest;
Into the which who looks, shall see
His temple of idolatry,
Where he of godheads has such store,
As Rome's Pantheon had not more.
His house of Rinnon this he calls,
Girt with small bones, instead of walls.
First, in a niche, more black than jet,
His idol-cricket there is set;
Then in a polished oval by,
There stands his idol beetle-fly;
Next, in an arch, akin to this,
His idol-canker seated is.
Then in a round, is placed by these
His golden god, Cantharides.
So that where'er ye look, ye see
No capital, no cornice free,
Or frieze, from this fine frippery.
Now, this the fairies would have known,
Theirs is a mixed religion :
And some have heard the elves it call
Part Pagan, part Papistical.
If unto me all tongues were granted,
I could not speak the saints here painted.
Saint Tit, Saint Nit, Saint Is, Saint Itis,
Who against Mab's state placed here right is.
Saint Will-o'-the-Wisp, of no great bigness,
But alias called here *fatuus ignis.*
Saint Frip, Saint Trip, Saint Fill. Saint Filly,
Neither those other saintships will I
Here go about for to recite
Their number, almost infinite ;
Which, one by one, here set down are
In this most curious calendar.

First, at the entrance to the gate,
A little puppet-priest doth wait,
Who squeaks to all the comers there.
" Favour your tongues, who enter here.
Pure hands bring hither, without stain."
A second pules, " Hence, hence, profane."
Hard by, i' th' shell of half a nut,
The holy-water there is put ;
A little brush of squirrels' hairs,
Composed of odd, not even pairs.
Stands in the platter or close by,
To purge the fairy family.
Near to the altar stands the priest,
There offering up the Holy Grist ;
Ducking in mood and perfect tense,
With (much good do't him) reverence.
The altar is not here four-square,
Nor in a form triangular ;
Nor made of glass, or wood, or stone,
But of a little transversed bone
Which boys and bruckelled children call
(Playing for points and pins) cockall.
Whose linen drapery is a thin,
Subtile, and ductile codlin's skin ;
Which o'er the board is smoothly spread
With little seal-work damasked.
The fringe that circumbinds it, too,
Is spangle-work of trembling dew,
Which, gently gleaming, makes a show,
Like frost-work glittering on the snow.
Upon this fetuous board doth stand
Something for show-bread, and at hand
(Just in the middle of the altar)
Upon an end, the Fairy-psalter,
Graced with the trout-fly's curious wings,
Which serve for watchet ribbonings.
Now, we must know, the elves are led
Right by the Rubric, which they read :
And if report of them be true,
They have their text for what they do,
Ay, and their book of canons too.
And, as Sir Thomas Parson tells,
They have their book of Articles ;
And if that Fairy knight not lies,
They have their Book of Homilies ;
And other Scriptures, that design
A short, but righteous discipline.
The basin stands the board upon
To take the Free Oblation,

A little pin-dust, which they hold
More precious than we prize our gold ;
Which charity they give to many
Poor of the parish, if there's any.
Upon the ends of these neat rails,
Hatched with the silver-light of snails,
The elves, in formal manner, fix
Two pure and holy candlesticks,
In either which a tall small bent
Burns for the altar's ornament.
For sanctity, they have to these
Their curious copes and surplices
Of cleanest cobweb, hanging by
In their religious vestery.
They have their ash-pans and their brooms,
To purge the chapel and the rooms ;
Their many mumbling mass-priests here,
And many a dapper chorister.
Their ushering vergers here likewise,
Their canons and their chanteries ;
Of cloister-monks they have enow,
Ay, and their abbey-lubbers too.
And if their legend do not lie,
They much affect the Papacy ;
And since the last is dead, there's hope
Elve Boniface shall next be Pope.
They have their cups and chalices,
Their pardons and indulgences,
Their beads of nuts, bells, books, and wax
Candles, forsooth, and other knacks ;
Their holy oil, their fasting spittle,
Their sacred salt here, not a little.
Dry chips, old shoes, rags, grease, and bones,
Beside their fumigations.
Many a trifle, too, and trinket,
And for what use, scarce man would think it.
Next then, upon the chanters' side
An apple's-core is hung up dried,
With rattling kernels, which is rung
To call to morn and even-song.
The saint, to which the most he prays
And offers incense nights and days,
The lady of the lobster is,
Whose foot-pace he doth stroke and kiss,
And humbly chives of saffron brings,
For his most cheerful offerings.
When, after these, he's paid his vows,
He lowly to the altar bows ;
And then he dons the silkworm shed,
Like a Turk's turban on his head,

And reverently departeth thence,
Hid in a cloud of frankincense ;
And by the glow-worm's light well guided,
Goes to the feast that's now provided.

To Mistress Katharine Bradshaw, the Lovely, that Crowned him with Laurel.

My Muse in meads has spent her many hours
Sitting, and sorting several sorts of flowers,
To make for others garlands ; and to set
On many a head here many a coronet.
But amongst all encircled here, not one
Gave her a day of coronation,
Till you, sweet mistress, came and interwove
A laurel for her, ever young as love.
You first of all crowned her ; she must, of due,
Render for that a crown of life to you.

The Plaudit ; or, End of Life.

If after rude and boisterous seas,
My wearied pinnace here finds ease ;
If so it be I've gained the shore,
With safety of a faithful oar ;
If having run my barque on ground,
Ye see the aged vessel crowned ;
What's to be done, but on the sands
Ye dance and sing, and now clap hands.
The first act's doubtful, but we say,
It is the last com'nends the play.

To the most Virtuous Mistress Pot, who many Times Entertained Him.

When I through all my many poems look,
And see yourself to beautify my book ;
Methinks that only lustre doth appear
A light fulfilling all the region here.
Gild still with flames this firmament, and be
A lamp eternal to my poetry,
Which, if it now, or shall hereafter shine,
'Twas by your splendour, lady, not by mine.
The oil was yours, and that I owe for yet :
He pays the half who does confess the debt.

To Music, to becalm his Fever.

CHARM me asleep, and melt me so
  With thy delicious numbers,
That being ravished, hence I go
  Away in easy slumbers,
    Ease my sick head,
    And make my bed,
  Thou power that canst sever
    From me this ill
    And quickly still
    Though thou not kill
      My fever.

Thou sweetly canst convert the same
  From a consuming fire
Into a gentle-licking flame,·
  And make it thus expire ;
    Then make me weep
    My pains asleep,
  And give me such reposes,
    That I, poor I,
    May think, thereby,
    I live and die
      'Mongst roses.

Fall on me like a silent dew,
  Or like those maiden showers
Which, by the peep of day, do strew
  A baptime o'er the flowers.
    Melt, melt my pains,
    With thy soft strains,
  That having ease me given,
    With full delight,
    I leave this light,
    And take my flight
      For Heaven.

Upon a Gentlewoman with a Sweet Voice.

So long you did not sing, or touch your lute,
We knew 'twas flesh and blood that there sat mute.
But when your playing and your voice came in,
'Twas no more you then, but a cherubin.

Upon Cupid.

As lately I a garland bound
'Mongst roses, I there Cupid found ;

I took him, put him in my cup,
And drunk with wine, I drank him up.
Hence then it is, that my poor breast
Could never since find any rest.

Best to be Merry.

FOOLS are they, who never know
How the times away do go ;
But for us, who wisely see
Where the bounds of black death be,
Let's live merrily, and thus
Gratify the genius.

The Changes.—To Corinna.

BE not proud, but now incline
Your soft ear to Discipline ;
You have changes in your life,
Sometimes peace, and sometimes strife ;
You have ebbs of face and flows,
As your health or comes or goes ;
You have hopes, and doubts, and fears,
Numberless as are your hairs ;
You have pulses that do beat
High, and passions less of heat ;
You are young, but must be old,
And to these ye must be told,
Time, ere long, will come and plough
Loathed furrows in your brow :
And the dimness of your eye
Will no other thing imply,
    But you must die
    As well as I.

Neglect.

ART quickens Nature ; Care will make a face ;
Neglected Beauty perisheth apace.

Upon Himself.

MOPE-EYED I am, as some have said,
Because I've lived so long a maid ;
But grant that I should wedded be,
Should I a jot the better see ?
No, I should think that marriage might
Rather than mend put out the light.

Upon a Physician.

Thou camest to cure me, Doctor, of my cold,
And caught'st thyself the more by twenty-fold;
Prithee go home; and for thy credit be
First cured thyself; then come and cure me.

To the Rose.—Song.

Go, happy rose, and interwove
With other flowers, bind my love.
 Tell her, too, she must not be,
 Longer flowing, longer free,
 That so oft has fettered me.

Say, if she's fretful, I have bands
Of pearl and gold to bind her hands;
 Tell her, if she struggle still,
 I have myrtle rods at will,
 For to tame, though not to kill,

Take thou my blessing thus, and go
And tell her this: but do not so,
 Lest a handsome anger fly
 Like a lightning from her eye,
 And burn thee up, as well as I.

Upon Guesse.—Epigram.

Guesse cuts his shoes, and limping goes about
To have men think he's troubled with the gout;
But 'tis no gout, believe it, but hard beer,
Whose acrimonious humour bites him here.

To his Book.

Thou art a plant, sprung up to wither never,
But like a laurel, to grow green for ever.

Upon a Painted Gentlewoman.

Men say ye are fair; and fair ye are, 'tis true;
But hark! We praise the painter now, not you.

Draw-Gloves.

AT Draw-Gloves we'll play,
And prithee let's lay
A wager, and let it be this :
Who first to the sum
Of twenty shall come,
Shall have for his winning a kiss.

To Music, to becalm a Sweet Sick Youth.

CHARMS, that call down the moon from out her sphere,
On this sick youth work your enchantments here ;
Bind up his senses with your numbers, so
As to entrance his pain, or cure his woe.
Fall gently, gently, and awhile him keep
Lost in the civil wilderness of sleep ;
That done, then let him, dispossessed of pain,
Like to a slumbering bride, awake again.

To the high and noble Prince George, Duke, Marquis, and Earl of Buckingham.

NEVER my book's perfection did appear,
'Till I had got the name of VILLIERS here ;
Now, 'tis so full, that when therein I look,
I see a cloud of glory fills my book.
Here stands it still to dignify our muse,
Your sober handmaid ; who doth wisely choose
Your name to be a laureate wreath to her,
Who doth both love and fear you, honoured sir.

His Recantation.

LOVE, I recant,
And pardon crave,
That lately I offended,
But 'twas,
Alas !
To make a brave,
But no disdain intended.

No more I'll vaunt,
For now I see
Thou only hast the power
To find
And bind
A heart that's free,
And slave it in an hour.

The Coming of Good Luck.

So Good-luck came, and on my roof did light,
Like noiseless snow, or as the dew of night;
Not all at once, but gently, as the trees
Are by the sunbeams tickled by degrees.

The Present; or, the Bag of the Bee.

FLY to my mistress, pretty pilfering bee,
And say thou bring'st this honey bag from me;
When on her lip thou hast thy sweet dew placed,
Mark if her tongue but slily steal a taste;
If so, we live; if not, with mournful hum,
Toll forth my death; next, to my burial come.

On Love.

LOVE bade me ask a gift,
  And I no more did move
But this, that I might shift
  Still with my clothes my love.
That favour granted was;
  Since which, though I love many,
Yet so it comes to pass,
  That long I love not any.

The Hock Cart; or, Harvest Home. To the Right Honourable Mildmay, Earl of Westmorland.

COME, sons of summer, by whose toil,
We are the lords of wine and oil;
By whose tough labours and rough hands,
We rip up first then reap our lands;
Crowned with the ears of corn, now come,
And, to the pipe, sing harvest home!
Come forth, my lord, and see the cart
Dressed up with all the country art.
See, here a maukin, there a sheet,
As spotless pure as it is sweet;
The horses, mares, and frisking fillies,
Clad all in linen white as lilies.
The harvest swains and wenches bound
For joy, to see the hock cart crowned.
About the cart hear how the rout
Of rural youngling raise the shout,
Pressing before, some coming after,
Those with a shout, and these with laughter.
Some bless the cart, some kiss the sheaves,
Some prank them up with oaken leaves;

Some cross the fill-horse, some with great
Devotion stroke the home-borne wheat,
While other rustics, less attent
To prayers than to merriment,
Run after with their breeches rent.
Well, on, brave boys, to your lord's hearth,
Glittering with fire, where, for your mirth,
Ye shall see first the large and chief
Foundation of your feast, fat beef;
With upper stories, mutton, veal,
And bacon, which makes full the meal,
With several dishes standing by,
As, here a custard, there a pie,
And here all tempting frumenty.
And for to make the merry cheer,
If smirking wine be wanting here,
There's that which drowns all care, stout beer.
Which freely drink to your lord's health,
Then to the plough, the commonwealth,
Next to your flails, your fans, your vats;
Then to the maids with wheaten hats;
To the rough sickle, and the crooked scythe,
Drink, frolic, boys, till all be blithe.
Feed and grow fat, and as ye eat,
Be mindful that the labouring neat,
As you, may have their full of meat;
And know, besides, ye must revoke
The patient ox unto the yoke,
And all go back unto the plough
And harrow, though they're hanged up now.
And, you must know, your lord's word's true,
Feed him ye must, whose food fills you.
And that this pleasure is like rain,
Not sent ye for to drown your pain,
But for to make it spring again.

The Perfume.

TO-MORROW, Julia, I betimes must rise,
For some small fault, to offer sacrifice;
The altar's ready; fire to consume
The fat; breathe thou, and there's the rich perfume.

Upon her Voice.

LET but thy voice engender with the string,
And angels will be born, while thou dost sing.

Not to Love.

HE that will not love, must be
My scholar, and learn this of me:

There be in love as many fears,
As the summer's corn has ears;
Sighs, and sobs, and sorrows more
Than the sand that makes the shore;
Freezing cold and fiery heats,
Fainting swoons and deadly sweats;
Now an ague, then a fever.
Both tormenting lovers ever.
Would'st thou know, besides all these,
How hard a woman 'tis to please;
How cross, how sullen, and how soon
She shifts and changes like the moon.
How false, how hollow she's in heart,
And how she is her own least part;
How high she's prized, and worth but small;
Little thou'lt love, or not at all.

To Music.—A Song.

MUSIC, thou queen of heaven, care-charming spell,
    That strik'st a stillness into hell;
Thou that tam'st tigers, and fierce storms that rise,
    With thy soul-melting lullabies;
Fall down, down, down, from those thy chiming spheres,
    To charm our souls, as thou enchant'st our ears.

To the Western Wind.

SWEET western wind, whose luck it is,
    Made rival with the air.
To give Perenna's lip a kiss,
    And fan her wanton hair.

Bring me but one, I'll promise thee,
    Instead of common showers,
Thy wings shall be embalmed by me,
    And all beset with flowers.

Upon the Death of his Sparrow: an Elegy.

WHY do not all fresh maids appear
To work love's sampler only here,
Where spring-time smiles throughout the year?
Are not here rosebuds, pinks, all flowers
Nature begets by the sun and showers,
Met in one hearse-cloth, to o'erspread
The body of the under-dead?
Phil, the late dead, the late dead dear,
O! may no eye distil a tear
For you once lost, who weep not here!

Had Lesbia, too too kind, but known
This sparrow, she had scorned her own;
And for this dead which underlies,
Wept out her heart, as well as eyes.
But endless peace, sit here, and keep
My Phil, the time he has to sleep,
And thousand virgins come and weep,
To make these flow'ry carpets show
Fresh as their blood, and ever grow,
Till passengers shall spend their doom;
Not Virgil's Gnat had such a tomb.

To Primroses filled with Morning Dew.

WHY do ye weep, sweet babes? Can tears
Speak grief in you,
Who were but born
Just as the modest morn
Teemed her refreshing dew?
Alas, thou have not known that shower
That mars a flower,
Nor felt the unkind
Breath of a blasting wind,
Nor are ye worn with years;
Or warped, as we,
Who think it strange to see
Such pretty flowers, like to orphans young,
To speak by tears before ye have a tongue.

Speak, whimpering younglings, and make known
The reason why
Ye droop and weep.
Is it for want of sleep,
Or childish lullaby?
Or that ye have not seen as yet
The violet?
Or brought a kiss
From that sweet heart to this?
No, no, this sorrow shown
By your tears shed
Would have this lecture read,
That things of greatest, so of meanest worth,
Conceived with grief are, and with tears brought forth.

How Roses came Red.

ROSES at first were white,
Till they could not agree,
Whether my Sappho's breast,
Or they more white should be.

But being vanquished quite,
  A blush their cheeks bespread;
Since which, believe the rest,
  The roses first came red.

Comfort to a Lady on the Death of her Husband.

DRY your sweet cheek, long drowned with sorrow's rain;
Since clouds dispersed, suns gild the air again.
Seas chafe and fret, and beat, and over-boil,
But turn soon after calm, as balm or oil.
Winds have their time to rage, but when they cease,
The leafy trees nod in a still-born peace.
Your storm is over.   Lady, now appear
Like to the peeping spring-time of the year.
Off then with grave clothes, put fresh colours on,
And flow and flame in your vermilion.
Upon your cheek sat icicles awhile;
Now let the rose reign like a queen, and smile.

How Violets came Blue.

LOVE on a day, wise poets tell,
  Some time in wrangling spent,
Whether the violets should excel,
  Or she, in sweetest scent.

But Venus having lost the day,
  Poor girls, she fell on you,
And beat ye so, as some dare say,
  Her blows did make ye blue.

Upon Groynes.—Epigram.

GROYNES, for his fleshly burglary of late,
Stood in the *Holy Forum Candidate;*
The word is Roman, but in English known;
Penance, and standing so, are both but one.

To the Willow Tree.

THOU art to all lost love the best,
  The only true plant found,
Wherewith young men and maids distressed,
  And left of love, are crowned.

When once the lover's rose is dead,
  Or laid aside forlorn,
Then willow garlands 'bout the head,
  Bedewed with tears, are worn.

When with neglect, the lover's bane,
  Poor maids rewarded be,
For their lost love, their only gain
  Is but a wreath from thee.

And underneath thy cooling shade,
  When weary of the light,
The love-spent youth and love-sick maid
  Come to weep out the night.

Mrs. Eliz. Wheeler, under the Name of the Lost Shepherdess.

AMONG the myrtles as I walked,
Love and my sighs thus intertalked:
" Tell me," said I, in deep distress,
Where I may find my shepherdess?"
" Thou fool," said Love, " know'st thou not this,
In everything that's sweet she is.
In yond' carnation go and seek,
There thou shalt find her lip and cheek;
In that enamelled pansy by,
There thou shalt have her curious eye;
In bloom of peach and rose's bud,
There waves th streamer of her blood."
" 'Tis true," said I, and thereupon
I went to pluck them one by one,
To make of parts an union;
But on a sudden all were gone.
At which I stopped. Said Love, " These be
The true resemblances of thee:
For as these flowers, thy joys must die,
And in the turning of an eye;
And all thy hopes of her must wither,
Like those short sweets ere knit together."

To the King.

IF when these lyrics, Cæsar, you shall hear,
And that Apollo shall so touch your ear,
As for to make this, that, or any one
Number, your own, by free adoption;
That verse, of all the verses here, shall be
The heir to this great realm of poetry.

To the Queen.

GODDESS of youth, and lady of the spring,
Most fit to be the consort to a king,
Be pleased to rest you in this sacred grove,
Beset with myrtles, whose each leaf drops love,

Many a sweet-faced wood-nymph here is seen,
Of which chaste order you are now the Queen.
Witness their homage when they come and strew
Your walks with flowers, and give their crowns to you.
Your leafy throne, with lily-work possess,
And be both princess here, and poetress.

The Poet's Good Wishes for the most hopeful and handsome Prince the Duke of York.

MAY his pretty Dukeship grow
Like t' a rose of Jericho ;
Sweeter far than ever yet
Showers or sunshines could beget.
May the Graces and the Hours
Strew his hopes and him with flowers ;
And so dress him up with love
As to be the chick of Jove.
May the thrice-three Sisters sing
Him the sovereign of their spring ;
And entitle none to be
Prince of Helicon but he.
May his soft foot, where it treads,
Gardens thence produce an meads ;
And those meadows full be set
With the rose and violet.
May his ample name be known
To the last succession :
And his actions high be told
Through the world, but writ in gold.

To Anthea, who may Command him Anything.

BID me to live, and I will live
    Thy Protestant to be ;
Or bid me love, and I will give
    A loving heart to thee.

A heart as soft, a heart as kind,
    A heart as sound and free,
As in the whole world thou canst find,
    That heart I'll give to thee.

Bid that heart stay, and it will stay,
    To honour thy decree ;
Or bid it languish quite away,
    And 't shall do so for thee.

Bid me to weep, and I will weep,
    While I have eyes to see ;
And having none, yet I will keep
    A heart to weep for thee.

Bid me despair, and I'll despair,
    Under that cypress tree ;
Or bid me die, and I will dare
    E'en death, to die for thee.

Thou art my life, my love, my heart,
    The very eyes of me ;
And hast command of every part,
    To live and die for thee.

Prevision, or Provision.

THAT prince takes soon enough the victor's room
Who first provides, not to be overcome.

Obedience in Subjects.

THE gods to kings the judgment give to sway ;
The subjects' only glory to obey.

More Potent, less Peccant.

HE that may sin, sins least ; leave to trangress
Enfeebles much the seeds of wickedness.

Upon a Maid that Died the Day she was Married.

THAT morn which saw me made a bride,
The ev'ning witnessed that I died.
Those holy lights, wherewith they guide
Unto the bed the bashful bride,
Served but as tapers, for to burn,
And light my reliques to their urn.
This epitaph, which here you see,
Supplied the epithalamie.

Upon Pink, an ill-faced Painter.—Epigram.

To paint the fiend, Pink would the devil see ;
And so he may, if he'll be ruled by me ;
Let but Pink's face i' th' looking-glass be shown,
And Pink may paint the devil's by his own.

Upon Brock.—Epigram.

To cleanse his eyes, Tom Brock makes much ado,
But not his mouth, the fouler of the two.
A clammy rheum makes loathsome both his eyes ;
His mouth worse furred with oaths and blasphemies.

To Meadows.

Ye have been fresh and green,
  Ye have been fill'd with flowers ;
And ye the walks have been
  Where maids have spent their hours.

You have beheld how they
  With wicker arks did come,
To kiss and bear away
  The richer cowslips home.

Ye've heard them sweetly sing,
  And seen them in a round ;
Each virgin, like a spring,
  With honeysuckles crowned.

But now, we see none here
  Whose silvery feet did tread
And with dishevelled hair
  Adorned this smoother mead.

Like unthrifts, having spent
  Your stock, and needy grown,
Ye're left here to lament
  Your poor estates, alone.

Crosses.

THOUGH good things answer many good intents,
Crosses do still bring forth the best events.

Miseries.

THOUGH hourly comforts from the gods we see,
No life is yet life-proof from misery.

Laugh and Lie Down.

YE'VE laughed enough, sweet, vary now your text,
And laugh no more ; or laugh, and lie down next.

To his Household Gods.

RISE, household gods, and let us go,
But whither, I myself not know.
First, let us dwell on rudest seas ;
Next, with severest salvages ;
Last, let us make our best abode,
Where human foot as yet ne'er trod ;
Search worlds of ice, and rather there
Dwell, than in loathed Devonshire.

To the Nightingale and Robin Redbreast.

WHEN I departed am, ring thou my knell,
Thou pitiful and pretty Philomel;
And when I'm laid out for a corpse, then be
Thou sexton, Redbreast, for to cover me.

To the Yew and Cypress to grace his Funeral.

BOTH you two have
Relation to the grave;
And where
The funeral trump sounds, you are there.

I shall be made
Ere long a fleeting shade;
Pray come.
And do some honour to my tomb.

Do not deny
My last request, for I
Will be
Thankful to you, or friends, for me.

I call and I call.

I CALL, I call: Who do ye call?
The maids to catch this cowslip ball;
But since these cowslips fading be,
Troth. leave the flowers, and maids take me.
Yet, if that neither you will do,
Speak but the word, and I'll take you.

On a perfumed Lady.

YOU say you're sweet; how should we know
Whether that you be sweet or no?
From powders and perfumes keep free,
Then we shall smell how sweet you be.

A Nuptial Song; or, Epithalamium on Sir Clipseby Crew and his Lady.

WHAT'S that we see from far? The spring of day
Bloomed from the east, or fair injewelled May
Blown out of April; or some new
Star filled with glory to our view,
Reaching at heaven,
To add a nobler planet to the seven?

Say, or do we not descry
Some goddess in a cloud of tiffany
    To move, or rather the
    Emergent Venus from the sea?

'Tis she! 'tis she! or else some more divine
Enlightened substance; mark how from the shrine
    Of holy saints she paces on,
    Treading upon vermilion
            And amber; spice-
Ing the chaste air with fumes of Paradise.
    Then come on, come on, and yield
A savour like unto a blessed field
            When the bedabbled morn
    Washes the golden ears of corn.

See where she comes, and smell how all the street
Breathes vineyards and pomegranates; O how sweet!
    As a fired altar, is each stone,
    Perspiring pounded cinnamon.
            The phœnix nest,
Built up of odours, burneth in her breast.
    Who therein would not consume
His soul to ash-heaps in that rich perfume?
        Bestroking fate the while
    He burns to embers on the pile.

Hymen, O Hymen! tread the sacred ground;
Show thy white feet, and head with marjoram crowned:
    Mount up thy flames, and let thy torch
    Display the bridegroom in the porch,
            In his desires
More towering, more disparkling then thy fires;
    Show her how his eyes do turn
And roll about, and in their motions burn
        Their balls to cinders; haste,
    Or else to ashes he will waste.

Glide by the banks of virgins then, and pass
The showers of roses, lucky four-leaved grass;
    The while the cloud of younglings sing,
    And drown ye with a flowery spring;
            While some repeat
Your praise, and bless you, sprinkling you with wheat,
    While that others do divine,
" Blest is the bride, on whom the sun doth shine;"
        And thousands gladly wish
    You multiply, as doth a fish.

And beauteous bride, we do confess ye're wise,
In dealing forth these bashful jealousies:

In Love's name do so, and a price
Set on your self, by being nice.
   But yet take heed :
What now you seem, be not the same indeed,
  And turn apostaté : Love will
Part of the way be met, or sit stone still.
   On then, and though you slow-
  Ly go, yet, howsoever, go.

And now you're entered, see the coddled cook
Runs from his torrid zone, to pry and look,
  And bless his dainty mistress; see,
  The aged point out, This is she
   Who now must sway
The house (love shield her) with her Yea and Nay ;
  And the smirk butler thinks it
Sin, in's napery, not to express his wit ;
   Each striving to devise
  Some gin, wherewith to catch your eyes.

By the bride's eyes, and by the teeming life
Of her green hopes, we charge ye, that no strife,
  Farther than gentleness tends, gets place
  Among ye, striving for her lace.
   O do not fall
Foul in these noble pastimes, lest ye call
  Discord in, and so divide
The youthful bridegroom and the fragrant bride ;
   Which love forefend ; but spoken
  Be 't to your praise, no peace was broken.

And to enchant ye more, see everywhere
About the roof a siren in a sphere,
  As we think, singing to the din
  Of many a warbling cherubin.
   O mark ye how
The soul of Nature melts in numbers ; now
  See, a thousand Cupids fly,
To light their tapers at the bride's bright eye.
   To bed, or her they'll tire,
  Were she an element of fire.

All now is hushed in silence ; midwife-moon,
With all her owl-eyed issue, begs a boon
  Which you must grant ; that's entrance ; with
  Which extract all we can call pith
   And quintessence
Of planetary bodies ; so commence
  All fair constellations
Looking upon ye, that, two nations
   Springing from two such fires,
  May blaze the virtue of their sires.

The Silken Snake.

FOR sport, my Julia threw a lace
Of silk and silver at my face ;
Watchet the silk was, and did make
A show, as if 't had been a snake.
The suddenness did me affright,
But though it scared, it did not bite.

Upon Himself.

I AM sieve-like, and can hold
Nothing hot, or nothing cold ;
Put in love, and put in, too,
Jealousy, and both will through ;
Put in fear, and hope, and doubt,
What comes in, runs quickly out ;
Put in secrecies withal,
Whate'er enters, out it shall.
But if you can stop the sieve,
For mine own part I'd as lieve,
Maids should say, or virgins sing,
Herrick keeps, as holds, nothing.

Upon Love.

LOVE's a thing, as I do hear,
Ever full of pensive fear ;
Rather than to which I'll fall,
Trust me, I'll not like at all :
If to love I should intend,
Let my hair then stand on end ;
And that terror likewise prove
Fatal to me in my love.
But if horror cannot slake
Flames, which would an entrance make ;
Then the next thing I desire,
Is to love, and live i' th' fire.

Reverence to Riches.

LIKE to the income must be our expense ;
Man's fortune must be had in reverence.

Devotion makes the Deity.

WHO forms a godhead out of gold or stone,
Makes not a god ; but he that prays to one.

To all Young Men that Love.

I COULD wish you all, who love,
That ye could your thoughts remove
From your mistresses, and be
Wisely wanton, like to me.
I could wish you dispossest
Of that fiend that mars your rest,
And with tapers comes to fright
Your weak senses in the night.
I could wish ye all who fry,
Cold as ice, or cool as I.
But if flames best like ye, then
Much good do 't ye, gentlemen.
I a merry heart will keep,
While you wring your hands and weep.

The Eyes.

'TIS a known principle in war,
The eyes be first that conquered are.

No Fault in Women.

No fault in women, to refuse
The offer which they most would choose.
No fault in women to confess,
How tedious they are in their dress ;
No fault in women, to lay on
The tincture of vermilion,
And there to give the cheek a dye
Of white, where Nature doth deny.
No fault in women, to make show
Of largeness, when they're a nothing s ;
When, true it is, the outside swells
With inward buckram, little else.
No fault in women, though they be
But seldom from suspicion free ;
No fault in womankind at all,
If they but slip, and never fall

Oberon's Feast.

" SHAPCOT ! to thee the fairy state
I with discretion dedicate ;
Because thou prizest things that are
Curious and unfamiliar.
Take first the feast ; these dishes gone,
We'll see the fairy-court anon."

A little mushroom table spread,
After short prayers they set on bread,

A moon-parched grain of purest wheat,
With some small glittering grit, to eat
His choice bits with; then in a trice
They make a feast less great than nice.
But all this while his eye is served,
We must not think his ear was starved;
But that there was in place to stir
His spleen, the chirping grasshopper,
The merry cricket, puling fly,
The piping gnat for minstrelsy.
And now, we must imagine first,
The elves present, to quench his thirst,
A pure seed-pearl of infant dew,
Brought and besweetened in a blue
And pregnant violet; which done,
His kitling eyes begin to run
Quite through the table, where he spies
The horns of papery butterflies,
Of which he eats; and tastes a little
Of that we call the cuckoo's spittle;
A little fuz-ball pudding stands
By, yet not blessed by his hands,
That was too coarse; but then forthwith
He ventures boldly on the pith
Of sugared rush, and eats the sag
And well bestrutted bees' sweet bag;
Gladding his palate with some store
Of emmets' eggs; what would he more,
But beards of mice, a newt's stewed thigh,
A bloated earwig, and a fly;
With the red-capped worm, that's shut
Within the concave of a nut,
Brown as his tooth.   A little moth,
Late fattened in a piece of cloth;
With withered cherries, mandrake's ears,
Mole's eyes; to these the slain stag's tears;
The unctuous dewlaps of a snail,
The broke-heart of a nightingale
O'er-come in music; with a wine
Ne'er ravished from the flattering vine,
But gently pressed from the soft side
Of the most sweet and dainty bride,
Brought in a dainty daisy, which
He fully quaffs up to bewitch
His blood to height; this done, commended
Grace by his priest; the feast is ended.

Event of Things not in our Power.

By time and counsel, do the best we can,
The event is never in the power of man.

Upon her Blush.

WHEN Julia blushes, she does show
Cheeks like to roses when they blow.

Merits make the Man.

OUR honours and our commendations be
Due to the merits, not authority.

To Virgins.

HEAR, ye Virgins, and I'll teach
What the times of old did preach.
Rosamond was in a bower
Kept, as Danaë in a tower;
But yet Love, who subtile is,
Crept to that, and came to this.
Be ye locked up like to these,
Or the rich Hesperides:
Or those babies in your eyes,
In their crystal nunneries;
Notwithstanding, love will win,
Or else force a passage in;
And as coy be as you can,
Gifts will get ye, or the man.

Virtue.

EACH must in virtue strive for to excel;
That man lives twice that lives the first life well.

The Bellman.

FROM noise of scare-fires rest ye free,
From murder's benedicite,   .
From all mischances that may fright
Your pleasing slumbers in the night;
Mercy secure ye all, and keep
The goblin from ye, while ye sleep.
Past one o'clock, and almost two,
My masters all, Good day to you.

Bashfulness.

OF all our parts, the eyes express
The sweetest kind of bashfulness.

To the most accomplished Gentleman, Master Edward Norgate, Clerk of the Signet to His Majesty.—Epigram.

FOR one so rarely tuned to fit all parts;
For one to whom espoused are all the Arts,
Long have I sought for; but could never see
Them all concentred in one man, but thee.
Thus thou that man art, whom the Fates conspired
To make but one, and that's thyself, admired.

Upon Prudence Baldwin, her Sickness.

PRUE, my dearest maid, is sick,
Almost to be lunatic:
Æsculapius, come and bring
Means for her recovering,
And a gallant cock shall be
Offered up by her to thee.

To Apollo.—A short Hymn.

PHŒBUS, when that I a verse,
Or some numbers more rehearse,
Tune my words, that they may fall
Each way smoothly musical;
For which favour, there shall be
Swans devoted unto thee.

A Hymn to Bacchus.

BACCHUS, let me drink no more,
Wild are seas that want a shore;
When our drinking has no stint,
There is no one pleasure in't.
I have drank up for to please
Thee, that great cup, Hercules.
Urge no more; and there shall be
Daffodil's gi'en up to thee.

Upon Bungie.

BUNGIE does fast; looks pale; puts sackcloth on;
Not out of conscience, or religion;
Or that this younker keeps so strict a Lent,
Fearing to break the King's commandement;
But being poor, and knowing flesh is dear,
He keeps not one, but many Lents i' th' year.

On Himself.

HERE down my wearied limbs I'll lay;
My pilgrim's staff, my weed of grey;
My palmer's hat, my scallop's shell;
My cross, my cord, and all farewell.
For having now my journey done,
Just at the setting of the sun,
Here have I found a chamber fit,
God and good friends be thanked for it,
Where if I can a lodger be
A little while from tramplers free;
At my uprising next, I shall,
If not requite, yet thank ye all.
Meanwhile, the Holy-rood hence fright
The fouler fiend and evil sprite,
From scaring you or yours this night.

Casualties.

GOOD things that come of course, far less do please
Than those which come by sweet contingencies.

Bribes and Gifts get all.

DEAD falls the cause, if once the hand be mute;
But let that speak, the client gets the suit.

The End.

IF well thou hast begun, go on for right;
It is the End that crowns us, not the Fight.

Upon a Child that Died.

HERE she lies, a pretty bud,
Lately made of flesh and blood;
Who, as soon fell fast asleep,
As her little eyes did peep.
Give her strewings; but not stir
The earth, that lightly covers her.

Upon Sneape.— Epigram.

SNEAPE has a face so brittle, that it breaks
Forth into blushes whensoe'er he speaks.

Content, not Cates.

'TIS not the food, but the content
That makes the table's merriment.

Where trouble serves the board, we eat
The platters there as soon as meat.
A little pipkin with a bit
Of mutton, or of veal in it,
Set on my table, trouble-free,
More than a feast contenteth me.

The Entertainment; or, Porch-verse, at the Marriage of Mr. H. Northly, and the most witty Mrs. Lettice Yard.

WELCOME! but yet no entrance, till we bless
First you, then you, and both for white success.
Profane no porch, young man and maid, for fear
Ye wrong the threshold-god that keeps peace here:
Please him, and then all good-luck will betide
You, the brisk bridegroom, you, the dainty bride.
Do all things sweetly, and in comely wise,
Put on your garlands first, then sacrifice;
That done, when both of you have seemly fed,
We'll call on night to bring ye both to bed;
Where being laid, all fair signs looking on,
Fish-like, increase then to a million;
And millions of spring-times may ye have,
Which spent, one death bring to ye both one grave.

The Good-Night, or Blessing.

BLESSINGS, in abundance come
To the bride and to her groom;
Pleasures many here attend ye,
And ere long a boy love send ye,
Curled and comely, and so trim,
Maids, in time, may ravish him.
Thus a dew of graces fall
On ye both.   Good-night to all.

Upon Leech.

LEECH boasts he has a pill, that can alone
With speed give sick men their salvation:
'Tis strange, his father long time has been ill,
And credits physic, yet not trusts his pill:
And why? he knows he must of cure despair
Who makes the sly physician his heir.

To Daffodils.

FAIR Daffodils, we weep to see
  You haste away so soon;
As yet the early rising sun
  Has not attained his noon.
      Stay, stay,
  Until the hasting day
      Has run
  But to the even-song;
And, having prayed together, we
  Will go with you along.

We have short time to stay, as you,
  We have as short a spring;
As quick a growth to meet decay,
  As you, or anything.
      We die
  As your hours do, and dry
      Away,
  Like to the summer's rain;
Or as the pearls of morning's dew,
  Ne'er to be found again.

To a Maid.

YOU say you love me; that I thus must prove;
If that you lie, then I will swear you love.

Upon a Lady that Died in Childbed, and left a Daughter behind her.

AS gillyflowers do but stay
To blow, and seed, and so away,
So you, sweet lady, sweet as May,
The garden's glory, lived a while,
To lend the world your scent and smile:
But when your own fair print was set
Once in a virgin flosculet,
Sweet as yourself, and newly blown,
To give that life resigned your own;
But so, as still the mother's power
Lives in the pretty lady-flower.

A New Year's Gift sent to Sir Simeon Steward.

NO news of navies burnt at seas;
No noise of late-spawned Tityries,
No closet plot or open vent,
That frights men with a Parliament:

No new device or late found trick,
To read by the stars the kingdom's sick;
No gin to catch the State, or wring
The free-born nostrils of the King,
We send to you; but here a jolly
Verse crowned with ivy and with holly;
That tells of winter's tales and mirth,
That milk-maids make about the hearth,
Of Christmas sports, the wassail-bowl,
That tost up after Fox-i' th' hole;
Of Blind-man-buff, and of the care
That young men have to shoe the mare;
Of Twelve-tide cake, of peas and beans,
Wherewith ye make those merry scenes,
When as ye choose your king and queen,
And cry out, " Hey for our town green."
Of ash-heaps, in the which ye use
Husbands and wives by streaks to choose;
Of crackling laurel, which fore-sounds
A plenteous harvest to your grounds;
Of these, and such like things, for shift,
We send instead of New-year's gift:
Read then, and when your faces shine
With buxom meat and cap'ring wine,
Remember us in cups full crowned,
And let our city-health go round,
Quite through the young maids and the men,
To the ninth number, if not ten;
Until the fired chestnuts leap
For joy to see the fruits ye reap
From the plump chalice and the cup
That tempts till it be tossed up.
Then as ye sit about your embers,
Call not to mind those fled Decembers;
But think on these that are to appear
As daughters to the instant year;
Sit crowned with rose-buds, and carouse,
Till *Liber Pater* twirls the house
About your ears, and lay upon
The year your cares, that's fled and gone.
And let the russet swains the plough
And harrow hang up resting now;
And to the bagpipe all address,
Till sleep takes place of weariness.
And thus, throughout, with Christmas plays
Frolic the full twelve holy-days.

Matins; or, Morning Prayer.

WHEN with the virgin morning thou dost rise
Crossing thyself, come thus to sacrifice:

First wash thy heart in innocence, then bring
Pure hands, pure habits, pure, pure everything.
Next to the altar humbly kneel, and thence
Give up thy soul in clouds of frankincense.
Thy golden censers, filled with odours sweet,
Shall make thy actions with their ends to meet.

Evensong.

BEGIN with Jove ; then is the work half done,
And runs most smoothly when 'tis well begun.
Jove's is the first and last ; the morn's his due,
The midst is thine, but Jove's the evening too,
As sure a matins does to him belong,
So sure he lays claim to the evensong.

The Bracelet to Julia.

WHY I tie about thy wrist,
Julia, this my silken twist ;
For what other reason is't,
But to show thee how in part
Thou my pretty captive art ?
But thy bond-slave is my heart.
'Tis but silk that bindeth thee,
Snap the thread and thou art free ;
But 'tis otherwise with me ;
I am bound, and fast bound so,
That from thee I cannot go ;
If I could, I would not so.

The Christian Militant.

A MAN prepared against all ills to come,
That dares to dead the fire of martyrdom ;
That sleeps at home, and sailing there at ease,
Fears not the fierce sedition of the seas ;
That's counter-proof against the farm's mishaps,
Undreadful, too, of courtly thunderclaps ;
That wears one face, like heaven, and never shows
A change, when fortune either comes or goes ;
That keeps his own strong guard, in the despite
Of what can hurt by day, or harm by night ;
That takes and re-delivers every stroke
Of chance, as made up all of rock and oak ;
That sighs at others' death, smiles at his own
More dire and horrid crucifixion.
Who for true glory suffers thus, we grant
Him to be here our Christian militant.

A Short Hymn to Lar.

THOUGH I cannot give thee fires
Glittering to my free desires ;
These accept, and I'll be free,
Offering poppy unto thee.

Another to Neptune.

MIGHTY Neptune, may it please
Thee, the rector of the seas,
That my barque may safely run
Through thy watery region,
And a tunny-fish shall be
Offered up with thanks to thee.

Upon Greedy.—Epigram.

AN old, old widow Greedy needs would wed,
Not for affection to her, or her bed ;
But in regard 'twas often said, this old
Woman would bring him more than could be told ;
He took her ; now the jest in this appears,
So old she was that none could tell her years.

His Embalming to Julia.

FOR my embalming, Julia, do but this,
Give thou my lips but their supremest kiss ;
Or else transfuse thy breath into the chest
Where my small reliques must for ever rest ;
That breath the balm, the myrrh, the nard shall be,
To give an incorruption unto me.

Gold before Goodness.

HOW rich a man is, all desire to know,
But none inquires if good he be, or no.

The Kiss.—A Dialogue.

1. AMONG thy fancies, tell me this,
What is the thing we call a kiss ?
2. I shall resolve ye what it is.

It is a creature born and bred
Between the lips, all cherry-red,
By love and warm desires fed.

It is an active flame, that flies
First to the babies of the eyes,
And charms them there with lullabies.

Then to the chin, the cheek, the ear,
It frisks and flies, now here, now there,
'Tis now far off, and then 'tis near,
  Chor. And here, and there, and everywhere.

1. Has it a speaking virtue ? 2. Yes.
1. How speaks it, say ? 2. Do you but this,
Part your joined lips, then speaks your kiss ;
  Chor. And this love's sweetest language is.

1. Has it a body ? 2. Aye, and wings,
With thousand rare encolourings ;
And as it flies it gently sings,
  Chor. Love honey yields, but never stings.

The Admonition.

SEEST thou those diamonds which she wears
    In that rich carcanet,
Or those on her dishevelled hairs,
    Fair pearls in order set ?
Believe, young man, all those were tears
    By wretched wooers sent,
In mournful hyacinths and rue,
    That figure discontent ;
Which, when not warmed by her view,
    By cold neglect each one
Congealed to pearl and stone ;
    Which precious spoils upon her,
    She wears as trophies of her honour.
Ah, then consider what all this implies ;
She that will wear thy tears, would wear thine eyes.

To his Honoured Kinsman, Sir William Soame.
Epigram.

I CAN but name thee, and methinks I call
All that have been, or are canonical
For love and bounty, to come near and see
Their many virtues volumed up in thee ;
In thee, brave man, whose incorrupted fame
Casts forth a light like to a virgin flame ;
And as it shines, it throws a scent about,
As when a rainbow in perfumes goes out.
So vanish hence, but leave a name as sweet
As benzoin and storax, when they meet.

On Himself.

    ASK me why I do not sing
    To the tension of the string

As I did not long ago
When my numbers full did flow?
Grief, ay me! hath struck my lute
And my tongue at one time mute.

To Lar.

No more shall I, since I am driven hence,
Devote to thee my grains of frankincense;
No more shall I from mantle-trees hang down,
To honour thee, my little parsley crown;
No more shall I, I fear me, to thee bring
My chives of garlic for an offering;
No more shall I, from henceforth, hear a quire
Of merry crickets by my country fire.
Go where I will, thou lucky Lar stay here,
Warm by a glittering chimney all the year.

The Departure of the Good Demon.

WHAT can I do in poetry,
Now the good spirit's gone from me?
Why nothing now, but lonely sit,
And over-read what I have writ.

Clemency.

FOR punishment in war, it will suffice
If the chief author of the faction dies;
Let but few smart, but strike a fear through all:
Where the fault springs, there let the judgment fall.

His Age, dedicated to his Peculiar Friend, M. John Wickes, under the name of Posthumus.

AH Posthumus! our years hence fly,
And leave no sound; nor piety,
          Or prayers, or vow
Can keep the wrinkle from the brow;
          But we must on,
As fate does lead or draw us; none,
None, Posthumus, could e'er decline
The doom of cruel Proserpine.

The pleasing wife, the house, the ground
Must all be left, no one plant found
          To follow thee,
Save only the curst-cypress tree;
          A merry mind
Looks forward, scorns what's left behind;

Let's live, my Wickes, then, while we may,
And here enjoy our holiday.

We've seen the past best times, and these
Will ne'er return; we see the seas,
      And moons to wane,
But they fill up their ebbs again;
      But vanished man,
Like to a lily lost, ne'er can,
Ne'er can repullulate, or bring
His days to see a second spring.

But on we must, and thither tend,
Where Ancus and rich Tullus blend
      Their sacred seed;
Thus has infernal Jove decreed;
      We must be made
Ere long a song, ere long a shade.
Why then, since life to us is short,
Let's make it full up by our sport.

Crown we our heads with roses, then,
And 'noint with Syrian balm; for when
      We two are dead,
The world with us is buried.
      Then live we free
As is the air, and let us be
Our own fair wind, and mark each one
Day with the white and lucky stone.

We are not poor, although we have
No roofs of cedar, nor our brave
      Baiæ, nor keep
Account of such a flock of sheep,
      Nor bullocks fed
To lard the shambles, barbels bred
To kiss our hands; nor do we wish
For Pollio's lampreys in our dish.

If we can meet, and so confer,
Both by a shining saltcellar,
      And have our roof,
Although not arched, yet weatherproof,
      And ceiling free,
From that cheap candle-baudery;
We'll eat our bean with that full mirth,
As we were lords of all the earth.

Well, then, on what seas we are tossed,
Our comfort is, we can't be lost.

　　　　　Let the winds drive
Our bark, yet she will keep alive
　　　　　Amidst the deeps;
'Tis constancy, my Wickes, which keeps
The pinnace up; which though she errs
I' th' seas, she saves her passengers.

Say, we must part; sweet mercy bless
Us both i' th' sea, camp, wilderness!
　　　　　Can we so far
Stray to become less circular
　　　　　Than we are now?
No, no, that self-same heart, that vow
Which made us one, shall ne'er undo,
Or ravel so, to make us two.

Live in thy peace; as for myself,
When I am bruised on the shelf
　　　　　Of time, and show
My locks behung with frost and snow;
　　　　　When with the rheum,
The cough, the ptisic, I consume
Unto an almost nothing; then,
The ages fled, I'll call again:

And with a tear compare these last
Lame and bad times with those are past,
　　　　　While Baucis by,
My old lean wife, shall kiss it dry;
　　　　　And so we'll sit
By the fire, foretelling snow and sleet,
And weather by our achés, grown
Now old enough to be our own

True calendars, as pussy's ear
Washed o'er 's to tell what change is near;
　　　　　Then, to assuage
The gripings of the chine by age,
　　　　　I'll call my young
Iülus to sing such a song
I made upon my Julia's breast,
And of her blush at such a feast.

Then shall he read that flower of mine
Enclosed within a crystal shrine;
　　　　　A primrose next.
A piece then of a higher text.

　　　*　　*　　*　　*

Thus frantic crazy man, God wot,
I'll call to mind things half forgot;
　　　　　And oft between
Repeat the times that I have seen;

Thus ripe with tears,
And twisting my Iulus' hairs,
Doting, I'll weep and say, " In truth,
" Baucis, these were my sins of youth."

Then next I'll cause my hopeful lad,
If a wild apple can be had
　　　To crown the hearth,
Lar thus conspiring with our mirth,
　　　Then to infuse
Our browner ale into the cruise ;
Which, sweetly spiced, we'll first carouse
Unto the genius of the house.

Then the next health to friends of mine,
Loving the brave Burgundian wine,
　　　High sons of pith,
Whose fortunes I have frolicked with ;
　　　Such as could well
Bear up the magic bough and spell ;
And dancing 'bout the mystic Thyrse,
Give up the just applause to verse.

To those, and then again to thee,
We'll drink, my Wickes, until we be
　　　Plump as the cherry,
Though not so fresh, yet full as merry
　　　As the cricket,
The untamed heifer, or the pricket,
Until our tongues shall tell our ears
We're younger by a score of years.

Thus, till we see the fire less shine
From the embers than the kitling's eyne,
　　　We'll still sit up,
Sphering about the wassail cup
　　　To all those times
Which gave me honour for my rhymes.
The coal once spent, we'll then to bed,
Far more than night-bewearied,

A Short Hymn to Venus.

GODDESS, I do love a girl
Ruby-lipped and toothed with pearl;
If so be I may but prove
Lucky in this maid I love,
I will promise there shall be
Myrtles offered up to thee.

The Hand and Tongue.

Two parts of us successively command;
The tongue in peace, but then in war the hand

Upon a Delaying Lady.

COME, come away,
Or let me go;
Must I here stay
Because you're slow,
And will continue so?
Troth, lady, no.

I scorn to be
A slave to state;
And since I'm free,
I will not wait
Henceforth at such a
For needy fate.

If you desire
My spark should glow,
The peeping fire
You must blow;
Or I shall quickly grow
To frost or snow.

To the Lady Mary Villiers, Governess to the Princess Henretta.

WHEN I of Villiers do but hear the name,
It calls to mind that mighty Buckingham,
Who was your brave exalted uncle here,
Binding the wheel of fortune to his sphere;
Who spurned at envy, and could bring with ease
An end to all his stately purposes.
For his love then, whose sacred reliques show
Their resurrection and their growth in you;
And for my sake, who ever did prefer
You above all those sweets of Westminster;
Permit my book to have a free access
To kiss your hand, most dainty governess.

Upon his Julia.

WILL ye hear what I can say
Briefly of my Julia?

Black and rolling is her eye,
Double chinn'd, and forehead high;
Lips she has, all ruby red,
Cheeks like cream enclareted;
And a nose that is the grace
And proscenium of her face.
So that we may guess by these
How she in all will richly please.

To Flowers.

IN time of life I graced ye with my verse;
Do now your flowery honours to my hearse.
You shall not languish, trust me; virgins here
Weeping, shall make ye flourish all the year.

To my Ill Reader.

THOU sayest my lines are hard,
    And I the truth will tell;
They are both hard and marr'd,
    If thou not read'st them well.

The Power in the People.

LET kings command, and do the best they may,
The saucy subject still will bear the sway.

A Hymn to Venus and Cupid.

SEA-BORN goddess, let me be,
By thy son thus graced and thee,
That whene'er I woo, I find
Virgins coy, but not unkind.
Let me, when I kiss a maid,
Taste her lips, so overlaid
With love's syrup, that I may
In your temple, when I pray,
Kiss the altar, and confess,
There's in love no bitterness.

On Julia's Picture.

HOW am I ravished when I do but see
The painter's art in thy sciography?
If so, how much more shall I dote thereon
When once he gives it incarnation?

Upon her Alms.

SEE how the poor do waiting stand
For the expansion of thy hand.
A wafer doled by thee will swell
Thousands to feed by miracle.

Rewards.

STILL to our gains our chief respect is had ;
Reward it is that makes us good or bad.

Nothing New.

NOTHING is new ; we walk where others went :
There's no vice now, but has his precedent.

The Rainbow.

LOOK how the rainbow doth appear
But in one only hemisphere ;
 So likewise after our decease,
No more is seen the arch of peace.
That covenant's here, the under-bow,
That nothing shoots but war and woe.

The Meadow Verse; or, Anniversary to Mistress Bridget Lowman.

COME with the spring-time forth, fair maid, and be
This year again the meadow's deity.
Yet ere ye enter, give us leave to set
Upon your head this flowery coronet ;
To make this neat distinction from the rest,
You are the prime and princess of the feast,
To which, with silver feet lead you the way,
While sweet-breath nymphs attend on you this day.
This is your hour, and best you may command,
Since you are lady of this fair land.
Full mirth wait on you, and such mirth as shall
Cherish the cheek, but make none blush at all.

The Parting Verse, the Feast there Ended.

LOTH to depart, but yet at last each one
Back must now go to 's habitation ;
Not knowing thus much, when we once do sever,
Whether or no that we shall meet here ever.
As for myself, since time a thousand cares
And griefs hath filled upon my silver hairs,

'Tis to be doubted whether I next year,
Or no, shall give ye a re-meeting here.
If die I must, then my last vow shall be,
You'll with a tear or two remember me,
Your sometime poet ; but if fates do give
Me longer date, and more fresh springs to live ;
Oft as your field shall her old age renew,
Herrick shall make the meadow-verse for you.

Upon Judith.—Epigram.

JUDITH has cast her old skin, and got new,
And walks fresh varnished to the public view.
Foul Judith was, and foul she will be known,
For all this fair transfiguration.

Long and Lazy.

THAT was the proverb.   Let my mistress be
Lazy to others, but belong to me.

Upon Ralph.—Epigram.

CURSE not the mice, no grist of thine they eat ;
But curse thy children, they consume thy wheat.

To the Right Honourable Philip, Earl of Pembroke and Montgomery.

How dull and dead are books, that cannot show
A Prince of Pembroke, and that Pembroke you !
You, who are high born, and a lord no less
Free by your fate, than fortune's mightiness,
Who hug our poems, honoured sir, and then
The paper gild, and laureate the pen.
Nor suffer you the poets to sit cold,
But warm their wits, and turn their lines to gold.
Others there be, who righteously will swear
Those smooth-packed numbers amble everywhere,
And these brave measures go a stately trot ;
Love those like these ; regard, reward them not.
But you, my lord, are one whose hand along
Goes with your mouth, or does outrun your tongue,
Paying before you praise, and cockering wit,
Give both the gold and garland unto it.

A Hymn to Juno.

STATELY goddess, do thou please,
Who art chief at marriages,

But to dress the bridal bed,
When my love and I shall wed;
And a peacock proud shall be
Offered up by us to thee.

Upon Sappho, Sweetly Playing and Sweetly Singing.

WHEN thou dost play, and sweetly sing,
Whether it be the voice or string,
Or both of them, that do agree
Thus to entrance and ravish me ;
This, this I know, I'm oft struck mute,
And die away upon thy lute.

Upon Paske, a Draper.

PASKE, though his debt be due upon the day,
Demands no money by a craving way ;
For why, says he, all debts and their arrears
Have reference to the shoulders, not the ears.

Chop-cherry.

THOU gav'st me leave to kiss,
Thou gav'st me leave to woo ;
Thou mad'st me think, by this
And that, thou lov'dst me too.

But I shall ne'er forget
How for to make thee merry,
Thou mad'st me chop, but yet
Another snapt the cherry.

To the Most Learned, Wise, and Arch-Antiquary Mr. John Selden.

I WHO have favoured many, come to be
Graced, now at last, or glorified by thee.
Lo, I, the lyric prophet, who have set
On many a head the Delphic coronet,
Come unto thee for laurel, having spent
My wreaths on those who little gave or lent.
Give me the Daphne, that the world may know it,
Whom they neglected thou hast crowned a poet.
A city here of heroes I have made
Upon the rock whose firm foundation laid
Shall never shrink ; where making thine abode,
Live thou a Selden, that's a demigod.

Upon Himself.

THOU shalt not all die ; for while love's fire shines
Upon his altar, men shall read thy lines ;
And learn'd musicians shall, to honour Herrick's
Fame, and his name, both set and sing his lyrics.

Upon Wrinkles.

WRINKLES no more are, or no less
Than beauty turned to sourness

Upon Prigg.

PRIGG, when he comes to houses, oft doth use,
Rather than fail, to steal from thence old shoes ;
Sound or unsound, or be they rent or whole,
Prigg bears away the body and the sole.

Upon Moon.

MOON is an usurer, whose gain
Seldom or never knows a wane ;
Only Moon's conscience, we confess,
That ebbs from pity less and less.

Pray and Prosper.

FIRST offer incense, then thy field and meads
Shall smile and smell the better by thy beads.
The spangling dew dredged o'er the grass shall be
Turned all to mel and manna there for thee.
Butter of amber, cream, and wine, and oil,
Shall run as rivers all throughout thy soil.
Would'st thou to sincere silver turn thy mould,
Pray once ; twice pray, and turn thy ground to gold.

His Lachrimæ; or, Mirth turned to Mourning.

CALL me no more,
As heretofore,
The music of a feast :
Since now, alas,
The mirth that was
In me, is dead or ceased.

Before I went
To banishment
Into the loathed West,
I could rehearse
A lyric verse,
And speak it with the best.

But time, Ai me !
Has laid, I see,
My organ fast asleep ;
And turned my voice
Into the noise
Of those that sit and weep.

Upon Shift.

SHIFT now has cast his clothes ; got all things new,
Save but his hat, and that he cannot mew.

Upon Cuts.

IF wounds in clothes, Cuts calls his rags, 'tis clear
His linings are the matter running there.

Gain and Gettings.

WHEN others gain much by the present cast,
The cobbler's getting time is at the last.

To the Most Fair and Lovely Mistress Anne Soame, now Lady Abdie.

So smell those odours that do rise
From out the wealthy spiceries ;
So smells the flower of blooming clove,
Or roses smothered in the stove ;
So smells the air of spiced wine,
Or essences of jessamine ;
So smells the breath about the hives,
When well the work of honey thrives,
And all the busy factors come
Laden with wax and honey home ;
So smell those neat and woven bowers,
All over-arched with orange flowers,
And almond blossoms, that do mix
To make rich these aromatics ;
So smell those bracelets, and those bands
Of amber chafed between the hands ;
When thus enkindled, they transpire
A noble perfume from the fire.
The wine of cherries, and to these
The cooling breath of raspberries,
The smell of morning's milk and cream,
Butter of cowslips mixed with them,
Of roasted warden, or baked pear,
These are not to be reckoned here ;
When as the meanest part of her
Smells like the maiden-pomander.

Thus sweet she smells, or what can be
More liked by her, or loved by me.

Upon his Kinswoman, Mistress Elizabeth Herrick.

SWEET virgin, that I do not set
The pillars up of weeping jet,
Or mournful marble ; let thy shade
Not wrathful seem, or fright the maid,
Who hither at her wonted hours
Shall come to strew thy earth with flowers.
No—know, blest maid, when there's not one
Remainder left of brass or stone,
Thy living epitaph shall be,
Though lost in them, yet found in me.
Dear, in thy bed of roses, then,
Till this world shall dissolve as men,
Sleep, while we hide thee from the light,
Drawing the curtains round : Good night.

A Panegyric to Sir Lewis Pemberton.

TILL I shall come again, let this suffice,
   I send my salt, my sacrifice
To thee, thy lady, younglings, and as far
   As to thy genius and thy lar ;
To the worn threshold, porch, hall, parlour, kitchen,
   The fat-fed smoking temple, which in
The wholesome savour of thy mighty chines,
   Invites to supper him who dines,
Where laden spits, warped with large ribs of beef,
   Not represent but give relief
To the lank stranger and the sour swain,
   Where both may feed and come again ;
For no black-bearded vigil from thy door
   Beats with a buttoned staff the poor ;
But from thy warm love-hatching gates, each may
   Take friendly morsels, and there stay
To sun his thin-clad members, if he likes,
   For thou no porter keep'st who strikes.
No comer to thy roof his guest-rite wants ;
   Or, staying there, is scourged with taunts
Of some rough groom, who, yerkt with corns, says, "Sir,
   You've dipped too long i' th' vinegar ;
And with our broth and bread and bits, Sir friend,
   You've fared well, pray make an end ;
Two-days you've larded here ; a third, ye know,
   Makes guests and fish smell strong ; pray go
You to some other chimney, and there take
   Essay of other giblets; make

Merry at another's hearth : you're here
    Welcome as thunder to our beer."
Manners knows distance, and a man unrude
    Would soon recoil, and not intrude
His stomach to a second meal.   No, no,
    Thy house, well fed and taught, can show
No such crabbed vizard : thou hast learnt thy train
    With heart and hand to entertain,
And by the arms-full, with a breast unhid,
    As the old race of mankind did,
When either's heart, and either's hand did strive
    To be the nearer relative.
Thou dost redeem those times ; and what was lost
    Of ancient honesty, may boast
It keeps a growth in thee, and so will run
    A course in thy fame's pledge, thy son.
Thus, like a Roman Tribune, thou thy gate
    Early sets hope to feast, and late ;
Keeping no currish waiter to affright,
    With blasting eye, the appetite,
Which fain would waste upon thy cates, but that
    The trencher creature marketh what
Best and more suppling piece he cuts, and by
    Some private pinch tells danger's nigh,
A hand too desperate, or a knife that bites
    Skin deep into the pork, or lights
Upon some part of kid, as if mistook,
    When checked by the butler's look.
No, no, thy bread, thy wine, thy jocund beer
    Is not reserved for Trebius here,
But all who at thy table seated are,
    Find equal freedom, equal fare ;
And thou, like to that hospitable god,
    Jove, joy'st when guests make their abode
To eat thy bullock's thighs, thy veals, thy fat
    Wethers, and never grudged at.
The pheasant, partridge, gotwit, reeve, ruff, rail,
    The cock, the curlew, and the quail,
These, and thy choicest viands do extend
    Their taste unto the lower end
Of thy glad table ; not a dish more known
    To thee, then unto any one.
But as thy meat, so thy immortal wine
    Makes the smirk face of each to shine,
And spring fresh rose-buds, while the salt, the wit
    Flows from the wine, and graces it ;
While reverence, waiting at the bashful board,
    Honours my lady and my lord.
No scurril jest, no open scene is laid
    Here, for to make the face afraid ;

But temp'rate mirth dealt forth, and so discreet-
    Ly, that it makes the meat more sweet,
And adds perfumes unto the wine, which thou
    Dost rather pour forth, then allow
By cruse and measure ; thus devoting wine,
    As the Canary Isles were thine ;
But with that wisdom and that method, as
    No one that's there his guilty glass
Drinks of distemper, or has cause to cry
    Repentance to his liberty.
No, thou knowest order, ethics, and hast read
    All economics, knowest to lead
A house-dance neatly, and canst truly show
    How far a figure ought to go,
Forward or backward, sideward, and what pace
    Can give, and what retract a grace ;
What gesture courtship, comeliness agrees,
    With those thy primitive decrees,
To give subsistence to thy house, and proof,
    What genii support thy roof,
Goodness and greatness, not the oaken piles ;
    For these, and marbles have their whiles
To last, but not their ever ; virtue's hand
    It is which builds 'gainst fate to stand.
Such is thy house, whose firm foundations' trust
    Is more in thee than in her dust,
Or depth ; these last may yield, and yearly shrink,
    When what is strongly built, no chink
Or yawning rupture can the same devour.
    But fixt it stands, by her own power,
And well-laid bottom, on the iron and rock,
    Which tries, and counter-stands the shock
And ram of time, and by vexation grows
    The stronger.   Virtue dies when foes
Are wanting to her exercise, but great
    And large she spreads by dust and sweat.
Safe stand thy walls, and thee, and so both will,
    Since neither's height was raised by th' ill
Of others ; since no stud, no stone, no piece
    Was reared up by the poor man's fleece ;
No widow's tenement was racked to gild
    Or fret thy ceiling, or to build
A sweating-closet to anoint the silk-
    Soft skin, or bathe in asses milk :
No orphan's pittance, left him, served to set
    The pillars up of lasting jet,
For which their cries might beat against thine ears,
    Or in the damp jet read their tears,
No plank from hallowed altar does appeal
    To yon Star-chamber, or does seal

A curse to thee, or thine ; but all things even
    Make for thy peace and pace to heaven.
Go on directly so, as just men may
    A thousand times, more swear, than say,
This is that princely Pemberton, who can
    Teach men to keep a God in man ;
And when wise poets shall search out to see
    Good men, they find them all in thee.

To his Valentine, on St. Valentine's Day.

OFT have I heard both youths and virgins say,
Birds choose their mates, and couple too, this day ;
But by their flight I never can divine
When I shall couple with my Valentine.

Upon Screw.—Epigram.

SCREW lives by shifts ; yet swears by no small oaths,
For all his shifts he cannot shift his clothes.

Upon Linnit.—Epigram.

LINNIT plays rarely on the lute, we know ;
And sweetly sings, but yet his breath says no.

Upon Mr. Ben Jonson.—Epigram.

AFTER the rare arch-poet Jonson died,
The sock grew loathsome, and the buskins' pride,
Together with the stage's glory, stood
Each like a poor and pitied widowhood.
The cirque profaned was, and all postures racked ;
For men did strut, and stride, and stare, not act.
Then temper flew from words, and men did squeak,
Look red, and blow, and bluster, but not speak :
No holy rage or frantic fires did stir,
Or flash about the spacious theatre.
No clap of hands, or shout, or praises-proof
Did crack the play-house sides, or cleave her roof.
Artless the scene was, and that monstrous sin
Of deep and arrant ignorance came in ;
Such ignorance as theirs was, who once hist
At thy unequall'd play, the Alchemist,
Oh fie upon 'em ! Lastly too, all wit
In utter darkness did and still will sit
Sleeping the luckless age out, till that she
Her resurrection has again with thee.

Another.

THOU had'st the wreath before, now take the tree ;
Then henceforth none be laurel-crowned but thee.

To his Nephew, to be Prosperous in his Art of Painting.

ON, as thou hast begun, brave youth, and get
The palm from Urbin, Titian, Tintoret,
Breugel, and Coxcie, and the works outdo
Of Holbein, and that mighty Rubens too.
So draw, and paint, as none may do the like,
No, not the glory of the world, Vandyke.

Upon Glass.—Epigram.

GLASS, out of deep and out of desp'rate want,
Turn'd from a Papist here, a Predicant.
A vicarage at last Tom Glass got here,
Just upon five-and-thirty pounds a year.
Add to that thirty five but five pounds more,
He'll turn a Papist, ranker than before.

A Vow to Mars.

STORE of courage to me grant,
Now I'm turn'd a combatant ;
Help me, so that I my shield,
Fighting, lose not in the field.
That's the greatest shame of all
That in warfare can befall.
Do but this, and there shall be
Offer'd up a wolf to thee.

To his Maid Prue.

THESE summer birds did with thy master stay
The times of warmth, but then they flew away,
Leaving their poet, being now grown old,
Expos'd to all the coming winter's cold.
But thou, kind Prue, did'st with my fates abide
As well the winter's as the summer's tide ;
For which thy love, live with thy master here,
Not one, but all the seasons of the year.

A Canticle to Apollo.

PLAY, Phœbus, on thy lute,
And we will sit all mute ;
By listening to thy lyre,
That set all ears on fire.

Hark, hark, the God does play ;
And as he leads the way
Through heaven, the very spheres,
As men, turn all to ears.

A Just Man.

A JUST man's like a rock that turns the wroth
Of all the raging waves into a froth.

Upon a Hoarse Singer.

SING me to death, for till thy voice be clear,
'Twill never please the palate of mine ear

How Pansies, or Heartsease, came first.

FROLIC virgins once these were,
Over-loving, living here ;
Being here their ends denied,
Ran for sweethearts mad, and died.
Love, in pity of their tears,
And their loss in blooming years,
For their restless here-spent hours.
Gave them heartsease turned to flowers.

To his Peculiar Friend, Sir Edward Fish, Knight Baronet.

SINCE for thy full deserts, with all the rest
Of these chaste spirits that are here possessed
Of life eternal, time has made thee one
For growth in this my rich plantation ;
Live here ; but know 'twas virtue, and not chance,
That gave thee this so high inheritance.
Keep it for ever ; grounded with the good,
Who hold fast here an endless lively food.

Lar's Portion and the Poet's Part.

AT my homely country-seat,
I have there a little wheat,

Which I work to meal, and make
Therewithal a holy cake ;
Part of which I give to Lar,
Part is my peculiar.

Upon Man.

MAN is composed here of a twofold part ;
The first of Nature, and the next of Art ;
Art presupposes Nature ; Nature she
Prepares the way for man's docility.

Liberty.

THOSE ills that mortal men endure,
So long are capable of cure
As they of freedom may be sure :
But that denied, a grief, though small,
Shakes the whole roof, or ruins all.

Lots to be Liked.

LEARN this of me, where'er thy lot doth fall :
Short lot, or not, to be content with all.

Griefs.

JOVE may afford us thousands of reliefs ;
Since man exposed is to a world of griefs.

Upon Eeles.—Epigram.

EELES winds and turns, and cheats and steals ; yet Eeles
Driving these sharking trades, is out at heels.

The Dream.

By dream, I saw one of the three
Sisters of Fate appear to me.
Close by my bedside she did stand,
Showing me there a firebrand ;
She told me, too, as that did spend,
So drew my life unto an end.
Three-quarters were consumed of it ;
Only remained a little bit,
Which will be burnt up by-and-by ;
Then Julia, weep, for I must die.

Upon Center, a Spectacle-maker, with a Flat Nose.

CENTER is known weak-sighted, and he sells
To others store of helpful spectacles.
Why wears he none? Because we may suppose,
Where leaven wants, there level lies the nose.

Upon Electra.

WHEN out of bed my love doth spring,
'Tis but as day a-kindling ;
But when she's up and fully dressed,
'Tis then broad day throughout the East.

Of Love.

I DO not love, nor can it be,
Love will in vain spend shafts on me ;
I did this Godhead once defy,
Since which I freeze, but cannot fry.
Yet out, alas ! the death's the same,
Killed by a frost or by a flame.

Upon Himself.

I DISLIKED but even now,
Now I love I know not how.
Was I idle, and that while
Was I fired with a smile ?
I'll to work, or pray ; and then
I shall quite dislike again.

Another.

LOVE he that will ; it best likes me,
To have my neck from Love's yoke free.

Upon Skinns.—Epigram.

SKINNS, he dined well to-day ; how do you think ?
His nails they were his meat, his rheum the drink.

Upon Peevish.—Epigram.

PEEVISH doth boast that he's the very first
Of English poets, and 'tis thought the worst.

The Mad Maid's Song.

GOOD morrow to the day so fair;
    Good morning, sir, to you;
Good morrow to mine own torn hair,
    Bedabbled with the dew.

Good morning to this primrose too;
    Good morrow to each maid
That will with flowers the tomb bestrew
    Wherein my love is laid.

Ah! woe is me, woe, woe is me,
    Alack, and well-a-day!
For pity, sir, find out that bee
    Which bore my love away.

I'll seek him in your bonnet brave;
    I'll seek him in your eyes;
Nay, now I think they'ave made his grave
    I'th' bed of strawberries.

I'll seek him there; I know, ere this,
    The cold, cold earth doth shake him;
But I will go, or send a kiss
    By you, sir, to awake him.

Pray hurt him not; though he be dead,
    He knows well who do love him;
And who with green turfs rear his head,
    And who do rudely move him.

He's soft and tender, pray take heed,
    With bands of cowslips bind him,
And bring him home; but 'tis decreed,
    That I shall never find him.

To Springs and Fountains.

I HEARD ye could cool heat; and came
With hope you would allay the same;
Thrice have I washed, but feel no cold,
Nor find that true which was foretold.
Methinks, like mine, your pulses beat,
And labour with unequal heat;
Cure, cure yourselves, for I descry
Ye boil with love as well as I.

Upon Julia's Unlacing Herself.

TELL, if thou canst, and truly, whence doth come
This camphor, storax, spikenard, galbanum;

These musks, these ambers, and those other smells,
Sweet as the vestry of the oracles.
I'll tell thee; while my Julia did unlace
Her silken bodice but a breathing space,
The passive air such odour then assumed,
As when to Jove great Juno goes perfumed;
Whose pure immortal body doth transmit
A scent that fills both heaven and earth with it.

To Bacchus.—A Canticle.

WHITHER dost thou worry me,
Bacchus, being full of thee?
This way, that way; that way, this;
Here and there a fresh love is;
That doth like me, this doth please:
Thus a thousand mistresses
I have now; yet I alone
Having all, enjoy not one.

The Lawn.

WOULD I see lawn, clear as the heaven, and thin?
It should be only in my Julia's skin;
Which so betrays her blood, as we discover
The blush of cherries when a lawn's cast over.

The Frankincense.

WHEN my off'ring next I make,
Be thy hand the hallowed cake;
And thy breast the altar, whence
Love may smell the frankincense.

Upon Patrick, a Footman.—Epigram.

Now, Patrick, with his footmanship has done,
His eyes and ears strive which should fastest run.

Upon Bridget.—Epigram.

OF four teeth only Bridget was possessed;
Two she spat out, a cough forced out the rest.

To Sycamores.

I'M sick of love; O let me lie
Under your shades, to sleep or die!
Either is welcome; so I have
Or here my bed, or here my grave.

Why do you sigh, and sob, and keep
Time with the tears that I do weep?
Say, have ye sense, or do you prove
What crucifixions are in love?
I know ye do ; and that's the why
You sigh for love as well as I.

A Pastoral sung to the King.

Montano, Silvio, and Mirtillo—shepherds.

Mon. BAD are the times.   *Sil.* And worse than they are we.
Mon. Troth, bad are both ; worse fruit, and ill the tree :
The feast of shepherds fail.   *Sil.* None crowns the cup
Of wassail now, or sets the quintell up :
And he, who used to lead the country round,
Youthful Mirtillo, here he comes, grief drowned.
Ambo. Let's cheer him up.   *Sil.* Behold him weeping ripe.
Mirt. Ah, Amarillis ! farewell mirth and pipe ;
Since thou art gone, no more I mean to play
To these smooth lawns, my mirthful roundelay.
Dear Amarillis ! *Mon.* Hark ! *Sil.* Mark ! *Mirt.* This earth
        grew sweet
Where, Amarillis, thou didst set thy feet.
Ambo. Poor pitied youth ! *Mirt.* And here the breath of
        kine
And sheep grew more sweet by that breath of thine.
This flock of wool, and this rich lock of hair,
This ball of cowslips, these she gave me here.
Sil. Words sweet as love itself. *Mon.* Hark !
Mirt. This way she came, and this way too she went ;
How each thing smells divinely redolent !
Like to a field of beans, when newly blown,
Or like a meadow being lately mown.
Mon. A sweet sad passion——
Mirt. In dewy mornings, when she came this way,
Sweet bents would bow, to give my love the day ;
And when at night she folded had her sheep,
Daisies would shut, and closing, sigh and weep.
Besides (Ai me !) since she went hence to dwell,
The voice's daughter ne'er spake syllable.
But she is gone.   *Sil.* Mirtillo, tell us whither?
Mirt. Where she and I shall never meet together.
Mon. Forefend it, Pan ; and Pales, do thou please
To give an end.   *Mirt.* To what ? *Sil.* Such griefs as these.
Mirt. Never, oh never ! Still I may endure
The wound I suffer, never find a cure.
Mon. Love, for thy sake, will bring her to these hills
And dales again.   *Mirt.* No, I will languish still ;
And all the while my part shall be to weep ;
And with my sighs call home my bleating sheep ;

And in the rind of every comely tree
I'll carve thy name, and in that name kiss thee.
Mon. Set with the sun thy woes.   *Sil.* The day grows old,
And time it is our full-fed flocks to fold.

    Chor.   The shades grow great; but greater grows our
        sorrow ;
            But let's go steep
            Our eyes in sleep,
            And meet to weep
                To-morrow.

Upon Flimsey.—Epigram.

WHY walks Nick Flimsey like a malcontent ?
Is it because his money all is spent ?
No, but because the ding-thrift now is poor,
And knows not where i' th' world to borrow more.

Upon Showbread.—Epigram.

LAST night thou didst invite me home to eat,
And show'st me there much plate, but little meat :
Prithee, when next thou dost invite, bar state,
And give me meat, or give me else thy plate.

The Willow Garland.

A WILLOW garland thou didst send
  Perfumed, last day, to me ;
Which did but only this portend,
  I was forsook by thee.

Since so it is ; I'll tell thee what,
  To-morrow thou shall see
Me wear the willow ; after that,
  To die upon the tree.

As beasts unto the altars go
  With garlands dressed, so I
Will, with my willow-wreath also,
  Come forth and sweetly die.

A Hymn to Sir Clipseby Crew.

    'TWAS not love's dart,
    Or any blow
    Of want or foe,
    Did wound my heart
With an eternal smart.

But only you,
My sometimes known
Companion,
My dearest Crew,
That me unkindly slew.

May your fault die,
And have no name
In books of fame ;
Or let it lie
Forgotten now as I.

We parted are,
And now no more,
As heretofore
By jocund Lar,
Shall be familiar.

But though we sever,
My Crew shall see
That I will be
Here faithless never,
But love my Clipseby ever.

Upon Roots.—Epigram.

ROOTS had no money ; yet he went o' th' score
For a wrought purse ; can any tell wherefore ?
Say, what should Roots do with a purse in print,
That had nor gold or silver to put in't ?

Empires.

EMPIRES of kings are now, and ever were,
As Sallust saith, coincident to fear.

Felicity, Quick of Flight.

EVERY time seems short to be
That's measured by Felicity ;
But one half-hour that's made up here
With grief, seems longer than a year.

Putrefaction.

PUTREFACTION is the end,
Of all that Nature doth intend.

Passion.

WERE there not a matter known,
There would be no Passion.

Jack and Jill.

SINCE Jack and Jill both wicked be,
It seems a wonder unto me,
That they no better do agree.

Upon Parson Beans.

OLD Parson Beans hunts six days of the week,
And on the seventh he has his notes to seek ;
Six days he halloos so much breath away,
That on the seventh he can nor preach or pray.

The Crowd and Company.

IN holy meetings, there a man may be
One of the Crowd, not of the Company.

Short and Long Both Likes.

THIS lady's short, that mistress she is tall ;
But long or short, I'm well content with all.

Policy in Princes.

THAT Princes may possess a surer seat,
'Tis fit they make no One with them too great.

Upon Rook.—Epigram.

ROOK, he sells feathers, yet he still doth cry,
Fie on this pride, this female vanity.
Thus, though the Rook does rail against the sin,
He loves the gain that vanity brings in.

To Daisies, not to Shut so Soon.

SHUT not so soon ; the dull-eyed night
    Has not as yet begun
To make a seizure on the light,
    Or to seal up the sun.

No marigolds yet closed are,
    No shadows great appear ;
Nor doth the early shepherd's star
    Shine like a spangle here.

Stay but till my Julia close
    Her life-begetting eye ;
And let the whole world then dispose
    Itself to live or die.

To the Little Spinners.

YE pretty Housewives, would ye know
The work that I would put ye to ?
This, this it should be, for to spin
A lawn for me, so fine and thin
As it might serve me for my skin.
For cruel love has me so whipped,
That of my skin I all am stripped,
And shall despair that any art
Can ease the rawness or the smart,
Unless you skin again each part.
Which mercy, if you will but do,
I call all maids to witness to
What here I promise, that no broom
Shall now, or ever after come,
To wrong a Spinner, or her loom.

Oberon's Palace.

AFTER the feast, my Shapcot, see
The Fairy Court I give to thee ;
Where we'll present our Oberon led
Half-tipsy to the Fairy bed,
Where Mab he finds, who there doth lie
Not without mickle majesty.
Which done, and thence remov'd the light,
We'll wish both them and thee good-night

Full as a bee with thyme, and red
As cherry harvest, now high fed
For lust and action ; on he'll go
To lie with Mab, though all say no.
Lust has no ears ; he's sharp as thorn,
And fretful, carries hay in 's horn,
And lightning in his eyes ; and flings
Among the elves, if mov'd, the stings
Of peltish wasps ; we'll know his guard ;
Kings, though they're hated, will be feared.
Wine lead him on.   Thus to a grove,
Sometimes devoted unto love,
Tinselled with twilight, he and they
Led by the shine of snails, a way
Beat with their numerous feet, which by
Many a neat perplexity,
Many a turn, and many a cross-
Track, they redeem a bank of moss
Spongy and swelling, and far more
Soft then the finest Leinster ore ;

E

Mildly disparkling, like those fires
Which break from the enjewelled tyres
Of curious brides ; or like those mites
Of candied dew in moony nights.
Upon this convex, all the flowers
Nature begets by th' sun and showers,
Are to a wild digestion brought,
As if Love's sampler here was wrought ;
Or Citherea's ceston, which
All with temptation doth bewitch.
Sweet airs move here, and more divine
Made by the breath of great-eyed kine,
Who, as they low, empearl with milk
The four-leav'd grass, or moss-like silk.
The breath of monkeys, met to mix
With musk-flies, are th' aromatics
Which 'cense this arch ; and here and there,
And farther off, and everywhere
Throughout that brave mosaic yard,
Those picks or diamonds in the card ;
With peeps of hearts, of club and spade,
Are here most neatly interlaid.
Many a counter, many a die,
Half-rotten and without an eye,
Lies hereabouts ; and for to pave
The excellency of this cave,
Squirrels' and children's teeth late shed,
Are neatly here enchequered,
With brownest toadstones, and the gum
That shines upon the bluer plum.
The nails fallen off by whit-flaws : Art's
Wise hand enchasing here those warts
Which we to others from ourselves)
Sell, and brought hither by the elves.
The tempting mole, stolen from the neck
Of the shy virgin, seems to deck
The holy entrance ; where within,
The room is hung with the blue skin
Of shifted snake ; enfriezed throughout
With eyes of peacocks' trains, and trout-
Flies' curious wings ; and these among
Those silver-pence, that cut the tongue
Of the red infant, neatly hung.
The glow-worm's eyes, the shining scales
Of silvery fish, wheat-straws, the snail's
Soft candle-light, the kitling's eyne,
Corrupted wood, serve here for shine.
No glaring light of bold-faced day,
Or other over-radiant ray,
Ransacks this room ; but what weak beams
Can make reflected from these gems,

And multiply ; such is the light,
But ever doubtful, day or night.
By this quaint taper-light, he winds
His errors up ; and now he finds
His moon-tanned Mab, as somewhat **sick**,
And, love knows, tender as a chick.
Upon six plump dandelions, high-
Reared, lies her elvish majesty,
Whose woolly bubbles seemed to drown
Her Mabship in obedient down ;
For either sheet was spread the caul
That doth the infant's face enthral,
When it is born, by some enstyled
The lucky omen of the child ;
And next to these, two blankets o'er-
Cast of the finest gossamer ;
And then a rug of carded wool,
Which, sponge-like, drinking in the **dull**
Light of the moon, seemed to comply,
Cloud-like, the dainty deity.
Thus soft she lies; and over-head
A spinner's circle is bespread
With cobweb curtains, from the **roof**
So neatly sunk, as that no proof
Of any tackling can declare
What gives it hanging in the air.

To his Peculiar Friend, Master Thomas Shapcott, Lawyer.

I've paid thee what I promised; that's not all;
Besides, I give thee here a verse that shall,
When hence thy circummortal part is gone,
Arch-like, hold up, thy name's inscription.
Brave men can't die, whose candid actions are
Writ in the poet's endless calendar :
Whose vellum and whose volume is the sky,
And the pure stars the praising poetry.

Farewell.

To Julia in the Temple.

Besides us two, i' th' Temple here's not one
To make up now a congregation.
Let's to the altar of perfumes then go,
And say short prayers : and when we have done **so**,
Then we shall see, how in a little space
Saints will come in to fill each pew and place.

E 2

To Œnone.

WHAT Conscience, say, is it in thee
  When I a heart had one,
To take away that heart from me,
  And to retain thy own ?

For shame or pity, now incline
  To play a loving part,
Either to send me kindly thine,
  Or give me back my heart.

Covet not both, but if thou dost
  Resolve to part with neither,
Why, yet to show that thou art just,
  Take me and mine together.

His Weakness in Woes.

I CANNOT suffer ; and in this, my part
Of patience wants.   Grief breaks the stoutest heart.

Fame makes us Forward.

To print our poems, the propulsive cause
Is Fame, the breath of popular applause.

To Groves.

YE silent shades, whose each tree here
Some relic of a saint doth wear,
Who for some sweetheart's sake did prove
The fire and martyrdom of love :
Here is the legend of those saints
That died for love, and their complaints ;
Their wounded hearts, and names we find
Encarved upon the leaves and rind :
Give way, give way to me, who come
Scorched with the self-same martyrdom ;
And have deserved as much, Love knows,
As to be canonized 'mongst those
Whose deeds and deaths here written are
Within your Greeny calendar.
By all those virgins' fillets hung
Upon your boughs, and requiems sung
For saints and souls departed hence,
Here honoured still with frankincense.
By all those tears that have been shed
As a drink-offering to the dead ;

By all those true love-knots that be
With mottoes carved on every tree,
By sweet St. Phillis, pity me!
By dear St. Phillis and the rest
Of all those other saints now blest,
Me, me forsaken, here admit
Among your myrtles to be writ;
That my poor name may have the glory
To live remembered in your story.

An Epitaph upon a Virgin.

HERE a solemn fast we keep,
While all beauty lies asleep,
Hushed be all things, no noise here
But the toning of a tear;
Or a sigh of such ... bring
Cowslips for her covering.

To the Right Gracious Prince, Lodwick, Duke of Richmond and Lennox.

OF all those three brave brothers, fallen i' th' war,
(Not without glory) noble sir, you are,
Despite of all concussions, left the stem,
To shoot forth generations like to them.
Which may be done, if, sir, you can beget
Men in their substance, not in counterfeit,
Such essences as those three brothers, known
Eternal by their own production.
Of whom, from Fame's white trumpet, this I'll tell,
Worthy their everlasting chronicle,
Never since first Bellona used a shield,
Such three brave brothers fell in Mars his field.
These were those three Horatii Rome did boast;
Rome's where these three Horatii we have lost.
One Cœur de Lion had that age long since;
This, three: which three you make up four, brave prince.

To Jealousy.

O JEALOUSY, that art
The canker of the heart;
And mak'st all hell
Where thou dost dwell;
For pity be
No fury, or no firebrand to me.

Far from me I'll remove
All thoughts of irksome love;

And turn to snow,
Or crystal grow,
To keep still free,
O soul-tormenting jealousy! from thee.

To Live Freely.

LET'S live in haste; use pleasures while we may;
Could life rèturn, 'twould never lose a day.

Upon Spunge.—Epigram.

SPUNGE makes his boasts that he's the only man
Can hold of beer and ale an ocean:
Is this his glory? then his triumph's poor:
I know the Tun of Heidelberg holds more.

His Alms.

HERE, here I live,
And somewhat give
Of what I have
To those who crave.
Little or much,
My alms is such;
But if my deal
Of oil and meal
shall fuller grow,
More I'll bestow.
Meantime, be it
E'en but a bit,
Or else a crumb,
The scrip hath some.

Upon Himself.

COME, leave this loathed country-life, and then
Grow up to be a Roman citizen.
Those mites of time, which yet remain unspent,
Waste thou in that most civil government.
Get their comportment, and the gilding tongue
Of those mild men thou art to live among:
Then being seated in that smoother sphere,
Decree thy everlasting topic there,
And to the farm-house ne'er return at all;
Though granges do not love thee, cities shall.

To Enjoy the Time.

WHILE Fate permits us, let's be merry;
Pass all we must the fatal ferry;

And this our life, too, whirls away,
With the rotation of the day.

Upon Love.

LOVE, I have broke
       Thy yoke ;
The neck is free :
But when I'm next
       Love-vexed,
Then shackle me.

'Tis better yet
       To fret
The feet or hands ;
Than to enthral
       Or gall
The neck with bands.

To the Right Honourable Mildmay, Earl of Westmoreland.

YOU are a lord, an earl, nay more, a man,
Who writes sweet numbers well as any can ;
If so, why then are not these verses hurled,
Like Sybil's leaves, throughout the ample world?
What is a jewel if it be not set
Forth by a ring or some rich carcanet ?
But being so, then the beholders cry,
See, see a gem as rare as Belus' eye !
Then public praise does run upon the stone,
For a most rich, a rare, a precious one.
Expose your jewels then unto the view,
That we may praise them, or themselves prize you.
Virtue concealed, with Horace you'll confess,
Differs not much from drowsy slothfulness.

The Plunder

I AM of all bereft,
Save but some few beans left,
Whereof, at last, to make
For me and mine a cake ;
Which eaten, they and I
Will say our grace, and die.

Littleness no Cause of Leanness.

ONE feeds on lard, and yet is lean ;
And I, but feasting with a bean,
Grow fat and smooth : the reason is,
Jove prospers my meat more than his.

Upon One who said She was always Young.

You say you're young; but when your teeth are told
To be but three, black-eyed, we'll think you're old.

Upon Huncks.—Epigram.

Huncks has no money; he does swear or say,
About him, when the tavern shot's to pay.
If he has none in 's pockets, trust me, Huncks
Has none at home in coffers, desks, or trunks.

The Gemmal Ring; or, True Loveknot.

Thou sent'st to me a true loveknot; but I
Returned a ring of gemmals, to imply
Thy love had one knot, mine a triple tie.

The Parting Verse; or, Charge to his Supposed Wife, when he Travelled.

Go hence, and with this parting kiss,
Which joins two souls, remember this :
Though thou be'st young, kind, soft, and fair,
And may'st draw thousands with a hair,
Yet let these glib temptations be
Furies to others, friends to me.
Look upon all; and though on fire
Thou set'st their hearts, let chaste desire
Steer thee to me ; and think, me gone,
In having all, that thou hast none.
Nor so immured would I have
Thee live, as dead and in thy grave ;
But walk abroad, yet wisely well
Stand for my coming, sentinel.
And think, as thou dost walk the street,
Me or my shadow thou dost meet.
I know a thousand greedy eyes
Will on thy features tyrannize,
In my short absence ; yet behold
Them like some picture, or some mould
Fashioned like thee ; which though 't have ears
And eyes, it neither sees or hears.
But if they woo thee, do thou say,
As that chaste Queen of Ithaca
Did to her suitors. this web done,
Undone as oft as done, I'm won.
I will not urge thee, for I know,
Though thou art young, thou canst say no.

I will not over-long enlarge
To thee, this my religious charge :
Take this compression, so by this
Means I shall know what other kiss
Is mixed with mine ; and truly know,
Returning, if 't be mine or no ;
Keep it till then. And now, my spouse,
For my wished safety pay thy vows
And prayers to Venus ; if it please
The great blue ruler of the seas,
Not many full-faced moons shall wane,
Lean-horned, before I come again
As one triumphant, when I find
In thee all faith of womankind.
Nor would I have thee think that thou
Hadst power thyself to keep this vow ;
But having 'scaped temptation's shelf,
Know Virtue taught thee, not thyself.

To his Kinsman, Sir Thomas Soame.

SEEING thee, Soame, I see a goodly man,
And in that good a great patrician ;
Next to which two, among the city powers
And thrones, thyself one of those senators
Not wearing purple only for the show,
As many conscripts of the city do,
But for true service, worthy of that gown,
The golden chain, too, and the civic crown.

To Blossoms.

FAIR pledges of a fruitful tree,
    Why do ye fall so fast ?
    Your date is not so past,
But you may stay yet here a while,
    To blush and gently smile,
        And go at last.

What, were ye born to be
    An hour or half's delight,
    And so to bid good-night ?
Twas pity Nature brought ye forth,
    Merely to show your worth,
        And lose you quite.

But you are lovely leaves, where we
    May read how soon things have
    Their end, though ne'er so brave ;

And after they have shown their pride
Like you a while, they glide
Into the grave.

Man's Dying-place Uncertain.

MAN knows where first he ships himself; but he
Never can tell where shall his landing be.

Nothing Free-cost.

NOTHING comes free-cost here; Jove will not let
His gifts go from him, if not bought with sweat.

Few Fortunate.

MANY we are, and yet but few possess
Those fields of everlasting happiness.

To Perenna.

HOW long, Perenna, wilt thou see
Me languish for the love of thee?
Consent and play a friendly part
To save, when thou may'st kill a heart.

To the Ladies.

TRUST me, ladies, I will do
Nothing to distemper you;
If I any fret or vex,
Men they shall be, not your sex.

The Old Wives' Prayer.

HOLY-ROOD, come forth and shield
Us i' th' city and the field;
Safely guard us, now and aye,
From the blast that burns by day,
And those sounds that us affright
In the dead of dampish night;
Drive all hurtful fiends us fro,
By the time the cocks first crow.

Upon a cheap Laundress.—Epigram.

FEACIE, some say, doth wash her clothes i' th' lye
That sharply trickles from her either eye.
The laundresses, they envy her good luck,
Who can with so small charges drive the buck.
What needs she fire and ashes to consume,
Who can scour linens with her own salt rheum?

Upon his Departure Hence.

THUS I
Pass by,
And die,
As one
Unknown
And gone :
I'm made
A shade,
And laid
I' th' grave,
There have
My cave :
Where tell
I dwell,
Farewell.

The Wassail.

GIVE way, give way, ye gates, and win
An easy blessing to your bin
An d basket, by our entering in.

May both with manchet stand replete,
Your larders, too, so hung with meat,
That thou a thousand, thousand eat.

Yet ere twelve moons shall whirl about
Their silvery spheres, there's none may doubt
But more's sent in than was served out.

Next, may your dairies prosper so
As that your pans no ebb may know ;
But if they do, the more to flow.

Like to a solemn sober stream,
Banked all with lilies, and the cream
Of sweetest cowslips filling them.

Then may your plants be pressed with fruit,
Nor bee or hive you have be mute,
But sweetly sounding like a lute.

Last, may your harrows, shares, and ploughs,
Your stacks, your stocks, your sweetest mows,
All prosper by your virgin-vows

Alas ! we bless, but see none here,
That brings us either ale or beer ;
In a dry house all things are near.

Let's leave a longer time to wait,
Where rust and cobwebs bind the gate;
And all live here with needy fate;

Where chimneys do for ever weep
For want of warmth, and stomachs keep
With noise the servants eyes from sleep.

It is in vain to sing, or stay
Our free feet here, but we'll away;
Yet to the Lares this we'll say:

The time will come when you'll be sad,
And reckon this for fortune bad,
T' have lost the good ye might have had.

How Springs Came First.

THESE springs were maidens once that loved,
But lost to that they most approved:
My story tells, by Love they were
Turned to these springs which we see here:
The pretty whimpering that they make
When of the banks their leave they take,
Tells ye but this, they are the same,
In nothing changed but in their name.

To Rosemary and Bays.

My wooing's ended: now my wedding's near;
When gloves are giving, gilded be you there.

Upon a Scar in a Virgin's Face.

'TIS heresy in others; in your face
That scar is no schism, but the sign of grace.

Upon his Eyesight Failing Him.

I BEGIN to wain in sight;
Shortly I shall bid good-night;
Then no gazing more about,
When the tapers once are out.

To his Worthy Friend, Mr. Thos. Falconbridge.

STAND with thy graces forth, brave man, and rise
High with thine own auspicious destinies;
Nor leave the search and proof till thou canst find
These, or those ends, to which thou wast designed.
Thy lucky genius, and thy guiding star,
Have made thee prosperous in thy ways thus far;

Nor will they leave thee till they both have shown
Thee to the world a prime and public one.
Then, when thou see'st thine age all turned to gold,
Remember what thy Herrick thee foretold,
When at the holy threshold of thine house
He boded good-luck to thyself and spouse.
Lastly, be mindful, when thou art grown great,
That towers high reared dread most the lightning's threat ;
Whenas the humble cottages not fear
The cleaving bolt of Jove the Thunderer.

Upon Julia's Hair filled with Dew.

DEW sat on Julia's hair,
    And spangled too,
Like leaves that laden are
    With trembling dew;
Or glittered to my sight
    As when the beams
Have their reflected light
    Danced by the streams.

Another on Her.

How can I choose but love, and follow her
Whose shadow smells like milder pomander !
How can I choose but kiss her, whence does come
The storax, spikenard, myrrh, and labdanum ?

Loss from the Least.

GREAT men by small means oft are overthrown;
He's lord of thy life who contemns his own.

Rewards and Punishments.

ALL things are open to these two events,
Or to rewards, or else to punishments.

Shame no Statist.

SHAME is a bad attendant to a state :
He rents his crown that fears the people's hate.

To Sir Clipseby Crew.

SINCE to the country first I came,
    I have lost my former flame ;
And, methinks, I not inherit,
    As I did, my ravished spirit.

If I write a verse or two,
'Tis with very much ado;
In regard I want that wine
Which should conjure up a line.
Yet, though now of muse bereft,
I have still the manners left
For to thank you, noble sir,
For those gifts you do confer
Upon him, who only can
Be in prose a grateful man.

Upon Himself.

I COULD never love indeed,
Never see mine own heart bleed ;
Never crucify my life,
Or for widow, maid, or wife.

I could never seek to please
One or many mistresses;
Never like their lips, to swear
Oil of roses still smelt there.

I could never break my sleep,
Fold mine arms, sob, sigh, or weep;
Never beg or humbly woo,
With oaths and lies, as others do.

I could never walk alone,
Put a shirt of sackcloth on;
Never keep a fast, or pray
For good luck in love that day.

But have hitherto lived free,
As the air that circles me;
And kept credit with my heart,
Neither broke i' th' whole or part.

An Eclogue, or Pastoral between Endymion Porter and Lycidas Herrick—set and sung.

Endym. AH, Lycidas, come tell me why
    Thy whilome merry oat
By thee doth so neglected lie,
    And never purls a note ?

I prithee speak. *Lyc.* I will. *End.* Say on.
    Lyc. 'Tis thou, and only thou
That art the cause, Endymion.
    End. For love's sake tell me how.

Lyc. In this regard, that thou dost play
    Upon another plain ;
And for a rural roundelay
    Strik'st now a courtly strain.

Thou leav'st our hills, our dales, our bowers,
    Our finer-fleeced sheep ;
Unkind to us, to spend thine hours,
    Where shepherds should not keep.

I mean the court : let Latmos be
    My loved Endymion's court ;
End. But I the courtly state would see.
    Lyc. Then see it in report.

What has the court to do with swains,
    Where Phillis is not known ?
Nor does it mind the rustic strains
    Of us, or Coridon.

Break, if thou lov'st us, this delay.
    End. Dear Lycidas, ere long,
I vow by Pan, to come away,
    And pipe unto thy song.

Then Jessamine, with Florabel,
    And dainty Amaryllis,
With handsome-handed Drosomel,
    Shall prank thy hook with lilies.

Lyc. Then Tityrus and Coridon,
    And Thyrsis, they shall follow,
With all the rest ; while thou alone
    Shalt lead, like young Apollo.

And till thou com'st, thy Lycidas,
    In every genial cup,
Shall write in spice, Endymion 'twas
    That kept his piping up.

And my most lucky swain, when I shall live to see
Endymion's moon to fill up full, remember me ;
Meantime, let Lycidas have leave to pipe to thee.

To a Bed of Tulips.

Bright tulips, we do know
You had your coming hither,
And fading time does show
That ye must quickly wither.

Your sisterhoods may stay,
And smile here for your hour ;
But die ye must away,
Even as the meanest flower.

Come, virgins, then, and see
Your frailties, and bemoan ye,
For lost like these 'twill be
As time had never known ye.

A Caution.

THAT love last long, let it thy first care be
To find a wife that is most fit for thee.
Be she too wealthy, or too poor, be sure
Love in extremes can never long endure.

To the Water Nymphs, Drinking at the Fountain.

REACH with your whiter hands to me
  Some crystal of the spring,
And I about the cup shall see
  Fresh lilies flourishing.

Or else, sweet nymphs, do you but this :
  To th' glass your lips incline ;
And I shall see by that one kiss
  The water turned to wine.

To his Honoured Kinsman, Sir Richard Stone.

To this white temple of my heroes, here
Beset with stately figures everywhere
Of such rare saintships who did here consume
Their lives in sweets, and left in death perfume ;
Come, thou brave man, and bring with thee a stone
Unto thine own edification.
High are these statues here, besides no less
Strong then the heavens for everlastingness ;
Where, built aloft, and being fixed by these,
Set up thine own eternal images.

Upon a Fly.

A GOLDEN fly one showed to me,
Closed in a box of ivory,
Where both seemed proud—the fly to have
His burial in an ivory grave ;
The ivory took state to hold
A corpse as bright as burnished gold.

One fate had both ; both equal grace,
The buried and the burying-place.
Not Virgil's Gnat, to whom the Spring
All flowers sent to 's burying ;
Not Martial's bee, which in a bead
Of amber quick was buried ;
Nor that fine worm that does inter
Herself i' th' silken sepulchre ;
Nor my rare Phil, that lately was
With lilies tombed up in a glass,
More honour had than this same fly,
Dead, and closed up in ivory.

To Julia.

JULIA, when thy Herrick dies,
Close thou up thy poet's eyes ;
And his last breath, let it be
Taken in by none but thee.

To Mistress Dorothy Parsons.

IF thou ask me, dear, wherefore
I do write of thee no more,
I must answer, sweet, thy part
Less is here than in my heart.

Upon Parrat.

PARRAT protests 'tis he, and only he,
Can teach a man the art of memory ;
Believe him not, for he forgot it quite,
Being drunk, who 'twas that caned his ribs last night.

How He would Drink his Wine.

FILL me my wine in crystal ; thus, and thus
I see 't in 's *puris naturalibus ;*
Unmixed, I love to have it smirk and shine,
'Tis sin, I know, 'tis sin to throttle wine.
What madman's he, that when it sparkles so,
Will cool his flames, or quench his fires with snow ?

How Marigolds came Yellow.

JEALOUS girls these sometimes were,
While they lived or lasted here :
Turned to flowers, still they be
Yellow, marked for jealousy.

The Broken Crystal.

To fetch me wine my Lucia went,
Bearing a crystal continent :
But, making haste, it came to pass,
She brake in two the purer glass,
Then smiled, and sweetly chid her speed ;
So with a blush beshrewed the deed.

Precepts.

GOOD precepts we must firmly hold,
By daily learning we wax old.

To the Right Honourable Edward, Earl of Dorset.

IF I dare write to you, my lord, who are
Of your own self a public theatre ;
And sitting, see the wiles, ways, walks of wit,
And give a righteous judgment upon it ;
What need I care, though some dislike me should,
If Dorset say, What Herrick writes is good ?
We know you're learned i' th' Muses, and no less
In our state-sanctions deep, or bottomless ;
Whose smile can make a poet, and your glance
Dash all bad poems out of countenance ;
So that an author needs no other bays
For coronation, than your only praise,
And no one mischief greater than your frown,
To null his numbers, and to blast his crown.
Few live the life immortal : he ensures
His fame's long life who strives to set up yours.

Upon Himself.

THOU'RT hence removing, like a shepherd's tent,
And walk thou must the way that others went :
Fall thou must first, then rise to life with these
Marked in thy book for faithful witnesses.

Hope Well and Have Well ; or, Fair after Foul Weather.

WHAT though the heaven be lowering now,
And look with a contracted brow ?
We shall discover, by-and-by,
A repurgation of the sky ;
And when those clouds away are driven,
Then will appear a cheerful heaven.

Upon Love.

I HELD Love's head while it did ache ;
  But so it chanced to be,
The cruel pain did his forsake,
  And forthwith came to me.

Ah me ! how shall my grief be stilled ?
  Or where else shall we find
One like to me, who must be killed
  For being too, too kind ?

To his Kinswoman, Mrs. Penelope Wheeler.

NEXT is your lot, fair, to be numbered one
Here, in my book's canonization ;
Late you come in, but you a saint shall be
In chief, in this poetic liturgy.

Another upon Her.

FIRST, for your shape, the curious cannot show
Any one part that 's dissonant in you ;
And 'gainst your chaste behaviour there's no plea,
Since you are known to be Penelope.
Thus fair and clean you are, although there be
A mighty strife 'twixt form and chastity.

Cross and Pile.

FAIR and foul days trip cross and pile ; the fair
Far less in number than our foul days are.

To the Lady Crew, upon the Death of her Child.

WHY, Madam, will ye longer weep,
When as your baby 's lulled asleep,
And, pretty child, feels now no more
Those pains it lately felt before ?
All now is silent ; groans are fled ;
Your child lies still, yet is not dead ;
But rather, like a flower hid here,
To spring again another year.

His Winding-sheet.

COME thou, who art the wine and wit
      Of all I've writ ;
The grace, the glory, and the best
      Piece of the rest ;
Thou art of what I did intend
      The all and end ;

And what was made, was made to meet
    Thee, thee my sheet ;
Come then, and be to my chaste side
    Both bed and bride.
We two, as relics left, will have
    One rest, one grave ;
And, hugging close, we will not fear
    Lust entering here.
Where all desires are dead or cold,
    As is the mould ;
And all affections are forgot,
    Or trouble not.
Here, here the slaves and prisoners be
    From shackles free,
And weeping widows, long oppressed,
    Do here find rest.
The wronged client ends his laws
    Here, and his cause ;
Here those long suits of Chancery lie
    Quiet, or die,
And all Star Chamber bills do cease,
    Or hold their peace.
Here needs no Court for our Request,
    Where all are best,
All wise, all equal, and all just
    Alike i' th' dust.
Nor need we here to fear the frown
    Of court or crown,
Where Fortune bears no sway o'er things,
    There all are kings.
In this securer place we'll keep,
    As lulled asleep ;
Or for a little time we'll lie,
    As robes laid by,
To be another day re-worn,
    Turned, but not torn ;
Or like old testaments engrossed,
    Locked up, not lost ;
And for a while lie here concealed,
    To be revealed
Next, at that great Platonic Year,
    And then meet here.

To Mistress Mary Willand.

ONE more by thee, Love, and Desert have sent,
T' enspangle this expansive firmament.
O flame of beauty, come, appear, appear,
A Virgin taper, ever shining here.

Change gives Content.

WHAT now we like, anon we disapprove ;
The new successor drives away old love.

Upon Magot, a Frequenter of Ordinaries.

MAGOT frequents those houses of good cheer,
Talks most, eats most, of all the feeders there.
He raves through lean, he rages through the fat ;
What gets the master of the meal by that ?
He who with talking can devour so much,
How would he eat were not his hindrance such.

On Himself.

BORN I was to meet with age,
And to walk life's pilgrimage.
Much, I know, of time is spent,
Tell I can't what's resident.
Howsoever, cares adieu !
I'll have nought to say to you ;
But I'll spend my coming hours,
Drinking wine, and crowned with flowers.

Fortune Favours.

FORTUNE did never favour one
Fully, without exception ;
Though free she be, there's something yet
Still wanting to her favourite.

To Phillis to Love, and Live with Him.

LIVE, live with me, and thou shalt see
The pleasures I'll prepare for thee ;
What sweets the country can afford
Shall bless thy bed, and bless thy board.
The soft sweet moss shall be thy bed,
With crawling woodbine overspread ;
By which the silver-shedding streams
Shall gently melt thee into dreams.
Thy clothing next shall be a gown
Made of the fleece's purest down ;
The tongues of kids shall be thy meat,
Their milk thy drink, and thou shalt eat
The paste of filberts for thy bread,
With cream of cowslips buttered.
Thy feasting-tables shall be hills
With daisies spread, and daffodils ;

Where thou shalt sit, and, redbreast by,
For meat shall give thee melody.
I'll give thee chains and carcanets
Of primroses and violets.
A bag and bottle thou shalt have,
That richly wrought, and this as brave ;
So that as either shall express
The wearer's no mean shepherdess.
At shearing-time, and yearly wakes,
When Themilis his pastime makes,
There thou shalt be, and be the wit,
Nay, more, the feast and grace of it.
On holy days, when virgins meet
To dance the hayes with nimble feet ;
Thou shalt come forth, and then appear
The Queen of Roses for that year ;
And having danced, 'bove all the best,
Carry the garland from the rest.
In wicker baskets maids shall bring
To thee, my dearest shepherdling,
The blushing apple, bashful pear,
And shame-faced plum, all simpering there.
Walk in the groves, and thou shalt find
The name of Phillis in the rind
Of every straight and smooth-skin tree ;
Where, kissing that, I'll twice kiss thee.
To thee a sheep-hook I will send,
Bepranked with ribbons, to this end,
This, this alluring hook might be
Less for to catch a sheep than me.
Thou shalt have possets, wassails fine,
Not made of ale, but spiced wine ;
To make thy maids and self free mirth,
All sitting near the glittering hearth.
Thou shalt have ribbons, roses, rings,
Gloves, garters, stockings, shoes, and strings
Of winning colours, that shall move
Others to lust, but me to love.
These, nay, and more, thine own shall be,
If thou wilt love and live with me.

To his Kinswoman, Mistress Susanna Herrick.

WHEN I consider, dearest, thou dost stay
But here awhile, to languish and decay ;
Like to these garden glories, which here be
The flowery sweet resemblances of thee :
With grief of heart, methinks, I thus do cry,
Would thou hast ne'er been born, or might'st not die.

Upon Mistress Susanna Southwell, her Checks.

RARE are thy checks, Susanna, which do show
Ripe cherries smiling, while that others blow.

Upon her Eyes.

CLEAR are her eyes,
Like purest skies ;
Discovering from thence
A baby there
That turns each sphere.
Like an intelligence.

Upon her Feet.

HER pretty feet
Like snails did creep
A little out, and then,
As if they playéd at bo-peep,
Did soon draw in again.

To his Honoured Friend, Sir John Mince.

FOR civil, clean, and circumcised wit,
And for the comely carriage of it,
Thou art the man, the only man best known.
Marked for the true wit of a million ;
From whom we 'll reckon wit came in, but since
The calculation of thy birth, brave Mince.

Upon his Grey Hairs.

FLY me not, though I be grey ;
Lady, this I know you'll say,
Better look the roses red
When with white commingled.
Black your hairs are ; mine are white ;
This begets the more delight,
When things meet most opposite ;
As in pictures we descry
Venus standing, Vulcan by.

Accusation.

IF Accustation only can draw blood,
None shall be guiltless, be he ne'er so good

Pride Allowable in Poets.

As thou deserv'st, be proud ; then gladly let
The Muse give thee the Delphic coronet.

A Vow to Minerva.

GODDESS, I begin an art ;
Come thou in with thy best part,
For to make the texture lie
Each way smooth and civilly ;
And a broad-faced owl shall be
Offered up with vows to thee.

On Jone.

JONE would go tell her hairs ; and well she might,
Having but seven in all—three black, four white.

Discord not Disadvantageous.

FORTUNE no higher project can devise,
Then to sow discord 'mongst the enemies.

Ill Goverment.

PREPOSTEROUS is that government, and rude,
When kings obey the wilder multitude.

To Marigolds.

GIVE way, and be ye ravished by the sun,
And hang the head whenas the act is done ;
Spread as he spreads ; wax less as he does wane :
And as he shuts, close up to maids again.

To Dianeme.

GIVE me one kiss,
    And no more :
If so be this
    Makes you poor,
To enrich you
    I'll restore
For that one, two
    Thousand score.

To Julia, the Flaminica Dialis ; or, Queen-Priest.

THOU know'st, my Julia, that it is thy turn
This morning's incense to prepare and burn

The chaplet and inarculum here be,
With the white vestures all attending thee.
This day the Queen-Priest thou art made, to appease
Love for our very many trespasses.
One chief transgression is, among the rest,
Because with flowers her temple was not dressed ;
The next, because her altars did not shine
With daily fires ; the last, neglect of wine
For which, her wrath is gone forth to consume
Us all, unless preserved by thy perfume,
Take then thy censer ; put in fire, and thus,
O pious Priestess ! make a peace for us.
For our neglect, Love did our death decree ;
That we escape, Redemption comes by thee.

Anacreontic.

BORN I was to be old,
  And for to die here ;
After that, in the mould
  Long for to lie here.
But before that day comes,
  Still I be bousing ;
For I know in the tombs
  There's no carousing.

Meat without Mirth.

EATEN I have ; and though I had good cheer,
I did not sup, because no friends were there.
Where mirth and friends are absent when we dine
Or sup, there wants the incense and the wine.

Large Bounds do but Bury Us.

ALL things o'erruled are here by chance ;
The greatest man's inheritance,
Where'er the lucky lot doth fall,
Serves but for place of burial.

Upon Ursley.

URSLEY, she thinks those velvet patches grace
The candid temples of her comely face ;
But he will say, whoe'er those circlets seeth,
They be but signs of Ursley's hollow teeth.

An Ode to Sir Clipseby Crew.

HERE we securely live, and eat
      The cream of meat ;

And keep eternal fires,
By which we sit, and do divine
As wine
And rage inspires.

If full, we charm ; then call upon
Anacreon
To grace the frantic thyrse :
And having drunk, we raise a shout
Throughout,
To praise his verse.

Then cause we Horace to be read,
Which sung or said,
A goblet, to the brim,
Of lyric wine, both swelled and crowned,
A round
We quaff to him.

Thus, thus we live, and spend the hours
In wine and flowers ;
And make the frolic year,
The month, the week, the instant day,
To stay
The longer here.

Come then, brave Knight, and see the cell
Wherein I dwell,
And my enchantments too;
Which love and noble freedom is,
And this
Shall fetter you.

Take horse, and come; or be so kind
To send your mind,
Though but in numbers few,
And I shall think I have the heart,
Or part,
Of Clipseby Crew.

To his Worthy Kinsman, Mr. Stephen Soame.

NOR is my number full, till I inscribe
Thee, sprightly Soame, one of my righteous tribe :
A tribe of one lip, leaven, and of one
Civil behaviour and religion :
A stock of saints, where every one doth wear
A stole of white, and canonized here ;
Among which holies be thou ever known.
Brave kinsman, marked out with the whiter stone
Which seals thy glory, since I do prefer
Thee here in my eternal calendar.

To his Tomb-maker.

Go I must; when I am gone,
Write but this upon my stone :
Chaste I lived, without a wife,
That's the story of my life.
Strewings need none, every flower
Is in this world, bachelor.

Great Spirits Survive.

OUR mortal parts may wrapt in cere-cloths lie ;
Great spirits never with their bodies die.

None Free from Fault.

OUT of the world he must, who once comes in ;
No man exempted is from death or sin.

Upon Himself being Buried.

LET me sleep this night away,
Till the dawning of the day ;
Then at th' opening of mine eyes
I and all the world shall rise.

Pity to the Prostrate.

TIS worse then barbarous cruelty to show
No part of pity on a conquered foe.

His Content in the Country.

HERE, here I live with what my board
Can with the smallest cost afford ;
Though ne'er so mean the viands be,
They well content my Prue and me :
Or pea or bean, or wort or beet,
Whatever comes, Content makes sweet.
Here we rejoice because no rent
We pay for our poor tenement,
Wherein we rest, and never fear
The landlord or the usurer.
The quarter-day does ne'er affright
Our peaceful slumbers in the night ;
We eat our own, and batten more,
Because we feed on no man's score ;
But pity those whose flanks grow great
Swelled with the lard of others' meat.
We bless our fortunes when we see
Our own beloved privacy ;
And like our living, where we're known
To very few, or else to none.

The Credit of the Conqueror.

HE who commends the vanquished, speaks the power,
And glorifies the worthy conquerer.

On Himself.

SOME parts may perish, die thou canst not all ;
The most of thee shall 'scape the funeral.

Upon One-eyed Broomsted.—Epigram.

BROOMSTED a lameness got by cold and beer,
And to the Bath went to be cured there;
His feet were helped, and left his crutch behind,
But home returned, as he went forth, half-blind.

The Fairies.

IF ye will with Mab find grace,
Set each platter in his place ;
Rake the fire up, and get
Water in, ere sun be set.
Wash your pails and cleanse your dairies,
Sluts are loathsome to the fairies ;
Sweep your house ; who doth not so,
Mab will pinch her by the toe.

To his Honoured Friend, Mr. John Weare, Counsellor.

DID I or love or could I others draw
To the indulgence of the rugged Law ;
The first foundation of that zeal should be
By reading all her paragraphs in thee,
Who does so fitly with the Laws unite,
As if you two were one hermaphrodite.
Nor courts thou her because she's well attended
With wealth, but for those ends she was intended :
Which were, and still her offices are known,
Law is, to give to every one his own ;
To shore the feeble up against the strong,
To shield the stranger and the poor from wrong.
This was the founder's grave and good intent :
To keep the outcast in his tenement ;
To free the orphan from that wolf-like man,
Who is his butcher more than guardian ;
To dry the widow's tears, and stop her swoons,
By pouring balm and oil into her wounds.

This was the old way, and 'tis yet thy course
To keep those pious principles in force.
Modest I will be, but one word I'll say,
Like to a sound that's vanishing away,
Sooner the inside of thy hand shall grow
Hisped and hairy, ere thy palm shall know
A postern-bribe took, or a forked fee
To fetter justice, when she might be free.
Eggs I'll not shave; but yet, brave man, if I
Was destined forth to golden sovereignty,
A prince I'd be, that I might thee prefer
To be my counsel both and chancellor.

The Watch.

MAN is a watch, wound up at first, but never
Wound up again; once down, he's down for ever.
The watch once down, all motions then do cease;
The man's pulse stopped, all passions sleep in peace.

Lines have their Linings, and Books their Buckram.

As in our clothes, so likewise he who looks,
Shall find much farcing buckram in our books.

Art above Nature.—To Julia.

WHEN I behold a forest spread
With silken trees upon thy head;
And when I see that other dress
Of flowers set in comeliness;
When I behold another grace
In the ascent of curious lace,
Which, like a pinnacle doth show
The top, and the top-gallant too;
Then, when I see thy tresses bound
Into an oval, square, or round,
And knit in knots far more than I
Can tell by tongue, or true love-tie;
Next, when those lawny films I see
Play with a wild civility,
And all those hairy silks to flow,
Alluring me, and tempting so,
I must confess, mine eye and heart
Dotes less on Nature than on Art.

Upon his Kinswoman, Mistress Bridget Herrick.

SWEET Bridget blushed, and therewithal,
Fresh blossoms from her cheeks did fall.
I thought at first 'twas but a dream,
Till after I had handled them,
And smelt them ; then they smelt to me
As blossoms of the almond tree.

Upon Love.

I PLAYED with Love as with the fire
   The wanton satyr did ;
Nor did I know, or could descry,
   What under there was hid.

That satyr he but burnt his lips ;
   But mine 's the greater smart,
For, kissing Love's dissembling chips,
   The fire scorched my heart.

Upon a Comely and Curious Maid.

IF men can say that beauty dies,
Marbles will swear that here it lies.
If, reader, then thou canst forbear
In public loss to shed a tear,
The dew of grief upon this stone
Will tell thee, pity thou hast none.

Upon the Loss of his Finger.

ONE of the five straight branches of my hand
Is lopped already ; and the rest but stand
Expecting when to fall ; which soon will be ;
First dies the leaf, the bough next, next the tree.

Upon Irene.

ANGRY if Irene be
But a minute's life with me,
Such a fire I espy
Walking in and out her eye,
As at once I freeze and fry.

Upon Electra's Tears.

UPON her cheeks she wept, and from those showers
Sprang up a sweet nativity of flowers.

Upon Tooly.

THE eggs of pheasants wry-nosed Tooly sells,
But ne'er so much as licks the speckled shells ;
Only, if one prove addled, that he eats
With superstition, as the cream of meats ;
The cock and hen he feeds, but not a bone
He ever picked, as yet, of any one.

A Hymn to the Graces.

WHEN I love, as some have told,
Love I shall when I am old,
O ye graces ! make me fit
For the welcoming of it.
Clean my rooms, as temples be,
To entertain that deity ;
Give me words wherewith to woo,
Suppling and successful too ;
Winning pastures, and withal,
Manners each way musical ;
Sweetness to allay my sour
And unsmooth behaviour :
For I know you have the skill
Vines to prune, though not to kill ;
And of any wood ye see,
You can make a Mercury.

To Silvia.

No more, my Silvia, do I mean to pray
For those good days that ne'er will come away.
I want belief ; O gentle Silvia ! be
The patient saint, and send up vows for me.

The Poet hath Lost his Pipe.

I CANNOT pipe as I was wont to do,
Broke is my reed, hoarse is my singing too ;
My wearied oat I'll hang upon the tree,
And give it to the sylvan deity.

True Friendship.

WILT thou my true friend be ?
Then love not mine, but me.

The Apparition of his Mistress calling him
to Elysium.

Desunt nonnulla——

COME then, and like two doves with silvery wings,
Let our souls fly to the shades, where ever springs
Sit smiling in the meads; where balm and oil,
Roses and cassia, crown the untilled soil;
Where no disease reigns, or infection comes
To blast the air, but ambergris and gums.
This, that, and evry thicket doth transpire
More sweet then storax from the hallowed fire;
Where every tree a wealthy issue bears
Of fragrant apples, blushing plums, or pears,
And all the shrubs, with sparkling spangles, show
Like morning sunshine, tinselling the dew.
Here in green meadows sits eternal May,
Purfling the margents, while perpetual day
So double gilds the air, as that no night
Can ever rust the enamel of the light:
Here naked younglings, handsome striplings, run
Their goals for virgins' kisses; which when done,
Then unto dancing forth the learned round
Commixed they meet, with endless roses crowned.
And here we'll sit on primrose-banks, and see
Love's chorus led by Cupid; and we'll be
Two loving followers too unto the grove
Where poets sing the stories of our love:
There thou shalt hear divine Musæus sing
Of Hero and Leander; then I'll bring
Thee to the stand, where honoured Homer reads
His Odysseys and his high Iliads;
About whose throne the crowd of poets throng
To hear the incantation of his tongue:
To Linus, then to Pindar; and that done,
I'll bring thee, Herrick, to Anacreon,
Quaffing his full-crowned bowls of burning wine,
And in his raptures speaking lines of thine,
Like to his subject; and as his frantic
Looks show him truly Bacchanalian like,
Besmear'd with grapes, welcome he shall thee thither,
Where both may rage, both drink and dance together.
Then stately Virgil, witty Ovid, by
Whom fair Corinna sits, and doth comply
With ivory wrists his laureat head, and steeps
His eye in dew of kisses while he sleeps;
Then soft Catullus, sharp-fanged Martial
And towering Lucan, Horace, Juvenal,

And snaky rods; these, and those whom rage,
Dropped from the jealous ears of heaven, filled t' engage
All times unto their frenzies; thou shalt there
Behold them in a spacious theatre.
Among which glories, crowned with sacred bays
And flattering ivy, to recite their plays,
Beaumont and Fletcher, swans, to whom all ears
Listen, while they, like sirens in their spheres,
Sing their Evadne : and still more for thee
There yet remains to know than thou canst see
By glimmering of a fancy; do but come,
And there I'll show thee that capacious room
In which thy father, Jonson, now is placed,
As in a globe of radiant fire and graced
To be in that orb crowned, that doth include
Those prophets of the former magnitude,
And he one chief.   But hark, I hear the cock,
The bellman of the night, proclaim the clock
Of late struck one ; and now I see the prime
Of daybreak from the pregnant east, 'tis time
I vanish ; more I had to say,
But night determines here.   Away !

Life is the Body's Light.

LIFE is the body's light ; which once declining,
Those crimson clouds i' th' cheeks and lips leave shining ;
Those counter-changed tabbies in the air,
The sun once set, all of one colour are :
So, when death comes, Fresh Tinctures lose their place,
And dismal darkness then doth smutch the face.

Upon Urles.—Epigram.

URLES had the gout so that he could not stand ;
Then from his feet it shifted to his hand ;
When 'twas in 's feet his charity was small ;
Now 'tis in 's hand, he gives no alms at all.

Upon Frank.

FRANK ne'er wore silk, she swears : but I reply,
She now wears silk to hide her bloodshot eye.

Love Lightly Pleased.

LET fair or foul my mistress be,
Or low, or tall, she pleaseth me ;
Or let her walk, or stand, or sit,
The posture hers, I'm pleased with it.

Or let her tongue be still, or stir,
Graceful is everything from her;
Or let her grant, or else deny,
My love will fit each history.

The Primrose.

Ask me why I send you here
This sweet Infanta of the year?
Ask me why I send to you
This Primrose, thus bepearled with dew?
I will whisper to your ears,
The sweets of love are mixed with tears.

Ask me why this flower does show
So yellow-green, and sickly too?
Ask me why the stalk is weak,
And bending, yet it doth not break?
I will answer, these discover
What fainting hopes are in a lover.

The Tithe.—To the Bride.

If nine times you your bridegroom kiss,
The tenth you know the parson's is;
Pay then your tithe; and doing thus,
Prove in your bride-bed numerous.
If children you have ten, Sir John
Won't for his tenth part ask you one.

A Frolic.

Bring me my rose-buds, drawer come
So while I thus sit crowned,
I'll drink the aged Cecubum
Until the roof turn round.

Change Common to All.

All things subjected are to Fate;
Whom this morn sees most fortunate.
The evening sees in poor estate.

To Julia.

The saints-bell calls; and Julia, I must read
The proper lessons for the saints now dead;
To grace which service, Julia, there shall be
One holy collect said or sung for thee.

Dead when thou art, dear Julia, thou shalt have
A trental sung by virgins o'er thy grave ;
Meantime we two will sing the dirge of these,
Who, dead, deserve our best remembrances.

No Luck in Love.

I DO love I know not what,
Sometimes this and sometimes that ;
All conditions I aim at.

But, as luckless, I have yet
Many shrewd disasters met,
To gain her whom I would get.

Therefore, now I'll love no more,
As I've doted heretofore :
He who must be, shall be poor.

A Charm, or an Allay for Love.

IF so be a toad be laid
In a sheep's skin newly flayed,
And that tied to man, 'twill sever
Him and his affections ever.

To his Brother-in-Law, Master John Wingfield.

FOR being comely, consonant, and free
To most of men, but most of all to me ;
For so decreeing, that thy clothes' expense
Keeps still within a just circumference ;
Then for contriving so to load thy board
As that the messes ne'er o'er-laid the Lord ;
Next, for ordaining that thy words not swell
To any one unsober syllable ;
These I could praise thee for, beyond another,
Wert thou a Wingfield only, not a brother.

The Headache.

MY head doth ache,
O Sappho ! take
   Thy fillet,
And bind the pain ;
Or bring some bane
   To kill it.

But less that part,
Than my poor heart,
   Now is sick :
One kiss from thee
Will counsel it,
   And physic.

On Himself.

LIVE by thy muse thou shalt, when others die
Leaving no fame to long posterity ;
When monarchies transhifted are, and gone,
Here shall endure thy vast dominion.

Upon a Maid.

HENCE a blessed soul is fled,
Leaving here the body dead ;
Which, since here they can't combine,
For the saint, we'll keep the shrine.

Upon Spalt.

OF pushes Spalt has such a knotty race,
He needs a tucker for to burl his face.

Of Horne, a Combmaker.

HORNE sells to others teeth, but has not one
To grace his own gums, or of box or bone.

Upon the Troublesome Times.

O TIMES most bad !
Without the scope
Of hope
Of better to be had !

Where shall I go,
Or whither run
To shun
This public overthrow ?

No places are,
This I am sure,
Secure
In this our wasting war.

Some storms wave past ;
Yet we must all
Down fall,
And perish at the last.

Cruelty Base in Commanders.

NOTHING can be more loathsome than to see
Power conjoined with Nature's cruelty.

Little and Loud.

LITTLE you are ; for woman's sake be proud ;
For my sake next, though little, be not loud.

Shipwreck.

HE who has suffered shipwreck, fears to sail
Upon the seas, though with a gentle gale.

Pains without Profit.

A LONG life's day I've taken pains
For very little or no gains ;
The evening's come here now I'll stop,
And work no more, but shut my shop.

To his Book.

BE bold, my book, nor be abashed, or fear
The cutting thumb-nail, or the brow severe ;
But by the Muses swear, all here is good,
If but well read—or, ill read, understood.

His Prayer to Ben Jonson.

WHEN I a verse shall make,
  Know I have prayed thee,
For old religion's sake,
  Saint Ben, to aid me.

Make the way smooth for me,
  When I, thy Herrick,
Honouring thee, on my knee
  Offer my Lyric.

Candles I'il give to thee,
  And a new altar ;
And thou, Saint Ben, shalt be
  Writ in my psalter.

Poverty and Riches.

GIVE want her welcome, if she comes ; we find
Riches to be but burthens to the mind.

Again.

WHO with a little cannot be content
Endures an everlasting punishment.

The Covetous still Captives.

LET'S live with that small pittance that we have;
Who covets more is evermore a slave.

Laws.

WHEN laws full power have to sway, we see
Little or no part there of tyranny.

Of Love.

I'LL get me hence,
Because no fence
Or fort that I can make here,
But Love by charms,
Or else by arms,
Will storm, or starving take here.

To his Muse.

Go woo young Charles no more to look
Than but to read this in my book,
How Herrick begs, if that he can-
Not like the Muse, to love the man,
Who by the shepherds, sung long since,
The star-led birth of Charles the Prince.

The Bad Season makes the Poet Sad.

DULL to myself, and almost dead to these
My many fresh and fragrant mistresses;
Lost to all music now, since everything
Puts on the semblance here of sorrowing;
Sick is the land to the heart; and doth endure
More dangerous faintings by her desperate cure.
But if that golden age would come again,
And Charles here rule, as he before did reign;
If smooth and unperplexed the seasons were,
As when the sweet Maria lived here;
I should delight to have my curls half drowned
In Syrian dews, and head with roses crowned:
And once more yet, ere I am laid out dead,
Knock at a star with my exalted head.

To Vulcan.

THY sooty godhead I desire
Still to be ready with thy fire ;
That should my book despised be,
Acceptance it might find of thee.

Like Pattern, like People.

THIS is the height of justice, that to do
Thyself, which thou put'st other men unto.
As great men lead, the meaner follow on,
Or to the good or evil action.

Purposes.

No wrath of men, or rage of seas
Can shake a just man's purposes ;
No threats of tyrants, or the grim
Visage of them, can alter him ;
But what he doth at first intend,
That he holds firmly to the end.

To the Maids to Walk Abroad.

COME, sit we under yonder tree,
Where merry as the maids we'll be ;
And as on primroses we sit,
We'll venture, if we can, at wit,
If not, at draw-gloves we will play,
So spend some minutes of the day ;
Or else spin out the thread of sands,
Playing at questions and commands,
Or tell what strange tricks love can do,
By quickly making one of two.
Thus we will sit and talk, but tell
No cruel truths of Philomel,
Or Phillis, whom hard fate forced on
To kill herself for Demophon
But fables we'll relate — how Jove
Put on all shapes to get a love,
As now a satyr, then a swan,
A bull but then, and now a man.
Next, we will act how young men woo,
And sigh and kiss as lovers do ;
And talk of brides, and who shall make
That wedding-smock, this bridal cake,
That dress, this sprig, that leaf, this vine,
That smooth and silken columbine.

This done, we'll draw lots who shall buy
And gild the bays and rosemary;
What posies for our wedding rings,
What gloves we'll give, and ribbonings;
And smiling at ourselves, decree
Who then the joining priest shall be;
What short sweet prayers shall be said,
And how the posset shall be made
With cream of lilies, not of kine,
And maiden's blush for spiced wine.
Thus having talked, we'll next commend
A kiss to each, and so we'll end.

His own Epitaph.

As wearied pilgrims, once possessed
Of longed-for lodging, go to rest;
So I, now having rid my way,
Fix here my buttoned staff and stay.
Youth, I confess, hath me misled,
But age hath brought me right to bed.

The Night-piece.—To Julia.

HER eyes the glow-worm lend thee,
The shooting stars attend thee;
   And the elves also,
   Whose little eyes glow,
Like the sparks of fire, befriend thee.

No Will-o'-the-Wisp mislight thee,
Nor snake or slow-worm bite thee;
   But on, on thy way,
   Not making a stay,
Since ghost there's none to affright thee.

Let not the dark thee cumber;
What though the moon does slumber?
   The stars of the night
   Will lend thee their light,
Like tapers clear, without number.

Then, Julia, let me woo thee,
Thus, thus to come unto me;
   And when I shall meet
   Thy silvery feet,
My soul I'll pour into thee.

To Sir Clipseby Crew.

GIVE me wine, and give me meat,
To create in me a heat,
That my pulses high may beat.

Cold and hunger never yet
Could a noble verse beget ;
But your bowls with sack replete.

Give me these, my knight, and try
In a minute's space how I
Can run mad, and prophesy.

Then if any piece proves new
And rare, I'll say, my dearest Crew,
It was full inspired by you.

Good Luck not Lasting.

IF well the dice run, let's applaud the cast ;
The happy fortune will not always last.

A Kiss.

WHAT is a kiss? Why this, as some approve,
The sure sweet cement, glue, and lime of love.

Glory.

I MAKE no haste to have my numbers read ;
Seldom comes glory till a man be dead.

Poets.

WANTONS we are ; and though our words be such,
Our lives do differ from our lines by much.

No Despite to the Dead.

REPROACH we may the living, not the dead ;
'Tis cowardice to bite the buried.

To his Verses.

What will ye, my poor orphans, do,
When I must leave the world and you ?

Who'll give ye then a shelt'ring shed,
Or credit ye, when I am dead ?
Who'll let ye by their fire sit,
Although ye have a stock of wit
Already coined to pay for it ?
I cannot tell ; unless there be
Some race of old humanity
Left, of the large heart and long hand,
Alive, as noble Westmoreland,
Or gallant Newark ; which brave two
May fost'ring fathers be to you.
If not, expect to be no less
Ill-used than babes left fatherless.

His Charge to Julia at his Death.

DEAREST of thousands, now the time draws near,
That with my lines my life must full stop here ;
Cut off thy hairs, and let thy tears be shed
Over my turf, when I am buried.
Then for effusions, let none wanting be,
Or other rites that do belong to me ;
As love shall help thee, when thou dost go hence
Unto thy everlasting residence.

Upon Love.

IN a dream, Love bade me go
To the galleys there to row ;
In the vision I asked why ?
Love as briefly did reply :
'Twas better there to toil, than prove
The turmoils they endure that love.
I awoke, and then I knew
What Love said was too, too true :
Henceforth therefore I will be
As from love, from trouble free :
None pities him that's in the snare,
And warned before, would not beware.

The Cobbler's Catch.

COME sit we by the fireside
And roundly drink we here,
Till that we see our cheeks ale-dyed,
And noses tanned with beer.

Upon Grudgings.

GRUDGINGS turns bread to stones, when to the poor
He gives an alms, and chides them from his door.

Connubii Flores ; or, the Well-wishes at Weddings.

Chorus Sacerdotum.

FROM the temple to your home
May a thousand blessings come ;
And a sweet concurring stream
Of all joys, to join with them !

Chorus Juvenum.

Happy day,
Make no long stay
Here
In thy sphere,
But give thy place to-night,
That she
As thee
May be
Partaker of the sight.
And since it was thy care
To see the younglings wed,
'Tis fit that night the pair
Should see safe brought to bed.

Chorus Senum.

Go to your banquet then, but use delight
So as to rise still with an appetite :
Love is a thing most nice, and must be fed
To such a height, but never surfeited.
What is beyond the mean is ever ill ;
'Tis best to feed love, but not over-fill :
Go then discreetly to the bed of pleasure,
And this remember, virtue keeps the measure.

Chorus Virginum.

Lucky signs we have descried
To encourage on the bride ;
And to these we have espied,
Not a kissing Cupid flies
Here about, but has his eyes,
To imply your love is wise.

Chorus Pastorum.

Here we present a fleece
To make a piece

Of cloth ;
Nor fair, must you be loth
Your finger to apply
To housewifery :
Then, then begin
To spin ;
And, sweetling, mark you, what a web will come
Into your chests, drawn by your painful thumb.

Chorus Matronarum.

Set you to your wheel and wax
Rich by the ductile wool and flax !
Yarn is an income, and the housewife's thread
The larders fills with meat, the bin with bread.

Chorus Senum.

Let wealth come in by comely thrift,
And not by any sordid shift ;
'Tis haste
Makes waste ;
Extremes have still their fault ;
The softest fire makes the sweetest malt ;
Who gripes too hard the dry and slippery sand,
Holds none at all, or little in his hand.

Chorus Virginum.

Goddess of pleasure, youth, and peace,
Give them the blessing of increase ;
And thou, Lucina, that dost hear
The vows of those that children bear;
When as her April hour draws near,
Be thou then propitious there.

Chorus Juvenum.

Far hence be all speech that may anger move ;
Sweet words must nourish soft and gentle love.

Chorus Omnium.

Live in the love of doves, and having told
The raven's years, go hence more ripe than old.

To his Lovely Mistresses.

ONE night i' th' year, my dearest beauties, come
And bring those dew-drink offerings to my tomb ;
When thence ye see my reverend ghost to rise,
And there to lick the effused sacrifice,
Though paleness be the livery that I wear,
Look ye not wan or colourless for fear ;

Trust me, I will not hurt ye, or once show
The least grim look, or cast a frown on you ;
Nor shall the tapers, when I'm there, burn blue.
This I may do, perhaps, as I glide by,
Cast on my girls a glance, and loving eye ;
Or fold mine arms, and sigh, because I've lost
The world so soon, and in it you the most :
Than these, no fears more on your fancies fall,
Though then I smile, and speak no words at all.

Upon Love.

A CRYSTAL vial Cupid brought,
  Which had a juice in it ;
Of which who drank, he said, no thought
  Of love he should admit.

I, greedy of the prize, did drink,
  And emptied soon the glass,
Which burnt me so, that I do think
  The fire of hell it was.

Give me my earthen cups again,
  The crystal I contemn ;
Which though enchased with pearls, contain
  A deadly draught in them.

And thou, O Cupid ! come not to
  My threshold, since I see,
For all I have, or else can do,
  Thou still wilt cozen me

The Beggar to Mab, the Fairy Queen.

PLEASE, your grace, from out your store
Give an alms to one that's poor.
That your mickle may have more.
Black I'm grown for want of meat,
Give me then an ant to eat,
Or the cleft ear of a mouse
Over-soured in drink of souce ;
Or, sweet lady, reach to me
The abdomen of a bee ;
Or commend a cricket's hip,
Or his huckson, to my scrip ;
Give for bread a little bit
Of a pease that 'gins to chit,
And my ful thanks take for it.
Flour of furze-balls, that's too good
For a man in needy-hood ;

But the meal of mill-dust can
Well content a craving man ;
Any oats the elves refuse
Well will serve the beggar's use.
But if this may seem too much
For an alms, then give me such
Little bits that nestle there
In the prisoner's pannier.
So a blessing light upon
You and mighty Oberon ;
That your plenty last till when
I return your alms again.

An End Decreed.

LET'S be jocund while we may ;
All things have an ending day ;
And when once the work is done,
Fates revolve no flax that have spun.

Upon a Child.

HERE a pretty baby lies
Sung asleep with lullabies ;
Pray be silent, and not stir
The easy earth that covers her.

Painting sometimes Permitted.

IF Nature do deny
Colours, let Art supply.

Farewell Frost; or, Welcome Spring.

FLED are the frosts, and now the fields appear
Reclothed in fresh and verdant diaper ;
Thawed are the snows, and now the lusty Spring
Gives to each mead a neat enamelling ;
The palms put forth their gems, and every tree
Now swaggers in her leafy gallantry.
The while the Daulian minstrel sweetly sings
With warbling notes, her Tercan sufferings,
What gentle winds perspire ! as if here
Never had been the northern plunderer,
To strip the trees and fields, to their distress,
Leaving them to a pitied nakedness.
And look how when a frantic storm doth tear
A stubborn oak or elm, long growing there,
But, lulled to calmness, then succeeds a breeze
That scarcely stirs the nodding leaves of trees ;

So when this war, which tempest-like doth spoil
Our salt, our corn, our honey, wine and oil,
Falls to a temper, and doth mildly cast
His inconsiderate frenzy off at last,
The gentle dove may, when those turmoils cease,
Bring in her bill, once more, the branch of peace.

The Hag.

THE hag is astride
This night for to ride,
The devil and she together ;
    Through thick and through thin,
    Now out and then in,
Though ne'er so foul be the weather.

A thorn or a burr
She takes for a spur ;
With a lash of a bramble she rides now,
    Through brakes and through briars,
    O'er ditches and mires,
She follows the spirit that guides now.

No beast, for his food,
Dares now range the wood,
But hushed in his lair he lies lurking ;
    While mischiefs by these,
    On land and on seas,
At noon of night are a-working.

The storm will arise
And trouble the skies
This night ; and, more for the wonder,
    The ghost from the tomb
    Affrighted shall come,
Called out by the clap of the thunder.

Upon an Old Man, a Residentiary.

TREAD, sirs, as lightly as ye can
Upon the grave of this old man.
Twice forty, bating but one year,
And thrice three weeks, he lived here ;
Whom gentle fate translated hence
To a more happy residence.
Yet, reader, let me tell thee this,
Which from his ghost a promise is,
If here ye will some few tears shed,
He'll never haunt ye now he's dead.

Upon Tears.

TEARS, though they're here below the sinner's brine,
Above they are the angels' spiced wine.

Physicians.

PHYSICIANS fight not against men, but these
Combat for men by conquering the disease.

The Primitiæ to Parents.

OUR household gods our parents be,
And manners good require, that we
The first-fruits give to them, who gave
Us hands to get what here we have.

Upon Cob.—Epigram.

COB clouts his shoes, and as the story tells,
His thumb-nails pared afford him sparables.

Upon Lucy.—Epigram.

SOUND teeth has Lucy, pure as pearl, and small,
With mellow lips, and luscious therewithal.

To Silvia.

I AM holy while I stand
Circum-crossed by thy pure hand ;
But when that is gone, again
I, as others, am profane.

To his Closet Gods.

WHEN I go hence, ye closet gods, I fear
Never again to have ingression here :
Where I have had, whatever things could be
Pleasant and precious to my muse and me.
Besides rare sweets, I had a book which none
Could read the intext but myself alone ;
About the cover of this book there went
A curious, comely, clean compartlement ;
And in the midst, to grace it more, was set
A blushing pretty-peeping rubylet ;
But now 'tis closed, and being shut and sealed,
Be it, oh be it never more revealed !
Keep here still, closet gods, 'fore whom I've set
Oblations oft of sweetest marmelet.

A Bacchanalian Verse.

FILL me a mighty bowl
    Up to the brim ;
    That I may drink
Unto my Jonson's soul.

Crown it again, again ;
    And thrice repeat
    That happy heat,
To drink to thee, my Ben.

Well I can quaff, I see,
    To th' number five,
    Or nine, but thrive
In frenzy ne'er like thee.

Long Looked-for Comes at Last.

THOUGH long it be, years may repay the debt;
None loseth that which he in time may get.

To Youth.

DRINK wine, and live here blitheful while ye may ;
The morrow's life too late is, Live to-day.

Never Too Late to Die.

NO man comes late unto that place from whence
Never man yet had a regredience.

A Hymn to the Muses.

O YOU the Virgins Nine,
That do our souls incline
To noble discipline,
Nod to this vow of mine :
Come then, an I now inspire
My viol and my lyre
With your eternal fire,
And make me one entire
Composer in your choir :
Then I'll your altars strew
With roses sweet and new ;
And ever live a true
Acknowledger of you.

On Himself.

I'LL sing no more, nor will I longer write
Of that sweet lady, or that gallant knight ;
I'll sing no more of frosts, snows, dews, and showers ;
No more of groves, meads, springs, and wreaths of flowers ;
I'll write no more, nor will I tell or sing
Of Cupid, and his witty cozening ;
I'll sing no more of death, or shall the grave
No more my dirges and my trentals have.

Upon Joan and Jane.

JOAN is a wench that's painted ;
Joan is a girl that's tainted ;
    Yet Joan she goes
    Like one of those
Whom purity had sainted.

Jane is a girl that's pretty ;
Jane is a wench that's witty ;
    Yet, who would think,
    Her breath does stink,
As so it doth—that's pity.

To Momus.

WHO read'st this book that I have writ,
And canst not mend, but carp at it ;
By all the Muses, thou shalt be
Anathema to it and me.

Ambition.

IN ways to greatness, think on this,
That slippery all ambition is.

The Country Life.

To the Honoured Mr. End. Porter, Groom of the Bedchamber to His Majesty.

SWEET country life, to such unknown
Whose lives are others', not their own,
But, serving courts and cities, be
Less happy less enjoying thee.
Thou never plough'st the ocean's foam
To seek and bring rough pepper home ;
Nor to the Eastern Ind dost rove
To bring from thence the scorched clove ;
Nor, with the loss of thy loved rest,
Bring'st home the ingot from the West :

No, thy ambition's masterpiece
Flies no thought higher than a fleece ;
Or how to pay thy hinds, and clear
All scores, and so to end the year :
But walk'st about thine own dear bounds,
Not envying others' larger grounds,
For well thou know'st, 'tis not the extent
Of land makes life, but sweet content.
When now the cock, the ploughman's horn,
Calls forth the lily-wristed morn,
Then to thy corn-fields thou dost go,
Which, though well soiled, yet thou dost know
That the best compost for the lands
Is the wise master's feet and hands.
There at the plough thou find'st thy team,
With a hind whistling there to them,
And cheer'st them up by singing how
The kingdom's portion is the plough.
This done, then to th' enamelled meads
Thou goest, and as thy foot there treads,
Thou seest a present Godlike power
Imprinted in each herb and flower,
And smell'st the breath of great-eyed kine,
Sweet as the blossoms of the vine.
Here thou behold'st thy large sleek neat
Unto the dewlaps up in meat ;
And as thou look'st, the wanton steer,
The heifer, cow, and ox draw near,
To make a pleasing pastime there.
These seen, thou goest to view thy flocks
Of sheep, safe from the wolf and fox,
And find'st their bellies there as full
Of short sweet grass as backs with wool,
And leav'st them, as they feed and fill,
A shepherd piping on a hill.
For sports, for pageantry, and plays,
Thou hast thy eves and holidays,
On which the young men and maids meet
To exercise their dancing feet,
Tripping the comely country round,
With daffodils and daisies crowned.
Thy wakes, thy quintals, here thou hast,
Thy Maypoles too with garlands graced,
Thy morris-dance, thy Whitsun-ale,
Thy shearing-feast, which never fail,
Thy harvest home, thy wassail bowl,
That's tossed up after fox-i'-th'-hole,
Thy mummeries, thy Twelfthtide kings
And queens, thy Christmas revellings,

Thy nut-brown mirth, thy russet wit,
And no man pays too dear for it.
To these thou hast thy times to go
And trace the hare i' th' treacherous snow;
Thy witty wiles to draw, and get
The lark into the trammel net ;
Thou hast thy cockrood and thy glade
To take the precious pheasant made ;
Thy lime-twigs, snares, and pitfalls then,
To catch the pilfering birds, not men.
O happy life ! if that their good
The husbandmen but understood,
Who all the day themselves do please,
And younglings, with such sports as these,
And, lying down, have nought t' affright
Sweet sleep, that makes more short the night.

Cætera desunt——

To Electra.

I DARE not ask a kiss,
  I dare not beg a smile ;
Lest having that or this,
  I might grow proud the while.

No, no, the utmost share
  Of my desire shall be
Only to kiss that air
  That lately kissed thee.

To his Worthy Friend, Mr. Arthur Bartly.

WHEN after many lustres thou shalt be
Wrapt up in cerecloth with thine ancestry ;
When of thy ragg'd escutcheons shall be seen
So little left as if they ne'er had been ;
Thou shalt thy name have, and thy fame's best trust
Here with the generation of my Just.

What kind of Mistress he would have.

BE the mistress of my choice
Clean in manners, clear in voice ;
Be she witty more than wise,
Pure enough, though not precise ;
Be she showing in her dress
Like a civil wilderness,
That the curious may detect
Order in a sweet neglect ;

Be she rolling in her eye,
Tempting all the passers-by,
And each ringlet of her hair
An enchantment or a snare,
For to catch the lookers-on,
But herself held fast by none ;
Be she such as neither will
Famish me nor over-fill.

The Rosemary Branch.

GROW for two ends, it matters not at all,
Be 't for my bridal or my burial.

Upon Madame Ursly.—Epigram.

FOR ropes of pearl, first Madame Ursly shows
A chain of corns, picked from her ears and toes,
Then next, to match Tradescant's curious shells,
Nails from her fingers mewed, she shows : what else ?
Why then, forsooth, a carcanet is shown
Of teeth as deaf as nuts, and all her own.

Upon Crab.—Epigram.

CRAB faces gowns with sundry furs ; 'tis known
He keeps the fox-fur for to face his own.

A Paranætical or Advisive Verse to his Friend, Mr. John Wicks.

IS this a life : to break thy sleep,
To rise as soon as day doth peep,
To tire thy patient ox or ass
By noon, and let thy good days pass,
Not knowing this that Jove decrees
Some mirth, t' adulce man's miseries ?
No, 'tis a life, to have thine oil
Without extortion from thy soil,
Thy faithful fields to yield thee grain
Although with some, yet little pain ;
To have thy mind and nuptial bed
With fears and cares uncumbered ;
A pleasing wife, that by thy side
Lies softly panting like a bride :
This is to live, and to endear
Those minutes time has lent us here.
Then while fates suffer live thou free
As is that air that circles thee,

And crown thy temples too ; and let
Thy servant, not thy own self, sweat
To strut thy barns with sheafs of wheat.
Time steals away like to a stream,
And we glide hence away with them :
No sound recalls the hours once fled,
Or roses being withered,
Nor us, my friend, when we are lost,
Like to a dew, or melted frost.
Then live we mirthful while we should,
And turn the iron age to gold ;
Let's feast and frolic, sing and play,
And thus less last than live our day.
Whose life with care is overcast,
That man's not said to live but last ;
Nor is't a life seven years to tell,
But for to live that half seven well ;
And that we'll do, as men who know,
Some few sands spent, we hence must go,
Both to be blended in the urn
From whence there's never a return.

Once Seen, and No More.

THOUSANDS each day pass by, which we
Once passed and gone, no more shall see.

Love.

THIS axiom I have often heard—
Kings ought to be more loved than feared.

To Mr. Denham, on his Prospective Poem.

OR looked I back unto the times hence flown,
To praise those Muses and dislike our own ;
Or did I walk those pean gardens through,
To kick the flowers and scorn their odours too ;
I might, and justly, be reputed here
One nicely mad or peevishly severe :
But, by Apollo ! as I worship wit
Where I have cause to burn perfumes to it,
So, I confess, 'tis somewhat to do well
In our high art, although we can't excel
Like thee ; or dare the buskins to unloose
Of thy brave, bold, and sweet Maronian muse.
But since I'm called, rare Denham, to be gone,
Take from thy Herrick this conclusion :
'Tis dignity in others, if they be
Crowned poets, yet live princes under thee ;

The while their wreaths and purple robes do shine,
Less by their own gems than those beams of thine.

A Hymn to the Lares.

IT was, and still my care is,
To worship ye, the Lares,
With crowns of greenest parsley,
And garlic chives not scarcely ;
For favours here to warm me,
And not by fire to harm me ;
For gladding so my hearth here
With inoffensive mirth here ;
That while the wassail bowl here
With Northdown ale doth troll here,
No syllable doth fall here,
To mar the mirth at all here.
For which, O chimney-keepers !
I dare not call ye sweepers,
So long as I am able
To keep a country table,
Great be my fare or small cheer,
I'll eat and drink up all here.

Denial in Women no Disheartening to Men.

WOMEN, although they ne'er so goodly make it,
Their fashion is, but to say no, to take it.

Adversity.

LOVE is maintained by wealth ; when all is spent,
Adversity then breeds the discontent.

To Fortune.

TUMBLE me down, and I will sit
Upon my ruins, smiling yet ;
Tear me to tatters, y t I'll be
Patient in my necessity ;
Laugh at my scraps of clothes, and shun
Me as a feared infection :
Yet, scarecrow like, I'll walk, as one
Neglecting thy derision.

Cruelties.

NERO commanded, but withdrew his eyes
From the beholding, death and cruelties.

Perseverance.

HAST thou begun an act? Ne'er then give o'er;
No man despairs to do what's done before.

Upon his Verses.

WHAT offspring other men have got,
The how, where, when, I question not;
These are the children I have left;
Adopted some, none got by theft;
But all are touched, like lawful plate,
And no verse illegitimate.

Distance Betters Dignities.

KINGS must not oft be seen by public eyes;
State at a distance adds to dignities.

Health.

HEALTH is no other, as the learned hold,
But a just measure both of heat and cold.

To Dianeme.—A Ceremony in Gloucester.

I'LL to thee a simnel bring,
'Gainst thou goest a-mothering;
So that when she blesseth thee,
Half that blessing thou'lt give me.

To the King.

GIVE way, give way! now, now my Charles shines here,
A public light, in this immensive sphere;
Some stars were fixed before, but these are dim,
Compared, in this my ample orb, to him.
Draw in your feeble fires, while that he
Appears but in his meaner majesty;
Where, if such glory flashes from his name,
Which is his shade who can abide his flame?
Princes, and such like public lights as these,
Must not be looked on but at distances;
For if we gaze on these brave lamps too near,
Our eyes they'll blind, or if not blind, they'll blear.

The Funeral Rites of the Rose.

THE rose was sick, and smiling died;
, being to be sanctified,

About the bed, there sighing stood
The sweet and flowery Sisterhood.
Some hung the head, while some did bring,
To wash her, water from the spring ;
Some laid her forth, while others wept,
But all a solemn fast there kept.
The Holy Sisters, some among,
The sacred dirge and trental sung ;
But ah ! what sweets smelt everywhere,
As heaven had spent all perfumes there.
At last, when prayers for the dead,
And rites were all accomplished ;
They, weeping, spread a lawny loom,
And closed her up as in a tomb.

The Rainbow ; or, Curious Covenant.

MINE eyes, like clouds, were drizzling rain ;
And, as they thus did entertain
The gentle beams from Julia's sight
To mine eyes levelled opposite,
O thing admired ! there did appear
A curious rainbow smiling there,
Which was the covenant that she
No more would drown mine eyes or me.

The Last Stroke Strikes Sure.

THOUGH by well-warding many blows we've past,
That stroke most feared is, which is struck the last.

Fortune.

FORTUNE 's a blind profuser of her own,
Too much she gives to some, enough to none.

Stool-ball.

AT stool-ball, Lucia, let us play,
    For sugar-cakes and wine ;
Or for a tansy let us pay
    The loss or thine or mine.

If thou, my dear, a winner be
    At trundling of the ball,
The wages thou shalt have, and me
    And my misfortunes all.

But if, my sweetest, I shall get,
    Then I desire but this,
That likewise I may pay the bet
    And have for all a kiss.

To Sappho.

LET us now take time and play,
Love, and live here while we may;
Drink rich wine, and make good cheer,
While we have our being here;
For, once dead, and laid i' th' grave,
No return from thence we have.

On Poet Prat.—Epigram.

PRAT he writes satires, but herein's the fault,
In no one satire there's a mite of salt.

Upon Tuck.—Epigram.

AT post and pair, or slam, Tom Tuck would play
This Christmas, but his want wherewith, says Nay.

Biting of Beggars.

WHO, railing, drives the lazar from his door,
Instead of alms, sets dogs upon the poor.

The Maypole.

THE Maypole is up,
Now give me the cup,
I'll drink to the garlands around it;
But first unto those
Whose hands did compose
The glory of flowers that crowned it.

A health to my girls
Whose husbands may earls
Or lords be, granting my wishes;
And when that ye wed
To the bridal bed,
Then multiply all, like to fishes.

Men Mind no State in Sickness.

THAT flow of gallants which approach .
To kiss thy hand from out the coach;
That fleet of lackeys which do run
Before thy swift postilion;
Those strong hoofed mules, which we behold
Reined in with purple, pearl, and gold,
And shod with silver, prove to be
The drawers of the axle-tree;

Thy wife, thy children, and the state
Of Persian looms and antique plate :
All these, and more, shall then afford
No joy to thee, their sickly lord.

Adversity.

ADVERSITY hurts none but only such
Whom whitest fortune dandled has too much.

Want.

NEED is no vice at all, though here it be
With men a loathed inconveniency.

Grief.

SORROWS divided amongst many, less
Discruciate a man in deep distress.

Love Palpable.

I PRESSED my Julia's lips, and in the kiss
Her soul and love were palpable in this.

No Action Hard to Affection.

NOTHING hard or harsh can prove
Unto those that truly love.

Mean Things Overcome Mighty.

BY the weak'st means things mighty are o'erthrown.
He's Lord of thy life, who contemns his own.

Upon Trigg.—Epigram.

TRIGG having turned his suit, he struts in state,
And tells the world, he's now regenerate.

Upon Smeaton.

HOW could Luke Smeaton wear a shoe or boot,
Who two and thirty corns had on a foot ?

The Bracelet of Pearl.—To Silvia.

I BRAKE thy bracelet 'gainst my will,
    And, wretched, I did see
Thee discomposed then, and still
    Art discontent with me.

One gem was lost, and I will get
  A richer pearl for thee
Than ever, dearest Silvia, yet
  Was drunk to Antony.

Or, for revenge, I'll tell thee what
  Thou for the breach shalt do ;
First, crack the strings, and after that
  Cleave thou my heart in two.

How Roses came Red.

'TIS said, as Cupid danced among
The gods, he down the nectar flung,
Which, on the white rose being shed,
Made it for ever after red.

Kings.

MEN are not born kings, but are men renowned,
Chose first, confirmed next, and at last are crowned.

First Work, and then Wages.

PREPOSTEROUS is that order, when we run
To ask our wages e'er our work is done.

Tears and Laughter.

KNEW'ST thou one month would take thy life away,
Thou'dst weep · but laugh, should it not last a day.

Glory.

GLORY no other thing is, Tully says,
Than a man's frequent fame spoke out with **praise.**

Possessions.

THOSE possessions short-lived are
Into the which we come by war.

Laxare Fibulam.

To loose the button is no less
Than to cast off all bashfulness.

His Return to London.

FROM the dull confines of the drooping West,
To see the day spring from the pregnant East,

Ravished in spirit I come, nay more, I fly
To thee, blessed place of my nativity!
Thus, thus with hallowed foot I touch the ground
With thousand blessings by thy fortune crowned.
O fruitful genius! that bestowest here
An everlasting p'enty year by year;
O place! O people! manners, framed to please
All nations, customs, kindreds, languages!
I am a free-born Roman; suffer then
That I amongst you live a citizen.
London my home is, though by hard fate sent
Into a long and irksome banishment;
Yet since called back, henceforward let me be,
O native country! repossessed by thee;
For, rather than I'll to the West return,
I'll beg of thee first here to have mine urn.
Weak I am grown, and must in short time fall,
Give thou my sacred relic burial.

Not Every Day Fit for Verse.

'Tis not every day that I
Fitted am to prophesy;
No, but when the spirit fills
The fantastic pannicles,
Full of fire, then I write
As the Godhead doth indite.
Thus enraged, my lines are hurled,
Like the Sybil's, through the world.
Look how next the holy fire
Either slakes, or doth retire;
So the fancy cools, till when
That brave spirit comes again.

Poverty the Greatest Pack.

To mortal men great loads allotted be,
But of all packs, no pack like poverty.

A Bucolic; or, Discourse of Neatherds.

1. COME, blitheful neatherds, let us lay
A wager, who the best shall play,
Of thee, or I, the roundelay
That fits the business of the day.

Chor. And Lalage the judge shall be,
To give the prize to thee or me.

2. Content, begin, and I will bet
A heifer, smooth and black as jet,
In every part alike complete,
And wanton as a kid as yet.

Chor. And Lalage, with cow-like eyes,
Shall be disposeress of the prize.

1. Against thy heifer, I will here
Lay to thy stake a lusty steer,
With gilded horns and burnished clear.

Chor. Why then begin, and let us hear
The soft, the sweet, the mellow note
That gently purls from either's oat.

2. The stakes are laid ; let's now apply
Each one to make his melody ;
Lal. The equal umpire shall be I,
Who'll hear, and so judge righteously.

Chor. Much time is spent in prate ; begin,
And sooner play, the sooner win.   [*He plays.*

1. That's sweetly touched ; I must confess
Thou art a man of worthiness ;
But hark how I can now express
My love unto my neatherdess.   [*He sings.*

Chor. A sugared note, and sound as sweet
As kine when they at milking meet.

1. Now for to win thy heifer fair,
I'll strike thee such a nimble air,
That thou shalt say, thyself, 'tis rare,
And title me without compare.

Chor. Lay by awhile your pipes, and rest,
Since both have here deserved best.

2. To get thy steerling once again,
I'll play thee such another strain,
That thou shalt swear my pipe does reign
Over thine oat, as sovereign.   [*He sings.*

Chor. And Lalage shall tell by this
Whose now the prize and wager is.

1. Give me the prize.   2. The day is mine.
1. Not so ; my pipe has silenced thine ;
And hadst thou wagered twenty kine,
They were mine own.   *Lal.* In love combine.

Chor. And lay we down our pipes together,
As weary, not o'ercome by either.

True Safety.

'TIS not the walls or purple that defends
A prince from foes, but 'tis his fort of friends.

A Prognostic.

As many laws and lawyers do express
Nought but a kingdom's ill-affectedness ;
Even so, those streets and houses do but show
Store of diseases where physicians flow.

Proof to no Purpose.

YOU see this gentle stream that glides,
Shoved on by quick succeeding tides ;
Try if this sober stream you can
Follow to the wilder ocean,
And see if there it keeps unspent
In that congesting element :
Next, from that world of waters then
By pores and caverns back again
Induct that inadulterate same
Stream to the spring from whence it came :
This with a wonder when ye do
As easy and else easier too,
Then may ye recollect the grains
Of my particular remains,
After a thousand lustres hurled
By ruffling winds, about the world.

Fame.

'TIS still observed, that Fame ne'er sings
The order but the sum of things.

By Use Comes Easiness.

OFT bend the bow, and thou with ease shalt do
What others can't with all their strength put to.

To the Genius of his House.

COMMAND the roof, great Genius, and from thence
Into this house pour down thy influence,
That through each room a golden pipe may run
Of living water by thy benison ;
Fulfil the larders, and with strengthening bread
Be evermore those bins replenished.

Next, like a bishop consecrate my ground,
That lucky fairies here may dance their round ;
And after that lay down some silver pence,
The master's charge and care to recompense ;
Charm then the chambers, make the beds for ease
More than for peevish pining sicknesses ;
Fix the foundation fast. and let the roof
Grow old with time, but yet keep weatherproof.

His Grange, or Private Wealth.

THOUGH clock,
To tell how night draws hence, I've none,
A cock
I have to sing how day draws on :
I have
A maid, my Prue, by good luck sent,
To save
That little Fates me gave or lent :
A hen
I keep, which, creeking day by day,
Tells when
She goes her long white egg to lay :
A goose
I have, which, with a jealous ear,
Lets loose
Her tongue to tell what danger's near :
A lamb
I keep, tame, with my morsels fed,
Whose dam
An orphan left him, lately dead :
A cat
I keep, that plays about my house,
Grown fat
With eating many a miching mouse ;
To these
A trasy I do keep, whereby
I please
The more my rural privacy :
Which are
But toys, to give my heart some ease.
Where care
None is, slight things do lightly please.

Good Precepts or Counsel.

IN all thy need be thou possessed
Still with a well-prepared breast,
Nor let the shackles make thee sad ;
Thou canst but have what others had.

And this for comfort thou must know,
Times that are won't still be so;
Clouds will not ever pour down rain,
A sullen day will clear again.
First peals of thunder we must hear,
Then lutes and harps shall stroke the ear.

Money Makes the Mirth.

WHEN all birds else do of their music fail,
Money s the still sweet-singing nightingale.

Charon and Philomel: a Dialogue Sung.

Ph. CHARON, O gentle Charon, let me woo thee,
By tears and pity now to come unto me.
Ch. What voice so sweet and charming do I hear?
Say, what thou art. *Ph.* I prithee first draw near.
Ch. A sound I hear, but nothing yet can see,
Speak where thou art. *Ph.* O Charon, pity me!
I am a bird, and though no name I tell,
My warbling note will say I'm Philomel.
Ch. What's that to me? I waft nor fish or fowls,
Nor beasts, fond thing but only human souls.
Ph. Alas, for me! *Ch.* Shame on thy witching note,
That made me thus hoist sail, and bring my boat:
But I'll return; what mischief brought thee hither?
Ph. A deal of love, and much, much grief together.
Ch. What's thy request? *Ph.* That since she's now beneath
Who fed my life, I'll follow her in death.
Ch. And is that all? I'm gone. *Ph.* By love, I pray thee.
Ch. Talk not of love; all pray, but few souls pay me.
Ph. I'll give thee vows and tears. *Ch.* Can tears pay scores
For mending sails, for patching boat and oars?
Ph. I'll beg a penny, or I'll sing so long
Till thou shalt say I've paid thee with a song.
Ch. Why, then begin, and all the while we make
Our slothful passage o'er the Stygian lake,
Thou and I'll sing to make these dull shades merry,
Who else with tears would doubtless drown my ferry.

Upon Paul.—Epigram.

PAUL'S hands do give—what? Give they bread or meat,
Or money? No, but only dew and sweat.
As stones and salt gloves use to give, even so
Paul's hands do give nought else, for aught we know.

Upon Sibb.—Epigram.

SIBB, when she saw her face how hard it was,
For anger spat on thee, her looking glass:

But weep not, crystal, for the shame was meant
Not unto thee, but that thou didst present.

A Ternary of Littles, upon a Pipkin of Jelly
sent to a Lady.

A LITTLE saint best fits a little shrine,
A little prop best fits a little vine ;
As my small cruse best fits my little wine.

A little seed best fits a little soil,
A little trade best fits a little toil ;
As my small jar best fits my little oil.

A little bin best fits a little bread,
A little garland fits a little head ;
As my small stuff best fits my little shed.

A little hearth best fits a little fire,
A little chapel fits a little choir ;
As my small bell best fits my little spire.

A little stream best fits a little boat,
A little lead best fits a little float ;
As my small pipe best fits my little note.

A little meat best fits a little belly,
As sweetly, lady, give me leave to tell ye,
This little pipkin fits this little jelly.

Upon the Roses in Julia's Bosom.

THRICE happy roses, so much graced, to have
Within the bosom of my love your grave !
Die when ye will, your sepulchre is known,
Your grave her bosom is, the lawn the stone.

Maid's Nays are Nothing

MAIDS nays are nothing ; they are shy,
But to desire what they deny.

The Smell of the Sacrifice.

THE gods require the thighs
Of beeves for sacrifice,
Which roasted, we the steam
Must sacrifice to them,
Who, though they do not eat,
Yet love the smell of meat.

Lovers, how they Come and Part.

A GYGES ring they bear about them still,
To be, and not, seen when and where they will ;
They tread on clouds, and though they sometimes fall,
They fall like dew, but make no noise at all :
So silently they one to th' other come,
As colours steal into the pear or plum,
And, air-like, leave no 'pression to be seen
Where'er they met, or parting-place has been.

In Praise of Women.

O JUPITER ! should I speak ill
Of womankind, first die I will ;
Since that I know, 'mong all the rest
Of creatures, woman is the best.

The Apron of Flowers.

To gather flowers Sappho went,
  And homeward she did bring
Within her lawny continent
  The treasure of the spring.

She smiling blushed, and blushing smiled,
  And sweetly blushing thus,
She looked as she'd been got with child
  By young Favonius.

Her apron gave, as she did pass,
  An odour more divine,
More pleasing, too, than ever was
  The lap of Proserpine.

The Candour of Julia's Teeth

WHITE as Zenobia's teeth, the which the girls
Of Rome did wear for their most precious pearls.

Upon Her Weeping.

SHE wept upon her cheeks, and weeping so,
She seemed to quench love's fires that there did glow.

Another upon Her Weeping

SHE by the river sat, and sitting there,
She wept, and made it deeper by a tear.

Delay.

BREAK off delay, since we but read of one
That ever prospered by cunctation.

To Sir John Berkley, Governor of Exeter.

STAND forth, brave man, since fate has made thee here
The Hector over aged Exeter,
Who for a long sad time has weeping stood,
Like a poor lady lost in widowhood,
But fears not now to see her safety sold,
As other towns and cities were, for gold,
By those ignoble births, which shame the stem
That gave progermination unto them,
Whose restless ghosts shall hear their children sing
Our sires betrayed their country and their king.
True, if this city seven times rounded was
With rock, and seven times circumflanked with brass,
Yet, if thou were not, Berkley, loyal proof,
The senators, down tumbling with the roof,
Would into praised, but pitied, ruins fall,
Leaving no show where stood the capital.
But thou art just and itchless, and dost please
Thy genius with two strength'ning buttresses,
Faith and Affection, which will never slip
To weaken this thy great Dictatorship.

To Electra.---Love looks for Love.

LOVE love begets ; then never be
Unsoft to him who's smooth to thee .
Tigers and bears, I've heard some say,
For proffered love will love repay ;
None are so harsh, but if they find
Softness in others, will be kind :
Affection will affection move ;
Then you must like because I love.

Regression spoils Resolution.

HAST thou attempted greatness? Then go on ;
Back-turning slackens resolution.

Contention.

DISCREET and prudent we that discord call
That either profits or not hurts at all.

Consultation.

CONSULT ere thou begin'st ; that done, go on
With all wise speed for execution.

Love dislikes Nothing.

WHATSOEVER thing I see,
Rich or poor although it be ;
'Tis a mistress unto me.

Be my girl or fair or brown,
Does she smile, or does she frown ;
Still I write a sweetheart down.

Be she rough or smooth of skin,
When I touch, I then begin
For to let affection in.

Be she bald, or does she wear
Locks incurled of other hair ;
I shall find enchantment there.

Be she whole or be she rent,
So my fancy be content,
She's to me most excellent.

Be she fat or be she lean,
Be she sluttish, be she clean ;
I'm a man for every scene.

Our own Sins Unseen.

OTHER men's sins we ever bear in mind ;
None sees the fardel of his faults behind.

No Pains, No Gains.

IF little labour, little are our gains ;
Man's fortunes are according to his pains.

Virtue Best United.

BY so much, virtue is the less,
By how much near to singleness.

The Eye.

A WANTON and lascivious eye
Betrays the heart's adultery.

To Prince Charles, upon his Coming to Exeter.

WHAT Fate decreed, Time now has made us see
A renovation of the West by thee :
That preternatural fever, which did threat
Death to our country, now hath lost his heat ;
And calms succeeding, we perceive no more
The unequal pulse to beat, as heretofore.
Something there yet remains for thee to do.
Then reach those ends that thou was destined to
Go on with Sylla's fortune ; let thy fate
Make thee, like him, this, that way fortunate !
Apollo's image side with thee to bless
Thy war, discreetly made, with white success !
Meantime, thy prophets watch by watch shall pray,
While young Charles fights, and fighting, wins the day :
That done, our smooth-paced poems all shall be
Sung in the high doxology of thee :
Then maids shall strew thee, and thy curls from them
Receive, with songs, a flowery diadem.

A Song.

BURN or drown me, choose ye whether,
So I may but die together,
Thus to slay me by degrees
Is the height of cruelties ;
What needs twenty stabs, when one
Strikes me dead as any stone ?
O, show mercy then, and be
Kind at once to murder me.

Princes and Favourites.

PRINCES and fav'rites are most dear, while they,
By giving and receiving, hold the play ;
But the relation then of both grows poor
When these can ask, and kings can give no more.

Examples ; or, Like Prince Like People.

EXAMPLES lead us, and we likely see,
Such as the prince is, will his people be.

Potentates.

LOVE and the Graces evermore do wait
Upon the man that is a potentate.

The Wake.

COME, Anthea, let us two
Go to feast, as others do :
Tarts and custards, creams and cakes,
Are the junkets still at wakes ;
Unto which the tribes resort,
Where the business is the sport.
Morris-dancers thou shalt see,
Marian, too, in pageantry ;
And a mimic to devise
Many grinning properties.
Players there will be, and those
Base in action as in clothes ;
Yet with strutting they will please
The incurious villages.
Near the dying of the day
There will be a cudgel-play,
Where a coxcomb will be broke,
Ere a good word can be spoke :
But the anger ends all here,
Drenched in ale or drowned in beer.
Happy rustics, best content
With the cheapest merriment,
And possess no other fear
Than to want the wake next year.

The Peter-penny.

FRESH strewings allow
To my sepulchre now,
To make my lodging the sweeter ;
A staff or a wand,
Put then in my hand,
With a penny to pay St. Peter.

Who has not a cross
Must sit with the loss,
And no whit further must venture ;
Since the porter he
Will paid have his fee,
Or else not one there must enter.

Who at a dead lift
Can't send for a gift
A cheese to the priest for a roaster,
Shall hear his clerk say,
By yea and by nay,
No penny, no paternoster.

To Doctor Alablaster.

Nor art thou less esteemed that I have placed,
Amongst mine honoured, thee almost the last :
In great processions many lead the way
To him who is the triumph of the day,
As these have done to thee, who art the one,
One only glory of a million ;
In whom the spirit of the gods does dwell,
Firing thy soul, by which thou dost foretell,
When this or that vast dynasty must fall
Down to a fillet more imperial ;
When this or that horn shall be broke, and when
Others shall spring up in their place again ;
When times and seasons, and all years must lie
Drowned in the sea of wild eternity ;
When the black Doomsday books, as yet unsealed
Shall by the mighty Angel be revealed ;
And when the trumpet which thou late hast found,
Shall call to judgment ; tell us when the sound
Of this or that great April day shall be,
And, next the Gospel, we will credit thee.
Meantime, like earthworms we will crawl below,
And wonder at those things that thou dost know.

Upon his Kinswoman, Mrs. M. S.

Here lies a virgin, and as sweet
As e'er was wrapped in winding-sheet ;
Her name, if next you would have known,
The marble speaks it Mary Stone,
Who dying in her blooming years,
This stone, for namesake, melts to tears.
If, fragrant virgins, you'll but keep
A fast while jets and marbles weep,
And, praying, strew some roses on her,
You 'll do my niece abundant honour.

Felicity knows no Fence.

Of both our fortunes, good and bad, we find
Prosperity more searching of the mind :
Felicity flies o'er the wall and fence,
While misery keeps in with patience.

Death ends all Woe.

Time is the bound of things ; where'er we go,
Fate gives a meeting ; death's the end of woe.

A Conjuration.—To Electra.

By those soft tods of wool,
With which the air is full;
By all those tinctures there,
That paint the hemisphere;
By dews and drizzling rain,
That swell the golden grain;
By all those sweets that be
I' th' flowery nunnery;
By silent nights, and the
Three forms of Hecate;
By all aspects that bless
The sober sorceress,
While juice she strains, and pith
To make her philtres with;
By time, that hastens on
Things to perfection;
And by yourself, the best
Conjurement of the rest;
Oh, my Electra! be
In love with none but me.

Courage Cooled.

I CANNOT love as I have lov'd before;
For I'm grown old, and with mine age grown poor.
Love must be fed by wealth; this blood of mine
Must needs wax cold, if wanting bread and wine.

The Spell.

HOLY water come and bring;
Cast in salt for seasoning;
Set the brush for sprinkling:
Sacred spittle bring ye hither;
Meal and it now mix together;
And a little oil to either;
Give the tapers here their light;
Ring the saints' bell, to affright
Far from hence the evil sprite.

His Wish to Privacy.

GIVE me a cell
  To dwell,
Where no foot hath
  A path;
There will I spend,
  And end
My wearied year
  In tears

A Good Husband.

A MASTER of a house, as I have read,
Must be the first man up and last in bed;
With the sun rising he must walk his grounds:
See this, view that, and all the other bounds;
Shut every gate, mend every hedge that's torn,
Either with old, or plant therein new thorn;
Tread o'er his glebe, but with such care, that where
He sets his foot he leaves rich compost there.

A Hymn to Bacchus.

I SING thy praise, Bacchus,
Who with thy Thyrse dost thwack us;
And yet thou so dost back us
With boldness, that we fear
No Brutus ent'ring here,
Nor Cato the severe.
What though the lictors threat us,
We know they dare not beat us,
So long as thou dost heat us.
When we thy orgies sing,
Each cobbler is a king,
Nor dreads he anything;
And though he do not rave,
Yet he'll the courage have
To call my Lord Mayor knave;
Besides, too, in a brave
Although he has no riches,
But walks with dangling breeches,
And skirts that want their stitches,
And shows his naked flitches;
Yet he 'll be thought or seen,
So good as George-a-Green,
And calls his blouze his queen,
And speaks in language keen.
Oh Bacchus! let us be
From cares and troubles free;
And thou shalt hear how we
Will chant new hymns to thee.

Blame the Reward of Princes.

AMONG disasters that dissension brings,
This not the least is which belongs to kings:
If wars go well, each for a part lays claim;
If ill, then kings, not soldiers, bear the blame.

Clemency in Kings.

KINGS must not only cherish up the good,
But must be niggards of the meanest blood.

Anger.

WRONGS, if neglected, vanish in short time ;
But beard with anger, we confess the crime.

A Psalm or Hymn to the Graces.

GLORY be to the Graces,
That do in public places,
Drive thence whate'er encumbers
The listening to my numbers !

Honour be to the Graces,
Who do with sweet embraces
Shew they are well contented
With what I have invented!

Worship be to the Graces,
Who do from sour faces,
And lungs that would infect me,
For evermore protect me !

An Hymn to the Muses.

HONOUR to you who sit
Near to the well of wit,
And drink your fill of it !

Glory and worship be
To you, sweet maids, thrice three,
Who still inspire me ;

And teach me how to sing,
Unto the lyric string,
My measures ravishing !

Then while I sing your praise,
My priesthood crown with bays,
Green to the end of days !

Upon Julia's Clothes.

WHEN as in silks my Julia goes,
Then, then, methinks, how sweetly flows,
That liquefaction of her clothes.
Next, when I cast mine eyes, and see
That brave vibration each way free ;
Oh, how that glittering taketh me !

Moderation.

In things a moderation keep ;
Kings ought to shear, not skin their sheep.

Upon Prue, his Maid.

In this little urn is laid
Prudence Baldwin, once my maid,
From whose happy spark here let
Spring the purple violet.

The Invitation.

To sup with thee thou didst me home invite,
And mad'st a promise that mine appetite
Should meet and tire on such lautitious meat,
The like not Heliogabalus did eat ;
And richer wine would'st give to me, thy guest,
Than Roman Sylla poured out at his feast.
I came, 'tis true, and looked for fowl of price,
The bastard phœnix, bird of Paradise ;
And for no less than aromatic wine
Of maiden's blush, commixed with jessamine.
Clean was the hearth, the mantel larded jet,
Which wanting Lar and smoke, hung weeping wet ;
At last, i' th' noon of winter, did appear
A ragg'd soused neat's foot with sick vinegar ;
And in a burnished flagonet stood by
Beer small as comfort, dead as charity :
At which amazed, and pondering on the food,
How cold it was, and how it chilled my blood,
I cursed the master and I damned the souse,
And swore I'd got the ague of the house.
Well, when to eat thou dost me next desire,
I'll bring a fever, since thou keep'st no fire.

Ceremonies for Christmas.

Come, bring with a noise,
My merry merry boys,
The Christmas log to the firing,
While my good dame, she
Bids ye all be free,
And drink to your hearts' desiring,

With the last year's brand
Light the new block, and
For good success in his spending,
On your psalteries play,
That sweet luck may
Come while the log is a-teending.

Drink now the strong beer,
Cut the white loaf here,
The while the meat is a-shreddin. ;
For the rare mince-pie,
And the plums stand by,
To fill the paste that's a-kneading.

Christmas Eve.—Another Ceremony.

COME, guard this night the Christmas-pie,
That the thief, though ne'er so sly,
With his flesh-hooks, don't come nigh
        To catch it

From him who alone sits there,
Having his eyes still in his ear,
And a deal of nightly fear,
        To watch it.

Another to the Maids.

WASH your hands, or else the fire
Will not teend to your desire ;
Unwashed hands, ye maidens, know,
Dead the fire, though ye blow.

Another.

WASSAIL the trees, that they may bear
You many a plum and many a pear ;
For more or less fruits they will bring
As you do give them wassailing.

Power and Peace.

'TIS never or but seldom known
Power and Peace to keep one throne.

To his dear Valentine, Mistress Margaret Falconbridge.

NOW is your turn, my dearest, to be set
A gem in this eternal coronet ;
Twas rich before. but since your name is down,
It sparkles now like Ariadne's crown.
Blaze by this sphere for ever, or this do,
Let me and it shine evermore by you.

To Œnone.

SWEET Œnone, do but say
Love thou dost, though Love says, Nay;
Speak me fair, for lovers be
Gently killed by flattery.

Verses.

WHO will not honour noble numbers, when
Verses outlive the bravest deeds of men?

Happiness.

THAT Happiness does still the longest thrive
Where joys and griefs have turns alternative.

Things of Choice, Long a Coming.

WE pray 'gainst war, yet we enjoy no peace;
Desire deferred is, that it may increase.

Poetry Perpetuates the Poet.

HERE I myself might likewise die,
And utterly forgotten lie,
But that eternal poetry,
Repullulation gives me here,
Unto the thirtieth thousand year,
When all now dead shall reappear.

Upon Trencherman.

TOM shifts the trenchers, yet he never can
Endure that lukewarm name of serving-man:
Serve or not serve, let Tom do what he can,
He is a serving who's a trencher-man.

Kisses.

GIVE me the food that satisfies a guest;
Kisses are but dry banquets to a feast.

Orpheus.

ORPHEUS he went, as poets tell,
To fetch Eurydice from hell,
And had her, but it was upon
This short but strict condition:

Backward he should not look while he
Led her through hell's obscurity.
But ah ! it happened, as he made
His passage through that dreadful shade,
Revolve he did his loving eye,
For gentle fear or jealousy.
And looking back, that look did sever
Him and Eurydice for ever.

Upon Comely, a Good Speaker but an Ill Singer.
Epigram.

COMELY acts well ; and when he speaks his part,
He doth it with the sweetest tones of art ;
But when he sings a psalm, there's none can be
More cursed for singing out of tune than he.

Any Way for Wealth.

E'EN all religious courses to be rich
Hath been rehearsed by Joel Michelditch ;
But now, perceiving that it still does please
The sterner fates to cross his purposes,
He tacks about ; and now he doth profess
Rich he will be by all unrighteousness.
Thus if our ship fails of her anchor hold,
We'll love the devil, so he lands the gold.

Upon an Old Woman.

OLD Widow Prouse, to do her neighbours evil,
Would give, some say, her soul unto the devil ;
Well, when she's killed that pig, goose, cock, or hen,
What would she give to get that soul again ?

Upon Pearch.—Epigram.

THOU writes in prose how sweet all virgins be,
But there's not one doth praise the smell of thee.

To Sappho.

SAPPHO, I will choose to go
Where the northern winds do blow
Endless ice and endless snow,
Rather than I once would see
But a winter's face in thee,
To benumb my hopes and me.

To his Faithful Friend, Master John Crofts, Cupbearer to the King.

For all thy many courtesies to me,
Nothing I have, my Crofts, to send to thee
For the requital, save this only one
Half of my just remuneration.
For since I've travelled all this realm throughout
To seek and find some few immortals out,
To circumspangle this my spacious sphere,
As lamps for everlasting shining here,
And having fixed thee in mine orb, a star,
Amongst the rest, both bright and singular,
The present age will tell the world thou art,
If not to the whole, yet satisfied in part ;
As for the rest, being too great a sum
Here to be paid, I'll pay 't i' th' world to come.

The Bridecake.

This day, my Julia. thou must make
For Mistress Bride the wedding-cake ;
Knead but the dough, and it will be
To paste of almonds turned by thee ;
Or kiss it thou but once or twice,
And for the bridecake there'll be spice.

To be Merry.

Let's now take our time,
While we are in our prime,
And old, old age is afar off ;
For the evil, evil days
Will come on apace,
Before we can be aware of.

Burial.

Man may want land to live in ; but for all
Nature finds out some place for burial.

Lenity.

'Tis the chirurgeon's praise and height of art,
Not to cut off but cure the vicious part.

Penitence.

Who after his transgression doth repent,
Is half or altogether innocent.

Grief.

CONSIDER sorrows, how they are aright;
Grief, if 't be great, 'tis short; if long, 'tis light.

The Maiden-Blush.

So look the mornings, when the sun
Paints them with fresh vermillion;
So cherries blush, and Kathrine pears,
And apricots in youthful years;
So corals look more lovely red,
And rubies lately polished;
So purest diaper doth shine,
Stained by the beams of claret wine;
As Julia looks when she doth dress
Her either cheek with bashfulness.

The Mean.

IMPARITY doth ever discord bring;
The mean the music makes in everything.

Haste Hurtful.

HASTE is unhappy: what we rashly do
Is both unlucky, aye, and foolish too;
Where war with rashness is attempted, there
The soldiers leave the field with equal fear.

Purgatory.

READERS, we entreat ye pray
For the soul of Lucia,
That in little time she be
From her Purgatory free;
In the interim she desires
That your tears may cool her fires.

The Cloud.

SEE'ST thou that cloud that rides in state,
Part ruby-like, part candidate!
It is no other than the bed
Where Venus sleeps, half-smothered.

The Amber Bead.

I SAW a fly within a bead
Of amber cleanly buried;
The urn was little, but the room
More rich than Cleopatra's tomb.

To my dearest Sister, Miss Mercy Herrick.

WHENE'ER I go, or whatsoe'er befalls
Me in mine age, or foreign funerals,
This blessing I will leave thee ere I go,
Prosper thy basket, and therein thy dough ;
Feed on the paste of filberts, or else knead
And bake the flour of amber for thy bread ;
Balm may thy tears drop, and thy springs run oil,
And everlasting harvest crown thy soil !
These I but wish for ; but thyself shall see
The blessing fall in mellow time on thee.

The Transfiguration.

IMMORTAL clothing I put on
So soon as, Julia, I am gone
To mine eternal mansion,

Thou, thou art here, to human sight,
Clothed all with incorrupted light,
But yet how more admiredly bright

Wilt thou appear, when thou art set
In thy refulgent thronelet,
That shinest thus in thy counterfeit?

Suffer that Thou canst not Shift.

DOES Fortune rend thee?   Bear with thy hard fate ;
Virtuous instructions ne'er are delicate.
Say, does she frown?   Still countermand her threats ;
Virtue best loves those children that she beats.

To the Passenger.

IF I lie unburied, sir,
These, my relics, pray inter ;
'Tis religious part to see
Stones or turfs to cover me.
One word more I had to say,
But it skills not ; go your way ;
He that wants a burial room,
For a stone has Heaven his tomb.

Upon Nodes.

WHEREVER Nodes does in the summer come,
He prays his harvest may be well brought home
What store of corn has careful Nodes, think you,
Whose field his foot is, and whose barn his shoe ?

To the King, upon his Taking of Leicester.
May 31, 1645.

THIS day is yours, great CHARLES ! and in this war
Your fate and ours alike victorious are.
In her white stole now Victory does rest,
Ensphered with palm on your triumphant crest ;
Fortune is now your captive ; other kings
Hold but her hands—you hold both hands and wings.

To Julia, in her Dawn or Daybreak.

BY the next kindling of the day,
  My Julia, thou shalt see,
Ere Ave-Mary thou canst say,
  I'll come and visit thee.

Yet, ere thou counsell'st with thy glass,
  Appear thou to mine eyes
As smooth and nak'd as she that was
  The prime of Paradise.

If blush thou must, then blush thou through
  A lawn, that thou may'st look
As purest pearls or pebbles do
  When peeping through a brook.

As lilies shrined in crystal, so
  Do thou to me appear ;
Or damask roses, when they grow
  To sweet acquaintance there.

Counsel.

'TWAS Cæsar's saying : kings no less conquerors are
By their wise counsel than they be by war.

Bad Princes Pill their People.

LIKE those infernal deities which eat
The best of all the sacrificed meat,
And leave their servants but the smoke and sweat ;
So many kings, and primates too, there are
Who claim the fat and fleshy for their share,
And leave their subjects but the starved ware.

Most Words, Less Works.

IN desperate cases, all or most are known
Commanders ; few for execution.

To Dianeme.

I COULD but see thee yesterday
　Stung by a fretful bee ;
And I the javelin sucked away,
　And healed the wound in thee.

A thousand thorns, and briars, and stings
　I have in my poor breast ;
Yet ne'er can see that salve which brings
　My passions any rest.

As love shall help me, I admire
　How thou canst sit and smile
To see me bleed, and not desire
　To stanch the blood the while.

If thou, composed of gentle mould,
　Art so unkind to me,
What dismal stories will be told
　Of those that cruel be ?

Upon Tap.

TAP, better known than trusted, as we hear,
Sold his old mother's spectacles for beer ;
And not unlikely, rather too than fail,
He'll sell her eyes and nose for beer and ale.

His Loss.

ALL has been plundered from me but my wit ;
Fortune herself can lay no claim to it.

Draw and Drink.

MILK still your fountains and your springs ; for why ?
The more they're drawn, the less they will grow dry.

Upon Punchin.—Epigram.

GIVE me a reason why men call
Punchin a dry plant animal ;
Because as plants by water grow,
Punchin by beer and ale spreads so.

To Œnone.

THOU say'st love's dart
Hath pricked thy heart,

And thou dost languish too ;
    If one poor prick
    Can make thee sick,
Say what would many do ?

Upon Blinks.—Epigram.

TOM BLINKS his nose is full of weals, and these
Tom calls not pimples, but pimpleides ;
Sometimes, in mirth, he says each whelk's a spark,
When drunk with beer, to light him home i' th' dark.

Upon Adam Peapes.—Epigram.

PEAPES he does strut, and pick his teeth, as if
His jaws had tired on some large shin of beef ;
But nothing so—the dinner Adam had,
Was cheese full ripe with tears, with bread as sad.

To Electra.

SHALL I go to Love and tell
Thou art all turned icicle ?
Shall I say, her altars be
Disadorned and scorned by thee ?
O beware ! in time submit ;
Love has yet no wrathful fit ;
If her patience turns to ire,
Love is then consuming fire.

To Mistress Amy Potter.

AH me ! I love ; give him your hand to kiss
Who both your wooer and your poet is.
Nature has precomposed us both to love ;
Your part 's to grant, my scene must be to move.
Dear, can you like, and liking, love your poet?
If you say aye, blush-guiltiness will show it.
Mine eyes must woo you, though I sigh the while,
True love is tongueless as a crocodile ;
And you may find in love these differing parts—
Wooers have tongues of ice, but burning hearts.

Upon a Maid.

HERE she lies, in bed of spice,
Fair as Eve in Paradise ;
For her beauty it was such,
Poets could not praise too much.

Virgins come, and in a ring
Her supremest requiem sing ;
Then depart, but see ye tread
Lightly, lightly o'er the dead.

Upon Love.

LOVE is a circle, and an endless sphere ;
From good to good, revolving here and there.

Beauty.

BEAUTY'S no other but a lovely grace
Of lively colours flowing from the face.

Upon Love.

SOME salve to every sore we may apply,
Only for my wound there's no remedy ;
Yet if my Julia kiss me, there will be
A sovereign balm found out to cure me.

Upon Hanch, a Schoolmaster.—Epigram.

HANCH, since he lately did inter his wife,
He weeps and sighs, as weary of his life ;
Say, is 't for real grief he mourns?   Not so ;
Tears have their springs from joy as well as woe.

Upon Peason.—Epigram.

LONG locks of late our zealot Peason wears.
Not for to hide his high and mighty ears—
No ; but because he would not have it seen
That stubble stands where once large ears have been.

To his Book.

MAKE haste away, and let one be
A friendly patron unto thee,
Lest wrapped from hence, I see thee lie
Torn for the use of pastery ;
Or see thy injured leaves serve well
To make loose gowns for mackerel ;
Or see the grocers, in a trice,
Make hoods of thee to serve out spice.

Readiness.

THE readiness of doing doth express
No other but the doer's willingness.

Writing.

WHEN words we want, love teacheth to indite,
And what we blush to speak she bids us write.

Society.

TWO things do make soci ty to stand—
The first commerce is, and the next command.

Upon a Maid.

GONE she is, a long, long way,
But she has decreed a day
Back to come, and make no stay ;
So we keep till her return
Here her ashes, or her urn.

Satisfaction for Sufferings.

FOR all our works a recompense is sure ;
'Tis sweet to think on what was hard t' endure.

To Mr. Henry Lawes.

TOUCH but thy lyre, my Harry, and I hear
From thee some raptures of the rare Gotire ;
Then if thy voice commingle with the string,
I hear in thee the rare Laniere to sing,
Or curious Wilson ; tell me, canst thou be
Less then Apollo, that usurp'st such three ?
Three unto whom the whole world give applause ;
Yet their three praises praise but one—that's Lawes.

Age unfit for Love.

MAIDENS tell me I am old ;
Let me in my glass behold
Whether smooth or not I be,
Or if hair remains to me.
Well, or be 't, or be 't not so,
This for certainty I know,
Ill it fits old men to play
When that death bids come away.

The Bedman, or Gravemaker.

THOU hast made many houses for the dead ;
When my lot calls me to be buried,
For love or pity, prithee let there be
I' th' churchyard made one tenement for me.

To Anthea.

ANTHEA, I am going hence
With some small stock of innocence ;
But yet those blessed gates I see
Withstanding entrance unto me !
To pray for me do thou begin,
The porter then will let me in.

Need.

WHO begs to die for fear of human need,
Wisheth his body, not his soul, good speed.

To Julia.

I AM zealous ; prithee pray
For my welfare, Julia,
For I think the gods require
Male perfumes, but female fire.

On Julia's Lips.

SWEET are my Julia's lips and clean,
As if o'erwashed in hippocrene.

Twilight.

TWILIGHT no other thing is, poets say,
Then the last part of night and first of day.

To his Friend Master J. Jinks.

LOVE, love me now, because I place
Thee here among my righteous race ;
The bastard slips may droop and die,
Wanting both root and earth, but thy
Immortal self shall boldly trust
To live for ever with my Just.

On Himself.

IF that my fate has has now fulfilled my year,
And so soon stopped my longer living here,
What was 't, ye gods, a dying man to save,
But while he met with his paternal grave ;
Though while we living 'bout the world do roam,
We love to rest in peaceful urns at home,
Where we may snug and close together lie
By the dead bones of our dear ancestry.

Kings and Tyrants.

'TWIXT kings and tyrants there's this difference known :
Kings seek their subjects' good, tyrants their own.

Crosses.

OUR crosses are no other than the rods,
And our diseases vultures, of the gods ;
Each grief we feel, that likewise is a kite
Sent forth by them. our flesh to eat or bite.

Upon Love.

LOVE brought me to a silent grove,
    And showed me there a tree,
Where some h. d hang'd themselves for love,
    And gave a twist to me.

The altar was of silk and gold
    That he reached forth unto me,
No otherwise than if he would
    By dainty things undo me.

He bade me then that necklace use,
    And told me too, he maketh
A glorious end by such a noose,
    His death for love that taketh.

'Twas but a dream ; but had I been
    There really alone,
My desperate fears, in love, had seen
    Mine execution.

No Difference i' th' Dark.

NIGHT makes no difference 'twixt the priest and clerk ;
Joan, as my lady, is as good i' th' dark.

The Body.

THE body is the soul's poor house or home,
Whose ribs the laths are, and whose flesh the loam.

To Sappho.

THOU say'st thou lov'st me, Sappho ; I say no ;
But would to Love I could believe 'twas so !
Pardon my fears, sweet Sappho ; I desire
That thou be righteous found, and I the liar.

Out of Time, out of Tune.

WE blame, nay, we despise her pains
That wets her garden when it rains ;
But when the drought has dried the knot,
Then let her use the watering-pot ;
We pray for showers, at our need,
To drench but not to drown our seed.

To his Book.

TAKE mine advice, and go not near
Those faces, sour as vinegar ;
For these the nobler numbers can
Ne'er please the supercilious man.

To his Honoured Friend Sir Thomas Heale.

STAND by the magic of my powerful rhymes,
'Gainst all the indignation of the times ;
Age shall not wrong thee, or one jot abate
Of thy both great and everlasting fate :
While others perish, here's thy life decreed,
Because begot of my immortal seed.

The Sacrifice, by way of Discourse betwixt Himself and Julia.

Herr. COME and let 's in solemn wise
Both address to sacrifice ;
Old religion first commands
That we wash our hearts and hands.
Is the beast exempt from stain,
Altar clean, do fire profane?
Are the garlands, is the nard
Ready here ?   *Jul.* All well prepar'd,
With the wine that must be shed,
'Twixt the horns, upon the head
Of the holy beast we bring
For our trespass-offering.
Herr. All is well : now, next to these,
Put we on pure surplices ;
And with chaplets crowned, we'll roast
With perfumes the holocaust ;
And while we the gods invoke,
Read acceptance by the smoke.

To Apollo.

THOU mighty lord and master of the lyre,
Unshorn Apollo, come and re-inspire
My fingers so the lyric strings to move
That I may play, and sing a hymn to Love.

On Love.

LOVE is a kind of war.   Hence those who fear !
No cowards must his royal ensigns bear.

Another.

WHERE Love begins, there dead thy first desire ;
A spark neglected makes a mighty fire.

An Hymn to Cupid.

THOU, thou that bear'st the sway,
With whom the sea-nymphs play,
And Venus, every way ;
When I embrace thy knee,
And make short prayers to thee,
In love ! then prosper me
This day I go to woo,
Instruct me how to do
This work thou put'st me to.
From shame my face keep free,
From scorn I beg of thee,
Love, to deliver me !
So shall I sing thy praise,
And to thee altars raise,
Unto the end of days.

To Electra.

LET not thy tombstone e'er be laid by me,
Nor let my hearse be wept upon by thee ;
But let that instant when thou die'st be known
The minute of mine expiration :
One knell be rung for both, and let one grave
To hold us two an endless honour have.

How his Soul came Ensnared

My soul would one day go and seek
For roses, and in Julia's cheek
A richess of those sweets she found,
As in another Rosamond.
But gathering roses as she was,
Not knowing what would come to pass,

It chanced a ringlet of her hair
Caught my poor soul, as in a snare,
Which ever since has been in thrall,
Yet freedom she enjoys withal.

Factions.

THE factions of the great ones call,
To side with them, the commons all.

Upon Reape.

REAPE'S eyes so raw are, that it seems the flies
Mistake the flesh, and fly-blow both his eyes ;
So that an angler, for a day's expense,
May bait his hook with maggots taken thence.

Upon Teage

TEAGE has told lies so long, that when Teage tells
Truth, yet Teage's truths are untruths, nothing else.

Upon Julia's Hair bundled up in a Golden Net.

TELL me, what needs those rich deceits,
These golden toils and trammel-nets,
To take thine hairs, when they are known
Already tame, and all thine own ?
'Tis I am wild, and more than hairs
Deserve these meshes and those snares.
Set free thy tresses ; let them flow
As airs do breathe or winds do blow;
And let such curious networks be
Less set for them than spread for me.

Upon Truggin.

TRUGGIN a footman was but now, grown lame,
Truggin now lives but to belie his name.

The Shower of Blossoms.

LOVE in a shower of blossoms came
Down, and half-drowned me with the same ;
The blooms that fell were white and red,
But with such sweets commingled,
As whether, this I cannot tell,
My sight was pleased more, or my smell ;
But true it was, as I rolled there,
Without a thought of hurt or fear,

Love turned himself into a bee,
And with his javelin wounded me,
From which mishap this use I make—
Where most sweets are, there lies a snake;
Kisses and favours are sweet things,
But those have thorns and these have stings.

Upon Spenke.

SPENKE has a strong breath, yet short prayers saith;
Not out of want of breath, but want of faith.

A Defence of Women.

NAUGHT are all women; I say no,
Since for one bad on good I know:
For Clytemnestra most unkind
Loving Alcestis there we find;
For one Medea that was bad
A good Penelope was had;
For wanton Laïs then we have
Chaste Lucrece, or a wife as grave;
And thus through womankind we see
A good and bad, Sirs, credit me.

Upon Lulls.

LULLS swears he is all heart, but you'll suppose
By his proboscis that he is all nose.

Slavery.

'TIS liberty to serve one lord, but he
Who many serves, serves base civility.

Charms.

BRING the holy crust of bread,
Lay it underneath the head;
'Tis a certain charm to keep
Hags away while children sleep.

Another.

LET the superstitious wife
Near the child's heart lay a knife,
Point be up and haft be down;
While she gossips in the town,
This, 'mongst other mystic charms,
Keeps the sleeping child from harms.

Another Charm for Stables.

HANG up hooks and shears to scare
Hence the hag that rides the mare,
Till they be all over wet
With the mire and the sweat ;
This observed, the manes shall be
Of your horses all knot-free.

Ceremonies for Candlemas Eve.

DOWN with rosemary and bays,
  Down with the misletoe ;
Instead of holly, now upraise
  The greener box, for show.

The holly hitherto did sway ;
  Let box now domineer
Until the dancing Easter Day
  Or Easter's eve appear.

Then youthful box, which now hath grace
  Your houses to renew,
Grown old, surrender must his place
  Unto the crisped yew.

When yew is out, then birch comes in,
  And many flowers beside,
Both of a fresh and fragrant kin,
  To honour Whitsuntide.

Green rushes then, and sweetest bents,
  With cooler oaken boughs,
Come in for comely ornaments,
  To re-adorn the house.
Thus times do shift, each thing his turn does hold ;
New things succeed as former things grow old.

The Ceremonies for Candlemas Day.

KINDLE the Christmas brand, and then
  Till sunset let it burn,
Which quenched, then lay it up again
  Till Christmas next return.

Part must be kept, wherewith to teend
  The Christmas log next year,
And where 'tis safely kept, the fiend
  Can do no mischief there.

Upon Candlemas Day.

END now the white-loaf and the pie,
And let all sports with Christmas die.

Surfeits.

BAD are all surfeits, but physicians call
That surfeit took my bread the worst of all.

Upon Nis.

NIS, he makes verses, but the lines he writes
Serve but for matter to make paper kites.

To Biancha, to Bless Him.

WOULD I woo, and would I win,
Would I well my work begin,
Would I evermore be crowned
With the end that I propound,
Would I frustrate or prevent
All aspects malevolent,
Thwart all wizards, and with these
Dead all black contingencies,
Place my words, and all works else
In most happy parallels,
All will prosper, if so be
I be kissed or blessed by thee.

Julia's Churching, or Purification.

PUT on thy holy filletings, and so
To the temple with the sober midwife go ;
Attended thus, in a most solemn wise,
By those who serve the childbed mysteries,
Burn first thine incense ; next, whenas thou see'st
The candid stole thrown o'er the pious priest,
With reverent curtsies come, and to him bring
Thy free and not decurted offering.
All rites well ended, with fair auspice come,
As to the breaking of a bridecake, home.
Where ceremonious Hymen shall for thee
Provide a second epithalamy ;
She who keeps chastely to her husband's side
Is not for one but every night his bride.

To his Book.

BEFORE the press scarce one could see
A little peeping part of thee,

But since thou'rt printed thou dost call
To show thy nakedness to all ;
My care for thee is now the less,
Having resigned thy shamefacedness :
Go with thy faults and fates, yet stay
And take this sentence then away—
Whom one beloved will not suffice,
She'll run to all adulteries.

Tears.

TEARS most prevail, with tears too thou may'st move
Rocks to relent and coyest maids to love.

To his Friend, to avoid Contention of Words.

WORDS beget anger, anger brings forth blows,
Blows make of dearest friends immortal foes ;
For which prevention, 'sociate, let there be
Betwixt us two no more logomachy ;
Far better 'twere for either to be mute,
Than for to murder friendship by dispute.

Truth.

TRUTH is best found out by the time and eyes ;
Falsehood wins credit by uncertainties.

Upon Prickles.—Epigram.

PRICKLES is waspish, and puts forth his sting,
For bread, drink, butter, cheese ; for everything
That Prickles buys puts Prickles out of frame :
How well his nature's fitted to his name !

The Eyes before the Ears.

WE credit most our sight ; one eye doth please
Our trust far more than ten ear-witnesses.

Want.

WANT is a softer wax, that takes thereon,
This, that, and every base impression.

To a Friend.

LOOK in my book, and herein see
Life endless sign'd to thee and me :
We o'er the tombs and fates shall fly,
While other generations die.

Upon Mr. William Lawes, the rare Musician.

SHOULD I not put on blacks, when each one here
Comes with his cypress, and devotes a tear?
Should I not grieve, my Lawes, when every lute,
Viol, and voice is, by thy loss, struck mute?
Thy loss, brave man! whose numbers have been hurled,
And no less praised than spread throughout the world:
Some have thee called Amphion; some of us
Named thee Terpander, or sweet Orpheus;
Some this, some that; but all in this agree,
Music had both her birth and death with thee.

The Honeycomb.

IF thou hast found an honeycomb,
Eat thou not all, but taste on some;
For if thou eat'st it to excess,
That sweetness turns to loathsomeness:
Taste it to temper, then 'twill be
Marrow and manna unto thee.

Upon Ben Jonson.

HERE lies Jonson with the rest
Of the poets, but the best.
Reader, wouldst thou more have known?
Ask his story, not this stone;
That will speak what this can't tell
Of his glory.   So farewell.

An Ode for Him.

AH, Ben!
Say how or when
Shall we, thy guests,
Meet at those lyric feasts
Made at the Sun,
The Dog, the Triple Tun;
Where we such clusters had
As made us nobly wild, not mad?
And yet each verse of thine
Outdid the meat, outdid the frolic wine.

My Ben!
Or come again,
Or send to us
Thy wit's great overplus;
But teach us yet
Wisely to husband it,
Lest we that talent spend,
And having once brought to an end
That precious stock, the store
Of such a wit the world should have no more,

Upon a Virgin.

SPEND, harmless shade, thy nightly hours,
Selecting here both herbs and flowers,
Of which make garlands here and there,
To dress thy silent sepulchre.
Nor do thou fear the want of these
In everlasting properties,
Since we fresh strewings will bring hither
Far faster than the first can wither.

Blame.

IN battles what disasters fall,
The king he bears the blames of all.

A Request to the Graces.

PONDER my words, if so that any be
Known guilty here of incivility ;
Let what is graceless, discomposed, and rude,
With sweetness, smoothness, softness, be endued;
Teach it to blush, to curtsey, lisp, and show
Demure, but yet full of temptation too.
Numbers ne'er tickle, or but lightly please,
Unless they have some wanton carriages :
This if ye do, each piece will here be good,
And graceful made by your neat sisterhood.

Upon Himself.

I LATELY fried, but now behold
I freeze as fast, and shake for cold,
And, in good faith, I'd thought it strange
T' have found in me this sudden change,
But that I understood by dreams,
These only were but love's extremes,
Who fires with hope the lover's heart,
And starves with cold the self-same part.

Multitude.

WE trust not to the multitude in war,
But to the stout and those that skilful are.

Fear.

MAN must do well out of a good intent,
Not for the servile fear of punishment.

To Mr. Kellam.

WHAT ! ! Can my Kellam drink his sack
  In goblets to the brim,
And see his Robin Herrick lack,
  Yet send no bowls to him ?

For love or pity to his Muse,
  That she may flow in verse,
Contemn to recommend a cruse,
  But send to her a tierce.

Cunctation in Correction.

THE lictors bundled up their rods ; beside,
Knit them with knots, with much ado untied,
That if, unknitting, men would yet repent,
They might escape the lash of punishment.

Present Government Grievous.

MEN are suspicious, prone to discontent ;
Subjects still loath the present government.

Rest Refreshes.

LAY by the good a while, a resting field
Will after ease a richer harvest yield ;
Trees this year bear : next, they their wealth withhold ;
Continual reaping makes a land wax old.

Revenge.

MAN'S disposition is for to requite
  An injury before a benefit ;
  Thanksgiving is a burden and a pain ;
  Revenge is pleasing to us, as our gain.

The First Mars or Makes.

IN all our high designments 'twill appear
The first event breeds confidence or fear.

Beginning, Difficult.

HARD are the two first stairs unto a crown,
Which got, the third bids him a king come down.

Faith Four-square.

FAITH is a thing that's four-square ; let it fall
This way or that, it not declines at all.

The Present Time best Pleaseth.

PRAISE they that will time past, I joy to see
Myself now live ; this age best pleaseth me.

Clothes are Conspirators.

THOUGH from without no foes at all we fear ;
We shall be wounded by the clothes we wear.

Cruelty.

'TIS but a dog-like madness in bad kings
For to delight in wounds and murderings ;
As some plants prosper best by cuts and blows,
So kings by killing do increase their foes.

Fair after Foul.

TEARS quickly dry ; griefs will in time decay ;
A clear will come after a cloudy day.

Hunger.

ASK me what hunger is, and I'll reply,
'Tis but a fierce desire of hot and dry.

Bad Wages for Good Service.

IN this misfortune kings do most excel,
To hear the worst from men, when they do well.

The End.

CONQUER we shall, but we must first contend ;
'Tis not the fight that crowns us, but the end.

The Bondman.

BIND me but to thee with thine hair,
   And quickly I shall be
Made, by that fetter or that snare,
   A bondman unto thee.

Or if thou tak'st that bond away,
   Then bore me through the ear,
And by the law I ought to stay
   For ever with thee here.

Choose for the Best.

GIVE house-room to the best ; 'tis never known
Virtue and pleasure both to dwell in one.

To Silvia.

PARDON my trespass, Silvia ; I confess
My kiss outwent the bounds of shamefacedness ;
None is discreet at all times—no, not Jove
Himself at one time can be wise and love.

Fair shows Deceit.

SMOOTH was the sea, and seemed to call
To pretty girls to play withal ;
Who paddling there, the sea soon frowned,
And on a sudden both were drowned.
What credit can we give to seas,
Who, kissing, kill such saints as these ?

His Wish.

FAT be my hind, unlearned be my wife,
Peaceful my night, my day devoid of strife :
To these a comely offspring I desire,
Singing about my everlasting fire.

A Mean in our Means.

THOUGH frankincense the deities require,
We must not give all to the hallowed fire ;
Such be our gifts, and such be our expense,
As for ourselves to leave some frankincense.

Upon Clunn.

A ROLL of parchment Clunn about him bears,
Charged with the arms of all his ancestors ;
And seems half-ravished when he looks upon
That Bar, this Bend, that Fess, this Cheveron ;
This Manch, that Moon, this Martlet and that Mound ;
This counterchange of Pearl and Diamond.
What joy can Clunn have in that coat or this,
Whenas his own still out at elbows is ?

Upon Cupid.

LOVE, like a beggar, came to me,
With hose and doublet torn,
His shirt bedangling from his knee,
With hat and shoes outworn.

He asked an alms ; I gave him bread,
  And meat too, for his need,
Of which, when he had fully fed,
  He wished me all good speed.

Away he went, but as he turned,
  In faith I know not how,
He touched me so as that I burn,
  And am tormented now.

Love's silent flames and fires obscure
  Then crept into my heart,
And though I saw no bow, I 'm sure
  His finger was the dart.

Upon Burr.

BURR is a smell-feast and a man alone
That, where meat is, will be a hanger-on.

An Hymn to Love.

I WILL confess
  With cheerfulness,
Love is a thing so likes me,
  That, let her lay
  On me all day
I'll kiss the hand that strikes me.

I will not, I
  Now blubb'ring cry ;
It, ah ! too late repents me.
  That I did fall
  To love at all,
Since love so much contents me.

No, no, I'll be
  In fetters free ;
While others they sit wringing
  Their hands for pain,
  I'll entertain
The wounds of love with singing.

With flowers and wine,
  And cakes divine,
To strike me I will tempt thee ;
  Which done, no more
  I'll come before
Thee and thine altars empty.

To his Honoured and most Ingenious Friend Mr. Charles Cotton.

FOR brave comportment, wit without offence,
Words fully flowing, yet of influence,
Thou art that man of men the man alone
Worthy the public admiration ;
Who with thine own eyes read'st what we do write,
And giv'st our numbers euphony and weight ;
Tell'st when a verse springs high, how understood
To be or not born of the royal blood ;
What state above, what symmetry below,
Lines have, or should have, thou the best can show ;
For which, my Charles, it is my pride to be
Not so much known as to be loved of thee ;
Long may I live so, and my wreath of bays
Be less another's laurel then thy praise.

Women Useless.

WHAT need we marry women, when
Without their use we may have men,
And such as will in short time be
For murder fit, or mutiny ?
As Cadmus once a new way found,
By throwing teeth into the ground,
From which poor seed, and rudely sown,
Sprung up a warlike nation ;
So let us iron, silver, gold,
Brass, lead, or tin, throw into th' mould,
And we shall see in little space
Rise up of men a fighting race.
If this can be, say then what need
Have we of women or their seed ?

Love is a Syrup.

LOVE is a syrup, and whoe'er we see
Sick and surcharged with this satiety,
Shall by this pleasing trespass quickly prove,
There 's loathsomeness e'en in the sweets of love.

Leaven.

LOVE is a leaven, and a loving kiss
The leaven of a loving sweetheart is.

Repletion.

PHYSICIANS say, repletion springs
More from the sweet than sour things.

On Himself.

WEEP for the dead, for they have lost this light ;
And weep for me, lost in an endless night ;
Or mourn or make a marble verse for me,
Who writ for many.   Benedicite.

No Man without Money.

No man such rare parts hath that he can swim
If favour or occasion help not him.

On Himself.

LOST to the world, lost to myself, alone
Here now I rest under this marble stone,
In depth of silence, heard and seen of none.

To Mr. Leonard Willan, his Peculiar Friend.

I WILL be short, and having quickly hurled
This line about, live thou throughout the world,
Who art a man for all scenes, unto whom
What's hard to others nothing's troublesome :
Canst write the comic strain, and fall
From these to pen the pleasing pastoral ;
Who fliest at all heights; prose and verse run'st through ;
Find'st here a fault, and mend'st the trespass too ;
For which I might extol thee, but speak less,
Because thyself art coming to the press ;
And then should I in praising thee be slow,
Posterity will pay thee what I owe.

To his Worthy Friend, Mr. John Hall, Student of Gray's Inn.

TELL me, young man, or did the Muses bring
Thee less to taste than to drink up their spring,
That none hereafter should be thought or be
A poet, or a poet like, but thee ?
What was thy birth, thy star that makes thee known,
At twice ten years, a prime and public one ?
Tell us thy nation, kindred, or the whence
Thou hadst and hast thy mighty influence,
That makes thee loved, and of the men desired,
And no less praised than of the maids admired.
Put on thy laurel then, and in that trim
Be thou Apollo, or the type of him ;
Or let the unshorn god lend thee his lyre,
And next to him be master of the choir.

To Julia.

OFFER thy gift; but first the law commands
Thee, Julia, first to sanctify thy hands:
Do that, my Julia, which the rites require,
Then boldly give thine incense to the fire.

To the most Comely and Proper Miss Elizabeth Finch.

HANDSOME you are, and proper you will be,
Despite of all your infortunity;
Live long and lovely, but yet grow no less
In that your own prefixed comeliness;
Spend on that stock, and when your life must fall,
Leave others beauty to set up withal.

Upon Ralph.

RALPH pares his nails, his warts, and corns, and Ralph
In several tills and boxes keeps 'em safe,
Instead of hartshorn, if he speaks the troth,
To make a lusty jelly for his broth.

To his Book.

IF hap it must that I must see thee lie
Absyrtus-like, all torn confusedly,
With solemn tears and with much grief of heart
I'll re-collect thee, weeping, part by part,
And having wash'd thee, close thee in a chest
With spice; that done, I'll leave thee to thy rest.

To the King, upon his Welcome to Hampton Court. Set and sung.

WELCOME, great Cæsar! welcome now you are
As dearest peace after destructive war;
Welcome as slumbers, or as beds of ease,
After our long and peevish sicknesses.
O pomp of glory! Welcome now, and come
To repossess once more your longed-for home;
A thousand altars smoke, a thousand thighs
Of beeves here ready stand for sacrifice;
Enter and prosper, while our eyes do wait
For an ascendant th'roughly auspiciate,
Under which sign we may the former stone
Lay of our safety's new foundation.
That done, O Cæsar! live, and be to us
Our Fate, our Fortune, and our Genius,

To whose free knees we may our temples tie,
As to a still protecting Deity :
That should you stir, we, and our altars too,
May, great Augustus, go along with you.
Chor. Long live the King ! and to accomplish this,
We'll from our own add far more years to his.

Ultimus Heroum ; or, to the most Learned and to the Right Honourable Henry, Marquis of Dorchester.

AND as, time past, when Cato the severe
Entered the circumspacious theatre,
In reverence of his person, every one
Stood as he had been turned from flesh to stone ;
E'en so my numbers will astonished be
If but looked on, struck dead, if scanned, by thee.

To his Muse.—Another to the same.

TELL that brave man, fain thou wouldst have access
To kiss his hands, but that for fearfulness,
Or else because thou'rt, like a modest bride,
Ready to blush to death should he but chide.

Upon Vinegar.

VINEGAR is no other, I define,
Than the dead corpse or carcase of the wine.

To his learned Friend Mr. John Harmar, Physician to the College of Westminster.

WHEN first I find those numbers thou dost write
To be most soft, terse, sweet, and perpolite,
Next, when I see thee towering in the sky,
In an expansion no less large than high,
Then in that compass, sailing here and there,
And with circumgyration everywhere,
Following with love and active heat thy game,
And then at last to truss the epigram ;
I must confess, distinction none I see
Between Domitian's Martial than to thee.
But this I know, should Jupiter again
Descend from heaven to reconverse with men,
The Roman language, full and superfine,
If Jove would speak, he would accept of thine.

Upon his Spaniel Tracy.

Now thou art dead, no eye shall ever see,
For shape and service, spaniel like to thee;
This shall my love do, give thy sad death one
Tear, that deserves of me a million.

The Deluge.

DROWNING, drowning, I espy
Coming from my Julia's eye;
'Tis some solace in our smart
To have friends to bear a part:
I have none, but must be sure
The inundation to endure.
Shall not times hereafter tell
This for no mean miracle,
When the waters by their fall
Threaten'd ruin unto all,
Yet the deluge here was known
Of a world to drown but one?

Upon Lupes.

LUPES for the outside of his suit has paid,
But, for his heart, he cannot have it made;
The reason is, his credit cannot get
The inward garbage for his clothes as yet.

Rags.

WHAT are our patches, tatters, rags, and rents,
But the base dregs and lees of vestiments?

Strength to support Sovereignty.

LET kings and rulers learn this line from me;
Where power is weak, unsafe is majesty.

Upon Tubbs.

FOR thirty years Tubbs has been proud and poor
'Tis now his habit, which he can't give o'er.

Crutches.

THOU seest me, Lucia, this year droop;
Three zodiacs filled more, I shall stoop;
Let crutches then provided be,
To shore up my debility.

Then while thou laugh'st I'll sighing cry,
A ruin underpropped am I ;
Don will I then my beadsman's gown,
And when so feeble I am grown
As my weak shoulders cannot bear
The burden of a grasshopper,
Yet with the bench of aged sires,
When I and they keep termly fires,
With my weak voice I'll sing or say
Some odes I made of Lucia ;
Then will I heave my withered hand
To Jove the mighty, for to stand
Thy faithful friend, and to pour down
Upon thee many a benison.

To Julia.

HOLY waters hither bring
For the sacred sprinkling ;
Baptise me and thee, and so
Let us to the altar go ;
And ere we our rites commence,
Wash our hands in innocence ;
Then I'll be the *Rex Sacrorum*,
Thou the Queen of Peace and Quorum.

Upon Case.

CASE is a lawyer that ne'er pleads alone,
But when he hears the like confusion
As when the disagreeing Commons throw
About their House their clamorous Aye or No,
Then Case, as loud as any sergeant there,
Cries out, " My lord, my lord, the case is clear;"
But when all's hushed, Case, than a fish more mute,
Bestirs his hand, but starves in hand the suit.

To Perenna.

I A DIRGE will pen for thee,
Thou a trental make for me,
That the monks and friars together
Here may sing the rest of either ;
Next, I'm sure the nuns will have
Candlemas to grace the grave.

To his Sister-in-Law, Miss Susanna Herrick.

THE person crowns the place ; your lot doth fall
Last, yet to be with these a principal ;
Howe'er it fortuned, know for truth I meant
You a foreleader in this testament.

Upon the Lady Crew.

THIS stone can tell the story of my life,
What was my birth, to whom I was a wife;
In teeming years how soon my sun was set,
Where now I rest, these may be known by jet;
For other things, my many children be
The best and truest chronicles of me.

On Tomasin Parsons.

GROW up in beauty, as thou dost begin,
And be of all admired, Tomasin.

Ceremony upon Candlemas Eve.

DOWN with the rosemary, and so
Down with the bays and mistletoe;
Down with the holly, ivy, all
Wherewith ye dressed the Christmas hall,
That so the superstitious find
No one least branch there left behind;
For look, how many leaves there be
Neglected there, maids, trust to me,
So many goblins you shall see.

Suspicion makes Secure.

HE that will live of all cares dispossessed
Must shun the bad, aye, and suspect the best.

Upon Spokes.

SPOKES, when he sees a roasted pig, he swears
Nothing he loves on 't but the chaps and ears;
But carve to him the fat flanks, and he shall
Rid these and those, and part by part eat all.

To his Kinsman, Mr. Thomas Herrick, who desired to be in his Book.

WELCOME to this my College, and though late,
Thou 'st got a place here, standing candidate,
It matters not, since thou art chosen one
Here of my great and good foundation.

A Bucolic betwixt Two: Lacon and Thyrsis.

Lacon. For a kiss or two, confess,
What doth cause this pensiveness,
Thou most lovely neatherdess?

Why so lonely on the hill,
Why thy pipe by thee so still,
That erewhile was heard so shrill?

Tell me, do thy kine now fail
To fulfil the milking-pail?
Say, what is 't that thou dost ail?

Thyr. None of these; but out, alas!
A mischance is come to pass,
And I'll tell thee what it was:
See, mine eyes are weeping ripe.
Lacon. Tell, and I'll lay down my pipe.

Thyr. I have lost my lovely steer,
That to me was far more dear
Than these kine which I milk here;
Broad of forehead, large of eye,
Party coloured like a pie,
Smooth in each limb as a die;
Clear of hoof, and clear of horn,
Sharply pointed as a thorn;
With a neck by yoke unworn,
From the which hung down by strings,
Balls of cowslips, daisy rings,
Interplaced with ribbonings;
Faultless every way for shape,
Not a straw could him escape;
Ever gamesome as an ape,
But yet harmless as a sheep.
Pardon, Lacon, if I weep;
Tears will spring where woes are deep.
Now, ah me! ah me!   Last night
Came a mad dog, and did bite,
Aye, and killed my dear delight.

Lacon. Alack, for grief!
Thyr. But I'll be brief.

Hence I must, for time doth call
Me, and my sad playmates all,
To his evening funeral.
Live long, Lacon; so adieu!
Lacon. Mournful maid, farewell to you;
Earth afford ye flowers to strew!

Upon Sappho.

LOOK upon Sappho's lip, and you will swear
There is a love-like leaven rising there.

Upon Faunus.

WE read how Faunus, he the shepherd's god,
His wife to death whipped with a myrtle rod ;
The rod, perhaps, was bettered by the name,
But had it been of birch, the death 's the same.

A Bacchanalian Verse.

DRINK up
Your cup,
But not spill wine ;
For if you
Do,
'Tis an ill sign,
That we
Foresee
You are cloy'd here ;
If so, no
Ho !
But avoid here.

Care a Good Keeper.

CARE keeps the conquest ; 'tis no less renown
To keep a city than to win a town.

Rules for our Reach.

MEN must have bounds how far to walk ; for we
Are made far worse by lawless liberty.

To Biancha.

AH, Biancha! now I see
It is noon and past with me ;
In a while it will strike one,
Then, Biancha, I am gone.
Some effusions let me have
Offer'd on my holy grave ;
Then, Biancha, let me rest
With my face towards the East.

To the Handsome Mistress Grace Potter.

As in your name so is your comely face,
Touched everywhere with such diffused grace,
As that in all that admirable round
There is not one least solecism found,
And as that part, so every portion else
Keeps line for line with beauty's parallels.

Anacreontic.

I MUST
Not trust
Here to any ;
Bereaved,
Deceived,
By so many ;
As one
Undone
By my losses,
Comply
Will I
With my crosses.
Yet still
I will
Not be grieving ;
Since thence
And hence
Comes relieving.
But this
Sweet is
In our mourning
Times bad
And sad
Are a turning ;
And he
Whom we
See dejected,
Next day
We may
See erected.

More Modest, More Manly.

'TIS still observ'd, those men more valiant are
That are most modest ere they come to war.

Not to Covet much where Little is the Charge.

WHY should we covet much, when as we know
We've more to bear our charge than way go to.

Anacreontic Verse.

BRISK, methinks I am, and fine,
When I drink my cap'ring wine ;
Then to love I do incline,
When I drink my wanton wine ;

And I wish all maidens mine
When I drink my sprightly wine;
Well I sup, and well I dine,
When I drink my frolic wine;
But I languish, lower, and pine,
When I want my fragrant wine.

Upon Pennie.

BROWN bread Tom Pennie eats, and must of right,
Because his stock will not hold out for white.

Patience in Princes.

KINGS must not use the axe for each offence;
Princes cure some faults by their patience.

Fear gets Force.

DESPAIR takes heart when there's no hope to speed;
The coward then takes arms, and does the deed.

Parcel-gilt Poetry.

LET'S strive to be the best; the gods, we know it,
Pillars and men hate an indifferent poet.

Upon Love, by way of Question and Answer.

I BRING ye love.   *Ques.* What will love do
   Ans. Like and dislike ye.
I bring ye love.   *Ques.* What will love do?
   Ans. Stroke ye, to strike ye.
I bring ye love.   *Ques.* What will love do?
   Ans. Love will befool ye.
I bring ye love.   *Ques.* What will love do?
   Ans. Heat ye, to cool ye.
I bring ye love.   *Ques.* What will love do?
   Ans. Love gifts will send ye.
I bring ye love.   *Ques.* What will love do?
   Ans. Stock ye, to spend ye.
I bring ye love.   *Ques.* What will love do?
   Ans. Love will fulfil ye.
I bring ye love.   *Ques.* What will love do?
   Ans. Kiss ye, to kill ye.

To the Lord Hopton, on his Fight in Cornwall.

Go on, brave Hopton, to effectuate that
Which we, and times to come, shall wonder at;
Lift up thy sword; next, suffer it to fall,
And by that one blow set an end to all.

His Grange.

How well contented in this private grange
Spend I my life, that's subject unto change ;
Under whose roof, with mosswork wrought, there I
Kiss my brown wife and black posterity.

Leprosy in Houses.

When to a house I come, and see
The Genius wasteful more than free ;
The servants thumbless, yet to eat
With lawless tooth the flour of wheat ;
The sons to suck the milk of kine
More than the teats of discipline ;
The daughters wild and loose in dress,
Their cheeks unstained with shamefacedness;
The husband drunk, the wife to be
A bawd to incivility;
I must confess I there descry
A house spread through with leprosy.

Anthea's Retractation.

Anthea laughed, and fearing lest excess
Might stretch the cords of civil comeliness,
She with a dainty blush rebuked her face,
And called each line back to his rule and space.

Comforts in Crosses.

Be not dismayed though crosses cast thee down,
Thy fall is but the rising to a crown.

Seek and Find.

Attempt the end, and never stand to doubt,
Nothing 's so hard but search will find it out.

Rest.

On with thy work, thou be'st hardly prest ;
Labour is held up by the hope of rest.

Leprosy in Clothes.

When flowing garments I behold,
Inspired with purple, pearl, and gold,
I think no other but I see
In them a glorious leprosy,

That does infect, and make the rent
More mortal in the vestiment.
As flowery vestures do descry
The wearer's rich immodesty,
So plain and simple clothes do show
Where virtue walks, not those that flow.

Upon Buggins.

BUGGINS is drunk all night—all day he sleeps ;
This is the level-coil that Buggins keeps.

Great Maladies, Long Medicines.

To an old sore a long cure must go on ;
Great faults require great satisfaction.

His Answer to a Friend.

YOU ask me what I do and how I live?
And, noble friend, this answer I must give .
Drooping, I draw on to the vaults of death,
O'er which you'll walk when I am laid beneath.

The Beggar.

SHALL I a daily beggar be,
For love's sake asking alms of thee ?
Still shall I crave, and never get
A hope of my desired bit ?
Ah, cruel maids ! I'll go my way
Whereas, perchance, my fortunes may
Find out a threshold or a door,
That may far sooner speed the poor.
Where thrice we knock and none will hear,
Cold comfort still I'm sure lives there.

His Change.

MY many cares and much distress
Has made me like a wilderness ;
Or, discomposed, I'm like a rude
And all confused multitude
Out of my comely manners worn,
And as in means, in mind all torn.

A Vow to Venus.

HAPPILY I had a sight
Of my dearest dear last night ;
Make her this day smile on me,
And I'll roses give to thee.

On his Book.

THE bound, almost, now of my book I see
But yet no end of those therein or me ;
Here we begin new life, while thousands quite
Are lost, and theirs, in everlasting night.

A Sonnet of Perilla.

THEN did I live when I did see
Perilla smile on none but me !
But, ah ! by stars malignant crossed,
The life I got I quickly lost ;
But yet a way there doth remain
For me embalmed to live again,
And that's to love me, in which state
I'll live as one regenerate.

Bad may be Better.

MAN may at first transgress, but next do well ;
Vice doth in some but lodge a while, not dwell.

Posting to Printing.

LET others to the printing-press run fast ;
Since after death comes glory, I'll not haste.

Rapine brings Ruin.

WHAT'S got by justice is established sure ;
No kingdoms got by rapine long endure.

Comfort to a Youth that had Lost his Love.

WHAT needs complaints,
When she a place
Has with the race
  Of saints ?
In endless mirth
She thinks not on
What's said or done
  In earth :
She sees no tears,
Or any tone
Of thy deep groan
  She hears ;
Nor does she mind,
Or think on 't now,
That ever thou
  Wast kind.

But changed above,
She likes not there,
As she did here,
Thy love.
Forbear, therefore,
And lull asleep
Thy woes, and weep
No more.

Upon Boreman.—Epigram.

BOREMAN takes toll, cheats, flatters, lies ; yet Boreman,
For all the devil helps, will be a poor man.

Saint Distaff's Day ; or, the Morrow after Twelfth Day.

PARTLY work and partly play
Ye must on St. Distaff's day;
From the plough soon free your team,
Then come home and fodder them ;
If the maids a-spinning go,
Burn the flax and fire the tow ;
Scorch their plackets, but beware
That ye singe no maiden-hair ;
Bring in pails of water then,
Let the maids bewash the men ;
Give St. Distaff all the right,
Then bid Christmas sport good-night,
And next morrow every one
To his own vocation.

Sufferance.

IN the hope of ease to come,
Let's endure one martyrdom.

His Tears to Thamesis.

I SEND, I send here my supremest kiss,
To thee, my silver-footed Thamesis ;
No more shall I reiterate thy strand,
Whereon so many stately structures stand,
Nor in the summer's sweeter evenings go,
To bathe in thee, as thousand others do ;
No more shall I along thy crystal glide
In barge, with boughs and rushes beautified,
With soft smooth virgins for our chaste disport,
To Richmond, Kingston, and to Hampton Court ;
Never again shall I with finny oar
Put from or draw unto the faithful shore ;

And landing here, or safely landing there,
Make way to my beloved Westminster,
Or to the golden Cheapside, where the earth
Of Julia Herrick gave to me my birth.
May all clean nymphs and curious water dames
With swan-like state float up and down thy streams;
No drought upon thy wanton waters fall,
To make them lean and languishing at all;
No ruffling winds come hither to disease
Thy pure and silver-wristed Naiades.
Keep up your state, ye streams, and as ye spring,
Never make sick your banks by surfeiting;
Grow young with tides, and though I see ye never,
Receive this vow; so fare ye well for ever.

Pardons.

THOSE ends in war the best contentment bring
Whose peace is made up with a pardoning.

Peace not Permanent.

GREAT cities seldom rest; if there be none
To invade from far, they'll find worse foes at home.

Truth and Error.

'TWIXT truth and error there's this difference known—
Error is fruitful, truth is only one.

Things Mortal still Mutable.

THINGS are uncertain, and the more we get,
The more on icy pavements we are set.

Studies to be Supported.

STUDIES themselves will languish and decay
When either price or praise is ta'en away.

Wit Punished Prospers most.

DREAD not the shackles; on with thine intent;
Good wits get more fame by their punishment.

Twelfth Night; or, King and Queen.

Now, now the mirth comes
With the cake full of plums,
Where Bean's the king of the sport here;
Beside, we must know
The Pea also
Must revel as queen in the court here.

Begin then to choose,
This night as ye use,
Who shall for the present delight here ;
Be a king by the lot,
And who shall not
Be Twelve-day queen for the night here.

Which known, let us make
Joy-sops with the cake,
And let not a man then be seen here,
Who unurged will not drink,
To the base from the brink,
A health to the king and the queen here.

Next crown the bowl full
With gentle lambs' wool,
Add sugar, nutmeg. and ginger,
With store of ale too ;
And thus ye must do
To make the wassail a swinger.

Give then to the king
And queen wassailing,
And though with ale ye be wet here,
Yet part ye from hence
As free from offence
As when ye innocent met here.

His Desire.

GIVE me a man that is not dull
When all the world with rifts is full,
But unamazed dares clearly sing
Whenas the roof's a-tottering,
And though it falls, continues still
Tickling the cittern with his quill.

Caution in Council.

KNOW when to speak, for many times it brings
Danger to give the best advice to kings.

Moderation.

LET moderation on thy passions wait ;
Who loves too much, too much the loved will hate.

Advice the best Actor.

STILL take advice ; though counsels, when they fly
At random, sometimes hit most happily.

Conformity is Comely.

CONFORMITY gives comeliness to things,
And equal shares exclude all murmurings.

Laws.

WHO violates the customs, hurts the health,
Not of one man, but all the commonwealth.

Like Loves his Like.

LIKE will to like ; each creature loves his kind ;
Chaste words proceed still from a bashful mind.

His Hope or Sheet-anchor.

AMONG these tempests, great and manifold,
My ship has here one only anchor-hold ;
That is my hope, which if that slip I'm one
Wilder'd in this vast watery region.

Comfort in Calamity.

'TIS no discomfort in the world to fall
When the great crack not crushes one, but all.

Twilight.

THE twilight is no other thing, we say,
Than night now gone, and yet not sprung the day.

False Mourning.

HE who wears blacks and mourns not for the dead,
Does but deride the party buried.

The Will makes the Work, or Consent makes the Cure.

NO grief is grown so desperate but the ill
Is half-way cured, if the party will.

Diet.

IF wholesome diet can recure a man,
What need of physic or physician ?

Smart.

STRIPES, justly given, yerk us with their fall,
But causeless whipping smarts the most of all.

The Tinker's Song.

ALONG, come along,
Let's meet in a throng
    Here of tinkers ;
And quaff up the bowl,
And big as a cowl,
    To beer-drinkers.
The pole of the hop
Place in the ale-shop,
    To bethwack us,
If ever we think
So much as to drink
    Unto Bacchus.
Who frolic will be
For little cost, he
    Must not vary
From beer-broth at all
So much as to call
    For canary.

His Comfort.

THE only comfort of my life
Is, that I never yet had wife,
Nor will hereafter, since I know
Who weds or buys his weal with woe.

Sincerity.

WASH clean the vessel, lest ye sour
Whatever liquor in ye pour.

To Anthea.

SICK is Anthea, sickly is the spring,
The primrose sick, and sickly everything ;
The while my dear Anthea does but droop,
The tulips, lilies, daffodils do stoop ;
But when again she's got her healthful hour,
Each bending then will rise a proper flower.

Nor Buying or Selling.

Now, if you love me, tell me.
For as I will not sell ye,
So not one cross to buy thee
I'll give, if thou deny me.

To his Peculiar Friend, Mr. John Wicks.

SINCE shed or cottage I have none,
I sing the more, that thou hast one,
To whose glad threshold and free door
I may a poet come, though poor,
And eat with thee a savoury bit,
Paying but common thanks for it.
Yet should I chance, my Wicks, fo see
An over-leaven look in thee,
To sour the bread and turn the beer
To an exalted vinegar;
Or shouldst thou prize me as a dish
Of thrice boiled worts, or third day's fish,
I'd rather hungry go and come,
Than to thy house be burdensome:
Yet in my depth of grief I'd be
One that should drop his beads for thee.

The more Mighty, the more Merciful.

WHO may do most, does least; the bravest will
Show mercy there where they have power to kill.

After Autumn, Winter.

DIE ere long I'm sure I shall;
After leaves the tree must fall.

A Good Death.

FOR truth I may this sentence tell,
No man dies ill that liveth well.

Recompense.

WHO plants an olive but to eat the oil?
Reward, we know, is the chief end of toil.

On Fortune.

THIS is my comfort, when she's most unkind,
She can but spoil me of my means, not mind.

To Sir George Parry, Doctor of the Civil Law.

I HAVE my laurel chaplet on my head,
If 'mongst these many numbers to be read
But one by you be hugged and cherished.

Peruse my measures thoroughly, and where
Your judgment finds a guilty poem, there
Be you a judge, but not a judge severe.

The mean pass by, or over—none contemn ;
The good applaud ; the peccant less condemn,
Since absolution you can give to them.

Stand forth, brave man, here to the public sight,
And in my book now claim a twofold right—
The first as Doctor and the last as Knight.

Charms.

THIS I'll tell ye by the way,
Maidens, when ye leavens lay,
Cross your dough, and your dispatch
Will be better for your batch.

Another.

IN the morning when ye rise,
Wash your hands and cleanse your eyes ;
Next, be sure ye have a care
To disperse the water far,
For as far as that doth light
So far keeps the evil sprite.

Another.

IF ye fear to be affrighted,
When ye are by chance benighted,
In your pocket, for a trust,
Carry nothing but a crust,
For that holy piece of bread
Charms the danger and the dread.

Gentleness.

THAT prince must govern with a gentle hand
Who will have love comply with his command.

A Dialogue betwixt Himself and Mistress Elizabeth Wheeler, under the name of Amarillis.

MY dearest love, since thou wilt go,
    And leave me here behind thee,
For love or pity, let me know
    The place where I may find thee.

Amaril. In country meadows, pearled with dew
    And set about with lilies,
There, filling maunds with cowslips, you
    May find your Amarillis.

Her. What have the meads to do with thee,
 Or with thy youthful hours?
Live thou at court, where thou may'st be
 The queen of men, not flowers.

Let country wenches make 'em fine
 With posies, since 'tis fitter
For thee with richest gems to shine,
 And like the stars to glitter.

Amaril. You set too high a rate upon
 A shepherdess so homely.
Her. Believe it, dearest, there's not one
 I' th' court that's half so comely.

I prithee stay. *Amaril.* I must away ;
 Let's kiss first, then we'll sever.
Ambo. And though we bid adieu to-day,
 We shall not part for ever.

To Julia.

HELP me, Julia, for to pray,
Matins sing, or matins say ;
This I know, the fiend will fly
Far away, if thou be'st by ;
Bring the holy water hither ;
Let us wash and pray together ;
When our beads are thus united,
Then the foe will fly affrighted.

To Roses in Julia's Bosom.

ROSES, you can never die,
Since the place wherein ye lie
Heat and moisture mixed are so
As to make ye ever grow.

To the Honoured Master Endymion Porter.

WHEN to thy porch I come, and, ravished, see
The state of poets there attending thee,
Those bards and I all in a chorus sing,
" We are thy prophets, Porter ; thou our king."

Speak in Season.

WHEN times are troubled, then forbear ; but speak
When a clear day out of a cloud does break.

Obedience.

THE power of princes rests in the consent
Of only those who are obedient,
Which if away, proud sceptres then will lie
Low, and of thrones the ancient majesty.

Another on the same.

No man so well a kingdom rules as he
Who hath himself obeyed the sovereignty.

Of Love.

1. INSTRUCT me now what love will do ;
2. 'Twill make a tongueless man to woo.
1. Inform me next what love will do ;
2. 'Twill strangely make a one of two.
1. Teach me besides what love will do ;
2. 'Twill quickly mar and make ye too.
1. Tell me, now last, what love will do ;
2. 'Twill hurt and heal a heart pierced through.

Upon Trap.

TRAP of a player turn'd a priest now is ;
Behold a sudden metamorphosis.
If tithe-pigs fail, then will he shift the scene,
And from a priest turn player once again.

Upon Grubs.

GRUBS loves his wife and children while that they
Can live by love, or else grow fat by play,
But when they call or cry on Grubs for meat,
Instead of bread, Grubs gives them stones to eat ;
He raves, he rends, and while he thus doth tear,
His wife and children fast to death for fear.

Upon Doll.

No question but Doll's cheeks would soon roast dry,
Were they not basted by her either eye.

Upon Hog.

HOG has a place i' th' kitchen, and his share
The flimsy livers and blue gizzards are.

The School or Pearl of Putney, the Mistress of all Singular Manners, Mistress Portman.

WHETHER I was myself, or else did see
Out of myself that glorious hierarchy ;
Or whether those, in orders rare, or these,
Made up one state of sixty Venuses ;
Or whether fairies, syrens, nymphs they were,
Or Muses, on their mountain sitting there ;
Or some enchanted place, I do not know ;
Or Sharon, where eternal roses grow ;
This I am sure, I ravished stood, as one
Confused in utter admiration.
Methought I saw them stir, and gently move,
And look as all were capable of love ;
And in their motion smelt much like to flowers
Inspired by the sunbeams after dews and showers.
There did I see the reverend Rectress stand,
Who with her eyes' gleam, or a glance of hand,
Those spirits raised, and with like precepts then,
As with a magic, laid them all again :
A happy realm ! when no compulsive law,
Or fear of it, but love keeps all in awe.
Live you, great mistress of your arts, and be
A nursing mother so to majesty,
As those your ladies may in time be seen
For grace and carriage every one a queen.
One birth their parents gave them, but their new
And better being they receive from you :
Man's former birth is graceless, but the state
Of life comes in when he's regenerate.

To Perenna.

THOU say'st I'm dull ; if edgeless so I be,
I'll whet my lips, and sharpen love on thee.

On Love.

THAT love 'twixt men does ever longest last,
Where war and peace the dice by turns do cast.

Another on Love.

LOVE'S of itself too sweet ; the best of all
Is, when love's honey has a dash of gall.

Upon Gut.

SCIENCE puffs up, says Gut, when either pease
Make him thus swell, or windy cabbages.

Upon Chub.

WHEN Chub brings in his harvest, still he cries,
" Aha, my boys ! here's wheat for Christmas pies !"
Soon after, he for beer so scores his wheat,
That at the tide he has not bread to eat.

Pleasures Pernicious.

WHERE pleasures rule a kingdom, never there
Is sober virtue seen to move her sphere.

On Himself.

A WEARIED pilgrim I have wandered here,
Twice five-and-twenty, bate me but one year ;
Long I have lasted in this world, 'tis true,
But yet those years that I have lived, but few.
Who by his grey hairs doth his lustres tell,
Lives not those years, but he that lives them well ;
One man has reached his sixty years, but he
Of all those threescore has not lived half three ;
He lives who lives to virtue ; men who cast
Their ends for pleasure, do not live, but last.

To Mr. Laurence Swettenham.

READ thou my lines, my Swettenham ; if there be
A fault, 'tis hid, if it be voiced by thee :
Thy mouth will make the sourest numbers please ;
How will it drop pure honey, speaking these ?

His Covenant or Protestation to Julia.

WHY dost thou wound and break my heart,
As if we should for ever part ?
Hast thou not heard an oath from me,--
After a day or two, or three.
I would come back and live with thee ?
Take, if thou dost distrust that vow,
This second protestation now
Upon thy cheek that spangled tear
Which sits as dew of roses there,
That tear shall scarce be dried before
I'll kiss the threshold of thy door ;

Then weep not, sweet, but this much know,
I'm half returned before I go.

On Himself.

I WILL no longer kiss,
  I can no longer stay ;
The way of all flesh is,
  That I must go this day.
Since longer I can't live,
  My frolic youths, adieu,
My lamp to you I'll give,
  And all my troubles too.

To the most Accomplished Gentleman, Master Michael Oulsworth.

NOR think that thou in this my book art worst
Because not placed here with the midst or first,
Since fame that sides with these, or goes before
Those, that must live with thee for evermore ;
That fame, and fame's reared pillar, thou shalt see
In the next sheet, brave man, to follow thee ;
Fix on that column then, and never fall,
Held up by fame's eternal pedestal.

To his Girls, who would have him Sportful.

ALAS ! I can't, for tell me how
Can I be gamesome, aged now ;
Besides, ye see me daily grow
Here, winter-like, to frost and snow,
And I, ere long, my girls, shall see
Ye quake for cold to look on me.

Truth and Falsehood.

TRUTH by her own simplicity is known,
Falsehood by varnish and vermilion.

His Last Request to Julia.

I HAVE been wanton and too bold, I fear,
To chafe o'ermuch the virgin's cheek or ear ;
Beg for my pardon, Julia ; he doth win
Grace with the gods who 's sorry for his sin ;
That done, my Julia, dearest Julia, come,
And go with me to choose my burial room.
My fates are ended ; when thy Herrick dies,
Clasp thou his book, then close thou up his eyes.

On Himself.

ONE ear tingles : some there be
That are snarling now at me.
Be they those that Homer bit,
I will give them thanks for it.

Upon Kings.

KINGS must be dauntless ; subjects will contemn
Those who want hearts, and wear a diadem.

To his Girls.

WANTON wenches, do not bring,
For my hairs, black colouring ;
For my locks, girls, let 'em be
Gray or white, all 's one to me.

Upon Spur.

SPUR jingles now, and swears by no mean oaths.
He 's double honoured since he 's got gay clothes :
Most like his suit, and all commend the trim,
And thus they praise the sumpter, but not him ;
As to the goddess people did confer
Worship, and not to the ass that carried her.

To his Brother, Nicholas Herrick.

WHAT others have with cheapness seen, and ease,
In varnished maps, by the help of compasses,
Or read in volumes, and those books, with all
Their large narrations, incanonical.
Thou hast beheld ; those seas and countries far,
And tell'st to us what once they were and are.
So that with bold truth thou canst now relate
This kingdom's fortune and that empire's fate ;
Canst talk to us of Sharon, where a spring
Of roses have an endless flourishing ;
Of Sion, Sinai, Nebo, and with them
Make known to us the new Jerusalem,
The Mount of Olives, Calvary, and where
Is, and hast seen, thy Saviour's sepulchre :
So that the man that will but lay his ears,
As inapostate, to the thing he hears,
Shall by his hearing quickly come to see
The truth of travels less in books than thee.

The Voice and the Viol.

RARE is the voice itself, but when we sing
To the lute or viol, then 'tis ravishing.

War.

IF kings and kingdoms once distracted be,
The sword of war must try the sovereignty.

A King and no King.

THAT prince who may do nothing but what's just,
Rules but by leave, and takes his crown on trust.

Plots not still Prosperous.

ALL are not ill plots that do sometimes fail,
Nor those false vows which oftimes don't prevail.

Flattery.

WHAT is 't that wastes a prince?   Example shows,
'Tis flattery spends a king more than his foes.

Excess.

EXCESS is sluttish; keep the mean—for why?
Virtue's clean conclave is sobriety.

Upon Croot.

ONE silver spoon shines in the house of Croot,
Who cannot buy or steal a second to 't.

The Soul is the Salt.

THE body's salt the soul is; which when gone,
The flesh soon sucks in putrefaction.

Upon Flood, or a Thankful Man.

FLOOD, if he has for him and his a bit,
He says his fore and after grace for it;
If meat he wants, then grace he says to see
His hungry belly borne by legs jail-free :
Thus have or have not, all alike is good
To this our poor yet ever patient Flood.

Upon Pimp.

WHEN Pimp's feet sweat, as they do often use,
There springs a soap-like lather in his shoes.

Upon Lusk.

IN De'nshire kersey, Lusk, when he was dead,
Would shrouded be, and therewith buried ;
When his assigns ask him the reason why,
He said, because he got his wealth thereby.

Foolishness.

IN's Tusc'lans, Tully doth confess
No plague there's like to foolishness.

Upon Rush.

RUSH saves his shoes in wet and snowy weather,
And fears in summer to wear out the leather ;
This is strong thrift that wary Rush doth use,
Summer and winter, still to save his shoes.

Abstinence.

AGAINST diseases here the strongest fence
Is the defensive virtue, abstinence.

No Danger to Men Desperate.

WHEN fear admits no hope of safety, then
Necessity makes dastards valiant men.

Sauce for Sorrows.

ALTHOUGH our suffering meet with no relief,
An equal mind is the best sauce for grief.

To Cupid.

I HAVE a leaden, thou a shaft of gold ;
Thou kill'st with heat, and I strike dead with cold :
Let's try of us who shall the first expire,
Or thou be frost, or I be quenchless fire.
Extremes are fatal where they once do strike,
And bring to the heart destruction both alike.

Distrust.

WHATEVER men for loyalty pretend,
'Tis wisdom's part to doubt a faithful friend.

The Hag.

IN a dirty hair lace
  She leads on a brace
Of black-boar cats to attend her,
  Who scratch at the moon,
  And threaten at noon
Of night from heaven for to rend her.

  A hunting she goes ;
  A cracked horn she blows,
At which the hounds fall a-bounding ;
  While the moon in her sphere
  Peeps trembling for fear,
And night 's afraid of the sounding.

The Mount of the Muses.

AFTER thy labour take thine ease
Here with the sweet Pierides ;
But if so be that men will not
Give thee the laurel crown for lot,
Be yet assured thou shalt have one
Not subject to corruption.

On Himself.

I'LL write no more of love, but now repent
Of all those times that I in it have spent ;
I'll write no more of life, but wish 'twas ended,
And that my dust was to the earth commended.

To his Book.

Go thou forth, my book, though late,
Yet be timely fortunate.
It may chance good luck may send
Thee a kinsman or a friend,
That may harbour thee, when I
With my fates neglected lie ;
If thou know'st not where to dwell,
See, the fire 's by. Farewell.

The End of his Work.

PART of the work remains, one part is past ;
And here my ship rides, having anchor cast.

To Crown it.

My wearied bark, O let it now be crowned !
The haven reached to which I first was bound.

On Himself.

THE work is done ; young men and maidens set
Upon my curls the myrtle coronet.
Washed with sweet ointments; thus at last I come
To suffer in the Muses' martyrdom,
But with this comfort, if my blood be shed,
The Muses will wear blacks when I am dead.

The Pillar of Fame.

FAME'S pillar here at last we set,
Out-during marble, brass, or jet ;
   Charmed and enchanted so,
   As to withstand the blow
      Of   overthrow ;
      Nor shall the seas,
      Or OUTRAGES
      Of storms o'erbear
      What we uprear ;
      Tho' kingdoms fall,
   This pillar never shall
   Decline or waste at all
But stand for ever by his own
Firm and well-fixed foundation.

To his book's end this last line he'd have placed :
JOCUND HIS MUSE WAS, BUT HIS LIFE WAS CHASTE.

His Noble Numbers;

OR, HIS PIOUS PIECES.

His Confession.

Look how our foul days do exceed our fair ;
And as our bad more than our good works are,
Ev'n so those lines, penned by my wanton wit,
Treble the number of these good I've writ.
Things precious are least numerous ; men are prone
To do ten bad for one good action.

His Prayer for Absolution.

For those my unbaptizéd rhymes,
Writ in my wild unhallowed times,
For every sentence, clause, and word,
That's not inlaid with thee, my Lord,
Forgive me, God, and blot each line
Out of my book that is not thine.
But if, 'mongst all, thou find'st here one
Worthy thy benediction,
That one of all the rest shall be
The glory of my work and me.

To Find God.

Weigh me the fire ; or canst thou find
A way to measure out the wind ;
Distinguish all those floods that are
Mixed in that watery theatre ;
And taste thou them as saltless there
As in their channel first they were ;
Tell me the people that do keep
Within the kingdoms of the deep ;

Or fetch me back that cloud again,
Beshivered into seeds of rain ;
Tell me the motes, dust, sands, and spears
Of corn, when summer shakes his ears ;
Show me that world of stars, and whence
They noiseless spill their influence ;
This if thou canst, then show me Him
That rides the glorious cherubim.

What God is.

GOD is above the sphere of our esteem,
And is the best known, not defining Him.

Upon God.

GOD is not only said to be
An Ens, but Supraentity.

Mercy and Love.

GOD hath two wings, which He doth ever move,
The one is Mercy, and the next is Love ;
Under the first the sinners ever trust,
And with the last he still directs the just.

God's Anger without Affection.

GOD, when He's angry here with any one,
His wrath is free from perturbation ;
And when we think His looks are sour and grim,
The alteration is in us, not Him.

God not to be Comprehended.

'Tis hard to find God, but to comprehend
Him as He is, is labour without end.

God's Part.

PRAYERS and praises are those spotless two
Lambs, by the law, which God requires as due.

Affliction.

GOD ne'er afflicts us more than our desert,
'Though He may seem to overact His part ;
Sometimes He strikes us more than flesh can bear,
But yet still less than grace can suffer here.

Three Fatal Sisters.

THREE fatal sisters wait upon each sin ;
First, Fear and Shame without, then Guilt within.

Silence.

SUFFER thy legs, but not thy tongue, to walk ;
God, the most wise, is sparing of His talk.

Mirth.

TRUE mirth resides not in the smiling skin :
The sweetest solace is to act no sin.

Loading and Unloading.

GOD loads and unloads ; thus His work begins,
To load with blessings, and unload from sins.

God's Mercy.

GOD's boundless mercy is to sinful man
Like to the ever-wealthy ocean,
Which, though it sends forth thousand streams, 'tis ne'er
Known, or else seen to be the emptier,
And though it takes all in, 'tis yet no more
Full, and filled-full, than when full-filled before.

Prayers must have Poise.

GOD, He rejects all prayers that are slight
And want their poise ; words ought to have their weight.

To God : an Anthem sung in the Chapel at Whitehall before the King.

Verse. MY GOD, I'm wounded by my sin,
And sore without and sick within,
Ver. Chor. I come to thee, in hope to find
Salve for my body and my mind.
Verse. In Gilead though no balm be found
To ease this smart or cure this wound
Ver. Chor. Yet, Lord, I know there is with thee
All saving health and help for me.

Verse. Then reach Thou forth that hand of thine,
That pours in oil as well as wine ;
Ver. Chor. And let it work, for I'll endure
The utmost smart, so thou wilt cure.

Upon God.

GOD is all fore-part, for we never see
Any part backward in the Deity.

Calling and Correcting.

GOD is not only merciful, to call
Men to repent, but when He strikes withal.

No Escaping the Scourging.

GOD scourgeth some severely, some He spares,
But all in smart have less or greater shares.

The Rod.

GOD's rod doth watch while men do sleep, and then
The rod doth sleep while vigilant are men.

God has a Twofold Part.

GOD when for sin He makes his children smart,
His own He acts not, but another's part ;
But when by stripes He saves them, then 'tis known,
He comes to play the part that is His own.

God is One.

GOD as He is most Holy known,
So He is said to be most One.

Persecutions Profitable.

AFFLICTIONS they most profitable are
To the beholder and the sufferer ;
Bettering them both, but by a double strain,
The first by patience, and the last by pain.

To God.

Do with me, God, as thou didst deal with John,
Who writ that heavenly Revelation ;
Let me, like him, first cracks of thunder hear,
Then let the harp's enchantments strike mine ear ;
Here give me thorns : there in thy kingdom set
Upon my head the golden coronet ;
There give me day, but here my dreadful night ;
My sackcloth here, but there my stole of white.

Whips.

God has his whips here to a twofold end,
The bad to punish, and the good t' amend.

God's Providence.

If all transgressions here should have their pay,
What need there then be of a reck'ning day ;
If God should punish no sin, here, of men,
His Providence who would not question then ?

Temptation.

Those saints which God loves best
The devil tempts not least.

His Ejaculation to God.

My God! look on me with thine eye
Of pity, not of scrutiny ;
For if thou dost, thou then shalt see
Nothing but loathsome sores in me.
O then, for mercy's sake, behold
These my irruptions manifold,
And heal me with thy look or touch ;
But if thou wilt not deign so much,
Because I'm odious in thy sight,
Speak but the word, and cure me quite.

God's Gifts Not Soon Granted.

God hears us when we pray, but yet defers
His gifts to exerci petitioners,
And though a while He makes requesters stay,
With princely hand He'll recompense delay.

Persecutions Purify.

GOD strikes His church, but 'tis to this intent,
To make not mar her, by this punishment ;
So where He gives the bitter pills, be sure
'Tis not to poison, but to make thee pure.

Pardon.

GOD pardons those who do through frailty sin,
But never those that persevere therein.

An Ode of the Birth of Our Saviour.

IN numbers, and but these few,
I sing thy birth, oh JESU !
Thou pretty Baby, born here,
With superabundant scorn here,
Who for thy princely port here,
    Hadst for thy place
    Of birth, a base
Out-stable for thy court here.

Instead of neat enclosures
Of interwoven osiers,
Instead of fragrant posies
Of daffodils and roses,
Thy cradle, Kingly Stranger,
    As Gospel tells,
    Was nothing else,
But, here, a homely manger.

But we with silks, not crewels,
With sundry precious jewels,
And lily-work, will dress thee ;
And as we dispossess thee
Of clouts, we'll make a chamber,
    Sweet Babe, for thee,
    Of ivory,
And plastered round with amber.

The Jews they did disdain thee,
But we will entertain thee
With glories to await here
Upon thy princely state here,
And more for love than pity ;
    From year to year
    We'll make thee here
A freeborn of our city.

Lip Labour.

IN the old Scripture I have often read,
The calf without meal ne'er was offered;
To figure to us nothing more than this,
Without the heart, lip-labour nothing is.

The Heart.

IN prayer the lips ne'er act the winning part
Without the sweet concurrence of the heart.

Earrings.

WHY wore th' Egyptians jewels in the ear,
But for to teach us, all the grace is there,
When we obey, by acting what we hear?

Sin Seen.

WHEN once the sin has fully acted been,
Then is the horror of the trespass seen.

Upon Time.

TIME was upon
The wing, to fly away ;
And I called on
Him but a while to stay ;
But he'd be gone,
For aught that I could say.

He held out then
A writing, as he went,
And asked me, when
False man would be content
To pay again
What God and nature lent.

An hour-glass,
In which were sands but few,
As he did pass,
He showed, and told me too
Mine end near was,
And so away he flew.

His Petition.

IF war or want shall make me grow so poor
As for to beg my bread from door to door,
Lord, let me never act that beggar's part,
Who hath Thee in his mouth, not in his heart.
He who asks alms in that so sacred Name,
Without due reverence, plays the cheater's game.

To God.

THOU hast promised, Lord, to be
With me in my misery :
Suffer me to be so bold
As to speak, Lord, say and hold.

His Litany to the Holy Spirit.

IN the hour of my distress,
When temptations me oppress,
And when I my sins confess,
      Sweet Spirit, comfort me !

When I lie within my bed,
Sick in heart and sick in head,
And with doubts discomforted,
      Sweet Spirit, comfort me !

When the house doth sigh and weep,
And the world is drowned in sleep,
Yet mine eyes the watch do keep,
      Sweet Spirit, comfort me !

When the artless doctor sees
No one hope, but of his fees,
And his skill runs on the lees,
      Sweet Spirit, comfort me !

When his potion and his pill,
His or none or little skill,
Meet for nothing but to kill,
      Sweet Spirit, comfort me !

When the passing-bell doth toll,
And the furies in a shoal
Come to fright a parting soul,
      Sweet Spirit, comfort me !

When the tapers now burn blue,
And the comforters are few,
And that number more than true,
      Sweet Spirit, comfort me !

When the priest his last hath prayed,
And I nod to what is said
'Cause my speech is now decayed,
    Sweet Spirit, comfort me !

When, God knows, I'm tossed about,
Either with despair or doubt,
Yet, before the glass be out,
    Sweet Spirit, comfort me !

When the tempter me pursueth
With the sins of all my youth,
And half damns me with untruth,
    Sweet Spirit, comfort me !

When the flames and hellish cries
Fright mine ears and fright mine eyes,
And all terrors me surprise,
    Sweet Spirit, comfort me !

When the Judgment is revealed,
And that opened which was sealed,
When to thee I have appealed,
    Sweet Spirit, comfort me !

Thanksgiving.

THANKSGIVING for a former doth invite
God to bestow a second benefit.

Cock-crow.

BELLMAN of night, if I about shall go
For to deny my Master, do thou crow.
Thou stopp'd'st St. Peter in the midst of sin.
Stay me, by crowing, ere I do begin ;
Better it is, premonished, for to shun
A sin, than fall to weeping when 'tis done.

All Things run well for the Righteous.

ADVERSE and prosperous fortunes both work on
Here for the righteous man's salvation ;
Be he opposed, or be he not withstood,
All serve to th' augmentation of his good.

Pain Ends in Pleasure.

AFFLICTIONS bring us joy in times to come,
When sins, by stripes, to us grow wearisome.

To God.

I'll come, I'll creep, though thou dost threat,
Humbly unto thy mercy-seat;
When I am there, this then I'll do,
Give thee a dart and dagger too;
Next, when I have my faults confessed,
Naked, I'll show a sighing breast,
Which, if that can't thy pity woo,
Then let thy justice do the rest,
      And strike it through.

A Thanksgiving to God for His House.

Lord, thou hast given me a cell
    Wherein to dwell,
A little house, whose humble roof
    Is weatherproof,
Under the spars of which I lie
    Both soft and dry;
Where thou, my chamber for to ward.
    Hast set a guard
Of harmless thoughts, to watch and keep
    Me while I sleep.
Low is my porch, as is my fate,
    Both void of state;
And yet the threshold of my door
    Is worn by th' poor,
Who thither come and freely get
    Good words or meat.
Like as my parlour so my hall
    And kitchen's small;
A little buttery, and therein
    A little bin,
Which keeps my little loaf of bread
    Unchipped, unfled;
Some brittle sticks of thorn or briar
    Make me a fire
Close by whose living coal I sit,
    And glow like it.
Lord, I confess too, when I dine,
    The pulse is thine,
And all those other bits that be
    There placed by thee;
The worts, the purslane, and the mess
    Of water-cress,
Which of thy kindness thou has sent;
    And my content

Makes those, and my beloved beet,
        To be more sweet
'Tis thou that crown'st my glittering hearth
        With guiltless mirth,
And giv'st me wassail bowls to drink,
        Spiced to the brink.
Lord, 'tis thy plenty-dropping hand
        That soils my land,
And giv'st me, for my bushel sown,
        Twice ten for one;
Thou mak'st my teeming hen to lay
        Her egg each day;
Besides my healthful ewes to bear
        Me twins each year;
The while the conduits of my kine
        Run cream, for wine.
All these, and better thou dost send
        Me, to this end,
That I should render, for my part,
        A thankful heart,
Which, fired with incense, I resign,
        As wholly thine;
But the acceptance,—that must be,
        My Christ, by Thee.

To God.

MAKE, make me thine, my gracious God,
Or with thy staff, or with thy rod;
And be the blow, too, what it will,
Lord, I will kiss it, though it kill;
Beat me, bruise me, rack me, rend me,
Yet in torments I'll commend thee;
Examine me with fire, and prove me
To the full, yet I will love thee;
Nor shalt thou give so deep a wound,
But I as patient will be found.

Another to God.

        LORD, do not beat me,
Since I do sob and cry,
And swoon away to die
        Ere thou dost threat me.

        Lord, do not scourge me,
If I, by lies and oaths,
Have soiled myself, or clothe,
        But rather purge me.

None Truly Happy Here.

HAPPY 's that man to whom God gives
A stock of goods, whereby he lives
Near to the wishes of his heart;
No man is blest through ev'ry part.

To his Ever-loving God.

CAN I not come to thee, my God, for these
So very many meeting hindrances,
That slack my pace, but yet not make me stay?
Who slowly goes, rids, in the end, his way.
Clear thou my paths, or shorten thou my miles,
Remove the bars, or lift me o'er the stiles;
Since rough the way is, help me when I call,
And take me up, or else prevent the fall.
I ken my home, and it affords some ease
To see far off the smoking villages.
Fain would I rest. yet covet not to die,
For fear of future biting penury;
No, no, my God, thou know'st my wishes be
To leave this life, not loving it, but thee.

Another.

THOU bidd'st me come; I cannot come; for why
Thou dwell'st aloft, and I want wings to fly.
To mount my soul, she must have pinions given,
For 'tis no easy way from earth to heaven.

To Death.

THOU bidd'st me come away,
And I'll no longer stay
Than for to shed some tears
For faults of former years,
And to repent some crimes
Done in the present times;
And next, to take a bit
Of bread, and wine with it;
To don my robes of love,
Fit for the place above;
To gird my loins about
With charity throughout,
And so to travel hence
With feet of innocence:
These done, I'll only cry,
" God, mercy !" and so die

Neutrality Loathsome.

GOD will have all or none; serve him, or fall
Down before Baal, Bel, or Belial :
Either be hot or cold, God doth despise,
Abhor, and spue out all neutralities.

Welcome what Comes.

WHATEVER comes, let's be content withal ;
Among God's blessings there is no one small.

To his Angry God.

THROUGH all the night
Thou dost me fright,
And hold'st mine eyes from sleeping ;
And day by day
My cup can say,
My wine is mixed with weeping.

Thou dost my bread
With ashes knead,
Each evening and each morrow;
Mine eye and ear
Do see and hear
The coming in of sorrow.

Thy scourge of steel,
Ah me ! I feel
Upon me beating ever;
While my sick heart
With dismal smart
Is disacquainted never.

Long, long, I'm sure,
This can't endure;
But in short time 'twill please thee,
My gentle God,
To burn the rod,
Or strike so as to ease me.

Patience, or Comforts in Crosses.

ABUNDANT plagues I late have had,
Yet none of these have made me sad;
For why? My Saviour, with the sense
Of suffering, gives me patience.

Eternity.

O YEARS and age, farewell !
  Behold I go
  Where I do know
Infinity to dwell.

And these mine eyes shall see
  All times, how they
  Are lost i' th' sea
Of vast eternity.

Where never moon shall sway
  The stars, but she
  And night shall be
Drowned in one endless day.

To his Saviour, a Child ; a Present, by a Child.

Go, pretty child, and bear this flower
Unto thy little Saviour;
And tell him, by that bud now blown,
He is the Rose of Sharon known.
When thou hast said so, stick it there
Upon his bib or stomacher ;
And tell him, for good handsel too,
That thou hast brought a whistle new,
Made of a clean strait oaten reed,
To charm his cries at time of need.
Tell him, for coral thou hast none,
But if thou hadst, he should have one;
But poor thou art, and known to be
Even as moneyless as he.
Lastly, if thou canst win a kiss
From those mellifluous lips of his ;
Then never take a second on,
To spoil the first impression.

The New Year's Gift.

LET others look for pearl and gold
Tissues, or tabbies manifold ;
One only lock of that sweet hay
Whereon the Blessed Baby lay,
Or one poor swaddling-clout, shall be
The richest New Year's gift to me.

To God.

IF anything delight me for to print
My book, 'tis this : that thou, my God, art in 't.

God and the King.

How am I bound to two ' God, who doth give
The mind; the King, the means whereby I live.

God's Mirth, Man's Mourning.

WHERE God is merry, there write down thy fears ;
What He with laughter speaks, hear thou with tears.

Honours are Hindrances.

GIVE me honours : what are these
But the pleasing hindrances,
Stiles, and stops, and stays, that come
In the way 'twixt me and home ?
Clear the walk, and then shall I
To my heaven less run than fly.

The Parasceve, or Preparation.

To a love-feast we both invited are ;
The figured damask or pure diaper.
Over the golden altar now is spread,
With bread, and wine, and vessels furnished ;
The sacred towel, and the holy ewer
Are ready by, to make the guests all pure ;
Let's go, my Alma ; yet ere we receive,
Fit, fit it is, we have our Par-sceve.
Who to that sweet bread unprepared doth come,
Better he starved than but to taste one crumb.

To God.

GOD gives not only corn for need,
But likewise sup'rabundant seed ;
Bread for our service, bread for show ;
Meat for our meals, and fragments too.

He gives not poorly, taking some
Between the finger and the thumb,
But for our glut and for our store
Fine flour pressed down and running o'er.

A Will to be Working.

ALTHOUGH we cannot turn the fervent fit
Of sin, we must strive 'gainst the stream of it ;

And howsoe'er we have the conquest missed,
'Tis for our glory that we did resist.

Christ's Part.

CHRIST, He requires still, wheresoe'er He comes
To feed or lodge, to have the best of rooms ;
Give him the choice, grant Him the nobler part
Of all the house : the best of all 's the heart.

Riches and Poverty.

GOD could have made all rich, or all men poor ;
But why he did not, let me tell wherefore :
Had all been rich, where then had patience been ?
Had all been poor, who had his bounty seen ?

Sobriety in Search.

To seek of God more than we well can find,
Argues a strong distemper of the mind.

Alms.

GIVE, if thou canst, an alms ; if not, afford,
Instead of that, a sweet and gentle word.
God crowns our goodness, wheresoe'er he sees,
On our part, wanting all abilities.

To his Conscience.

CAN I not sin but thou will be
My private protonotary ?
Can I not woo thee to pass by
A short and sweet iniquity ?
I'll cast a mist and cloud upon
My delicate transgression,
So utter dark as that no eye
Shall see the hugged impiety.
Gifts blind the wise, and bribes do please,
And wind all other witnesses ;
And wilt not thou with gold be tied
To lay thy pen and ink aside,
That in the mirk and tongueless night
Wanton I may, and thou not write ?
It will not be ; and therefore now,
For times to come, I'll make this vow,

From aberrations to live free,
So I'll not fear the judge or thee.

To his Saviour.

LORD, I confess that thou alone art able
To purify this my Augean stable ;
Be the seas water and the land all soap,
Yet if thy blood not wash me, there's no hope.

To God.

GOD is all-sufferance here ; here He doth show
No arrow notched, only a stringless bow ;
His arrows fly, and all his stones are hurled
Against the wicked in another world.

His Dream.

I DREAMT last night thou didst transfuse
Oil from thy jar into my cruse,
And pouring still thy wealthy store,
The vessel full, did then run o'er ;
Methought I did thy bounty chide,
To see the waste ; but 'twas replied
By thee, dear God, God gives men seed
Oftimes for waste, as for his need.
Then I could say, that house is bare
That has not bread, and some to spare.

God's Bounty.

GOD'S bounty, that ebbs less and less,
As men do wane in thankfulness.

To his Sweet Saviour.

NIGHT hath no wings to him that cannot sleep,
And Time seems then not for to fly, but creep ;
Slowly her chariot drives, as if that she
Had broke her wheel or cracked her axletree.
Just so it is with me, who list'ning, pray
The winds to blow the tedious night away,
That I might see the cheerful peeping day.
Sick is my heart ; O Saviour ! do Thou please
To make my bed soft in my sicknesses ;
Lighten my candle, so that I beneath,
Sleep not for ever in the vaults of death ;

Let me thy voice betimes i' th' morning hear ;
Call, and I'll come ; say Thou the when and where :
Draw me but first, and after Thee I'll run,
And make no one stop till my race be done.

His Creed.

I DO believe that die I must,
And be returned from out my dust ;
I do believe that when I rise,
Christ I shall see with these same eyes ;
I do believe that I must come
With others to the dreadful doom ;
I do believe the bad must go
From thence to everlasting woe ;
I do believe the good, and I,
Shall live with Him eternally ;
I do believe I shall inherit
Heaven by Christ's mercies, not my merit ;
I do believe the One in Three,
And Three in perfect Unity ;
Lastly, that JESUS is a deed
Of gift from God : and here's my Creed.

Temptations.

TEMPTATIONS hurt not, though they have access :
Satan o'ercomes none but by willingness.

The Lamp.

WHEN a man s faith is frozen up as dead,
Then is the lamp and oil extinguished.

Sorrows.

SORROWS our portion are ; ere hence we go,
Crosses we must have, or hereafter woe.

Penitence.

A MAN'S transgression God does then remit
When man he makes a Penitent for it.

The Dirge of Jephthah's Daughter.—Sung by the Virgins.

O THOU, the wonder of all days !
O paragon, and pearl of praise !

O Virgin martyr, ever blest
        Above the rest
Of all the maiden-train! We come,
And bring fresh strewings to thy tomb.

Thus, thus, and thus we compass round
Thy harmless and unhaunted ground,
And as we sing thy dirge, we will
        The daffodil
And other flowers lay upon
The altar of our love, thy stone.

Thou wonder of all maids, list here,
Of daughters all the dearest dear;
The eye of virgins; nay, the queen
        Of this smooth green,
And all sweet meads from whence we get
The primrose and the violet.

Too soon, too dear did Jephthah buy,
By thy sad loss, our liberty;
His was the bond and covenant, yet
        Thou pa'd'st the debt:
Lamented Maid! He won the day,
But for the conquest thou didst pay.

Thy father brought with him along
The olive branch and victor's song;
He slew the Ammonites, we know,
        But to thy woe,
And in the purchase of our peace.
The cure was worse than the disease.

For which obedient zeal of thine
We offer here, before thy shrine.
Our sighs for storax, tears for wine;
        And to make fine
And fresh thy hearse-cloth, we will here
Four times bestrew thee every year.

Receive, for this thy praise, our tears;
Receive this offering of our hairs;
Receive these crystal vials, filled
        With tears distilled
From teeming eyes; to these we bring,
Each maid, her silver filleting,

To gild thy tomb, besides, these cauls,
These laces, ribbons, and these falls,
These veils wherewith we use to hide
        The bashful bride
When we conduct her to her groom—
All, all we lay upon thy tomb.

No more, no more, since thou art dead,
Shall we e'er bring coy brides to bed ;
  No more, at yearly festivals,
      We cowslip balls
Or chains of columbines shall make
For this or that occasion's sake.

No, no ; our maiden pleasures be
Wrapt in the winding-sheet with thee ;
'Tis we are dead, though not i' th' grave,
      Or if we have
One seed of life left, 'tis to keep
A Lent for thee, to fast and weep.

Sleep in thy peace, thy bed of spice,
And make this place all paradise ;
May sweets grow here, and smoke from hence
      Fat frankincense ;
Let balm and cassia send their scent
From out thy maiden monument.

May no wolf howl, or screech-owl stir
A wing about thy sepulchre ;
No boisterous winds or storms come hither,
      To starve or wither
Thy soft sweet earth, but like a spring
Love keep it ever flourishing.

May all shy maids at wonted hours
Come forth to strew thy tomb with flowers ;
May virgins, when they come to mourn,
      Male incense burn
Upon thine altar, then return
And leave thee sleeping in thy urn.

To God, on his Sickness.

WHAT though my harp and viol be
Both hung upon the willow-tree?
What though my bed be now my grave,
And for my house I darkness have ?
What though my healthful days are fled,
And I lie numbered with the dead ?
Yet I have hope, by Thy great power
To spring, though now a withered flower.

Sins Loathed, and yet Loved.

SHAME checks our first attempts ; but then 'tis proved,
Sins first disliked are after that beloved.

Sin.

SIN leads the way, but as it goes it feels
The following plague still treading on his heels.

Upon God.

GOD, when He takes my goods and chattels henco,
Gives me a portion, giving patience ;
What is in God is God ; if so it be
He patience gives, He gives Himself to me.

Faith.

WHAT here we hope for, we shall once inherit ;
By faith we all walk here, not by the spirit.

Humility.

HUMBLE we must be, if to heaven we go;
High is the roof there, but the gate is low.
Whene'er thou speak'st, look with a lowly eye ;
Grace is increased by humility.

Tears.

OUR present tears here, not our present laughter,
Are but the handsels of our joys hereafter.

Sin and Strife.

AFTER true sorrow for our sins, our strife
Must last with Satan to the end of life.

An Ode or Psalm to God.

DEAR GOD !
If Thy smart rod
Here did not make me sorry,
I should not be
With Thine or Thee,
In Thy eternal glory.

But since
Thou didst convince

My sins by gently striking ;
And still to those
First stripes, new blows,
According to Thy liking.

Fear me,
Or scourging tear me,
That thus from vices driven,
I may from hell
Fly up to dwell
With Thee and Thine in heaven.

Graces for Children.

WHAT God gives, and what we take,
'Tis a gift for Christ His sake ;
Be the meal of beans and peas,
God be thanked for those and these ;
Have we flesh or have we fish,
All are fragments from His dish.
He His church save, and the king,
And our peace, here like a spring
Make it ever flourishing.

God to be First Served.

HONOUR thy parents ; but good manners call
Thee to adore thy God, the first of all.

Another Grace for a Child.

HERE a little child I stand,
Heaving up my either hand ;
Cold as paddocks though they be,
Here I lift them up to Thee,
For a benison to fall
On our meat and on us all.   Amen.

A Christmas Carol, sung to the King in the Presence at Whitehall.

Chor. WHAT sweeter music can we bring
Than a carol, for to sing
The birth of this our heavenly King?
Awake the voice, awake the string !
Heart, ear, and eye, and every thing,
Awake, the while the active finger
Runs division with the singer.

From the Flourish they came to the Song.

1. Dark and dull night, fly hence away,
And give the honour to this day,
That sees December turned to May.

2. If we may ask the reason, say
The why and wherefore all things here
Seem like the spring-time of the year?

3. Why does the chilling winter's morn
Smile like a field beset with corn ;
Or smell like to a mead new-shorn,
Thus on the sudden?   4. Come and see
The cause why things thus fragrant be.
'Tis He is born, whose quickening birth
Gives life and lustre, public mirth,
To heaven and the under earth.

Chor. We see Him come, and know Him ours,
Who, with His sunshine and His showers,
Turns all the patient ground to flowers.

1. The Darling of the world is come,
And fit it is we find a room
To welcome Him.   2. The nobler part
Of all the house here is the heart,

Chor. Which we will give him, and bequeath
This holly and this ivy wreath,
To do Him honour, who's our King,
And Lord of all this revelling.

The musical part was composed by
Mr. Henry Lawes.

The New Year's Gift, or Circumcision's Song.—
Sung to the King in the Presence at Whitehall.

1. PREPARE for songs ; He's come, He's come,
And be it sin here to be dumb,
And not with lutes to fill the room.

2. Cast holy water all about,
And have a care no fire goes out,
But cense the porch and place throughout.

3. The altars all on fire be ;
The storax fries, and ye may see
How heart and hand do all agree
To make things sweet.   *Chor.* Yet all is less sweet
     than He.

4. Bring Him along, most pious priest,
And tell us then, whenas thou see'st
His gently-gliding dove-like eyes,
And hear'st his whimp'ring and his cries,
How canst thou this babe circumcise?

5. Ye must not be more pitiful than wise ;
For, now unless ye see Him bleed,
Which makes the baptism, 'tis decreed
The birth is fruitless.   *Chor.* Then the work God speed.

1. Touch gently, gently touch, and here
Spring tulips up through all the year ;
And from his sacred blood, here shed,
May roses grow, to crown his own dear head.

Chor. Back, back again ; each thing is done
With zeal alike, as 'twas begun ;
Now, singing, homeward let us carry
The Babe unto his mother Mary,
And when we have the Child commended
To her warm bosom, then our rites are ended.

Composed by Mr. Henry Lawes.

Another New Year's Gift, or Song for the Circumcision.

1. HENCE, hence, profane, and none appear
With anything unhallowed here ;
No jot of leaven must be found
Concealed in this most holy ground.

2. What is corrupt, or soured with sin,
Leave that without, then enter in ;
Chor. But let no Christmas mirth begin
Before ye purge and circumcise
Your hearts and hands, lips, ears, and eyes.

3. Then like a perfumed altar see
That all things sweet and clean may be,
For here's a Babe that, like a bride,
Will blush to death if aught be spied
Ill-scenting or unpurified.

Chor. The room is censed ; help, help t' invoke
Heaven to come down the while we choke
The temple with a cloud of smoke.

4. Come then, and gently touch the birth
Of Him who's Lord of heaven and earth ;

5. And softly handle Him ; ye'd need,
Because the pretty Babe does bleed.

Poor pitied Child ! who from thy stall
Bring'st in thy blood a balm that shall
Be the best New Year's gift to all.

1. Let's bless the Babe, and as we sing
His praise, so let us bless the King.

Chor. Long may he live, till he hath told
His New Years trebled to his old,
And when that's done, to reaspire,
A new-born Phœnix from his own chaste fire.

God's Pardon.

WHEN I shall sin, pardon my trespass here,
For once in hell, none knows remission there.

Sin

SIN once reached up to God's eternal sphere,
And was committed, not remitted, there.

Evil.

EVIL no nature hath ; the loss of good
Is that which gives to sin a livelihood.

The Star Song ; a Carol to the King.—Sung at Whitehall.

The flourish of music ; then followed the song.

1. TELL us, thou clear and heavenly tongue,
Where is the Babe but lately sprung?
Lies He the lily-banks among?

2. Or say, if this new Birth of ours
Sleeps, laid within some ark of flowers,
Spangled with dew-light : thou can't clear
All doubts, and manifest the where.

3. Declare to us, bright star, if we shall seek
Him in the morning's blushing cheek,
Or search the bed of spices through
To find Him out ?
Star. No, this ye need not do ;
But only come and see Him rest,
A princely Babe, in 's mother's breast

Chor. He's seen ! He's seen ! Why then around
Let's kiss the sweet and holy ground,
And all rejoice that we have found
A King before conception crowned.

4. Come then, come then, and let us bring
Unto our pretty Twelfth-tide King
Each one his several offering ;

Chor. And when night comes we'll give him wassailing ;
And that his treble honours may be seen,
We'll choose him King, and make his mother Queen.

To God.

WITH golden censers and with incense here
Before thy virgin altar I appear,
To pay thee that I owe, since what I see
In or without, all, all belongs to Thee.
Where shall I now begin to make, for one
Least loan of thine, half restitution ?
Alas ! I cannot pay a jot ; therefore
I'll kiss the tally, and confess the score.
Ten thousand talents lent me thou dost write
'Tis true, my God, but I can't pay one mite.

To his dear God.

I'LL hope no more
For things that will not come,
And if they do, they prove but cumbersome.
Wealth brings much woe,
And, since it fortunes so,
'Tis better to be poor
Than so t' abound
As to be drowned
Or overwhelmed with store.

Pale care, avaunt !
I'll learn to be content
With that small stock thy bounty gave or lent.
What may conduce
To my most healthful use,
Almighty God, me grant ;
But that or this
That hurtful is,
Deny thy suppliant.

To God, his Good Will.

GOLD I have none, but I present my need,
O Thou that crown'st the will where wants the deed.

Where rams are wanting, or large bullocks' thighs,
There a poor lamb 's a plenteous sacrifice.
Take then his vows, who, if he had it, would
Devote to thee both incense, myrrh, and gold,
Upon an altar reared by him, and crowned
Both with the ruby, pearl, and diamond.

On Heaven.

PERMIT mine eyes to see
Part or the whole of thee,
    O happy place!
Where all have grace
And garlands shared,
 For their reward;
Where each chaste soul
In long white stole,
And palms in hand,
Do ravished stand;
So in a ring
The praises sing
Of Three in One,
That fill the throne,
While harps and viols then
To voices say, Amen.

The Sum and the Satisfaction.

LAST night I drew up mine account,
And found my debits to amount
To such a height as for to tell
How I should pay, 's impossible.
Well, this I'll do: my mighty score
Thy mercy-seat I'll lay before;
But therewithal I'll bring the band,
Which in full force did daring stand.
Till my Redeemer, on the tree,
Made void for millions, as for me:
Then, if thou bidst me pay, or go
Unto the prison, I'll say, No;
Christ having paid, I nothing owe;
For this is sure, the debt is dead
By law, the bond once cancelled.

Good Men Afflicted Most.

GOD makes not good men wantons, but doth bring
Them to the field, and there to skirmishing;
With trials those, with terrors these He proves,
And hazards those most whom the most He loves.

K

For Sceva, darts ; for Cocles, dangers ; thus
He finds a fire for mighty Mutius ;
Death for stout Cato ; and besides all these
A poison too He has for Socrates ;
Torments for high Attilius ; and with want
Brings in Fabricius for a combatant ;
But bastard-slips, and such as He dislikes,
He never brings them once to th' push of pikes.

Good Christians.

PLAY their offensive and defensive parts,
Till they be hid o'er with a wood of darts.

The Will the Cause of Woe.

WHEN man is punished, he is plagued still,
Not for the fault of nature, but of will.

To Heaven.

OPEN thy gates
To him who weeping waits,
And might come in
But that held back by sin.
Let mercy be
So kind to set me free,
And I will straight
Come in, or force the gate.

The Recompense.

ALL I have lost that could be rapt from me,
And fare it well ; yet, Herrick, if so be
Thy dearest Saviour renders thee but one
Smile, that one smile's full restitution.

To God.

PARDON me, God, once more I thee entreat,
That I have placed thee in so mean a seat,
Where round about thou see'st but all things vain,
Uncircumcised, unseasoned, and profane.
But as heaven's public and immortal eye
Looks on the filth, but is not soiled thereby ;
So thou, my God, may'st on this impure look
But take no tincture from my sinful book.
Let but one beam of glory on it shine,
And that will make me and my work divine.

To God.

LORD, I am like to misletoe,
Which has no root, and cannot grow
Or prosper, but by that same tree
It clings about ; so I by thee.
What need I then to fear at all
So long as I about thee crawl ?
But if that tree should fall and die,
Tumble shall heaven, and down will I.

His Wish to God.

I WOULD to God that mine old age might have,
Before my last, but here a living grave ;
Some one poor alms-house, there to lie or stir,
Ghost-like, as in my meaner sepulchre,
A little piggin and a pipkin by,
To hold things fitting my necessity,
Which rightly used, both in their time and place,
Might me excite to fore and after grace.
Thy cross, my Christ, fixed 'fore mine eyes should be
Not to adore that, but to worship thee.
So here the remnant of my days I'd spend,
Reading Thy Bible and my book ; so end.

Satan.

WHEN we 'gainst Satan stoutly fight, the more
He tears and tugs us than he did before ;
Neglecting once to cast a frown on those
Whom ease makes his, without the help of blows.

Hell.

HELL is no other but a soundless pit,
Where no one beam of comfort peeps in it.

The Way.

WHEN I a ship see on the seas,
Cuffed with those watery savages,
And therewithal behold it hath
In all that way no beaten path,
Then with a wonder I confess
Thou art our way i' th' wilderness,
And while we blunder in the dark,
Thou art our candle there, or spark.

Great Grief, Great Glory.

THE less our sorrows here and sufferings cease,
The more our crowns of glory there increase.

Hell.

HELL is the place where whipping-cheer abounds,
But no one jailor there to wash the wounds.

The Bellman.

ALONG the dark and silent night,
With my lantern and my light,
And the tinkling of my bell,
Thus I walk, and this I tell :
Death and dreadfulness call on
To the gen'ral session,
To whose dismal bar we there
All accounts must come to clear.
Scores of sins we 've made here many,
Wiped out few, God knows, if any.
Rise ye debtors then, and fall
To make payment while I call.
Ponder this, when I am gone ;
By the clock 'tis almost one.

The Goodness of his God..

WHEN winds and seas do rage,
    And threaten to undo me,
Thou dost their wrath assuage,
    If I but call unto thee.

A mighty storm last night
    Did seek my soul to swallow ;
But by the peep of light
    A gentle calm did follow.

What need I then despair
    Though ills stand round about me,
Since mischiefs neither dare
    To bark or bite without thee?

The Widow's Tears; or, Dirge of Dorcas.

COME, pity us, all ye who see
Our harps hung on the willow-tree ;
Come pity us, ye passers-by,
Who see or hear poor widows cry ;

Come pity us, and bring your ears
And eyes to pity widows' tears.
  Chor. And when you are come hither,
      Then we will keep
      A fast, and weep
  Our eyes out all together,

For Tabitha ; who dead lies here,
Clean washed, and laid out for the bier.
O modest matrons, weep and wail,
For the corn and wine must fail,
The basket and the bin of bread,
Wherewith so many souls were fed,
  Chor. Stand empty here for ever ;
      And ah ! the poor
      At thy worn door
  Shall be relieved never.

Woe worth the time, woe worth the day,
That reaved us of thee, Tabitha,
For we have lost with thee the meal,
The bits, the morsels, and the deal
Of gentle paste and yielding dough,
That thou on widows did bestow.
  Chor. All's gone, and death hath taken
      Away from us
      Our maundy ; thus
  Thy widows stand forsaken.

Ah, Dorcas, Dorcas ! now adieu
We bid the cruse and pannier too ;
Aye, and the flesh, for and the fish,
Doled to us in that lordly dish.
We take our leaves now of the loom
From whence the housewives' cloth did come ;
  Chor. The web affords now nothing :
      Thou being dead,
      The worsted thread
  Is cut that made us clothing.

Farewell the flax and reaming wool,
With which thy house was plentiful ;
Farewell the coats, the garments, and
The sheets, the rugs, made by thy hand ;
Farewell thy fire and thy light
That ne'er went out by day or night.
  Chor. No, or thy zeal so speedy,
      That found a way,
      By peep of day,
  To feed and clothe the needy.

But ah, alas ! the almond bough,
And olive branch is wither'd now,
The wine-press now is ta'en from us,
The saffron and the calamus ;
The spice and spikenard hence is gone,
The storax and the cinnamon ;
 Chor. The carol of our gladness
   Has taken wing,
   And our late spring
 Of mirth is turn'd to sadness.

How wise wast thou in all thy ways !
How worthy of respect and praise !
How matron-like didst thou go dressed !
How soberly above the rest
Of those that prank it with their plumes,
And jet it with their rich perfumes !
 Chor. Thy vestures were not flowing,
   Nor did the street
   Accuse thy feet
 Of mincing in their going.

And though thou here liest dead, we see
A deal of beauty yet in thee.
How sweetly shows thy smiling face,
Thy lips with all diffused grace !
Thy hands, though cold, yet spotless, white,
And comely as the chrysolite.
 Chor. Thy belly like a hill is,
   Or as a neat
   Clean heap of wheat,
All set about with lilies.

Sleep with thy beauties here, while we
Will show these garments made by thee ;
These were the coats, in these are read
The monuments of Dorcas dead :
These were thy acts, and thou shalt have
These hung as honours o'er thy grave,
 Chor. And after us, distressed,
   Should fame be dumb,
   Thy very tomb
Would cry out, Thou art blessed.

To God, in Time of Plundering.

RAPINE has yet took nought from me ;
But if it please my God I be
Brought at the last to th' utmost bit,
God make me thankful still for it.
I have been grateful for my store;
Let me say grace when there 's no more.

To his Saviour.—The New Year's Gift.

THAT little pretty bleeding part
  Of foreskin send to me,
And I'll return a bleeding heart
  For New Year's gift to thee.

Rich is the gem that thou didst send,
  Mine's faulty too, and small ;
But yet this gift thou wilt commend,
  Because I send thee all.

Doomsday.

LET not that day God's friends and servants scare ;
The bench is then their place, and not the bar.

The Poor's Portion.

THE superabundance of my store,
That is the portion of the poor ;
Wheat, barley, rye, or oats, what is 't
But he takes toll of? All the grist.
Two raiments have I ? Christ then makes
This law, that He and I part stakes.
Or have I two loaves ? Then I use
The poor to cut, and I to choose.

The White Island ; or, Place of the Blessed.

IN this world the Isle of Dreams,
While we sit by sorrow's streams,
Tears and terrors are our themes,
    Reciting ;

But when once from hence we fly,
More and more approaching nigh
Unto young eternity,
    Uniting :

In that whiter island where
Things are evermore sincere,
Candour here and lustre there,
    Delighting ;

There no monstrous fancies shall
Out of hell an horror call,
To create or cause at all
    Affrighting.

There in calm and cooling sleep
We our eyes shall never steep,
But eternal watch shall keep,
　　　　Attending

Pleasures such as shall pursue
Me immortalized, and you,
And fresh joys, as never too
　　　　Have ending.

To Christ.

I CRAWL, I creep, my Christ, I come
To Thee for curing balsamum ;
Thou hast, nay more, Thou art, the tree
Affording salve to sovereignty.
My mouth I'll lay unto thy wound,
Bleeding, that no blood touch the ground;
For rather than one drop shall fall
To waste, my JESU, I'll take all.

To God.

GOD ! to my little meal and oil,
Add but a bit of flesh, to boil,
And thou my pipkinet shalt see
Give a wave-offering unto thee.

Free Welcome.

GOD, He refuseth no man, but makes way
For all that now come, or hereafter may.

God's Grace.

GOD'S grace deserves here to be daily fed,
That, thus increased, it might be perfected.

Coming to Christ.

To him who longs unto his CHRIST to go
Celerity even itself is slow.

Correction.

GOD had but one son free from sin, but none
Of all His sons free from correction.

God's Bounty.

GOD, as He 's potent, so He 's likewise known
To give us more than hope can fix upon.

Knowledge.

SCIENCE in God is known to be
A substance, not a quality.

Salutation.

CHRIST, I have read, did to his chaplains say,
Sending them forth, Salute no man by the way ;
Not that He taught his ministers to be
Unsmooth or sour to all civility ;
But to instruct them, to avoid all snares
Of tardidation in the Lord's affairs.
Manners are good, but till his errand ends,
Salute we must nor strangers, kin, or friends.

Lasciviousness.

LASCIVIOUSNESS is known to be
The sister to saturitie.

Tears.

GOD from our eyes all tears hereafter wipes,
And gives his children kisses then, not stripes

God's Blessing.

IN vain our labours are, whatsoe'er they be,
Unless God gives the benedicite.

God and Lord.

GOD, is his name of nature ; but that word
Implies his power, when he 's called the LORD.

The Judgment Day.

GOD hides from man the reckoning day, that he
May fear it ever for uncertainty ;
That being ignorant of that one, he may
Expect the coming of it every day.

Angels.

ANGELS are called Gods; yet of them none
Are Gods but by participation;
As just men are entitled Gods, yet none
Are Gods of them, but by adoption.

Long Life.

THE longer thread of life we spin,
The more occasion still to sin.

Tears.

THE tears of saints more sweet by far
Than all the songs of sinners are.

Manna.

THAT manna which God on his people cast,
Fitted itself to every feeder's taste.

Reverence.

TRUE reverence is, as Cassiodore doth prove,
The fear of God commixed with cleanly love.

Mercy.

MERCY, the wise Athenians held to be
Not an affection, but a Deity.

Wages.

AFTER this life the wages shall,
Not shared alike, be unto all.

Temptation.

GOD tempteth no one, as St. Augustine saith,
For any ill, but for the proof of faith;
Unto temptation God exposeth some,
But none of purpose to be overcome.

God's Hands.

GOD'S hands are round and smooth, that gifts may fall
Freely from them, and hold none back at all.

Labour.

LABOUR we must, and labour hard,
I' th' forum here, or vineyard.

Mora Sponsi, the Stay of the Bridegroom.

THE time the bridegroom stays from hence
Is but the time of penitence.

Roaring.

ROARING is nothing but a weeping part,
Forced from the mighty dolour of the heart.

The Eucharist.

HE that is hurt seeks help ; sin is the wound ;
The salve for this i' th' Eucharist is found.

Sin Severely Punished.

GOD in His own day will be then severe
To punish great sins, who small faults whipped here.

Montes Scripturarum, the Mounts of the Scriptures.

THE mountains of the Scriptures are, some say,
Moses and Jesus, called Joshua ;
The Prophets mountains of the Old are meant,
The Apostles mounts of the New Testament.

Prayer.

A PRAYER that is said alone,
Starves, having no companion.
Great things ask for when thou dost pray,
And those great are which ne'er decay.
Pray not for silver, rust eats this ;
As not for gold, which metal is;
Nor yet for houses, which are here
But earth ; such vows ne'er reach God's ear.

Christ's Sadness.

CHRIST was not sad i' th' garden for His own
Passion, but for His sheep's dispersion.

God Hears Us.

GOD, who's in heaven, will hear from thence,
If not to th' sound, yet to the sense.

God.

GOD, as the learned Damascene doth write,
A sea of substance is, indefinite.

Clouds.

HE that ascended in a cloud shall come
In clouds, descending to the public doom.

Comforts in Contentions.

THE same who crowns the conqueror will be
A coadjutor in the agony.

Heaven.

HEAVEN is most fair ; but fairer He
That made that fairest canopy.

God.

IN God there 's nothing, but 'tis known to be
E'en God himself, in perfect entirety.

His Power.

GOD can do all things, save but what are known
For to imply a contradiction.

Christ's Words on the Cross, " My God, My God."

CHRIST, when he hung the dreadful cross upon,
Had, as it were, a dereliction,
In this regard : in those great terrors he
Had no one beam from God's sweet majesty.

Jehovah.

JEHOVAH, as Boetius saith,
No number of the plural hath.

Confusion of Face.

GOD then confounds man's face, when He not hears
The vows of those who are petitioners.

Another.

THE shame of man's face is no more
Than prayers repelled, says Cassiodore.

Beggars.

JACOB, God's beggar was : and so we wait,
Though ne'er so rich, all beggars at His gate.

Good and Bad.

THE bad among the good are here mixed ever ;
The good without the bad are here placed never.

Sin.

SIN no existence; Nature none it hath,
Or good at all, as learned Aquinas saith.

Martha, Martha.

THE repetition of the name made known
No other than Christ's full affection.

Youth and Age.

GOD on our youth bestows but little ease,
But on our age most sweet indulgences.

God's Power.

GOD is so potent as His power can
Draw out of bad a sovereign good to man.

Paradise.

PARADISE is, as from the learned I gather,
A choir of blest souls circling in the Father.

Observation.

THE Jews, when they built houses, I have read,
One part thereof left still unfinished,
To make them thereby mindful of their own
City's most sad and dire destruction.

The Ass.

GOD did forbid the Israelites to bring
An ass unto him, for an offering ;
Only, by this dull creature to express
His detestation to all slothfulness.

Observation.

THE Virgin-mother stood at distance there
From her Son's cross, not shedding once a tear,
Because the law forbade to sit and cry
For those who did as malefactors die.
So she, to keep her mighty woes in awe,
Tortured her love not to transgress the law.
Observe, we may, how Mary Joses then,
And the other Mary, Mary Magdalen,
Sat by the grave, and sadly sitting there,
Shed for their Master many a bitter tear ;
But 'twas not till their dearest Lord was dead,
And then to weep they both were licensed.

Tapers.

THOSE tapers which we set upon the grave
In funeral pomp, but this importance have,
That souls departed are not put out quite,
But as they walked here in their vestures white,
So live in Heaven, in everlasting light.

Christ's Birth.

ONE birth our Saviour had, the like none yet
Was, or will be a second like to it.

The Virgin Mary.

TO work a wonder, God would have her shown
At once a bud, and yet a rose full-blown.

Another

As sunbeams pierce the glass, and streaming in,
No crack or schism leave i' th' subtile skin ;
So the divine hand worked, and brake no thread,
But in a mother kept a maidenhead.

God.

God, in the holy tongue they call
The place that filleth all in all.

Another of God.

God 's said to leave this place, and for to come
Nearer to that place than to other some,
Of local motion in no least respect,
But only by impression of effect.

Another.

God is Jehovah called, which name of His
Implies or essence or the He that Is.

God's Presence.

God 's evident, and may be said to be
Present with just men to the verity ;
But with the wicked, if he doth comply,
'Tis, as St. Bernard saith, but seemingly.

God's Dwelling.

God 's said to dwell there, wheresoever He
Puts down some prints of His high majesty ;
As when to man He comes, and there doth place
His holy Spirit, or doth plant His grace.

The Virgin Mary.

The Virgin Mary was, as I have read,
The House of God, by Christ inhabited ;
Into the which He entered, but the door,
Once shut, was never to be opened more.

To God.

GOD's undivided, One in Persons Three,
And Three in inconfused Unity ;
Original of essence, there is none
'Twixt God the Father, Holy Ghost, and Son,
And though the Father be the first of Three,
'Tis but by order, not by entity.

Upon Woman and Mary.

So long, it seem'd, as Mary's faith was small,
Christ did her Woman, not her Mary call ;
But no more Woman, being strong in faith,
But Mary call'd then, as St. Ambrose saith.

Sabbaths.

SABBATHS are threefold, as St. Austin says,
The first of time, or Sabbath here of days ;
The second is a conscience trespass-free ;
The last the Sabbath of eternity.

The Fast, or Lent.

NOAH the first was, as tradition says,
That did ordain the fast of forty days.

Sin.

THERE is no evil that we do commit
But hath th' extraction of some good from it,
As when we sin, God, the great Chemist, thence
Draws out the elixir of true penitence.

God.

GOD is more here then in another place,
Not by His essence, but commerce of grace.

This and the Next World.

GOD hath this world for many made, 'tis true ;
But he hath made the world to come for few.

Ease.

God gives to none so absolute an ease,
As not to know or feel some grievances.

Beginnings and Endings.

Paul, he began ill, but he ended well ;
Judas began well, but he foully fell.
In godliness, not the beginning so
Much as the ends are to be looked unto.

Temporal Goods.

These temp'ral goods, God the most wise commends
To th' good and bad in common, ior two ends :
First, that these goods none here may o'er-esteem,
Because the wicked do partake of them ;
Next, that these ills none cowardly may shun,
Being oft here the just man's portion.

Hell Fire.

The fire of hell this strange condition hath,
To burn, not shine, as learned Basil saith.

Abel's Blood.

Speak, did the blood of Abel cry
To God for vengeance? Yes, say I.
Ev'n as the sprinkled blood called on
God for an expiation.

Another.

The blood of Abel was a thing
Of such a reverend reckoning,
As that the old world thought it fit
Especially to swear by it.

A Position in the Hebrew Divinity.

ONE man repentant, is of more esteem
With God, than one that never sinned 'gainst Him.

Penitence.

THE doctors in the Talmud say,
That in this world one only day,
In true repentance spent, will be
More worth than heaven's eternity.

God's Presence.

GOD'S presence everywhere, but most of all
Present by union hypostatical ;
God, He is there where 's nothing else, schools say,
And nothing else is there where He 's away.

The Resurrection Possible and Probable.

FOR each one body that i' th' earth is sown,
There 's an uprising but of one for one,
But for each grain that in the ground is thrown,
Threescore or fourscore spring up thence for one ;
So that the wonder is not half so great
Of ours, as is the rising of the wheat.

Christ's Suffering.

JUSTLY our dearest Saviour may abhor us,
Who hath more suffered by us far than for us.

Sinners.

SINNERS confounded are a twofold way,
Either as when, the learned schoolmen say,
Men's sins destroyed are when they repent,
Or when for sins men suffer punishment.

Temptations.

No man is tempted so, but may o'ercome,
If that he has a will to masterdom.

Pity and Punishment.

GOD doth embrace the good with love, and gains
The good by mercy, as the bad by pains.

God's Price and Man's Price.

GOD bought man here with his heart's blood expense ;
And man sold God here for base thirty pence.

Christ's Action.

CHRIST never did so great a work, but there
His human nature did in part appear ;
Or ne'er so mean a piece, but men might see
Therein some beams of His divinity ;
So that in all He did there did combine
His human nature and His part divine.

Predestination.

PREDESTINATION is the cause alone
Of many standing, but of fall to none.

Another.

ART thou not destined ? Then, with haste go on
To make thy fair predestination ;
If thou canst change thy life, God then will please
To change or call back His past sentences.

Sin.

SIN never slew a soul, unless there went
Along with it some tempting blandishment.

Another.

SIN is an act so free that if we shall
Say 'tis not free, 'tis then no sin at all.

Another.

SIN is the cause of death ; and sin 's alone
The cause of God's predestination ;
And from God's prescience of man's sin doth flow
Our destination to eternal woe

Prescience.

GOD'S prescience makes none sinful, but the offence
Of man's the chief cause of God's prescience.

Christ.

To all our wounds here, whatsoe'er they be,
Christ is the one sufficient remedy.

Christ's Incarnation.

CHRIST took our nature on Him, not that He
'Bove all things loved it, for the purity;
No, but he dressed Him with our human trim,
Because our flesh stood most in need of Him.

Heaven.

HEAVEN is not given for our good works here,
Yet it is given to the labourer.

God's Keys.

GOD has four keys which he reserves alone;
The first of rain: the key of hell next known;
With the third key He opes and shuts the womb;
And with the fourth key He unlocks the tomb.

Sin.

THERE'S no constraint to do amiss,
Whereas but one enforcement is.

Alms.

GIVE unto all, lest He whom thou deniest
May chance to be no other man but Christ.

Hell Fire.

ONE only fire has hell, but yet it shall,
Not after one sort, there excruciate all;
But look how each transgressor onward wen
Boldly in sin, shall feel more punishment.

To Keep a True Lent.

Is this a fast to keep
  The larder lean,
    And clean
From fat of veals and sheep?

Is it to quit the dish
  Of flesh, yet still
    To fill
The platter high with fish?

Is it to fast an hour,
  Or ragg'd to go,
    Or show
A downcast look, and sour?

No; 'tis a fast, to dole
  Thy sheaf of wheat
    And meat
Unto the hungry soul.

It is to fast from strife,
  From old debate
    And hate
To circumcise thy life.

To show a heart grief-rent;
  To starve thy sin,
    Not bin;
And that's to keep thy Lent.

No Time in Eternity.

By hours we all live here; in heaven is known
No spring of time, or time's succession.

His Meditation upon Death.

Be those few hours which I have yet to spend
Blessed with the meditation of my end;
Though they be few in number, I'm content,
If otherwise, I stand indifferent;
Nor makes it matter Nestor's years to tell,
If man lives long, and if he live not well.
A multitude of days still heaped on
Seldom brings order, but confusion.
Might I make choice, long life should be withstood,
Nor would I care how short it were, if good;

Which, to effect, let every passing bell
Possess my thoughts, next comes my doleful knell ;
And when the night persuades me to my bed,
I'll think I'm going to be buried ;
So shall the blankets which come over me
Present those turfs which once must cover me,
And with as firm behaviour I will meet
The sheet I sleep in as my winding-sheet.
When sleep shall bathe his body in mine eyes,
I will believe that then my body dies ;
And if I chance to wake, and rise thereon,
I'll have in mind my resurrection,
Which must produce me to that general doom
To which the peasant so the prince must come,
To hear the Judge give sentence on the throne,
Without the least hope of affection.
Tears at that day shall make but weak defence,
When hell and horror fright the conscience.
Let me, though late, yet at the last, begin
To shun the least temptation to a sin ;
Though to be tempted be no sin, until
Man to th' alluring object gives his will.
Such let my life assure me, when my breath
Goes thieving from me, I am safe in death,
Which is the height of comfort ; when I fall
I rise triumphant in my funeral.

Clothes for Continuance.

THOSE garments lasting evermore,
Are works of mercy to the poor ;
Which neither tetter, time, or moth,
Shall fray that silk or fret this cloth.

To God.

COME to me, God ; but do not come
To me as to the general doom,
In power ; or come thou in that state
When thou thy laws didst promulgate,
Whenas the mountains quaked for dread,
And sullen clouds bound up his head.
No, lay Thy stately terrors by,
To talk with me familiarly ;
For if Thy thunder-claps I hear,
I shall less swoon than die for fear.
Speak Thou of love, and I'll reply
By way of epithalamy ;

Or sing of mercy, and I'll suit
To it my viol and my lute.
Thus let Thy lips but love distil,
Then come my God, and hap what will.

The Soul.

WHEN once the soul has lost her way,
O then how restless does she stray !
And having not her God for light,
How does she err in endless night !

The Judgment Day.

IN doing justice God shall then be known,
Whom, showing mercy here, few priz'd, or none.

Sufferings.

WE merit all we suffer, and by far
More stripes than God lays on the sufferer.

Pain and Pleasure.

GOD suffers not His saints and servants dear
To have continual pain or pleasure here,
But look how night succeeds the day, so He
Gives them by turns their grief and jollity.

God's Presence.

GOD is all-present to whate'er we do,
And as all-present so all-filling too.

Another.

THAT there 's a God we all do know,
But what God is we cannot show.

The Poor Man's Part.

TELL me, rich man, for what intent
Thou load'st with gold thy vestiment?
Whenas the poor cry out, To us
Belongs all gold superfluous.

The Right Hand.

GOD has a right hand, but is quite bereft
Of that which we do nominate the left.

The Staff and Rod.

TWO instruments belong unto our God,
The one a staff is, and the next a rod,
That if the twig should chance too much to smart,
The staff might come to play a friendly part.

God Sparing in Scourging.

GOD still rewards us more than our desert,
But when He strikes He quarter-acts His part.

Confession.

CONFESSION twofold is, as Austin says,
The first of sin is, and the next of praise ;
If ill it goes with thee, thy faults confess,
If well, then chant God's praise with cheerfulness.

God's Descent.

GOD is then said for to descend when He
Doth here on earth some thing of novity ;
As when in human nature He works more
Than ever yet the like was done before.

No Coming to God without Christ.

GOOD and great God !   How should I fear
To come to Thee, if Christ not there ?
Could I but think He would not be
Present, to plead my cause for me,
To hell I'd rather run than I
Would see Thy face and He not by.

Another to God.

THOUGH thou be'st all that active love
Which heats those ravished souls above,
And though all joys spring from the glance
Of Thy most winning countenance,
Yet sour and grim Thou'dst seem to me,
If through my Christ I saw not Thee.

The Resurrection.

THAT Christ did die the Pagan saith ;
But that He rose, that's Christians' faith.

Co-heirs.

WE are co-heirs with Christ, nor shall His own
Heirship be less by our adoption ;
The number here of heirs shall from the state
Of His great birthright nothing derogate.

The Number of Two.

GOD hates the dual number—being known
The luckless number of division ;
And when He blessed each several day whereon
He did His curious operation,
'Tis never read there, as the Fathers say,
God blessed his work done on the second day,
Wherefore two prayers ought not to be said,
Or by ourselves, or from the pulpit read.

Hardening of Hearts.

GOD 's said our hearts to harden then
When as His grace not supples men.

The Rose.

BEFORE man's fall the Rose was born,
St. Ambrose says, without the thorn ;
But for man's fault then was the thorn
Without the fragrant rosebud born ;
But ne'er the rose without the thorn.

God's Time must End our Trouble.

GOD doth not promise here to man that He
Will free him quickly from his misery ;
But in His own time, and when He thinks fit,
Then He will give a happy end to it.

Baptism.

THE strength of Baptism that 's within,
It saves the soul by drowning sin.

Gold and Frankincense.

GOLD serves for tribute to the King,
The frankincense for God's offring.

To God.

God, who me gives a will for to repent,
Will add a power to keep me innocent,
That I shall ne'er that trespass recommit
When I have done true penance here for it.

The Chewing the Cud.

When well we speak, and nothing do that's good,
We not divide the hoof, but chew the cud;
But when good words by good works have their proof,
We then both chew the cud and cleave the hoof.

Christ's Twofold Coming.

Thy former coming was to cure
My soul's most desperate calenture;
Thy second advent, that must be
To heal my earth's infirmity.

To God, his Gift.

As my little pot doth boil,
We will keep this level coil,
That a wave, and I will bring
To my God, a heave-offering.

God's Anger.

God can't be wrathful, but we may conclude,
Wrathful He may be by similitude;
God's wrathful said to be when He doth do
That without wrath which wrath doth force us to.

God's Commands.

In God's commands ne'er ask the reason why;
Let thy obedience be the best reply.

To God.

If I have played the truant, or have here
Failed in my part, oh Thou that art my dear,
My mild, my loving tutor, Lord and God,
Correct my errors gently with thy rod.
I know that faults will many here be found,
But where sin dwells, there let thy Grace abound.

To God.

THE work is done ; now let Thy laurel be
Given by none but by Thyself to me :
That done, with honour Thou dost me create
Thy poet and Thy prophet laureate.

Good Friday; Rex Tragicus, or Christ going To His Cross.

PUT off thy robe of purple, then go on
To the sad place of execution ;
Thine hour is come, and the tormentor stands
Ready to pierce thy tender feet and hands.
Long before this the base, the dull, the rude,
Th' inconstant and unpurged multitude
Yawn for thy coming ; some ere this time cry,
How He defers, how loth He is to die !
Amongst this scum, the soldier with his spear,
And that sour fellow with his vinegar,
His sponge and stick, do ask why thou dost stay ?
So do the scurf and bran too.   Go thy way,
Thy way, thou guiltless man, and satisfy
By thine approach, each their beholding eye.
Not as a thief shalt thou ascend the mount,
But like a person of some high account :
The cross shalt be thy stage, and thou shalt there,
The spacious field have for thy theatre.
Thou art that Roscius, and that marked-out man
That must this day act the tragedian,
To wonder and affrightment.   Thou art He
Whom all the flux of nations comes to see ;
Not those poor thieves that act their parts with thee :
Those act without regard, when once a King
And God, as thou art, comes to suffering.
No, no, this scene from thee takes life and sense,
And soul and spirit plot, and excellence.
Why then begin, Great King ! Ascend thy throne,
And thence proceed to act Thy Passion
To such an height, to such a period raised,
As Hell, and Earth, and Heav'n may stand amazed.
God and good angels guide Thee, and so bless
Thee in thy several parts of bitterness ;
That those who see Thee nailed unto the tree
May, though they scorn Thee, praise and pity Thee
And we, thy lovers, while we see thee keep
The laws of action, will both sigh and weep,
And bring our spices to embalm Thee dead ;
That done, we'll see Thee sweetly buried.

His Words to Christ, going to the Cross.

WHEN thou wast taken, Lord, I oft have read,
All Thy disciples thee forsook and fled ;
Let their example not a pattern be
For me to fly, but now to follow Thee.

Another to his Saviour.

IF thou be'st taken, God forbid
I fly from Thee as others did ;
But if Thou wilt so honour me
As to accept my company,
I'll follow Thee, hap, hap what shall,
Both to the judge and judgment-hall ;
And if I see Thee posted there
To be all flayed with whipping-cheer,
I'll take my share, or else, my God,
Thy stripes I'll kiss, or burn the rod.

His Saviour's Words, going to the Cross

HAVE, have ye no regard, all ye
Who pass this way, to pity Me,
Who am a Man of misery ?

A Man both bruis'd and broke, and One
Who suffers not here for Mine own,
But for My friend's transgression.

Ah ! Sion's daughters, do not fear
The cross, the cords, the nails, the spear,
The myrrh, the gall, the vinegar ;

For Christ, your loving Saviour, hath
Drunk up the wine of God's fierce wrath ;
Only, there 's left a little froth,

Less for to taste than for to show
What bitter cups had been your due,
Had He not drank them up for you.

His Anthem to Christ on the Cross.

WHEN I behold Thee, almost slain,
With one and all parts full of pain ;
When I Thy gentle heart do see
Pierced through and dropping blood for me,
I'll call and cry out, Thanks to Thee.

Verse But yet it wounds my soul to think
That for my sin Thou. Thou must drink,
Even Thou alone, the bitter cup
Of fury and of vengeance up.

Chor. Lord, I'll not see Thee to drink all
The vinegar, the myrrh, the gall ;

Ver Chor. But I will sip a little wine.
Which done, Lord say, The rest is mine.

THIS CROSS-TREE HERE
DOTH   JESUS   BEAR
WHO SWEETENED FIRST
THE DEATH ACCURSED.

HERE all things ready are ; make haste, make haste, away,
For long this work will be, and very short this day.
Why then, go on to act ; here's wonders to be done
Before the last least sand of thy ninth hour be run
Or ere dark clouds do dull or dead the mid-day's sun.

Act when thou wilt,
Blood will be spilt ;
Pure balm, that shall
Bring health to all.
Why, then, begin
To pour first in
Some drops of wine,
Instead of brine,
To search the wound,
So long unsound ;
And when that's done,
Let oil next run,
To cure the sore
Sin made before.
And, O dear Christ !
E'en as thou diest
Look down and see
Us weep for Thee.
And though love knows
Thy dreadful woes
We cannot ease,
Yet do Thou please,
Who mercy art,
T' accept each heart,
That gladly would
Help, if it could.
Meanwhile let me,
Beneath this tree,
This honour have,
To make my grave.

To his Saviour's Sepulchre.—His Devotion.

HAIL, holy and all-honoured tomb,
By no ill haunted, here I come,
With shoes put off, to tread thy room.
I'll not profane by soil of sin,
Thy door, as I do enter in,
For I have washed both hand and heart,
This, that, and every other part;
So that I dare, with far less fear
Than full affection, enter here.
Thus, thus I come to kiss thy stone
With a warm lip and solemn one;
And as I kiss I'll here and there
Dress thee with flowery diaper.
How sweet this place is! As from hence
Flowed all Panchaia's frankincense,
Or rich Arabia did commix
Here all her rare aromatics.
Let me live ever here, and stir
No one step from this sepulchre.
Ravished I am, and down I lie,
Confused in this brave ecstasy.
Here let me rest, and let me have
This for my heaven, that was thy grave;
And coveting no higher sphere,
I'll my eternity spend here.

His Offering, with the Rest, at the Sepulchre.

To join with them who here confer
Gifts to my Saviour's sepulchre,
Devotion bids me hither bring
Somewhat for my thank-offering.
Lo! thus I bring a virgin-flower
To dress my maiden Saviour.

His Coming to the Sepulchre.

HENCE they have borne my Lord; behold, the stone
Is rolled away, and my sweet Saviour's gone.
Tell me, white angel, what is now become
Of Him we lately sealed up in his tomb?

Is he from hence gone to the shades beneath,
To vanquish hell, as here he conquered death?
If so, I'll thither follow without fear,
And live in hell, if that my Christ stays there.

Of all the good things whatsoe'er we do,
God is the ΑΡΧΉ and the ΤΕΛΟΣ́ too.

THE BEGINNING AND

THE END.

PRINTED BY BALLANTYNE, HANSON AND CO.
LONDON AND EDINBURGH

www.ingramcontent.com/pod-product-compliance
Lightning Source LLC
Chambersburg PA
CBHW031024120726
47905CB00007B/2033